AND THE WINNER IS . . .

The sword came to rest wedged between two rocks. Kevin and the bandit both scuffled after it, but the bandit got there first, stomping down hard. To the bardling's horror, the sword snapped halfway up the blade.

For a moment, Kevin and his foe stared at each other, frozen. Then the bandit slowly grinned, revealing a mouthful of ugly teeth.

"Too bad, boy. I win, you lose!"

With that, the man leaped at him. Kevin scrambled to his feet, looking frantically about for another weapon. Out of the corner of his eye, the bardling saw the bandit's knife flash again, this time aimed at his unprotected neck. He twisted about, just barely managing to catch the man's wrist in time.

But I . . . can't . . . hold him . . . he's just . . . too strong . . . .

The bandit continued to grin. Slowly he began bending the bardling's wrists back and back . . . Kevin gasped as renewed pain shot through his bruised hand, and lost his grip. The knife began its plunge —

But then the bandit froze as a dark-skinned hand closed on his neck. The man's eyes widened, gaping in sudden blind horror. As Kevin stared in sheer disbelief, he saw the man's hair fade from black to gray to white. The leathery skin sagged, wrinkled. The bandit let the bardling go so suddenly Kevin fell, dragging himself frantically away as what had been a living man a moment before crumbled to ancient dust.

Naitachal stood revealed, eyes still blazing red from the force of his spell.

The Bard's Tale
Castle of Deception

MERCEDES LACKEY
&
JOSEPHA SHERMAN

BAEN FANTASY

CASTLE OF DECEPTION

This is a work of fiction. All the characters and events portrayed in this book are fictional, and any resemblance to real people or incidents is purely coincidental.

A Baen Books Original

Baen Publishing Enterprises
P.O. Box 1403
Riverdale, NY 10471

ISBN: 0-671-72125-9

Cover art by Larry Elmore

First Printing, July 1992

Printed in the United States of America

Distributed by Simon & Schuster
1230 Avenue of the Americas
New York, NY 10020

Chapter I

Twang!

The lute string snapped, whipping across Kevin's hand. He yelped, just barely managing not to drop the lute. Instead, he placed the instrument gently down on his cot, then brought his stinging hand to his mouth. Blast it all, that had *hurt*! Of course it had. He knew better by now than to try tightening a string too far. After all, he'd been a bardling, an apprentice Bard, for what seemed like all his nearly sixteen years.

The welt finally stopped smarting. Kevin got to his feet with an impatient sigh. He didn't really mind practicing; it was something every musician had to do every day, even his Master. He didn't even mind being stuck in his cramped little room. Or at least he wouldn't mind practicing and being cooped up in this stupid room in this stupid inn if only he knew this was all leading somewhere!

If something doesn't happen soon, something exciting . . .

Picking his way across the piles of clothes and music scrolls littering the floor, the bardling stared out the one window, down to the Blue Swan's cobblestone courtyard. A merchant was climbing onto his fine bay horse, his travelling robes rich purple in the springtime sunlight. With him rode his bodyguard, two men and a woman in plain leather armor, straight-backed and alert as falcons, hands never straying too far from the swords at their sides. Kevin sighed in envy. They were probably nothing more heroic than common mercenaries, and the journey they were taking was probably nothing more exciting than a ride to the next town, but at least they were *going* somewhere, they were doing something! While he —

"Blast it!" the bardling swore under his breath.

He couldn't stand being stuck here a moment longer. Clattering down the inn's wooden staircase, Kevin hurried across the common room — empty at this early hour — and headed out into the courtyard. But then he stopped short on the cobblestones. What was he hoping to see? The merchant and his party were already out of sight, riding down the old North Road that ran just outside the inn's gateway, and there probably weren't going to be any more travellers today. Discouraged, the bardling turned and went back through the inn to the back entrance, stepping out into town.

Ha. Some town.

Bracklin was little more than a collection of a dozen small, thatched-roof houses clustered behind the inn. A neat, pretty, orderly place, one where nothing different had ever happened and nothing ever would.

And people here actually like *it that way!*

Kevin leaned back against the inn's half-timbered side, the wall chilly on his back, the sun warm on his face. There had never been a day he could remember when he hadn't dreamed of being a Bard, of singing wonderful songs and travelling to wonderful places, maybe even working the rare, powerful Bardic Magic, healing people with his music or even banishing demons. How could those dreams have turned into something so unbearably *dull*?

"Morning, Kevin," a woman's cheerful voice called from across the unpaved street.

The bardling started. "Uh, good morning, Ada."

"That's just like you bard-folk, always off in a world all your own."

Ada was a round, chubby, middle-aged hen of a

woman. Right now her brown hair was tucked up out of her way in an untidy bun, and the sleeves of her plain white blouse were pushed back above the elbows as she filled a washtub full of soapy water. "Come for Master Aidan's clothes, have you? Told you they couldn't be ready till this afternoon. Had to spend all day yesterday washing the travel dust off the robes of His Nibs." Ada's jerk of the head took in the departed merchant and his party. "Eh, won't bad-mouth the fellow; paid me down to the last coin, with extra added." Her bright black eyes studied Kevin. "What's with you, lad?"

"Nothing."

"Oh, don't give me 'nothing.' What is it?"

Kevin sighed. "Ada, you remember when I first came here."

The woman smiled warmly. "Don't I, though. You were such a little boy, almost too small for the lute on your back, clinging to your music teacher's hand and all wide-eyed with wonder."

"Mistress Malen was very kind."

"Well, of course she was! Imagine after all the years of having to teach merchants' kids without a drop of talent to them coming across someone like you with the true gift for music! No, no, don't start blushing like that. You know it's true."

Ada plopped a shirt into her washtub and started scrubbing. "Look you, lad, before she left, Mistress Malen told me all about you: how you were plucking at the strings of your family's old lute the minute you were old enough to hold it, making up your own little tunes till they didn't have a choice but to hire her."

Kevin had to smile. Mistress Malen had been a wonderful first teacher, endlessly patient with her eager pupil. She had also been honest enough to admit his talent was more than she could shape. A little shiver of wonder raced through the bardling as he remembered how she'd shaken her head and told him, "You have the makings of a Bard, boy, a true Bard."

Ada's chuckle dragged him back to the present. "So there you were, poor chick, standing in the courtyard of the Blue Swan, full of wonder, yes, but maybe just a touch scared, too. And no surprise, being apprenticed to Master Aidan like that, a Bard — *and* a hero as well!"

Kevin glanced up at his Master's room. "You remember how it was, don't you? When my Master helped King Amber keep his throne, I mean."

"Bless you, child, how old do you think I am? That was a good thirty years ago! I was a chick myself back then, much younger than you." She paused thoughtfully. "But I do remember all the celebrating. My, yes! Everyone couldn't stop chattering about how it had been a Bard, your Bard, who'd used his magical songs to stop that witch of a would-be usurper."

"Princess Carlotta."

"Oh, she might have been a princess, the nasty little creature, but she was a sorceress, all right, darkhearted as they come! She turned our good king into stone — stone, can you imagine that! And if it hadn't been for Master Aidan, stone, King Amber would have remained. Bah! Good riddance to her, I say — and all praise to Master Aidan for stopping her."

Kevin sighed. "That must have been a wonderful time. . . ."

"Wonderful! Those were the most dangerous days nobody ever wanted! And I don't blame your Master for coming here after it was all over. If anyone ever earned some peace and quiet, it was he!"

That wasn't what Kevin wanted to hear. At first every day with his Master had seemed wild with excitement. After all, with a hero Bard to teach him, why shouldn't he, too, do great deeds someday! But it hadn't taken long to learn that his Master had, somewhere over the years, forgotten all about heroism.

"Ada, you've lived here in Bracklin all your life, haven't you?"

"You know it. Never left this town. Never saw any need to!"

"But don't you ever want to meet new people?"

"I do! Enough travellers come into the inn for that."

"That's not what I mean. Don't you ever get bored? Want to see new places, do new things?"

Ada looked at him as though he'd gone mad. "Why should I want something as foolish as that? I have a nice house, good, steady work. Love you, lad, I think the spring's gotten into you." She shooed him away with soapy hands. "Now, get along with you, Kevin. I have work to do."

The bardling wandered on down Bracklin's one street to the end. It didn't take long. He stood looking out over the fields beyond the edge of town, each neatly plowed strip of land exactly like the next, and shuddered. Making his way back towards the Blue Swan, Kevin politely returned the greetings of baker and seamstress and butcher. All of them, he realized, were quite peacefully going about their various tasks just as they did every day. And not a one of them seemed to mind! Suddenly frustrated to the point of screaming, Kevin hurried back into the inn and his room. At least he could learn a new song!

There wasn't a sound out of his Master's room. Of course not. The old Bard probably had his nose buried in old manuscripts, just as he had whenever he wasn't playing himself, or giving the bardling a music lesson —just as he had for almost all the time Kevin had studied with him.

I know he's hunting for something important. But he won't tell me what it is! And while he hunts through all those dusty books, I'm stuck here in Bracklin with him. I'm not a child anymore! I can't be content like this!

The bardling snatched up his lute and struck a few

savage chords. But he couldn't play anything with that broken string.

"Blast it all to Darkness!"

Kevin rummaged through the mess on floor and table till he found a replacement string. This was ridiculous! All Master Aidan had to do was say the word, and King Amber would gladly name him the royal bard. They could be living in the royal palace right now.

And wouldn't *that* be grand? Kevin pictured his Master in elegant Bardic robes, people bowing respectfully as he passed. He would be a major power in court. And his brave young apprentice would be a figure of importance too. . . .

"Right," Kevin muttered. "And pigs could fly."

His Master had tremendous musical talent, no doubt about that; every time the old Bard took his own well-worn mandolin and showed the boy how a song should be played, a little shiver of wonder ran through Kevin, and with it a prayer: *Ah, please, please, let me someday play like that, with such grace, such — such glory!* Of late he had begun to hope that his prayers, if not answered, had at least begun to be heard. But even Ada insisted Master Aidan was also an adept at Bardic Magic. . . .

I don't understand it! If I had such a gift, I'd be using it, not — not hiding it away in the middle of nowhere!

Oh yes, "if," Kevin thought darkly. It wasn't as though every Bard had the innate gift for Bardic Magic, after all. Master Aidan seemed to believe he possessed it, had assured Kevin over and over that in some bardlings the gift blossomed fairly late. But surely if he was going to show any sign of magic, it would have surfaced by now. After all, he was nearly a man! Yet so far he hadn't felt the slightest tingle of Power no matter how hard he'd tried. To him, the potentially magical songs his Master had taught him remained just that: songs.

The bardling gave the lute an impatient strum, then winced. Sour! Lute strings went out of pitch all too easily.

As he retuned them, Kevin admitted to himself that yes, he did take a great deal of joy in creating music, and in creating it well. But aside from that music, what did he have? Of course it was true that a musician seldom had time for much else; if he was to succeed at all, a musician must give himself totally to his craft. Kevin could accept that. But did the rest of life have to be so — drab? What did he do from day to day, really, but run his Master's errands like a little boy, keep all those old manuscripts dusted, see the same dull town and the same dull people?

I might as well be apprenticed to a — a baker!

"Kevin," a weary voice called from across the hall, and the bardling straightened, listening. "Come here, please."

"Yes, Master."

Now what? Maybe he was supposed to order their supper from the innkeeper? Or go find out from Ada exactly when their wash would be done?

But when the bardling saw the old Bard's pale face, his impatience slipped away, replaced by a pang of worry. He had never known the Master as anything but a white-bearded old man, but surely he'd never seen him look quite *this* tired. Quite this . . . fragile.

It's because he never goes out, Kevin tried to persuade himself. *Never even gets any sunlight, cooped up in here with his books.* "Master? Is — is something wrong?"

"No, Kevin. Not exactly."

But a hint of fire flickered in the man's weary blue eyes, and Kevin tensed, all at once so wild with hope he nearly cheered. "You've found what you were looking for!"

"Alas, no."

"Then . . . what is it? Are we going somewhere?" *Oh please, oh please, say yes!*

"We? No, boy. You."

Kevin felt his heart thunder in his chest. Yes! At last

something *new* was going to happen! "You w-won't regret this!" he stammered. "Just tell me what the quest is, and I — "

The old Bard chuckled faintly. "I'm afraid it isn't a quest, my fine young hero. More of an errand. A longer one than usual, and further away than most, but an errand never the less."

"Oh." Kevin struggled to keep the disappointment from his face. *I should have known better. Just another stupid errand.*

"What I want you to do," the Bard continued, "is go to the castle of Count Volmar — "

"And deliver a message from the King?" At least that would be something halfway dramatic!

"And copy a manuscript for me," his Master corrected, looking down his long nose at the bardling. "You're to copy it — copy it exactly, understand — and bring the copy back to me."

Kevin barely silenced a groan. "Is it very long?"

"I believe so."

And it was probably unbearably dull, too. "But, Master," Kevin asked desperately, "why don't you just ask them to send the manuscript to you?"

"No! It's too valuable to be moved."

Naturally. "If you want it copied exactly," the bardling said as casually as he could, "why not hire a trained scribe — "

"No!" For a startling moment, the Bard's face was so fierce Kevin could almost believe the heroic tales. But then the fierceness faded, leaving only a weary old man behind. "I have given you your orders. The manuscript you are to copy is known as *The Study of Ancient Song*. It is approximately three hands high and one and a half hands wide, and is bound in plain, dark brown leather that, I imagine, must be fairly well worn by now. The title may or may not be embossed on the spine, but it should be printed clearly enough on the cover." He paused. "In brief: the manuscript cannot be moved from the count's library. And only you are to copy it. Each day's work must be hidden. It must *not* be shown to anyone. Is that understood?"

Kevin frowned. Had the old Bard's mind turned? Or, more likely, was he simply trying to enliven a dull job for his apprentice with a touch of the dramatic?

The bardling bowed in resignation. "Yes, Master," he muttered.

"Good. Now, here's a letter of introduction to the count from me. He should recognize my seal. Be sure you keep it safe in your belt pouch; nobles are suspicious sorts, and unless they know you're really from me, you'll never get past the castle gates."

Kevin obediently stuffed the parchment into his pouch. Ah well, he'd try to make the most of this. At least it meant getting out of this dull old inn for a few days. Yes, and he would be staying in a castle. Hey now, maybe even rubbing elbows with the nobility!

The bardling fought down a sudden grin, imagining himself at court, impressing somebody important, maybe even the count himself, with his talent. Who knew? If he was really lucky, he might get a chance to really prove himself. He might even end up being named a true Bard!

Oh, right. If he didn't wind up spending all his time stuck in the count's library.

"Kevin? Kevin! Listen to me, boy," his Master fussed. "You must hurry. I have a way to get you to the count safely—friends are coming through—but time is short. Can't have a lad your age travelling all by himself."

The bardling straightened, insulted. "Your pardon, Master, but I'm not a baby. I'll be all right, don't worry."

"It's not *you* I'm worried about, boy. It's what you might meet along the way. You're a bardling, not a trained warrior."

"I can handle a sword!"

"But you won't," the Bard ordered bluntly. "A musician doesn't dare risk injuring his hands."

"Well, yes, of course, but— "

"I repeat, you are *not* a trained warrior. If someone attacked you, you wouldn't stand a chance of defending yourself."

"I'm nearly sixteen!" Kevin began hotly. "I can take care of myself!"

But the Bard was no longer listening to him. Head cocked, the old man murmured, "Well now, do you hear that?"

"Singing?" the bardling said in surprise. Who in that quiet town would suddenly be frivolous enough to burst into song? And raucous song at that!

"I wonder," the Bard murmured to himself. "Can it be . . . so soon?"

He moved slowly to the window. Kevin followed, looking over the man's shoulder at a laughing group of folks on horseback clattering into the courtyard, surrounding two gaudy red and blue wagons. The riders' cloaks and tunics fluttered in the wind, their many colors so bright he could have sworn they were cut from scraps of rainbows. The man who seemed to be the leader, driving the first wagon, wore a robe that glittered like the sun itself.

"It's just a troop of minstrels," Kevin began, but his Master was already calling out the window: "Berak!"

The leader glanced up, his sharp-featured, green-eyed face suddenly alert. "So it *was* your Summons, old man!" he yelled back. "You're still alive and kicking, I see!"

Kevin gasped, but his Master only laughed. "And you're still the same disrespectful soul as ever! Come up here, if you would."

Berak brought his whole troop with him, twenty men and women and their offspring, all with sharp, suntanned faces and bright, wild eyes. Chattering and laughing, they filled the small room almost to overflow, their gaudy clothing making it look even shabbier than it was.

Berak held up a hand for silence. "What would you, old Bard?" he asked, making the man a fantastic bow.

The Bard didn't seem at all disturbed by the curious stares. "A favor, Berak, if you would. My apprentice here, young Kevin, needs to travel to Count Volmar's castle— "

"A far way for such a child," a woman murmured, and Kevin gave her an indignant glare.

"Exactly," his Master said. "I doubt you restless butterflies will be staying here longer than one night."

"Not in *this* dull town!"

"Then since your route seems to be taking you along the North Road anyhow, if you might happen to see your way to the count's castle, and take Kevin with you when you go . . . ?"

For a moment, the Bard's eyes met Berak's fierce green gaze.

Almost, Kevin thought in sudden confusion, *as though they're exchanging secret information.*

But in the next moment Berak laughed and bowed another of his intricate bows, and Kevin told himself not to be ridiculous. The man was nothing more than a common minstrel.

"Of course, old man," Berak said. "Kevin, bardling, we leave at sunrise tomorrow!"

Whether I like it or not, the boy thought drily.

That night, the troop of minstrels sang for their supper, standing to one side of the open fireplace, the gaudy colors of their clothing turned muted and glowing by the flickering firelight. Kevin listened to their music for a long time, trying to figure out exactly what they were doing. No two singers seemed to be following the same tune, and the two harpers, three fiddlers and one flutist all seemed to be playing their own melodies as well. And yet somehow all that wild sound managed to blend into one whole, intricate song. He couldn't say whether or not it was a beautiful song, he couldn't even say whether or not he liked it, but the bardling had to admit it certainly was interesting!

The innkeeper and his wife didn't seem to know what to make of the music, either, nor did their guests. When the troop had finished, there was a fair amount of applause, and everyone agreed they had earned their dinners, but Kevin suspected from their uncertain glances that the rest of the audience was as confused as he.

"How did you like it?" The old Bard had appeared so suddenly at Kevin's shoulder that the bardling had to bite back a yell.

"I'm not sure . . . I mean, it was music, all right, not just sound, but . . . well . . . it was *wild*. Like something the forest would sing, if trees could only — I mean — I'm sounding stupid, aren't I?"

His Master chuckled. "No. Not at all. You sound like a youngster who's suddenly realized that the world's a good deal wider, with a good deal more strangeness in it, than he ever suspected." He patted Kevin's shoulder. "Come along, bardling. The night's growing late, and you must be up early in the morning."

Kevin stood in the courtyard of the inn, clad in good, serviceable tunic, breeches and boots, the whole thing covered by a woollen cloak, its warmth welcome in the chilly morning air. His lute was in its waterproof travelling case, slung across his back, because no Bard, not even a bardling, ever travelled without his instrument.

All around the bardling, the minstrels were chattering and scuttling about, somehow never getting in each other's way, reloading their wagons, scooping up giggling children, tightening a saddle girth here, readjusting a pack there. But Kevin didn't really notice all the bustle. He was too busy staring at the animal placidly looking back at him. His heart sank.

A mule! The Master hadn't even trusted him with a horse. An adventurer needed a stallion, a destrier, a war horse — not a stupid old long-eared mule!

"Eh, bardling!" Berak called from his wagon seat. "Mount up, boy! We have a long way to travel."

"My name is Kevin, not 'bardling,' " Kevin muttered, but Berak didn't seem to hear him.

"That's a wise old mule, bardling. He'll carry you safe and sound to Count Volmar's castle. If he doesn't decide to dump you in the mud instead!"

The minstrels all burst into laughter. His cheeks flaming, Kevin made sure the saddle pack with his spare clothes was secure, then climbed into the saddle. As he did, the lute whacked him painfully across the back. The mule wiggled a long ear back at him as though it too was laughing at him.

"If you bray at me, I'll whack *you!*" Kevin warned it, but the mule only shook its head, ears flapping.

As the minstrels rode out of the inn's courtyard, hoofs clopping and wagon wheels rattling against cobblestones, Kevin glanced up at his Master's window. But if the old Bard was watching, the bardling couldn't see him.

Feeling abandoned and very sorry for himself, Kevin kicked the mule's sides to get it moving. The mule rolled a reproachful eye back at him, but started grudgingly forward.

"Hey-ho, off to adventure!" Berak laughed, and burst into song.

Some adventure, Kevin thought bitterly.

Chapter II

As the minstrel troop rode and rattled along the wide dirt road, the day was as bright and cheery as something out of a story, full of bird song and pleasant little breezes.

Kevin hardly noticed. He was too busy struggling with his mule to keep it from lagging lazily behind.

"Here, boy." One of the musicians, a red-clad fiddler with instrument case strapped to his back like Kevin, handed the bardling a switch broken from a bush. "Wave this at him. He'll keep moving."

The fiddler's eyes were kind enough, but it seemed to Kevin that his voice practically dripped with condescension. *Thinks I've never ridden before*, Kevin thought, but he managed a tight smile and a "Thanks." It didn't help that the man was right; as long as the mule could see the switch out of the corner of an eye, it kept up a nice, brisk pace.

The North Road cut through brushland for a time, then through stands of saplings, then at last through true forest, green and lush in the springtime. This was royal land, not ceded to any of the nobles, and the road was kept clear, Kevin knew, by the spells of royal magicians. But those nice, neat spells hardly applied to the wildness on either side. The bardling, trying to pretend he'd travelled this way a hundred times, couldn't help wondering if bandits or even dark creatures, orcs or worse, were hiding in there.

Oh, nonsense! He was letting his Master's fussing get to him. It was forest, only forest. No one could see anything sinister in that tranquil greenery.

He'd let the switch drop and the mule was lagging again. Kevin waved it at the beast yet again. When that didn't seem to do any good, he gave it a good whack on the rump. The mule grunted in surprise and broke into a bone-jarring trot, overtaking the wagons and most of the riders. The equally surprised bardling jounced painfully in the saddle, lute banging against his back. For a moment Kevin wished he'd kept it in its case rather than out for quick playing. Struggling to keep his stirrups and his balance, he was sure he heard snickers from the troop.

Then, just as suddenly, the mule dropped back into its easygoing walk. Kevin nearly slammed his face into the animal's neck. This time, as he straightened himself in the saddle, he *knew* he'd heard muffled laughter. Without a word, he pulled the mule back into the troop.

Although the minstrels kept up a steady patter of cheerful conversation and song all around him, Kevin clamped his lips resolutely together after that. He had given them enough entertainment already!

It wasn't helping his increasingly sour mood that every time someone looked his way, he could practically hear that someone thinking, *Poor little boy, out on his own!*

"I'm *not* a baby!" he muttered under his breath.

"What's that?" A plump, motherly woman, bright yellow robes making her look like a buttercup, brought her mare up next to his mule. "Is something wrong, child?"

"I am not a child." Kevin said the words very carefully. "I am not a full Bard yet, I admit it, but I am the apprentice to — "

"Oh, well, bardling, then!" Her smile was so amused that Kevin wanted to shout at her, Leave me alone! Instead, he asked, as levelly as he could:

"Just how far away is Count Volmar's castle?"

"Oh, two days' ride or so, weather permitting, not more."

"And we're going to stay on this road?"

"Well, of course! We can hardly go cross-country through the woods with the wagon! Besides, that would be a silly thing to do: the North Road leads right to the castle. Very convenient."

"Very," Kevin agreed, mind busy. He hadn't dared hope that the castle would be so easy to find, even for someone who'd never been there before. Even for someone who just might happen to be travelling alone.

That night, the minstrels made camp in a circle of song and firelight that forced back the forest's shadow. Dinner had been cheese and only slightly stale bread from the inn, water from a nearby stream, and rabbits the older children had brought down with their slings. Now Kevin, sitting on a dead log to one side, nearly in darkness, watched the happy, noisy circle with a touch of envy. What must it be like to be part of a group like that? They were probably all related, one big, wild, merry family.

But then the bardling reminded himself that these were only minstrels, wandering folk whose musical talents just weren't good enough to let them ever be Bards. He should be pitying them, not envying them. Maybe they even envied him . . . ?

No. Two of the women were gossiping about him, he was sure of it, glancing his way every now and then, hiding giggles behind their hands. Kevin straightened, trying to turn his face into a regal mask. Unfortunately, the log on which he sat picked that moment to fall apart, dumping him on the ground in a cloud of moldy dust.

Predictably, every one of the troop was looking his way just then. Predictably, they all burst into laughter. Kevin scrambled to his feet, face burning. He'd had it with being babied and laughed at and made to feel a fool!

"Hey, bardling!" Berak called. "Where are you going?"

"To sleep," Kevin said shortly.

"Out there in the dark? You'll be warmer — and safer — here with us."

Kevin pretended he hadn't heard. Wrapping himself in his cloak, he settled down as best he could. The ground was harder and far colder than he'd expected. He really would have been more comfortable with the minstrels.

But then, he didn't really intend to sleep . . . not really. . . . It was just that he was weary from the day's riding. . . .

Kevin woke with a start, almost too cold and stiff to move. What — where — All around him was forest, still dark with night, but overhead he could see patches of pale, blue-gray sky through the canopy of leaves and realized it wasn't too far from morning. He struggled to his feet, jogging in place to warm himself up, wincing as his body complained, then picked up his lute. Safe and dry in its case, it hadn't suffered any harm.

Stop stalling! he told himself.

Any moment now, one of the minstrels was bound to wake up, and then it would be too late. Kevin ducked behind a tree to answer his chilly body's demands, then tiptoed over to where the horses and his mule were tied. One horse whuffled at him, but to his relief, none of them whinnied. Although his hands were still stiff with cold, the bardling managed to get his mule bridled and saddled. He hesitated an uncertain moment, looking back at the sleeping camp, wondering if he really was doing the right thing.

Of course I am! I don't want the count to think I'm a baby who can't take care of himself.

Kevin led the mule as silently as he could down the

road till the camp was out of sight, then swung up into the saddle.

"Come on, mule," he whispered. "We have a lot of ground to cover."

The minstrels would be discovering his absence any moment now. But, encumbered with their wagons and children as they were, they would never be able to overtake him. Kevin kicked the mule; frisky from the still chilly air, it actually broke into a prance. The bardling straightened proudly in the saddle.

At last! He finally felt like a hero riding off into adventure.

By nightfall, Kevin wasn't so sure of that. He was tired and sore from being in the saddle all day, and hungry as well. If only he had thought to take some food with him! The mule wasn't too happy with its snatches of grass and leaves, but at least it could manage, but the few mouthfuls of whatever berries Kevin had been able to recognize hadn't done much to fill his stomach.

Overhead, the sky was still clear blue, but the forest on either side was already nearly black, and a chill was starting up from the cooling earth. Kevin shivered, listening to the twitter of birds settling down for the night and the faint, mysterious rustlings and stirrings that could have been made by small animals or . . . other things. He shivered again, and told himself not to be stupid. He was probably already on Count Volmar's lands, and there wasn't going to be anything dangerous this close to a castle.

He hoped.

"We're not going to be able to go much further today," he told the mule reluctantly. "We'd better find a place to camp for the night."

At least he had flint and steel in his pouch. After stumbling about in the dim light for a time, Kevin managed to find enough dead branches to build himself a decent little fire in the middle of a small, rocky clearing. The firelight danced off the surrounding trees as the bardling sat huddling before the flames, feeling the welcome warmth steal through him.

The fire took off the edge of his chill. But it couldn't help the fact that he was still tired and so hungry his stomach ached. The bardling tried to ignore his discomfort by taking out his lute and working his way through a series of practice scales.

As soon as he stopped, the night flowed in around him, his small fire not enough to hold back the darkness, the little forest chirpings and rustlings not enough to break the heavy silence. Kevin struck out bravely into the bouncy strains of "The Miller's Boy." But the melody that had sounded so bright and sprightly with the inn around it seemed thin and lonely here. Kevin's fingers faltered, then stopped. He sat listening to the night for a moment, feeling the weight of the forest's indifference pressing down on him. He roused himself with an effort and put his lute back in its case, safe from the night's gathering mist. Those nice, dull, safe days back at the inn didn't seem quite so unattractive right now. . . .

Oh, nonsense! What sort of hero are you, afraid of a little loneliness?

He'd never, Kevin realized, been alone before, really alone, in his life. Battling with homesickness, the bardling banked the fire and curled up once more in his cloak.

After what seemed an age, weariness overcame misery, and he slipped into uneasy sleep.

Scornful laughter woke him. Kevin sat bolt upright, staring up into eyes that glowed an eerie green in the darkness. Demons!

No, no, whatever these beings were, they weren't demonic. After that first terrified moment, he could make out the faces that belonged with those eyes, and gasped in wonder. The folk surrounding him were tall and graceful, a touch too graceful, too slender, to be human. Pale golden hair framed fair, fine-boned, coldly beautiful faces set with those glowing, slanted eyes, and Kevin whispered in wonder:

"Elves . . ."

He had heard about them of course, everyone had. They were even supposed to share some of King Amber's lands with humans — though every now and then bitter feelings surfaced between the two races. But Kevin had never seen any of the elf-folk, White or Dark, good or evil, never even dreamed he might.

"Why, how clever the child is!" The elvish voice was clear as crystal, cold with mockery.

"Clever in one way, at least!" said another.

"So stupid in all other ways!" a third mocked. "Look at the way he sleeps on the ground, like a poor little animal."

"Look at the trail he left, so that anyone, anything could track him."

"Look at the way he sleeps like a babe, without a care in the world."

"A human child."

"A careless child!"

The elf man who'd first spoken laughed softly. "A foolish child that anyone can trick!"

So alien a light glinted in the slanted eyes that Kevin's breath caught in his throat. Everyone knew elvish whims were unpredictable; it was one of the reasons there could never be total ease between elf and human. If these folk decided to loose their magic on him, he wouldn't have a chance of defending himself. "My lords," he began, very, very carefully, "if I have somehow offended you, pray forgive me."

"Offended!" the elf echoed coldly. "As if anything a child such as you could do would be strong enough to offend us!"

That stung. "My lord, I — I know I may not look like much to someone like you." To his intense mortification, his empty stomach chose that moment to complain with a loud gurgle. Kevin bit his lip, sure that those keen, pointed elf ears had picked up the sound. All he could do was continue as best he could, "But — but that doesn't give you the right to insult me."

"Oh, how brave it is!" The elf man rested one foot lightly on a rock and leaned forward, fierce green gaze flicking over Kevin head to foot. "Bah, look at yourself! Sleeping on bare ground when there are soft pine boughs to make you a bed. Aching with hunger when the forest holds more than enough to feed one scrawny human. Leaving a trail anyone could follow and carrying no useful weapon at all. How could we *not* insult such ignorance?"

The elf straightened, murmuring a short phrase in the elvish tongue to the others. They laughed and faded soundlessly into the night, but not before one of them had tossed a small sack at Kevin's feet.

"Our gift, human," the elf man said. "Inside is food enough to keep you alive. And no, it is not bespelled. We would not waste magic on you."

With that, the elf turned to leave, then paused, looking back over his shoulder at the bardling. With inhuman bluntness, he said, "I hope, child, for your sake that you are simply naive and not stupid. In time, either flaw will get you killed, but at least the first can be corrected."

The alien eyes blazed into Kevin's own for a moment longer. Then the elf was gone, and the bardling was left alone in the night, more frightened than he would ever have admitted.

He's wrong! Kevin told himself defiantly once his heart had stopped racing. *Just because I'm a bardling, not a — a woodsman who's never known anything but the forest doesn't make me naive* or *stupid!*

Deciding that didn't stop him from rummaging in the little sack. The elvish idea of food that would keep him alive seemed to be nothing more exciting than flat wafers of bread. But when he managed to choke one of the dry things down, it calmed his complaining stomach so nicely that the bardling sighed with relief and actually slipped back into sleep.

Kevin stood with head craned back, sunlight warm on his face, feeling the last of last night's fears melting away. How could he possibly hold onto fear when it was bright, clear morning and all around him the air was filled with bird song?

Maybe the whole thing had been only a dream?

No. The sack of wafers was quite real. Kevin gnawed thoughtfully on one, then gave another to his mule, which lipped it up with apparent delight. He saddled and bridled the animal, then climbed aboard, still trying to figure out what the purpose of that midnight meeting had been.

At last he shook his head in dismissal. All the stories said the elf folk, being the nonhuman race they were, had truly bizarre senses of humor, sometimes outright cruel by human standards. What had happened last night must surely have been just another nasty elvish idea of a joke.

"Come on, mule. Let's get going." At least he wasn't hungry.

The road sloped up, first gently then more steeply, much to the mule's distaste. When it grew too steep, Kevin dismounted now and again to give the animal a rest, climbing beside it.

But at last, after a quiet day of riding and walking, they reached the crest. Kevin stared out in awe at a wild mountain range of tall gray crags, some of them high enough to be snowcapped even in spring. They towered over rolling green fields neatly sectioned into farms. On the nearest crag, surrounded by open space stood:

"Count Volmar's castle!" Kevin cried triumphantly. "It has to be!"

The castle hadn't been built for beauty. Heavy and squat, it seemed to crouch possessively on its crag like some ancient grey beast of war staring down at the count's lands. But Kevin didn't care. It was the first castle he had ever seen, and he thought it was wonderful, a true war castle dating from the days when heroes held back the forces of Darkness. Bright banners flew from the many towers, softening some of the harshness, and the bardling could see from here that the castle's gates were open. By squinting he could make out the devices on those banners: the count's black boar on an azure field.

"We've done it," he told the mule. "That is definitely the castle of Count Volmar."

He forgot about elves and hunger, loneliness and mocking minstrels. Excitement shivering through him, the bardling kicked his mule forward. Soon, soon, the real adventure was going to begin!

Chapter III

The closer Kevin got to Count Volmar's castle, the more impressive it seemed, looming up over him till he had to crane his head back to see the tops of the towers. The North Road ran right past the base of the crag, but the count's own road led its winding way up and up to the castle gates. Just when the bardling had almost reached the top (riding all the way this time, in case someone in the castle was watching him), the mule stopped short, long ears shooting up. In the next moment, two knights in gleaming mail, faces hidden by their helms, came plunging skillfully down the steep road on their powerful destriers, trailed by two younger, more cautious, riders — squires, Kevin guessed — on smaller horses.

"Get out of the way, boy!" they shouted.

Kevin hastily kneed his mule aside. With a shout of "Peasant fool!" the riders were past him, showering him with dirt and pebbles, and gone.

"Peasant fool, is it?" Kevin muttered, brushing himself off. "At least I know better than to force a horse down a steep hill at full speed!"

The bardling glanced down at himself. He had saved his best tunic and breeches for now; the neat red tunic and brown breeches and cloak might not be of the most noble quality, but they were, he thought, quite suitable. Definitely not what a peasant would wear. Not even a rich one who owned his farm; the cloth might in such a case be finer, but there was such a thing as style and taste.

Feeling better about the whole thing, Kevin prodded his mule up the last few feet to the open gates, huge, heavy brass-sheathed things—

Which were slowly shut in his face.

"Hey!" he yelled indignantly.

"Servants use the postern gate," an officious voice called down from one of the narrow tower windows.

"But I'm not—"

"Use the postern gate," the voice repeated.

Kevin sighed. He was hardly about to shout out his business here for everyone to hear. *This is just someone's mistake,* he told himself. *They'll correct it once I'm inside.*

He rode around the massive base of the castle to the humble little servants' entrance, which was sealed by a heavy, brass-bound oaken door. Standing in the stirrups, Kevin gave it a solid rap with his fist, then, when that got no results, managed a more satisfying thump with a foot.

"Hey! Anybody in there?"

A tiny window creaked open high in the door. "State your business," a voice demanded. This one, Kevin thought, sounded more bored than officious.

"My business," he said firmly, "is with Count Volmar. I have a message here from my Master."

The bardling drew out the sealed parchment the old Bard had given him and held it up so whoever was behind the door could see it. There was a long moment of silence. Then Kevin heard the sound of a heavy bolt being drawn. The door creaked open.

"Enter."

"At last!" the bardling muttered, and kicked his mule through the doorway.

As he'd expected, he was faced by a long stone tunnel; the outer walls of a war castle could hardly be anything but thick!

I'll never get the mule in there.

But the animal, after a brief hesitation about entering this narrow, shadowy cave, sniffed the air and moved eagerly forward, so eagerly Kevin suspected it must have smelled oats.

As they came out from the tunnel, the bardling found himself in what looked almost like a small town, tucked into the outer ward, the space between the ring of the outer walls and the inner walls of the count's keep. To one side was the castle stables, and the mule did its best to get Kevin to let it head off that way. But the bardling kept a tight hold on the reins, trying to see everything without making it look like he was gawking.

So many people!

He'd never seen so many crowded into so small a space, not even on market day. Here was the blacksmith's forge, the smith hard at work shoeing a restless gray destrier, calmly avoiding the war horse's attempts to bite; there, the carpenter's workshop echoed with hammering; and next to that, the armorer sat in the sunlight before his shop, mending the links in a mail shirt. A tangled crowd of castle folk chattered away as they did their tasks, while their children ran squealing and laughing all around the ward. Maybe the whole place did smell a bit too strongly of horse and dung and humanity, but it was still such a lively place that it took Kevin's breath away. He drank it all in, only to come back to himself with a shock when someone asked shortly:

"Name and business?"

Kevin glanced down to see a guard watching him warily. Mail glinted under a surcoat embroidered with the count's crest, and the weather-worn face held not a trace of warmth.

"Uh, yes. My — my name is Kevin, I'm a bardling, and my Master has sent me here with a message for Count Volmar."

He showed the guard the sealed parchment. To his dismay, the man snatched it from his hand. "Hey!"

"Leave your mule with the stablehands. Your bags will be brought to you — Arn!"

A small boy, a page clad in the count's blue livery, came running. "Sir?"

"Take this bardling to the squires' quarters."

"But my message!" Kevin protested.

"It will be given to Count Volmar." The guard's contemptuous stare said without words, Did you really think a mere bardling would be allowed to bother a count? "Go get your mule stabled."

With that, the man turned and disappeared into the keep. Kevin hesitated, toying with the idea of hurrying after the guard and insisting he be admitted to the count *at once*!

Oh no. Not only would something like that destroy what little was left of his dignity, it would probably get him thrown out of the castle!

Kevin's shoulders sagged. So much for being able to rub elbows with nobility!

"I'm supposed to wait *here*?"

"That's what I was told," little Arn answered. "In the squires' quarters."

"But *here*?" the bardling repeated. "There's nobody —Arn! Wait!"

The boy had already scurried away. Kevin, feeling helpless, stood looking uneasily about. The squires' quarters was nothing more than this long, dark, chilly hall broken up by a row of cots and clothes chests. The high roof was supported by thick columns, and the only light came from narrow windows set high in the walls. The silence was heavier than anything back in the forest.

The bardling sat down on the edge of one of the cots to wait. And wait. And wait.

Kevin had just about decided he'd been abandoned, and was wondering what would happen if he went hunting for Count Volmar himself when he heard a sudden rush of cheerful voices and sprang to his feet. A crowd of boys in their late teens came ambling into the hall, all of them in blue livery.

These must surely be the missing squires. Kevin watched them in sudden uneasiness, painfully aware that his secluded musician's life hadn't given him many chances to spend time with anyone his own age.

A stocky blond boy stopped short, staring at Kevin with bright blue eyes. "Holla! Who's this?"

"My name is Kevin," the bardling began, "and I — "

"You've got a lute. You a minstrel?"

"No!"

"You seem kinda young to be a Bard."

The boy's voice was brusque, but a hint of respect shone in his eyes. For a moment Kevin toyed with the idea of claiming that yes, he *was* a Bard. But he could picture his Master's disapproval only too well. A Bard, after all, was always supposed to be truthful. With a sigh, Kevin admitted:

"I'm not. Not yet. I'm apprenticed to a Bard, but — "

"A bardling," someone said in a scornful voice. "He's nobody."

The squires turned away. Blatantly ignoring him, they set about changing their clothes or cleaning their boots, chattering and joking as though he wasn't even there.

"Did you see me in the tilting yard?"

"Sure did. Saw you fall off, too!"

"The saddle slipped!"

"S-u-r-e it did! Like this!"

He pounced on the other boy and they wrestled, laughing. Watching them, totally excluded, Kevin ached with a loneliness more painful even than what he'd felt in the forest. As the horseplay broke off, he heard the squires argue over which of them was most skilled with sword or lance, or who would be the first to be knighted. A great surge of resentment swelled up within him.

Listen to them boast! I bet there isn't one of them who knows anything but *weaponry and fighting, the empty-headed idiots.*

But as the squires began to boast instead about the exploits of the knights they served, of Sir Alamar who'd taken on an entire bandit band and bested them, or Sir Theomard, who might be aging but who had still managed to slay three enemy knights in battle, one right after the other, Kevin's heart sank. These boys who were his own age had already done more than he'd even imagined. As squires to their knights, they had almost certainly shared in those mighty deeds. They would probably soon be heroes themselves.

Kevin bit his lip as resentment turned to envy. No wonder the squires scorned him! Here he was, a bardling, a mere music apprentice, someone who hadn't done *anything*! He must seem like a weakling to them, a coward, no better than a peasant.

A small hand shook his sleeve and he started. "Bardling?" It was little Arn. "Follow me, if you would. Master D'Krikas, Count Volmar's seneschal, wishes to speak with you."

D'Krikas? What an odd name!

Who cares how odd it is! At least I haven't been forgotten.

The bardling followed Arn through a maze of corridors, across the rush-strewn stretch of the Great Hall, and up a winding stairway, stopping before a closed door. "Here we are," Arn said, and scurried away once more. Kevin took a deep breath and knocked on the door.

"Enter!" a scratchy voice commanded.

Within was a cozy room, hung with thick hangings of deep red velvet and furnished with a scroll-filled bookcase and a massive desk, behind which sat a truly bizarre figure. Although it sat upright and had the right number of arms and head, it most definitely was not human. Kevin stared at the shiny, chitinous green skin, set off by a glittering golden gorget, and the large, segmented eyes and gasped out:

"You're an Arachnia!"

"The boy is a marvel of cleverness," the insectoid being chittered. "If he has satisfied his curiosity?"

"Oh, uh, of course. I'm sorry, I — I didn't mean to stare."

"Why not? You have plainly never seen one of my kind before. Why should you not stare?"

"I . . ."

Kevin blinked. The Arachnia had snatched what looked like a handful of sugar cubes from a small bowl on the desk and popped them into its beaked mouth. The crunching sound reminded him uncomfortably of praying mantises devouring beetles. In fact, now that he thought of it, the being *did* look a good deal like a giant mantis. . . .

"Now you wonder anew." The dry chitter might have been a laugh. "Have you never heard that my kind are always hungry? For logic as well as food. Boy, time is a precious thing, and we have already wasted enough of it. I am, as I am sure you have already realized, D'Krikas, seneschal, major-domo if you wish, to Count Volmar."

"My lord." Belatedly, Kevin bowed, but D'Krikas, writing busily in a huge open ledger, hardly seemed to notice.

"Here are the arrangements that have been made for you. Yes, yes, I know why you are here. You are to be housed and fed with the squires, and you will be permitted to copy the manuscript in the library between dawn and dusk. You are not to intrude upon the count's private quarters. You are not to bother any of the knights. You are not to interfere with any of the castle personnel. You are not to handle any weapons. You are not to enter the tilting grounds. You are not to interfere with any of the servants. You are not to steal food from the kitchen . . ."

As the list of prohibitions went on and on, Kevin

thought wryly he could almost wish he was back with his Master — at least there'd been fewer rules!

I can't stand this place! he decided suddenly. *The sooner I finish the stupid job, the better.*

"Master D'Krikas," Kevin asked as soon as the being fell silent, "is there any reason I can't continue my copying after dark? I mean," he added cajolingly, "it would save precious time."

"No, no, no!" the seneschal snapped. "Have you no idea of how expensive candles are? Have you? No! Burning candles so a human can do some copy work would be a waste of good wax." D'Krikas stood, gray cloak swirling, tall, thin body towering over Kevin. "And no one your age, boy, can be trusted with open flame around so many fragile manuscripts!"

The seneschal folded himself back behind the desk. Once more writing in the huge ledger, D'Krikas said curtly, "That is all. You may leave."

Kevin hardly wanted to return to the squires' quarters. But where else was there? By now, it was too late to start copying the manuscript. And after D'Krikas' never-ending list of prohibitions, he hardly dared go exploring! Since Arn didn't seem to be anywhere around, Kevin retraced his steps as best he could, and didn't get lost more than once or twice.

Dinner, he suspected, wasn't going to be any brighter than anything else that had happened this day.

It wasn't. Dinner was a miserable affair served on rough trestle tables set up in the squires' quarters. Even though the bardling had been assigned a seat among the squires, he'd might as well have been in the middle of a desert, because no one would talk to him. Kevin busied himself in trying to chew the stringy beef, and in trying to convince himself the squires' coldness didn't matter; as soon as he'd finished copying that cursed manuscript, he would never have to see any of these idiots again.

Once they had finished eating and the food scraps and trestle tables had been cleared away, the squires disappeared, still without a word to Kevin. He gathered, from the bits of their conversations he overheard, that they were going off to wait on their knights.

Who are probably just as brainless.

Left alone in the now empty hall, the bardling shivered, grabbing for his cloak. The place seemed even more silent than before, and twice as chilly. Evidently Count Volmar didn't believe in pampering youngsters, because there wasn't a fireplace anywhere in the hall.

Never mind, Kevin told himself. *A true hero doesn't mind a little discomfort.*

Or a little loneliness.

The silence was getting on his nerves. The bardling took out his lute and practiced for a long, long while, trying to ignore everything but his music. At last, warmed a little by his own exertions, Kevin put the instrument back in its case and stretched out on the lumpy cot he'd been assigned. The hour, he thought, was probably still fairly early — not that there was any way to tell in here, without so much as a water clock or hourglass. But there wasn't anything else to do but sleep. The pillow was so thin it felt as though the feathers had been taken from a very scrawny bird. The one blanket was too thin for real comfort, but by adding his cloak to it, the bardling was almost warm.

He had nearly drifted off to sleep when the squires returned. Kevin heard their whispers and muffled laughter, and felt his face redden in the darkness. They were laughing at him. He knew they were laughing at him.

Miserable all over again, Kevin turned over, and buried his face in the pillow.

INTERLUDE THE FIRST

Count Volmar, tall, lean and graying of brown hair and beard, sat seemingly at ease in his private solar before a blazing fireplace, a wine-filled goblet of precious glass in his hand. He looked across the small room at the woman who sat there, and raised the goblet in appreciation. She nodded at the courtesy, her dark green eyes flickering with cold amusement in the firelight.

Carlotta, princess, half-sister to King Amber himself, could not, Volmar knew, be much younger than his own mid-forties, and yet she could easily have passed for a far younger woman. Not the slightest trace of age marred the pale, flawless skin or the glorious masses of deep red hair turned to bright flame by the firelight.

Sorcery, he thought, and then snickered at his own vapid musings so that he nearly choked on his own wine. Of course it was sorcery! Carlotta was an accomplished sorceress, and about as safe, for all her beauty, as a snake.

About as honorable, too.

Not that he was one to worry overmuch about honor.

"The boy is safely ensconced, I take it?" Carlotta's smile was as chill as her lovely eyes.

"Yes. He has a place among the squires. Who, I might add, have been given to understand that he's so far beneath them they needn't bother even to acknowledge his presence — that to do so, in fact, would demean their own status. By now, the boy is surely thoroughly disillusioned about nobility and questioning his own worth."

"He suspects nothing, then? Good. We don't want him showing any awkward sparks of initiative." Carlotta sipped delicately from her goblet. "We don't want him copying his Master."

Volmar's mouth tightened. Oh, yes, the Bard, that cursed Bard. He could remember so clearly, even though it was over thirty years ago, how it had been, himself just barely an adult and Carlotta only . . . how old? Only thirteen? Maybe so, but she had already been as ambitious as he. More so. Already mistress of the Dark Arts despite her youth, the princess had attempted to seize the throne from her half-brother.

And almost made it, Volmar thought, then corrected that to: We *almost made it.*

Amber had been only a prince back then, on the verge of the succession. His father had been old, and there hadn't been any other legal heir; Carlotta, as the court had been so eager to gossip, was only Amber's half-sister, her mother quite unknown.

But there were always ways around such awkward little facts. Once Amber had been declared dead — or so it had been believed — in heroic battle (when actually, Volmar thought wryly, Carlotta's magics had turned him to stone), the poor old king would surely have . . . pined away. Volmar grinned sharply. Why, the shock alone would have finished him; Carlotta wouldn't have needed to waste a spell. The people, even if they had, by some bizarre chance, come to suspect her of wrongdoing, would have had no choice but to accept Carlotta, with her half-share of the Blood Royal, as queen.

Ambitious little girl . . . Volmar thought with approval. *What a pity she didn't succeed. Sorceress or no, she would have been too wise to try ruling alone. She would have taken a consort.*

And who better than one of her loyal supporters?

Even one whose role in the attempted usurpation had never become public.

Volmar suddenly realized he was grimacing, and forced himself to relax. His late father had been an avid supporter of the old king, and if he had ever found out his own son was a traitor . . .

But he hadn't. And of course if only Carlotta had safely become queen, it wouldn't have mattered. The only traitors then would have been those who failed to acknowledge her!

If only . . . Bah!

Carlotta *would* have become queen if it hadn't been for the boy's Master, that accursed Bard and his allies. . . .

"Forget the past, Volmar."

The count started, thrown abruptly back into the present. "You . . . have learned to read minds . . . ?" If the sorceress suspected he planned to use her to place a crown on his own head, he was dead. Worse than dead.

"You must learn to guard your expressions, my lord. Your thoughts were there for anyone with half an eye to read."

Not all *my thoughts,* the count thought, giddy with relief.

Carlotta got restlessly to her feet, dark green gown swirling about her elegant form. Volmar, since she was, after all, a princess and he only a count, stood as well: politic courtesy.

She never noticed. "Enough of the past," the sorceress repeated, staring into the flames. "We must think of what can be done *now*."

Volmar moved warily to stand beside her, and caught a flicker of alien movement in the flames. Faces . . . ah. Carlotta was absently creating images of the boy, the bardling. "Why do you suppose he sent the boy here?" the princess murmured. "And why just now? What purpose could the old man possibly have? You've convinced me the manuscript is merely a treatise on lute music." She glanced sharply at Volmar. "It *is*, isn't it?"

"Of course," Volmar said easily, hiding the fact that he wasn't really sure which of the many manuscripts stored in the library it might be; his father had been the scholar, not he. "My father collected such things."

"Yes, yes, but why send the boy *now*? Why is it suddenly so urgent that the thing be copied?"

"Ah . . . it could be merely coincidence."

"No, it couldn't!" The flames roared up as Carlotta whirled, eyes blazing. Volmar shrank back from her unexpected surge of rage, half expecting a sorcerous attack, but the princess ignored him, returning to her chair and dropping into it with an angry flounce. "You're the only one who knows how I've been in hiding all these years, lulling suspicions, making everyone think I was dead."

"Of course." Though Volmar never had puzzled out why Carlotta had hidden for quite so many years. Oh, granted, she had been totally drained after the breaking of her stone-spell on Amber, but even so . . .

"Maybe that's it." Carlotta's musings broke into Volmar's wonderings. "Maybe now that I've come out of hiding, begun moving again, the Bard has somehow sensed I'm still around. He *is* a Master of that ridiculous Bardic Magic, after all."

Volmar was too wise to remind her it was the Bardic Magic she so despised that had blocked her path so far. "Eh, well, the bardling is safe among the squires," he soothed. "I've been debating simply telling him the manuscript isn't here and sending him away."

"Don't be a fool!" Sorcery crackled in the air around Carlotta, her hair stirring where there was no breeze. "The boy was sent here for a purpose, and we will both be better off when we find out just what that purpose might be!"

"But how can we learn the truth? If the boy becomes suspicious, he'll never say a thing. And I can hardly order the imprisonment or torment of an innocent bardling. My people," Volmar added with a touch of contempt, "wouldn't stand for it."

"Don't be so dramatic. The boy is already quite miserable, you say. No one will talk to him, no one will treat him kindly, and he's faced with a long, boring, lonely task." Carlotta smiled slowly. "Just think how delighted he would be if someone was *nice* to him! How eager he would be to confide in that someone!"

"I don't understand. An adult — "

"No, you idiot! Don't you remember what it's like being that young? The boy is only going to confide in someone his own age."

As usual, Volmar forced down his rage at her casual insults. *Ah, Carlotta, you superior little witch, if ever I gain the throne beside you, you had better guard your back!* As innocuously as he could, he asked, "Who are you suggesting? One of the squires?"

"Oh, hardly that."

Her shape blurred, altered . . . Volmar rubbed a hand over his eyes. He'd known from the start that Carlotta was as much a master of shape-shifting as any fairy, but watching her in action always made him dizzy.

"You can look now, poor Volmar." Her voice was an octave higher than before, and so filled with sugar he dropped his hand to stare.

Where the adult Carlotta had sat was now a coyingly sweet little blonde girl of, Volmar guessed, the bardling's own age, though it was difficult to tell age amid all the golden ringlets and alabaster skin and large, shining blue eyes.

"How do I look?" she cooed.

Honest words came to his lips before he could stop them. "Sweet enough to rot my teeth."

She merely threw back her head and laughed. *Her* teeth, of course, were flawless. "I *am* a bit sickening, aren't I? Let me try a more plausible form."

The sickening coyness faded. The girl remained the

same age, but the blonde hair was now less perfectly golden, the big blue eyes a bit less glowing, the pale skin just a touch less smooth. As Volmar grit his teeth, determinedly watching despite a new surge of dizziness, he saw the perfect oval of her face broaden ever so slightly at the forehead, narrow at the chin, until she looked just like . . .

"Charina!" the count gasped.

"Charina," the princess agreed. "Your darling little niece."

Too amazed to remember propriety, Volmar got to his feet and slowly circled her. "Marvelous!" he breathed at last. "Simply marvelous! I would never know you weren't the real — But what do we do with the real Charina?"

Her voice was deceptively light. "I'm sure you'll think of something."

"Ah, yes." Volmar smiled thinly. "Poor Charina. She always *has* been a bit of a nuisance, wandering about the castle like a lonely wraith. How unfortunate that my sister and her fool of a husband had the bad taste to die. Poor little creature: too far from the main line of descent to be of any use as a marriage pawn. No political value at all. Just another useless girl."

"Not so useless now." Carlotta/Charina dimpled prettily.

"Poor Charina," Volmar repeated without any warmth at all. "So easily disposed of. She never *will* be missed."

Chapter IV

Kevin woke with a jolt as something smothering landed smack across his face, molding itself over his nose and mouth. Gasping, he clawed the monster aside — and found himself holding a damp towel.

"Very funny!" he began angrily, only to find himself talking to empty space. The last of the squires was just leaving the hall, laughing with the others.

Fuming, Kevin got to his feet and found the garde-robe facilities, grateful that at least the count didn't insist his underlings use lowly chamber pots. Going to the communal washing trough, he discovered the squires hadn't left him more than a few inches of water, barely enough to splash on his face.

I should just be glad the water's clean!

Grumbling, he dressed, pulling his clothes from the chest at the foot of his bed, and sat down to a solitary breakfast — at least they'd left him *something* to eat! — of a roll and some scraps of cheese, washed down with a lukewarm goblet of *khafe*.

Now, all he had to do was find the count's library.

Easily said. Kevin wandered helplessly through the castle corridors for a time, sure he was going to be shouted at by D'Krikas for being where he shouldn't be. At last, to his relief, he intercepted a page, a wide-eyed boy even younger than Arn, who shyly gave him directions, then hurried away.

At last, the bardling thought wryly. *Someone whose status here is even lower than mine.*

The library was a large, dusty room lined with tall

shelves piled high with scrolls and books of all sizes. It was so redolent with the scent of dusty old parchment and leather that Kevin sneezed. Obviously scholarship wasn't high on the count's list of priorities!

As he glanced about the crowded room, the bardling shook his head in gloom. The room faced onto an inner courtyard, safely away from attack, so at least the windows were large enough to let him see what he was doing. But there wasn't a title anywhere, not on books or scroll cases. There wasn't any sign of a librarian, either. There probably wasn't one, judging from the dustiness of the room.

All right. The sooner he started looking, the sooner he'd get this whole stupid job finished.

By mid-afternoon, Kevin was dusty, weary of climbing up and down the rickety library ladder and sick to death of the whole room. Ha, by now he probably knew more about the contents of the count's library than anyone, including the count! And what a weird collection it was, without any logic to it! Why in the world would anyone want to keep not one but three copies of *The Agricultural Summaries of Kendall County for the First Twenty Years of King Sendak's Reign*? And what was a treatise on politics doing tucked in between two volumes of rather bad love poetry?

How can the Master even know for sure the manuscript's in here?

By Bardic Magic, of course. Kevin started to sigh, then coughed instead. Blast this dust!

The bardling stopped his hunt long enough to snag some lunch from a startled page, then dove into the library once more. A book about farm tools. Another. A catalog of cattle diseases. One on swine, wild and domestic. A book on —

"Ow!"

Kevin nearly fell off the ladder, just barely managing

to catch his balance in time. Something in the shelves had bit him!

No, no, it hadn't been a bite at all, more of a weird tingling in his fingertips. Kevin looked warily at the last book he'd touched — and let out a whoop of joy. Yes, yes, *yes,* he'd found the manuscript he needed at last!

The bardling scurried down the ladder clutching his prize, and took it over to the library's one desk, wiping off dust from the manuscript's leather binding as he went. A good chunk of the day was already gone, but at least he could get the copying started. Someone, presumably at D'Krikas' command, had left him supplies. Kevin found an inkwell and two quill pens on the desk, and a nice stack of parchment in a drawer. Sitting with the manuscript open before him, the bardling paused for one anticipatory moment, then dove into his work.

But after a moment, Kevin straightened again, blinking in confusion. He could have sworn the whole manuscript had been written in the common script used by most of the human lands here in the West — yet now some of the words seemed to be in a different language completely.

The bardling rubbed his eyes. He'd spent too much time in this dusty place, peering at old books. Manuscripts did *not* change themselves from one language to another.

Yet when Kevin took a second look, he saw, without any doubt about it, that some of the letters were actually, slowly and gracefully, changing before his eyes, altering from the human script into elaborate, beautiful, alien figures.

Elvish, he realized with a shock, recognizing the script from some of his Master's music books.

Kevin bit back a groan as he realized what lay ahead. He could only read a few words in elvish. That meant he'd have to copy the symbols line for line, much more slowly and carefully than he would the script of a language that meant something to him.

Oh, wonderful. More time wasted.

But as the bardling started copying the manuscript word by word and symbol by symbol, a sudden little shiver of wonder raced through him. Even though the elvish wasn't miraculously translating itself for him, even though he had no idea what he was copying, the very fact that he'd been able to see the letters transform could only mean one thing: his long-sleeping gift for Bardic Magic had finally started to wake up! His fingers fairly itched to try his lute and see if the magical songs finally had some Power to them!

First things first. There was still the manuscript to finish.

Maybe his magic was starting to wake, but his eyes were beginning to ache. It was getting more and more difficult to see the pages. Kevin looked up, mildly surprised to realize how dark the library had become; he hadn't been aware of the passing hours, but by now it was very obviously too late to do any more copying. Still, he'd made a good start. And . . . magic, he thought with a renewed thrill of wonder, Bardic Magic was going to be his.

Kevin got slowly to his feet. But in the middle of stretching stiff muscles, he froze. Acting on an impulse he didn't quite understand, the bardling warily hid the manuscript behind a shelf of books.

There. That should keep it safe till tomorrow.

He scooped up his copy. Returning to the squires' quarters, the bardling followed his Master's orders (though they seemed unnecessarily wary) and hid the copy in a secret pocket in his saddlebags, which in turn he hid under his clothes in the chest. With a tired sigh, he sat down on the cot and picked up his lute. Warily, he tried one of the magical songs. Nothing much happened — except for a faint, yet very real tingling in his fingers.

It was true. Grinning, Kevin knew he really did have the gift for Bardic Magic. And who knew where that might lead?

"Bard," Kevin whispered joyously.

* * *

In the morning, not even noticing how the squires continued to snub him, Kevin ate and dressed in a rush and hurried to the library, eager to start the day's copying. Let's see, he'd hidden the manuscript behind this row...

"No, oh no!"

The manuscript was gone.

That's impossible. I — I must have just mistaken which row it was.

The bardling started searching in the next row and then the next, carefully at first, then more and more frantically. It *had* to be here! Elvish words or no, manuscripts just didn't get up and walk!

Kevin was on his knees, facing denuded shelves and surrounded by piles of books when a gentle cough made him start. He whirled so sharply he lost his balance, sitting down hard on some of the books, and stared up at...

At one of the loveliest girls he'd ever seen. Her long plaits of hair were such a beautiful gold, her eyes were the clearest blue, the same shade as her silky gown, while her face and figure were . . . were . . .

Reddening, Kevin scrambled to his feet, trying to brush off as much dust as possible. "I . . . uh . . . was working in the library." *Oh, you idiot! She can see that for herself.* "I mean, I was copying out a manuscript. For my Master. He's a Bard. And I — I'm Kevin, I mean his apprentice, I mean, a bardling."

The lovely eyes widened. "How wonderful! I've never met anyone studying to be a Bard before. You must be very wise."

"Uh . . . well, I don't know about that. It's not easy being a bardling, though."

"I can imagine! All that music to learn — I never *could* manage to do more than pick out the simplest tunes on the harp, no matter *how* my tutors insisted. Are you a harper, too? No? What instrument do you play?"

For a moment, staring into those warm blue depths,

Kevin couldn't remember to save his life. "The — the lute," he stammered out at last.

"My goodness," she said respectfully. "That's a very difficult instrument, isn't it?"

"Not for me." *Wonderful. Now, instead of an idiot I sound like a braggart.*

"I'd love it if you'd play for me. If you want to, that is."

"Oh, I do!" Kevin exclaimed.

The girl gave the most delightful little giggle. "But I'm forgetting my manners! Here I'm asking you to play for me, and you don't even know who I am. My name is Charina, and I am Count Volmar's niece."

Kevin hastily bowed. "My lady."

"Please!" Her sweet laugh sent a little shiver through him. "I hear enough formalities at my uncle's court. But I didn't mean to startle you, or interrupt you in . . . " Her glance took in the empty shelves and piles of books. "In whatever it is you're doing. Please, continue."

How could he, with such a wonderful creature watching him? One eye on Charina, Kevin did his best to look for the missing manuscript, but at last sank back on his heels with a groan. "I can't find it."

To his wonder, she knelt by his side in a faint, sweet cloud of perfume. He heard himself say, "You'll get your gown all dusty," even as he was hoping she wouldn't listen.

Charina shrugged impatiently. "Gowns can be cleaned. Now, if you'll tell me what the manuscript looks like, I'll help you look."

He couldn't concentrate with her face so close to his, her eyes so earnest, her lips . . .

To his horrified embarrassment, his body was responding. Kevin turned hastily away, praying she hadn't noticed. "It's c-called *The Study of Ancient Song*, but I don't think that's its real name, and it's about so big, so wide, in a worn brown leather binding."

"You don't think that's its real name?" Charina echoed softly. "Why ever not?"

Kevin felt her warmth like a fire against his arm. He hastily moved that arm away, and the girl laughed.

"Why, bardling, are you *afraid* of me?"

She made it sound so ridiculous that Kevin found himself starting to laugh, too. "No, of course not," he lied. "But I . . . you . . . " Quickly he changed to a safer subject. "The manuscript's too weird to be just a study. I mean, part of it's in elvish."

"How odd! But I said I'd help you look, and I will."

It was, Kevin thought, as they searched together, easily turning out to be both the worst and the most wonderful day of his life.

A day that ended all too soon.

"I'm sorry we couldn't find the manuscript," Charina said. A smudge of dirt covered the very tip of her nose, and Kevin had to fight down the impulse to brush it away, to touch her soft cheek — No! He didn't dare. If he touched her once, he wouldn't be able to stop. And she *was* the count's niece, after all.

"Yes, uh, right," he got out. "Blast the thing! It has to be here *somewhere*!"

"I know what you need," Charina told him with a smile. "You need a day away from this dusty old place."

"I can't — "

"You can! You'll be more likely to find the manuscript if you get out in the nice, fresh air. I know! I'm going riding tomorrow. Why don't you join me? You . . . do ride, don't you?"

He wasn't about to tell her about the mule. "Of course."

"Well, then! Meet me by the stables tomorrow morning, and we'll make a whole day of it."

I shouldn't. I should stay here and find the manuscript and finish copying it, and — and —

And a day away from it couldn't possibly matter.

"I'll be there," Kevin promised, and smiled.

Of course they weren't allowed to ride out alone. A dull-faced groom went with them, several tactful strides behind so they could at least pretend to be alone.

Kevin hardly noticed the man. Charina sat her pretty white palfrey with graceful ease, her deep blue riding gown matching the little mare's blue-dyed bridle and saddle, her hair tucked neatly up under a feathered cap. As for the bardling, well, he was mounted not on a mule but on a horse, a real, spirited horse! Maybe it wasn't so easy to keep his seat, maybe he nearly fell a dozen times, but at last he was riding a proper hero's mount.

They didn't ride very far, only as far as a flowery hillside.

"I thought this would make a lovely picnic site," Charina said, jumping lightly down before the embarrassed Kevin could help her. As they munched on fresh, buttery bread and the first peaches of springtime, the girl coaxed, eyes bright, "But there's so much more in my uncle's demesne! Tomorrow is market day. We can ride down into the town and see all the sights."

"Well . . ."

"Oh, you can't say no! Please! It'll be such fun. Besides, I see so few people my own age!"

"There *are* the squires," Kevin said, hating himself for reminding her.

To his delight, she dismissed them all with a contemptuous wave of the hand. "Mere boys. Servants no better than their masters. While *you* are almost a Bard. *You* are going to be somebody. You *are* somebody! Besides," she added shyly, "I like you."

Another day away from the library can't hurt, either, Kevin told himself.

But two days stretched into three, then four. A full week passed, then another without him noting it, a time out of time during which Kevin and Charina rode together all over the count's lands, hunting out pretty glades and awesome mountain vistas. He played his lute for her, searching for the most romantic songs he knew, half amazed to hear how wonderfully alive his music sounded, how full of strength. This was the true dawning of his Bardic Magic, Kevin realized with a touch of awe. And surely Charina, just by being her own sweet, wonderful self, was helping it awaken. Surely he wouldn't have long to wait before it woke completely. When it did . . .

Kevin smiled, seeing himself released from apprenticeship, seeing himself returning in triumph to Charina, no longer a mere bardling but a full Bard, the equal of almost any rank of nobility.

"Kevin." His Master was facing him, looking so reproachful the bardling asked warily:

"What's wrong? What have I done?"

"It's what you haven't *done, Kevin. Where is the manuscript, boy? Where is the copy I asked you to make?"*

"I'll make it, Master, don't fear!"

"You must. Your life depends on it. Do you hear me, Kevin? Your life depends on it."

"No, I— "

"No!"

Kevin's eyes shot open, staring up at a stone ceiling high overhead. What — Where —

A dream, he realized, sinking back in relief. He was in the squires' quarters in Count Volmar's castle, and he'd merely had a bad dream.

And yet, Kevin thought uneasily, there had been a germ of truth to it. He really had been neglecting his duty for . . . how long had it been? Mentally adding up the days, the bardling gasped to realized he hadn't even thought of the manuscript for nearly two weeks.

Overwhelmed by guilt, he sprang to his feet — and gasped anew.

Someone in the night had most thoroughly gone through his belongings.

My lute!

To his immense relief, though its case had been opened, the lute hadn't been harmed.

But what about the copy of the manuscript? If anyone's taken it . . .

The bardling hastily knelt by the clothes chest. His clothes were strewn all about, but nothing at all seemed to have been taken. Suddenly wary, Kevin deliberately didn't grab at the saddlebags. Instead, he slipped his hand casually into the hidden pocket, just in case he was being watched, as though he was merely rummaging through the clothing.

Ah! The copy was still in there, undisturbed.

The bardling straightened, glaring about at the squires. "All right, whose idea of a joke was this?"

"Look at the poor little boy!" someone jeered. "Musta been sleepwalking."

"Sleep rummaging, you mean!" someone else yelled. "Just like some ragpicking peasant!"

The squires all burst into raucous laughter, and Kevin turned away in disgust. He wasn't going to learn which one of them was the jester, not without fighting the whole pack. Which would be truly stupid; every one of these buffoons practiced combat daily. Besides, although he burned to wipe some of those grins off a few of those jeering faces, he'd been a bardling too long to risk damaging his hands in a fight, particularly not now, when his magic was starting to blossom.

I wish I could really use it! Then we'd see who had the final laugh!

No. A true Bard never used his talents for harm.

Blast it to Darkness!

Clenching his jaws in frustration, Kevin set about

putting his belongings back in place. By the time he was done, he was alone in the hall, and by the time he had eaten and dressed, he'd gotten his emotions under control.

After all, he had been spending his time with Count Volmar's niece, equal to equal. Nothing these silly boys, these . . . mere servants could do was worth his notice!

At least Kevin *thought* he believed all that.

As he was on his way to the library, determined once and for all to find the missing manuscript and copy it, a sweet voice called to him, "Where are you going in such a hurry?"

Why did he suddenly feel so guilty? "Charina, I — "

"The weather's so nice and warm today! And I have a wonderful idea for a picnic, just the two of us."

Oh, how could he resist those lovely blue eyes? Grimly, Kevin reminded himself of the dream and his neglected duty. "I'm sorry, Charina," he said with very real regret. "I can't. I really would love to go riding or picnicking or anything else with you, truly. But, well, I have a job to do, and I'd better do it."

Charina stared at him as though he'd just told her something obscene. "You'd turn *me* down?" she gasped.

"Please, I didn't mean — "

"You would! No, no, don't try to argue. I quite understand. You're bored with me."

"No!"

"Yes, you are." She tossed her head. "If you don't want to come with me, you don't have to. I can do very well without you, you — you *boy*!"

With that, Charina flounced angrily away, leaving Kevin standing lost and unhappy behind her.

INTERLUDE THE SECOND

Count Volmar looked up in surprise as Carlotta stormed into the solar, shedding the persona of Charina like a cloak and throwing herself down in a chair, eyes wild, red hair crackling about her.

"I cannot *bear* being that simpering little fool of a girl a moment longer!" she raged.

She looked so totally inhuman in her sorcerous fury that Volmar shuddered. "I can't say I blame you," he said soothingly, and saw just a touch of that fury fade. "I never did like little girls. All sweetness and cuteness—Bah." He moved to the small table by the wall that held decanters of wine. Without asking her, Volmar filled a goblet and handed it to her. As Carlotta sipped, he took his seat again and asked, "Do you really need to be her any longer?"

The princess glared at him over the goblet's rim in suddenly renewed anger, sorcerous hair like wildfire about her. "*I* don't know!" she snapped. "I feel as though I don't know anything any more!"

Warily, like a man tiptoeing on the edge of a fiery pit, Volmar asked, "You haven't been able to find the manuscript, I take it?"

"Curse the thing, no! You either, obviously."

"Obviously." Ambitious though he was, Volmar admitted to himself, he was not about to do anything as reckless as trying to hide a probably magical artifact from a sorceress. Particularly one who right now was ablaze with rage and frustration. "You're sure the boy isn't deliberately hiding it somewhere in the library."

Carlotta shook her head. "He may have tried to do

so at first, but he was quite definitely on the verge of panic while hunting for the thing when I entered as Charina. No . . . " she added thoughtfully, "he has nothing to do with its disappearance. There is almost certainly a spell surrounding the manuscript."

"A spell! I thought you could detect such things."

"Oh, it's a very subtle one if even my sorceries haven't been able to sense it. And, since the manuscript seems to be designed to deliberately hide itself, even from me, it must be a very powerful spell indeed."

Volmar fought down a new shudder. Bad enough to have a sorcerous ally; he understood Carlotta and the dangers she represented after all these years. Or at least he hoped he did. But the thought that there might be some new, unknown, alien magic lurking in his castle as well, magic even Carlotta couldn't identify, just waiting to strike . . .

"What about the boy?" That came out more sharply than he'd intended; he was struggling to keep his voice from shaking. "You told me he has the rudiments of Bardic Magic about him. Could he have somehow — "

"The *rudiments*. It's a nuisance that it should have begun waking now, but the boy hasn't yet mastered even the least Powerful of magic songs."

"He still might know more than he admits."

"I doubt it." Carlotta sighed impatiently. "I've seen more of him in the past two weeks than I ever want to see of anyone. Still, he *is* the only clue we have to the manuscript."

"But what if his magic *does* come to life?" Volmar stirred uneasily in his chair. "I don't like the boy. He's too . . . too . . . "

"Honest?" Carlotta's voice was sly.

"Unpredictable," the count countered. "I think we should be rid of him now, while we still can."

"Not yet." Her glance held a disconcerting hint of contempt. "Volmar, you always were a nervous sort.

Let me try to explain this to you as clearly as I can: the boy is not a threat to us."

"Not yet," the count echoed darkly.

Carlotta's eyes flashed. "Challenging my wisdom?" she asked, ever so softly. "Volmar, dear little Volmar, don't try to cross me. I could destroy you, little man, with a glance."

The count froze, all at once very much aware of how close Death could be. One wrong word . . . "Why, Princess!" He forced the words from a mouth that suddenly seemed too dry for speech. "Have I ever been anything but your loyal ally?"

"To serve your own goals."

"Well, yes, I won't lie about that. But in doing so I serve yours as well, for both our sakes! Someday, my princess, you will wrest the throne from that fool— "

" 'That fool,' as you so charmingly put it, is my brother."

"Your half-brother only. Carlotta, we both know you aren't bound by any misguided sisterly love. Someday you *will* take the throne. And when you do, my dear princess, I know you will remember your friends."

"Friends." Carlotta's glance flicked over him, the contempt now only just barely hidden. But then she shrugged. "We shall watch the boy a bit longer. I will make one last effort to win him, body and mind. And if I still cannot subvert him to my side, I give you permission to rid us of him." She paused. "Even as you did our poor, sweet Charina."

Volmar waved that off. A girl hadn't any business being up on the ramparts anyhow, not without even a guard for company, let alone doing something as foolish as leaning over the edge of the crenellations to watch birds fly by. It had almost been too easy to help her join that flight. However briefly. And not a soul could say it had been anything but an accident. "We shouldn't wait," the count insisted. "I have a feeling— "

"Come now! Leave prescience to me. We can't be rid of him just yet. We still may need him to find the manuscript if we cannot." She shuddered delicately. "Even if it means I must once more take on the persona of that pretty little fool of a — No, wait . . . " The princess straightened in her chair, eyes fierce. "That may not be necessary. The boy has a head full of wild romance. What if . . . ? Ha, yes, of course! I already laid the groundwork without realizing it when I told him I would go riding alone."

"My princess, what *are* you talking about?"

"You'll learn, soon enough. Yes, I do believe that I shall go riding alone again tomorrow." Her smile was all at once so alien, so full of dark, sorcerous promise, that Volmar's heart turned chill. "And then," Carlotta added softly, "we . . . shall see what we shall see."

More than that, she would not say, leaving Count Volmar cold with nameless dread.

Chapter V

Kevin sat on a wobbly pile of books, head in hands. He'd searched the library from end to end; the manuscript just wasn't here!

No one could have taken it. Not even the count knew which manuscript I was copying!

Right. No one had taken the thing. The dust that covered much of the floor showed pretty clearly that, save for that one brief visit by Charina, no one other than he had even been in the library recently: her neat footprints were in a direct line in and out of the room, his were all over the place, but had a distinctive cleft in one sole. If anyone else had entered, they'd done so in mid-air.

This was insane! Nobody around here could fly — but manuscripts didn't up and vanish all by themselves!

I should have gone riding with Charina, Kevin thought in misery.

He had passed her in the hall — or, rather, she had passed him, on her way for another solitary ride, sweeping regally by with her head in the air as if he hadn't even existed. Kevin winced, wondering if she would ever even speak to him again. He had been right, of course, painful though it was; he was here to do a job, not enjoy himself with a beautiful young woman —

A job he couldn't do because the cursed manuscript was gone!

A sudden frantic pounding on the library door brought Kevin to his feet in alarm.

"Bardling!" a voice shouted. "Count Volmar wishes to see you!"

The count! The bardling stiffened in sudden panic. Why did Count Volmar want to see him *now*? Was it something about the manuscript — or about Charina? Kevin hastily smoothed his hair with his hands and brushed the dust off himself as best he could, wishing he had time to make himself more presentable, then hurried out of the library.

His first impression was of an anthill someone had kicked. The usually quiet corridors were packed with people rushing back and forth, panic in their eyes and voices.

"What is it?" he asked. "Are — are we under attack?"

"No, no." The servant who'd knocked on the door was in a frenzy of impatience. "No time to talk, bardling. Hurry!"

Kevin had expected Count Volmar to be holding court in the Great Hall, as was usual for the lord of a castle. Instead, to the bardling's surprise, he was bustled up to the count's private solar and practically shoved inside. A tall, lean, richly dressed man who could only be Count Volmar was pacing restlessly back and forth.

He stopped short as Kevin entered, staring at the bardling with frantic eyes. "Good, good, you're here. Bardling, I know you and my niece have become friends. No, no, don't look so guilty! I know you haven't done anything dishonorable."

The count resumed his nervous pacing. "It's Charina." The words were choked out. "She's gone."

"Gone! What — how — "

"Charina went riding this morning," Count Volmar said softly, "with only her groom to protect her. I — I never should have let her go, but . . . " He held up a helpless hand. "Charina can be so very persuasive. And I never really believed she could come to any harm, never! Not on my lands!"

"My lord, please!" Kevin cried. "What happened?"

"Her horse returned without her, its coat all sweaty with fright. I thought there had been an accident, that Charina had been thrown and the groom was staying with her. But when I sent men out to hunt for my niece, they returned white-faced and trembling. They had found the groom, all right. Dead. Killed by sorcery — elvish sorcery." The count shuddered. "There was no sign at all of Charina."

"Elvish?" Kevin protested, remembering the elves who'd appeared to him back in the forest. He never doubted those so-superior beings could have been capable of great cruelty if the fancy moved them. But surely they never would have committed murder! They were alien, not evil! "Are you sure? I mean, why would elves — "

"Don't you know anything?" Count Volmar snapped. "Don't you have the slightest idea of what the world is like out there? Bardlings! All wound up in your music — Did you think that *everyone* in the land is loyal to the King?"

"I . . . suppose not. But — "

"There are rebel elves throughout the king's realm — yes, and not just White Elves, either! At least those *have* a code of honor, even if a man can't understand it. But there are others far worse!"

"Dark Elves, you mean?" Kevin wanted desperately to show he knew *something* about the world.

"Of course Dark Elves! Necromancers, the lot of them!" The count shook his head in disgust. "Should have been exterminated years ago!"

"I don't understand! I always thought the elf-folk, even the — the Dark Elves, kept pretty much to themselves. Why would they — "

"They aren't human!" the count exploded. "These are Others; who can comprehend anything they do? They hate humans, bardling, every one of them, particularly any who try to rule 'their' country. And they have Powers we can't hope to understand. The Dark Elves, with their foul, foul sorceries . . . " He shuddered. "Yes, and even the White Elves wield magic strong enough to twist human minds! They can turn child against parent, friend against friend — They can even destroy a human mind and soul, leaving nothing behind but an empty shell to be filled with whatever they will."

Volmar broke off abruptly, turning sharply away. After a moment, he muttered, "Forgive me. I didn't mean to shout at you, bardling. It's simply that I — I am so very worried about Charina. . . . "

"They wouldn't dare harm her!" Kevin said inanely.

"You think not? Look you, at first I hoped she had simply been kidnapped. But there have been no ransom demands, no messages at all! I fear they hate humans so much they're not going to even try to get anything from me. No, ah no, they'll hurt her just because she is who she is!"

"They can't!" Kevin cried in anguish. "I — uh, we won't let them!"

The count let out a long, shuddering sigh. "No," he said, "we won't. Bardling . . . Kevin, is it? Kevin, I plan to mount several expeditions to find her. And I want you to lead one."

"*Me?*"

"Yes. You and Charina became such good friends in so short a time that there must be some psychic link between you. And that will certainly help you use Bardic Magic to find her."

Somehow Kevin forgot that what magic he happened to possess was only now starting to wake, its range still unknown. "I'll do it!" he cried. "When do we leave?"

"Tomorrow." The count smiled faintly. "Thank you, Kevin. I'm sure a talented young man like yourself will succeed where knights, with all their brainless heroics, would only fail."

A small part of Kevin's mind wasn't so sure of that. What, he, an untrained bardling, succeed over battle-proven warriors? But he didn't dare let himself start to doubt, for Charina's lovely sake. "Your niece will be safely returned to you, Count Volmar," the bardling said somberly, and bowed his most courtly bow.

That night, Kevin slept not at all. His mind kept insisting on conjuring dreadful images of Charina in her captors' hands. He couldn't shake the count's dark words: *"They can destroy a human mind and soul!"* The thought of Charina left so hopelessly . . . empty bit at his soul. "No! I won't let that happen to you! I'll save you, I swear it!" Or die trying . . .

He wanted to shout it, but such hysteria would only bring the castle folk rushing around him, wanting to know why he was making so much noise. So Kevin lay still, aching with impatience, and waited as the slow, slow hours passed.

As soon as the sun was just barely lightening the sky, he was down in the courtyard, so wild with excitement he couldn't stand still, eager to meet his fellow searchers and get going. His lute was slung across his back, since no Bard could work Bardic Magic without the aid of an instrument, and the few pages he'd managed to copy from the missing manuscript were safely tucked into the case as well. But now a mail shirt burdened Kevin's shoulders with unaccustomed weight — though fortunately it was dwarven work, lighter than human-made armor — and a sword from the castle armory hung at his side. Kevin closed his hand about the hilt, trying to feel like a seasoned warrior but guiltily remembering his Master's warning: a musician must always be careful of his hands.

I will, he promised the old Bard silently. *But . . . well . . . this is something that I must do.*

Odd. He had expected the courtyard to be full of

knights and squires preparing to set out on their own rescue missions. Yet there didn't seem to be anyone around but himself. Suddenly panicky, Kevin wondered if, early though the morning was, he was already too late. Had everyone left without him?

No. That was ridiculous. Even the boldest knight wasn't going to try riding down the castle's steep hill in the dark. Evidently the count meant to send the different parties out at different times during the day. His must be the first. And that had to mean the count truly trusted him!

Yes, but where were his —

"You?" the bardling said in dismay. "You're my troop?"

"You?" a throaty voice echoed in wry humor. "You're our leader?"

The woman who'd spoken was tall and rangy, a hunter and warrior, quiver on her back, sword at her side. Her short, curly black hair was held back from her face by a leather thong, and her dark eyes were the most devilish Kevin had ever seen. Her olive skin was deeply tanned — and a good deal of that skin was revealed, because her leather armor and breeches didn't seem to be hiding very much of her lithe form. Kevin realized how (and where) he was staring, and reddened. The woman only laughed.

"Never mind, boy. Nothing to be ashamed of, not you, not me." She held out a rough hand for him to shake; for all her undeniably feminine shape, there was nothing fragile about her grip. "I'm Lydianalanthis, but let's make things easier on you: Call me Lydia."

"I'm Kevin." He added with reluctant honesty, "A bardling."

"A bardling, huh? Count couldn't afford a full Bard?" She grinned at his look of dismay, teeth dazzlingly white against her skin. "Don't look so hot and heavy, boy! I'm only teasing."

"I knew that," he muttered.

"He *is* paying you, isn't he?" Lydia asked with a note of genuine concern in her voice. "I mean, a kid like you — he isn't trying to cheat you?"

The bardling straightened indignantly. Yes, the count had given him a purse of coins, but it had been for travelling expenses, not payment! "I'm not a — a kid! Or a mercenary!"

Lydia shrugged. "In other words, he's not paying you. Powers save me from idealistic youngsters!"

"The count's niece is in terrible danger! How can you possibly be worried about money!"

"Because," the woman drawled, "I've gotten into the habit of eating regularly. Can't do that very well without coin in the purse."

"You're not one of Count Volmar's subjects?"

"Powers, no! I'm subject to *me*, boy, not to any count! I was making my way across the world — never did it before, that's why!" she added before he could ask. "Anyhow, I got as far as this castle when I heard the news about the count's niece and a reward for her safe return."

"Oh."

Lydia grinned again, but this time Kevin thought it looked more like a snarl than a smile. "Let's set things straight from the start. Yes, I'm a mercenary. But don't you look down your nose at me, boy! I earn my own way, give good value for service bought, honor my agreements, and sleep nice and sound at night. You find anything wrong with that, or with me, best get it out in the open now."

"I don't. And I didn't mean to insult you. It's just that . . . well, I've never met anyone like you before."

She gave a bark of a laugh. "I bet you haven't! Look, Kevin, I'm not angry at you. It's just I've seen too many men — and boys like you — try to take advantage of any woman who isn't under some man's protection. I'm lucky; my people believe in letting a girl grow up knowing how to defend herself. But I've travelled enough to know it sure as hell isn't an easy world for most of my sex."

"And so you're trying to protect other women?"

"Hell, no! I'm trying to protect *any* helpless soul! Damned if I'm going to let anyone, male, female or whatever, be turned into a — a thing to be used, not if I can do something to stop it. Besides," she added, her quick grin back so suddenly Kevin wondered if she was ashamed of having been serious for even a moment, "the pay is good!"

"But what — "

"Look," she interrupted brusquely, "here comes the rest of our party."

The bardling watched them leaving the keep, first one, then another, then . . . two? Only two? Staring in dismay, Kevin realized that despite all those encouraging words, the count couldn't have trusted him that much after all.

Ah well, what was, as the saying went, was. Trying to keep the disappointment out of his voice, he waited till they were within earshot, then began as firmly as he could, "Welcome. I am Kevin, a bardling, and this warrior is Lydia."

As the first figure shook back the hood of its gray-green cloak, revealing slanted green eyes, pale, silken hair and fair-skinned, ageless features so fine-boned and elegant they never could have been human, the bardling added with a gasp, "You're an elf!"

The elf-man looked at him without expression. Except, Kevin thought glumly, for a hint of contempt in those slanted eyes. "You are observant."

Oh yes, this was an elf, all right. The sarcasm in the cool voice reminded Kevin all too well of that night in the forest. "I'm sorry," the bardling said as courteously as he could. "I didn't mean to be rude. I was just surprised."

That earned him the barest dip of the head from the elf. "Understandably. I am Eliathanis, of the Moonspirit clan of White Elves." He was also obviously a warrior, his lithe figure clad in silvery scales of elvish armor, a straight sword with an intricately wrought silver hilt at his side. "My people do *not* enjoy being accused by humans of harm. I was here at court when the girl was stolen — and I intend to prove those accusations wrong."

I bet you haven't got a crumb of humor in your whole body, Kevin thought, eyeing that rigidly controlled face. Stealing from one of the old ballads, the bardling said formally, "We shall be glad of your help, good warrior," and gave a formal little bow.

"But will you be so glad of *my* help?" the second figure wondered softly. Slowly, with a fine sense of drama, it drew back the hood of its black cloak, revealing a face just as inhumanly fine-boned and elegant as that of Eliathanis, framed by a fall of straight, silvery-blond hair — but this face was so dark of skin it was nearly as black as the cloak. The elf was dressed entirely in black as well, tunic, hose, boots, all save for a thin silver belt. The clasp, Kevin noted uneasily, was worked in the shape of a skull. Blue eyes, eerie against so much darkness, glinted coldly.

"A Dark Elf!" Lydia yelped, hand flying to the hilt of her sword.

"*Nithathil!*" the White Elf hissed, eyes blazing.

The Dark Elf bowed, so very graciously it was an insult. "Yes," he said in his soft voice, "*Nithathil,* Dark Elf, indeed." The blue glance flicked lightly over Kevin and Lydia, then back to the other elf. "Call me Naitachal if you must have a specific name for me."

"I have a name for you!" Eliathanis snapped. "Necromancer!"

Kevin stepped hastily between the angry elves, hoping he wasn't about to get blasted by either side. "Uh . . . might we ask what you wish, my . . . uh . . . my lord Naitachal?"

"Why, I am here to help you return the lost human girl to her uncle, even as you," the Dark Elf purred.

But Kevin, being as close to the elf as he was, caught the barest glint of pain in the eerie blue eyes. *He* expects *us to hate him!* the bardling realized in surprise. *And the idea hurts him. I didn't think Dark Elves cared what* anyone *thought of them!*

As Kevin hesitated, uncertain, Naitachal drew back the barest step, drawing his cloak about his lean form. "I do not wish to force myself on you," he murmured to Kevin. "But even as you, White Elf, I will not see my people accused of a crime that is not theirs."

"Since when did your kind worry about what others thought?" Eliathanis challenged.

"Since the humans have become so numerous," the Dark Elf answered. "Even the mightiest of dragons can be brought down by a large enough pack of hounds."

"Ah. Well. Yes," Kevin said. Great, here was his first big decision as a leader, and he was stammering like an idiot! "Lydia, Eliathanis, we can hardly deny a man the right to defend the honor of his people."

"They have no — "

"Of his people," Kevin repeated hastily, before the White Elf could finish his insult. "Whatever we may think of each other, we've been thrown together on the orders of Count Volmar. Do any of you wish to back out now? Well? Do you? You'd better speak now, because I don't want to find myself in the middle of — " Of what? Thinking frantically, the bardling continued, almost smoothly — "of some heroic battle only to see my supposed comrades battling each other instead. Or running away like little boys yelling, 'I don't wanna play with him!' "

"How dare you!" Eliathanis began in outrage, but Kevin continued, using his trained musician's voice to swell over the White Elf's words, "Look at you two elves! You think yourself superior to us humans? Well, maybe you are —but I haven't seen any sign of that superiority yet!"

"Bravo," murmured Lydia, but the bardling ignored her, continuing hotly, "While you two waste precious time by bickering, an innocent girl may be suffering, may even be dying! We all want the same thing, and that's to free her! I ask you, all three of you: will you or will you not stay with me?"

There was a long, tense silence. Then:

"Hell, I'm willing," Lydia said with a shrug.

"And I," murmured Naitachal.

Eliathanis hesitated a moment longer, glaring at the Dark Elf, then shrugged. "No one has spoken of abandoning you, human. Besides, I would not have it said I was less brave than a *Nithathil*."

Kevin nearly laughed aloud, all at once so shaky with relief he wasn't sure he could move. "Good! And together we shall stay — until the Lady Charina is returned safely to her uncle!"

Chapter VI

"What do you mean, this is all we get?" Lydia thundered at the startled stable hand.

"But — but my lady, there are four of you. The count's offering you four horses — "

"And what about grain for those horses? And supplies for us? Hell, I can hunt down enough meat to keep us going, and I'm sure the boy or one of these elves knows how to find nuts and berries, but I am *not* going to sleep on bare ground or go without a change of clothes! You throw in at least one pack horse, fully provisioned, mind you — and do it now!"

As the terrified servant scurried off, Lydia winked at Kevin. "That's the way to do it," she murmured. "Act as if you know what you're doing, keep 'em off balance, and they'll give you anything you want."

"I — I see." The bardling struggled to imitate Eliathanis and keep his face an impassive mask. But he was sure everyone knew exactly how inept he felt! Here he was supposed to be the leader of the group and it hadn't even occurred to him to ask for grain!

"Don't worry, kid." The woman gave his shoulder a light punch. "I'll look out for you."

Wonderful. Just what he wanted: a babysitter. Kevin tried not to scowl as he watched Lydia prowl up and down the rows of stalls. "Which is Lady Charina's horse?" she called out. "This? Should have known. Dainty little creature. A real lady's palfrey. Couldn't stand a day on the trail.... Hold still, horse."

She lifted a foreleg, examining the hoof and shoe, then waved the others to her side.

"Distinctive shoeing. See the slight ridging here, and here? If this beast left hoofprints, I can follow them."

"My . . . uh . . . lady?"

Lydia glanced up and grinned. "Ah, here we go!"

As she had ordered, the stable hand had brought them not only their horses, but a laden pack horse as well.

As they rode down from the castle and out over the fields, Lydia crouched low over the neck of her horse, studying the ground, finally dismounting to study what looked like a perfectly unremarkable patch of earth to Kevin.

"This is where the girl was seized, all right," she said. "See how the grass has been torn up?"

Eliathanis dismounted as well, then drew back in distaste. "It stinks of sorcery."

"It does," Naitachal agreed softly, joining him. "Sorcery cold enough to slay a man." Wrapped in his black cloak, hood up against the sun (which must be uncomfortably bright, Kevin thought, to someone used to darker lands), the Dark Elf was a sinister, faceless figure. "Do you not feel the echo of his death?" Naitachal sighed in regret. "Were it only a tiny bit stronger, I could call his spirit to us and learn the truth."

"Necromancy!" Eliathanis spat.

"Oh, indeed." Kevin thought he caught the barest hint of a sardonic smile from under that black hood. "What was worked here," the Dark Elf continued softly, "was not the magic of my folk, nor yours, nor even that of the humans. Not . . . quite, at any rate. Intriguing. But I can't pick up a clear enough trace for it to be very helpful. What of you, White Elf?"

Eliathanis shook his head. "Whoever it was took great pains to cover his tracks."

"His?"

"Or hers. Or even theirs. I can't be sure."

Lydia glanced from one elf to the other, then shrugged. "We didn't expect things to be easy, did we?" Bending to examine the ground, the woman gave a soft laugh of triumph. "Maybe there aren't any clear magical traces, but at least there *is* a physical track. See, here's where Charina's palfrey bolted back to its stable. But here . . . these are the tracks of a different horse. Bigger . . . heavier . . . maybe a destrier?" She swung lithely back into the saddle. "It has to be the horse the kidnapper was riding. Look, the tracks are faint enough as they are. Let's get going before something destroys them altogether."

As the small party rode on out of field into scrubland then forest, following an overgrown trail that must originally have been cut by woodsmen, Kevin wondered bitterly if he really *was* the leader. Lydia was doing the tracking, and the two elves had their magic to help them, while he — he was nothing but an untried bardling who didn't even know about —

Hey, wait a minute! "Naitachal?"

The Dark Elf had pushed back his hood as soon as the first trees had screened off the sun. His fair hair gleamed, startling bright against the darkness of skin and clothing, as he brought his horse up beside Kevin's. "Yes?"

Naitachal's eyes, disconcertingly, glinted red in the dim light, sending echoes of every eerie tale he'd ever heard flashing through Kevin's mind. *Don't be stupid!* he scolded himself. *He's an ally.* For now, anyhow. "Were you in the castle when the groom's body was brought in?"

"I was," Naitachal said softly. "And yes, I did ask to be allowed to examine it."

Eliathanis' keen elf ears caught that murmur. "To work your spells on it, you mean!"

The Dark Elf smiled without rancor. "Exactly. I have

been well trained in the sorceries that can draw back the dead. One would think Count Volmar would have been anxious to learn anything that might have helped him recover his niece. And yet I was refused."

"Not surprising," the White Elf snapped. "He didn't want anything tainted by Darkness in his castle."

"Ah, my touchy cousin-elf, you don't understand. One would also think the groom would have been buried with honor, having died defending his lady. But there *was* no public burial, and even I have no idea what became of his body."

Odd, Kevin admitted to himself uneasily, *very odd.*

But before he could continue that thought, a small, shrill voice called out:

"Here you are! It took you long enough!"

With a laugh, Lydia reined in her horse. "Well, forgive me, Tich'ki! You knew it was going to take some time! I went as fast as I could."

"A fairy!" Kevin cried.

"A human!" the fairy mocked in return. "My, my, what a *clever* little boy!"

The bardling tried in vain not to stare. As with all her kind, Tich'ki was small, barely coming up to his horse's knee. She was undeniably female, an adult woman of her kind, almost beautiful in a sharp-edged, predatory wild creature way. Her bright, sharply slanted eyes, green as those of a White Elf, seemed enormous in her triangular face, her hair was caught up in a tangle of auburn braids, and even her irridescent wings seemed to have a predatory glint to them, like those of a dragonfly.

She was, if half the stories about her kind were true, just as likely to stab a human with that gleaming little spear she bore as talk to one.

That didn't seem to bother Lydia. *I never heard of any human making friends with a fairy,* Kevin thought. But friends they did seem to be, or at least acquaintances. "We're off on an adventure," the warrior woman said.

"No-o," Tich'ki drawled, "*really*? I thought you were just out for a ride in the woodland." Her green gaze sharpened. "With a White and Dark Elf together, no less. So, Lydia? Are you going to give me a hand up?"

"You — you're going with us?" Kevin asked, then had to hold fast to his startled horse's reins as Tich'ki darted upward in a blur and buzz of wings, landing lightly behind the warrior woman.

"You going to stop me?"

"No, no, of course not. It's just . . . well . . . I never knew one of your people to be friendly with one of mine."

"No, and you're not likely to again."

Lydia laughed. "Tich'ki and me, we're a lot alike. Don't like staying cooped up in one place too long. I first met her when she was pinned down by a hunting hound."

"And I saved you later from the angry hunters." Tich'ki gave the woman a sharp little pinch. "So don't go getting all superior." She squirmed about to stare at Kevin with her hard green gaze. "That's it, boy. Lydia and me, we sometimes travel together. But don't think because I tolerate her, I have a love for all you humans."

"Ah." For a fairy to be out on her own like this, travel lust or no, could only mean she'd been cast out from her people—possibly for associating with a mere human. Not knowing what else to say, Kevin stammered, "Uh, welcome to our group. We're searching for the niece of—"

"I know all that!" Tich'ki said impatiently, wings stirring. "I have every bit as strong a scrying talent as those hulking elf-men. The only reason I wasn't up there in that castle with you is because I didn't want to get stepped on by some clumsy lout of a human."

More likely, Kevin thought, the humans wouldn't let such a perilous little creature in!

Tich'ki settled herself more comfortably sidesaddle behind Lydia, folding her wings, too small to ride astride. "I want to find out what happened to that simpering little girl, too."

"She doesn't simper!" Kevin said hotly, then stopped short at Tich'ki's sly grin. Too late, he remembered another nasty little trait about fairies: they delighted in tormenting humans, one way or another. *And I fell right into her trap.*

"Now we are five," Naitachal murmured wryly.

Tich'ki glared. "And you'll be glad of it, Dark Elf! All right, enough of this. Let's go!"

As they rode deeper into the forest, dense brush all but engulfed the trail, forcing them to ride single file. Thick canopies of leaves shut out more and more of the light. At last, surrounded by dim green twilight, Lydia swore under her breath and dismounted, peering at the ground in disgust. "Damn."

"What's wrong?" Kevin asked. "You've lost the track?"

"No, no, the track's still there — I just can't see it in all this gloom."

"A torch — "

"Torches flicker too much, create too many distorting shadows." She glanced up at the elves. "One of you give me some nice, steady light."

Eliathanis hesitated, then admitted reluctantly, "I can't. I'm a warrior, not a magician. The only magic I possess is that innate to my race."

"No light-spells, eh? Tich'ki, I know you don't have any, either."

The fairy shrugged. "Can't know everything. Better things to do with my time than waste it studying spells."

A fairy who wasn't too much of a magician? Kevin had never heard of such a thing. Maybe *that* was why she'd been cast out by her people.

Lydia was turning to Naitachal. "What about you, Dark Elf?"

Naitachal's eyes glinted eerily in the darkness. "My people have no need for light-spells."

"Oh, great." Lydia got to her feet. "Might as well make camp, then. We're not going anywhere."

"Wait." Heart racing, Kevin took out his lute, tuning it carefully. One of the magical songs his Master had taught him was known as the Watchwood Melody, and its purpose was to create light. "I don't know if this is going to work, but . . ."

He cleared his throat, took a deep breath, and started to sing.

At first nothing happened. But halfway through the melody, Kevin felt a tingle run through him, head to foot. *Magic,* he prayed, *let it be magic . . .*

And it was. For the first time in all the weary years of study he *felt* the song, felt each syllable, each note, as a separate wonder ringing in his mind. Listening to that wonder, he slid more and more deeply into his music . . . though he was vaguely aware of something outside himself being different . . . the darkness . . . ? Surely it wasn't quite as dark . . . ?

Powers! He and his lute were — *glowing*! They were actually glowing with a pale, steady light!

"Terrific!" Lydia yelled. "Keep it going, just like that."

But all at once Kevin was terrified of what he had done. A childish part of his mind jibbered that he should stay what he'd been, ordinary, unimportant, safe. The bardling's concentration slipped. His fingers stumbled on the strings, breaking the spell. As the pale light began to fade, his voice faltered to a stop. Kevin slumped, suddenly so weary from the energy loss of a failed spell he could barely stay in the saddle.

"Sorry," he muttered.

"Sorry!" Lydia echoed. "That was *amazing*!"

"No, it wasn't. If I'd done it right, the light would have lasted even after I stopped singing."

"Well, never mind," the woman said cheerfully. "You'll get it right next time."

Kevin clenched his jaws before he could say something he'd regret. The last thing he wanted right now was to be patronized, even by someone who meant well.

What was I trying to prove? I couldn't hold onto even the simplest song-spell. I'm not a Bard. Maybe I never will be.

At least the two elves weren't trying to be kind. But it didn't help to hear Tich'ki chortling to herself, "Just like a human! Disappointed because he's been de-lighted!"

Once the party had fed and watered the horses, and picketed them in a line, and eaten a dinner of cold meat and bread, there wasn't much else to do. Kevin tried to start a conversation with the others, but nobody else seemed to want to talk. He sat back, disgruntled. This camp was hardly like those in the old songs: those songs in which a cheery group of comrades on the road gathered beneath the stars. If there were stars, they were totally hidden by the roof of leaves. And except for Lydia and Tich'ki, the comrades were strangers to each other, and not in a very cheery mood.

Naitachal sat as silently as a black-wrapped statue, a darker part of the night just outside the ring of firelight. Eliathanis, polishing his silvery elf-sword with slow, methodical strokes, light glinting off the blade with each upstroke, was almost as silent, though he kept shooting wary, hostile glances at the Dark Elf. Kevin attempted a few practice scales on his lute, not daring to try any magic lest it fail, just keeping his fingers limber. But he gave up after Tich'ki sneered every time he missed a note. And Lydia prowled round and round their camp like some cautious wild thing until the bardling couldn't stand it any longer.

"What *are* you doing?"

"Checking," came the short answer, "just checking. Don't like the idea of something sneaking up on us without us having some way out."

"Nothing lurks out there." Naitachal's soft voice

made everyone start. "Nothing living." With superb timing, the Dark Elf waited till the others had a chance to imagine undead horrors before adding lightly, "Except, of course, for the small, normal creatures of the forest."

"Oh, thank you," Lydia muttered.

Naitachal glanced up as the woman passed him in her circlings. "There is a rather large skeleton under the leaves just to your left. It was a wolf, I believe, and it is still in fairly good condition. If you wish, Lydia, I can summon it up to stand guard."

She gave him a look of sheer horror. "Uh, no, that won't be necessary. I — "

"We will have none of your foul sorceries!" Eliathanis' sword glinted in his hand.

"You melodramatic fool." Naitachal's voice was quietly deadly. "Don't ever point a weapon at me. Not unless you intend to use it."

"Push me too far, Dark Elf, and I will."

"Go ahead, White Elf. Try."

"I — "

"Stop that!" Kevin snapped, and both elves turned to him in surprise. "You sound like little boys daring each other to fight! Look, I know you two don't like each other, but we're stuck with each other. For the sake of our mission, can't you declare a truce?"

Eliathanis frowned sternly. "It is not in elf natures to lie."

"Well then at least *pretend*! And you, Lydia, will you please stop pacing? Naitachal told you there's nothing dangerous out there. We have three Faerie-kin here and five horses; surely one of them will be able to warn us if anything's approaching." He glared at them all. "Is that all right with everyone? Yes? Fine! And now, *good night*!"

There was startled silence. Amazed at his own boldness, Kevin wrapped himself in a blanket, turned away, and curled up to sleep.

I didn't mean to explode like that. But I couldn't stand listening to that stupid bickering any longer! Charina would have laughed and said —

Charina, who might not even still be alive. Kevin swallowed hard. *You are alive. I — I know it, Charina. You are alive. And we'll find you, I promise.*

Bit by bit, he managed to relax. All around him was quiet, save for the peaceful chirpings and rustlings of a forest at night, soothing sounds . . .

But just as the bardling was drifting off, timed to exactly the right moment to annoy him the most, Tich'ki murmured, "Cute little puppy dog. Thinks he has fangs!"

Kevin sat bolt upright. The fairy was watching him from beyond the banked campfire, her green eyes the eyes of a sly predator. As he stared, she smiled. "Sleep well," Tich'ki whispered, and blew him a kiss.

Kevin woke, disoriented, somewhere in the small hours of the night. There, just barely visible in the darkness, were Naitachal and Tich'ki, talking softly together in the elvish tongue as though they were old friends.

But as though they felt him watching them, they turned as one. Two pairs of alien eyes, glowing eerily, looked at him, sending a shiver through the bardling at the thought that the darkness was no barrier to them. Why had they been whispering together? The Dark Elf and the perilous fairy: what could they be plotting? Kevin swallowed drily, trying to find an innocuous way to ask them, but before he could open his mouth, Naitachal murmured:

"Go back to sleep, Kevin."

A trace of sorcery must have hidden behind the simple words, because for all his sudden worry, Kevin found himself sliding helplessly back into slumber.

Chapter VII

"Oh, hell," Lydia said.

For two full days they had been riding through forest so dense Kevin thought that any one of them could have followed the track. The trail had been so overgrown a horse's body could hardly have kept from breaking telltale branches; there had been no way for the kidnapper to avoid leaving a track, let alone to leave the trail. But the forest had been thinning for some time as the land grew increasingly more rocky.

And now they had broken out of forest altogether. The trail melted into a series of paths and one true road winding their way through a limestone wilderness, a time-eroded maze of tall, gray-white stone walls.

"Are we out of luck?" Kevin asked.

Lydia shrugged. "Can't follow a trace over solid rock! Still, it's not *all* rock. . . . "

She dismounted, searching with her face so close to the ground that the bardling was reminded of a hunting hound searching for an elusive scent.

"Yes . . . " the woman said at last. "This way. I think."

They rode on, following the road, the only sounds the creak of saddle leather and the click of their horses' hoofs against stone. Kevin glanced at Lydia, not at all happy about the uncertainty he saw on her face.

The walls of the gorge towered over them as they rode, weighing down his spirit. Staring up at the narrow slash of sky, Kevin couldn't shake the sense of being a very small, insignificant creature in the middle of a very small, insignificant party. Now that he wasn't so overwhelmed by the mere thought of adventure, he had to admit that five . . . ah . . . beings hardly seemed a big enough group to have any hope of success. Yet if the count had sent out any larger expeditions, the bardling hadn't seen any sign of them.

I don't understand that. I don't understand any of this! We don't even know for sure that whoever we're following actually has *Charina!*

Kevin sighed. None of his doubts were going to matter if he couldn't hold his team together long enough to accomplish something.

Team, ha! The last thing they were was a team. Oh, everyone was nicely polite to each other — if you ignored the subtle snipings of White and Dark Elf at each other, or the jibes of Lydia at these silly males, or the nasty little jokes of the fairy.

The bardling gritted his teeth. Tich'ki seemed to have decided he was the best butt for her humor she'd ever seen. She never said anything out-and-out hostile. Oh no, that would have been too simple! Instead, the fairy would wait till he'd finished practicing a particularly difficult melody on his lute, then ask innocently, "Are you going to actually play something now?" Or worse: "When are you going to work some Bardic Magic?" knowing he was too scared of failure to risk trying another spell. Or perhaps she would simply wonder aloud what it was like to be a leader when he hadn't really had a chance to be one. Anything, Kevin thought, to undermine what little self-confidence he had left!

The only two who did seem to be getting along were Naitachal and Tich'ki. After that first night, Kevin was still keeping a wary eye on those two, but so far they hadn't done anything even remotely suspicious.

Except . . . last night, there had been that bizarre whatever-it-had-been. Kevin frowned, remembering how he had caught the Dark Elf and the fairy huddling together mysteriously, so involved in what they were doing they hadn't even noticed him. The bardling had gotten close enough to hear Tich'ki urge, "Try it again." And Naitachal had actually responded with, "Pick a card, any card."

At that moment, they'd spotted him. The Dark Elf had suddenly straightened, looking important and mysterious, but Kevin could have sworn Naitachal was embarrassed. And hadn't he caught a glimpse of Tich'ki hastily hiding a fairy-size deck of cards?

Card tricks? A necromancer learning card tricks?

It made about as much sense as anything else so far.

"We're not still on Count Volmar's lands, are we?" Kevin asked warily.

"Hardly." Lydia glanced up at the sky, judging direction. "I'm pretty sure we're on the outskirts of crown lands. If we keep riding east like this, we'll probably wind up in the city of Westerin."

"If we get that far." Eliathanis glanced up at the steep, brooding walls on either side, his usually unreadable eyes glittering with uneasiness. "I don't like this place. Anyone could be lurking up there."

"Claustrophobic elf!" Tich'ki taunted. "Scared of the shadows in his mind!"

The White Elf glared at her. "I'm not imagining things! Westerin is an important trading city, is it not? Thanks to the rocks, this must surely be one of the only roads available for anyone who wishes to reach the city from the west. What better place for an ambush?"

"Don't say something like that!" Lydia snapped. "It's bad — "

A savage shout from overhead cut into her words.

" — luck," she finished ironically, whipping out her sword.

Kevin didn't have a chance to act, to think, before a heavy body hurtled into him, hurling him from his horse.

My lute!

The bardling twisted frantically sideways to save it as

he fell, by luck slamming into earth rather than rock, mail shirt bruising his ribs. Aching and breathless, Kevin struggled to draw his sword, handicapped by the lute case's strap. The bandit's face leered into his own, foul-smelling and ugly as an ogre — and as deadly. Kevin saw the man raise the club that was going to bash out his brains, but he couldn't get the stupid sword free —

So the bardling did the only thing he could, smashing his fist up into the ugly face.

Ow! Oh — damn!

He hadn't been able to get much force into the blow, not lying sprawled on the ground, but it was enough to send pain flaming up his arm, because he'd connected with the man's battered helmet, not his face. The bandit grunted in surprise, falling back just enough for the bardling to wriggle free. He squirmed out of the lute case, leaving the instrument safe — please, let it be safe! — behind a rock.

As Kevin frantically tugged at the hilt of his sword, the weapon came free of its scabbard so suddenly he nearly dropped it. Hearing the bandit rushing him, the bardling whirled — and the man impaled himself on the blade.

For what seemed like an eternity Kevin stared helplessly into his foe's disbelieving eyes, too horrified to move. Then those eyes glazed and the bandit slowly sagged, nearly dragging the sword from Kevin's hand. The bardling swallowed hard and pulled the blade free, trying not to look at the blood darkening it, trying not to think about how dreadfully easily metal had slid into flesh. His hand still throbbed with pain, and part of his mind was yammering, *It's broken, it has to be broken!* But it wasn't, not if he could grip the sword hilt so tightly, and there wasn't any time to worry about what other damage he might have done.

Panting, Kevin glanced wildly about. For one confused moment he was reminded of a dog pack dragging down its prey. But these dogs were armed with clubs, knives, and homemade spears — and this prey was fighting back. Lydia, swearing fiercely, sword flashing, still sat her horse, taking advantage of its greater height, or trying to: the confused, frightened animal, unused to battle, was more of a hindrance than a help. At least its frantic whirling and kicking kept anyone from closing with the woman. Tich'ki, her wings a blur, darted in and out of the battle with waspish speed, her spear jabbing savagely at bandit eyes. The two elves had given up their mounts and stood fighting back to back, White and Dark forgetting their differences for the moment. Eliathanis' blade shone clear silver, mere human blood unable to stain it, while Naitachal —

Kevin stared. Naitachal was wielding a night-black sword that seemed to swallow up the light and that laughed softly every time it struck a foe. After the first few blows, the bandits, understandably, cringed away, putting themselves within Lydia's reach.

He didn't have that sword before, I know *he didn't!*

But the sight of that eerie sorcery reminded the bardling that he, too, had some combat magic. Granted, the song-spell wasn't strong enough to hurt anyone. All it could do was confuse a foe's attack. But surely that would help — if the magic would only work for him.

No, no, there wasn't time to doubt! Kevin dove for his lute, for a moment terrified that his bruised hand wasn't going to let him play. Forcing his stiff fingers over the strings, he started at full speed into the opening bars. His voice was almost too dry for song, rasping out desperately, and he knew that even if he did summon his Bardic Magic, it wasn't going to last long. It didn't even seem to be coming out right! But something was happening, because the whole battle was beginning to glow a faint but very real blue.

Oh, great. All I'm doing is making pretty colors!

"Damned sorcerer!" a voice muttered. Before Kevin could turn, a harsh arm was about his throat, choking him. The bardling lost his grip on the lute, heard it hit the ground —

Please, please, don't let it break!

He kicked back and felt his boot hit bone. The bandit swore, losing his strangling grip. Kevin felt a jolt against his already sore ribs as the man tried to stab him but hit the mail shirt instead. The bardling pulled free, lunging for his sword, then cried out in pain as the bandit kicked it viciously away, tearing the hilt from Kevin's aching hand. The sword came to rest wedged between two rocks. Kevin and the bandit both scuffled after it, but the bandit got there first, stomping down hard. To the bardling's horror, the sword snapped halfway up the blade.

For a moment, Kevin and his foe stared at each other, frozen. Then the bandit slowly grinned, revealing a mouthful of ugly teeth.

"Too bad, boy. I win, you lose!"

With that, the man leaped at him. Kevin scrambled to his feet, looking frantically about for another weapon. Out of the corner of his eye, the bardling saw the bandit's knife flash again, this time aimed at his unprotected neck. He twisted about, just barely managing to catch the man's wrist in time.

But I . . . can't . . . hold him . . . he's just . . . too strong . . .

The bandit continued to grin. Slowly he began bending the bardling's wrists back and back . . . Kevin gasped as renewed pain shot through his bruised hand, and lost his grip. The knife began its plunge —

But then the bandit froze as a dark-skinned hand closed on his neck. The man's eyes widened, gaping in sudden blind horror. As Kevin stared in sheer disbelief, he saw the man's hair fade from black to gray to white. The leathery skin sagged, wrinkled. The bandit let the bardling go so suddenly Kevin fell, dragging himself frantically away as what had been a living man a moment before crumbled to ancient dust.

Naitachal stood revealed, eyes still blazing red from the force of his spell. But in those eerie eyes, Kevin saw such bitter despair that for a moment the bardling could do nothing but stare in helpless fascination. Then, with a quick flip of his wrist, the Dark Elf pulled up the hood of his black cloak, hiding his face.

Only then did Kevin realize what was happening around them. That last horrific sorcery had been too much for what was left of the bandit gang. Yelling in terror, they fled back down the gorge. Lydia started to knee her horse after them, then reined the animal in again.

"Nah," she muttered. "Not worth it. Everyone all right?"

Tich'ki fluttered to a landing behind Lydia. Cleaning her spear with a scrap of cloth from a bandit's tunic, she grinned fiercely. "No problems here."

"I am unhurt." Eliathanis was disheveled, golden hair wild, cloak gashed and elven mail darkly stained, but his voice was as calmly formal as ever.

"And I," added Naitachal softly. "What of you, Kevin?"

The bardling snatched up his fallen lute, examining it carefully, then let out a sigh of relief. "It's only scratched a little."

"Yes, bardling, but what of you? I saw how carefully you moved your hand."

Reaction set in, as abruptly as though the words had been a spell. Kevin clutched the lute to him, trying to hide his sudden trembling, realizing only now how narrowly he'd escaped permanently damaging his fingers. Powers, oh Powers, Master Aidan had been right to warn him. He'd come so close to ending his Bardic career before it had started. . . .

"It's nothing," the bardling said gruffly. "Just a

bruise." He retrieved what was left of his sword, glancing ruefully at the fragments, then slipping them back into their scabbard. "C-come on, let's get out of here before the bandits recover."

"They're not going to recover so quickly!" Tich'ki jeered, pointing with her spear at crumpled bodies. "But the boy's right. Let's go."

"Wait," Eliathanis said softly, approaching the Dark Elf. Naitachal stiffened, murmuring something in the elvish tongue that was plainly a wary question, but the White Elf shook his head. "No. Let the humans understand this as well. Naitachal, I have always believed that the *Nithathili*, the Dark Elves, hated life, that they cared nothing for any but themselves."

"Well?"

"You had no need to risk yourself guarding my back. Yet you did. You had no need to risk yourself saving the bardling. Yet you did."

"What are you trying to say, Eliathanis?"

"Just that I . . . " The fair skin reddened. "I may have been too hasty in judging you."

He held out a hand. The Dark Elf hesitated for a long moment, then raised his own hand. As they pressed palm to palm in the elvish version of a handshake, Tich'ki snickered.

"Touching," she said. "Now, can we please get going?"

A lilting call in the elvish language coaxed the strayed horses back to them. As they rode off, Kevin resolutely refused to look at the dissipating mound of dust that had been a living man.

To the bardling's relief, the gorge widened again after a short time of uneasy riding, the stone walls dropping off into a tangle of greenery. Dazed by shock and exhaustion, he sank into a weary stupor, clinging blindly to the saddle, barely aware of the world around him.

"Hey, Kevin! Kevin!"

Lydia was calling him. The bardling roused himself, realizing with a start that night had stolen up on them. They were stopped in the middle of a small meadow, their horses grabbing greedily at the lush weeds and grass. "We're stopping for the night?"

"I think that's a good idea, boy, don't you?"

Oh, he did, indeed.

Lydia, experienced traveller and adventurer that she was, carried a pouch of healing herbs with which she treated everyone's cuts and bruises, including the bardling's sore hand.

"Now let's try to get some sleep," she ordered after they'd finished a brief meal of cold rabbit and stale bread. "It's been one hell of a tiring day!"

But for all his weariness, Kevin couldn't sleep. He kept seeing death, and blood, and a man dying on the point of his sword, another man withering to dust. . . . At last he moved away from the others to sit wrapped in darkness without and within.

After a time a shadow stirred: Naitachal, moving silently to join him.

"What's wrong, Kevin?" the Dark Elf asked softly.

"Nothing. I just can't sleep."

"You're still thinking of the battle, aren't you?"

"No — Yes — " The bardling broke off with a choked little gasp. "Naitachal, t-this isn't going to mean much to you, I mean you're a Dark Elf and a necromancer, you're used to death and all that, but I . . . killed a man today."

"So you did."

Kevin stiffened at the casual reply. "That really *doesn't* mean anything to you, does it?"

"Oh, it does." It was the barest whisper. "I cannot remember the first time I was forced to take a life. But I have never totally forgotten the horror of it."

"You c-can't remember? How could you not remember — "

"Kevin, I don't know how much you know of my people. Humans tell some truly bizarre stories about the *Nithathili*, those you call the Dark Elves. But one thing they say of us is quite true: we are indeed raised without love, without anything that might weaken us. I was singled out early in my childhood as one who held sorcerous promise. That means only one thing to the *Nithathili*. For all the years of my life I have studied dark magic, the magic of death. Necromancy, as you call it. But . . . ah, Powers, I am so very weary of it!"

Kevin glanced at the Dark Elf in surprise. "Then I was right, wasn't I? You were every bit as horrified as I was when that bandit died from — from age."

"When I killed him, you mean? That life-draining spell is called *Archahai Necrazach,* Spectre Touch in your language." Naitachal shuddered, ever so faintly. "It is a very dark thing, indeed. But there wasn't much time to act, not with that knife about to slay you, and I couldn't think of any other way to save you."

"You had a . . . sword."

"A Death Sword, Kevin, a temporary thing drawn from sorcery's heart. You heard its joy in taking life, did you not? That soft and empty laughter? I couldn't run the risk of even scratching you with it."

Hearing the bitter self-loathing in the Dark Elf's voice, the bardling cried, "I don't understand! If you don't want to work death-spells, why do it? Why not try something else?"

"There *is* nothing else, not for one of my kind. Not yet, at any rate," the Dark Elf added softly. "I meant it when I told you I intended to prove my people had nothing to do with the stealing of Count Volmar's niece. Love or hate, they *are* my people. But I have no intention of ever returning to them."

"What will you do?"

"Aye, bardling! I don't know, not yet." Naitachal paused. "You don't know how I envy you."

"Me?"

"You know what you want from life. You have the joy that is your music, and with it, the promise of bright, happy, living magic."

"I don't understand! Surely your people have music, too? I mean, they're elves, and I thought all elves — "

"We are not like the other elven races. We alone have no music."

"No music! B-but that's terrible!"

"Oh, it is. Listening to your songs, bardling, has been untold delight for me." The Dark Elf gave a soft, rueful laugh. "Ay me. Here I try to help you, and end up telling you my problems instead!"

Kevin blinked, all at once realizing that somewhere during this strange conversation, the specter of the bandit he'd killed had ceased to haunt him. "You *have* helped."

"Misery loving company, eh?" Whatever else he might be, Naitachal was still Dark Elf enough to be ashamed of showing weakness. "Ah, enough of this!" he said abruptly, getting to his feet. "The night is late, boy. Go get some sleep."

But then Naitachal paused, teeth flashing in a sudden grin. "And if you tell anyone about this conversation," he said, a touch too lightly, "I shall deny it all!"

Chapter VIII

Something damp was hitting his face. For a sleepy moment, Kevin thought he was back in the castle, with the squires playing one of their pranks on him. He opened his eyes with a cry of:

"*Will* you stop — "

"The rain?" Lydia cut in wryly. "Don't think any of us can manage that."

Kevin sat up in dismay, clutching his cloak about him. It wasn't much of a rain, more of a light but persistent drizzle. "But it's going to wash away the tracks!"

"Probably. Let's get going, boy. I want to get as far as we can before that happens."

Gathering up his damp belongings, the bardling muttered, "It never rains in the songs." At least the day wasn't cold, but the ride was still going to be an unpleasant one.

He hadn't guessed just how unpleasant. As though the previous day had never happened, the two elves began bristling towards each other once more. And Naitachal showed not the slightest sign of the lonely, music-hungry soul of the night before.

I give up! Kevin thought. *I just give up!*

Of course the weather had a good deal to do with deteriorating tempers. Kevin knew that. Not that such wisdom helped him any. Discovering that even a relatively lightweight mail shirt became incredibly uncomfortable when wet, the bardling had to keep a tight rein on anything he said, particularly when Tich'ki made some waspish remark.

She can't help it, he forced himself to accept.

The fairy, after all, had to be the most uncomfortable of them all, constantly fluttering her wings in a vain attempt to keep them dry. No wonder she was snapping at elf and human indiscriminately! Too waterlogged for flight, she must feel frighteningly helpless.

Lydia, meanwhile, fairly radiated angry frustration, bent nearly double over her horse, muttering under her breath as she hunted for the rapidly fading trail.

It didn't help uncertain tempers to realize that they were almost out of supplies for people and horses both. Granted, the animals would probably be able to find enough forage to keep them going, but it wasn't going to be much fun hunting for game in this weather.

At least, Kevin thought, struggling for any sign of good humor, the drizzle did seem to be letting up. Who knew? Maybe the sun would even deign to put in an appearance and dry everybody off.

But even as the first feeble rays did at last break through the clouds, Lydia threw up her hands in disgust. "That does it."

"I take it the rain washed away the tracks?" Naitachal asked.

"Hell, no! They aren't washed away, they simply disappear, just like that! As though horse and rider, up and vanished into the air." Lydia let out her breath in an angry hiss. "I've had trails go cold on me before, but I've never had one just — stop!"

"Wonderful," Tich'ki said flatly. "Now what?"

What, indeed? After a moment, Kevin began, "I think — "

"We're going to have to go on to Westerin," Lydia said, just as if he wasn't there.

Eliathanis shook his head. "There's no evidence they rode that way."

"There's no evidence they didn't! Besides, the horses need grain, and a hot meal and a bath wouldn't hurt any of us, either."

"Ah, I think — " Kevin began again, but Naitachal cut in:

"Lydia has a point. We would be more likely to learn something important in a city than out here in the middle of open country."

"That's a human city!" Eliathanis snapped. "How willingly do you think they're going to admit a Dark Elf?"

Naitachal shrugged. "About as willingly as they would a White Elf in these uncertain days. But our cloaks are hooded, after all. No one need know our races, as long as we're careful."

"Huh! No one's going to bother a fairy!" Tich'ki boasted.

"No one's going to bother *with* a fairy!" Lydia corrected with a grin. "Not a little thing like you!"

"Little, is it?" Tich'ki pinched Lydia so hard the woman jumped. "Little, is it?"

"Well, you *are* little — Aie, stop that! I apologize!"

"Hey, remember me?" the bardling asked. "I've got some say in this, too, and I — "

"This is nonsense." Eliathanis shook his head again, stubbornly. "I think we should continue to search out here."

"Search *what*?" Lydia exploded. "I tell you, there isn't the slightest clue. There isn't even the slightest *trace* of a clue! In the city, it'll be a different matter. Give 'em enough money, and we'll be able to bribe nearly anyone to tell us whatever we need to know."

The White Elf straightened, staring at her as though she'd uttered an obscenity. "Humans lie," he said shortly. "How much truth do you think you will get out of anyone who can be bought?"

"He's scared," Tich'ki taunted. "Poor elf is scared the

humans will throw things at him. Dirty his pretty face."

Eliathanis took a furious swipe at her, but the fairy, fluttering heavily because of her still-damp wings, still managed to evade him, mocking him with, "Temper, temper!"

"Stop that, Tich'ki!" Lydia caught one small foot and pulled the fairy back down behind her on the horse. "I say we go to Westerin."

"And I," Naitachal voted.

"Me, too." Tich'ki grinned sharply. "I *like* human cities. So many folks careless with their belongings. So many . . . opportunities."

"Huh," Lydia muttered. "Just don't get us thrown into prison."

"Have I ever?"

"Yes!"

The fairy ruffled her wings. "Thought you'd forgotten all about that. It wasn't *my* fault the gems fell into your pouch!"

"Oh no. The pouch just happened to come open at just the right time."

"Well . . . it might have had a little help . . . "

"And it's not going to have any more help! If I find your fingers anywhere near that pouch, Tich'ki, I swear I'll cut 'em off!"

"Spoilsport."

"I sure hope so! What about you, Eliathanis? Are you with us or not?"

After a reluctant moment, the White Elf nodded. "Not that it will do any good."

"Hey!" Kevin shouted with all his breath, and the others stared at him as though seeing him for the first time. "Remember me? I get some say in this, too!"

"All right, Kevin," Lydia said, a little too cheerfully. *As though she's humoring a child!* Kevin fumed. "What do *you* say?"

What *could* he say? No matter what Count Volmar

had said, Kevin knew he certainly wasn't the leader of this group! "I say," the bardling grumbled, "we go to Westerin."

Kevin reined in his horse without even being aware he'd done it, staring in sheer wonder.

"Westerin," he breathed.

Oh, he had been taught his geography as a child. He knew that the walled city lay at the junction of two trading routes, on a wide, fertile plain fed by a tranquil river. But hearing about it and actually seeing it were two very different things! Westerin was a beautifully picturesque sight beneath the dramatically cloudy sky, the thick, crenellated wall that girded it broken at regular intervals by pointed towers topped in bronze that gleamed like gold in the shifting rays of sunlight.

The city was also much larger than the bardling had ever imagined —no, no, he thought, it wasn't merely large, it was *enormous*!

Particularly, Kevin added wryly to himself, compared to quiet little Bracklin.

The others were riding on. The bardling urged his horse after them, trying to ignore Tich'ki's mocking, "Boy acts like he's never seen a city before."

Well, all right, maybe he hadn't! What of it?

With an indignant sniff, Kevin straightened in the saddle, doing his best to pretend there was nothing at all amazing about those thick stone walls towering over them as they approached, nothing at all amazing about the mass of buildings he glimpsed through the open gates.

But for all his attempts at keeping calm, the bardling's heart had begun pounding wildly.

Westerin. Westerin!

Why, the very name rang with adventure!

Chapter IX

Despite Eliathanis' worries, they had no trouble at all getting into Westerin. In fact, the city guards hardly glanced their way, waving the party inside with bored indifference.

Kevin struggled to copy that indifference. But how could he possibly keep from gawking? The street up which they were riding was wide enough to hold them easily even if they had been riding abreast. And it was paved with cobblestones! Only the innkeeper of the Blue Swan back in Bracklin had been able to afford those expensive things.

And how could Kevin not stare at all the buildings? He'd never seen so many in one place. He'd never dreamed so many could exist! They seemed to have been set out helter-skelter, as though each owner had put his house wherever *he* wanted it, without worrying about how the whole thing was going to look. The casual jumble of buildings created a maze of smaller streets branching out in all directions.

Kevin shook his head in confusion. Not only was there no pattern to the way the buildings were laid out, no two houses looked alike. Some of those he glimpsed were small, low to the ground, looking somehow meek amid all the bustle, of the homey, wattle-and-daub sort familiar to him from Bracklin, even if their roofs here were of red tile rather than thatch. Other houses were eccentrically painted half-timbered buildings, their upper stories leaning drunkenly together over their narrow streets, only wooden props keeping them apart. Kevin gave up trying to be aloof and stared openly when he saw a row of out and out mansions of beautifully worked stone, some of them, amazingly, three or four stories high.

And the people! There must be thousands here inside the encircling city walls, all of them speaking a jumble of languages. Their tunics and gowns and cloaks were a dazzling confusion of colors: red, blue, gold, even some hues he couldn't name.

And despite the White Elf's uneasiness, not all those folks were human. In one block alone, Kevin saw two haughty, elegant White Elves stride arrogantly by, acting as though humans didn't even exist, a couple of more relaxed people whose not-quite human features and ever so slightly pointed ears revealed them as half-elven, three hulking guards who almost certainly were nearly full-blooded ogres, even a pair of Arachnia dressed in priestly robes, chittering together in a language that seemed made up only of consonants.

Rows of shops lined the street, and the air rang with the cries of merchants bawling out their wares in half a dozen dialects. The bardling ached to examine the pile of scrolls one dealer offered, or the harps and lutes hanging in another booth, but he didn't dare let the rest of his party get too far ahead. He'd never be able to find them again in this crowd!

"It stinks," Eliathanis muttered.

Well, maybe it did, of animal and cooking oil and too many people of all sorts crowded in together, but overwhelmed by wonder as he was, Kevin hardly minded.

Lydia unerringly led the way to a livery stable, a well-kept place warm with the friendly smells of horses and hay.

"Smells better than the city," the White Elf muttered.

"Stop complaining." As Kevin dismounted, the woman asked in an undertone, "Before we start spending: you *do* have the bribe money with you, don't you?"

The bardling started to pat the purse Count Volmar had given him, but Lydia caught his hand in an angry grip. "Don't be a fool! You want to bring every thief in town down on us?"

Stung, he straightened. "I am *not* a fool."

But Lydia, bargaining with the stablekeep, ignored him. Only after she was finished, and she and the stolid man had shaken on the deal, did she turn back to Kevin.

"I don't like the idea of you wandering around without a weapon. The first thing we do, kid, is get you a new sword." She glanced at the elves. "We'll be back as soon as we can, okay?"

They nodded. Lydia grinned.

"Come on, Kevin."

As they stepped back out onto the streets of Westerin, the bardling was overwhelmed — and this time not by wonder. While he'd been up on a horse's back, he'd been raised up out of the worst of it, but now the crowd surrounded him like a noisy, smelly ocean trying to drown him.

"This way," Lydia called, and he struggled after her. After the first few "Excuse me's" and "Pardon me's," Kevin gave up and pushed and shoved his way like everybody else, elbows jabbing his ribs and feet tromping on his toes. City life might be exciting, but he guessed it wasn't so glamorous after all!

"Looks like a likely place," Lydia noted.

Kevin frowned, puzzled. The only indication that this might be a weaponry shop was the sign creaking back and forth over the door, roughly painted with a weather-worn picture of crossed swords. Ah, of course! With all the different races in Westerin, who knew how many of them could actually read the common tongue — or read at all? But anyone could figure out what a simple picture meant!

He followed Lydia inside, and found himself in a

small, crowded room, facing a counter piled with a staggering variety of knives. Behind the counter a curtained doorway presumably led to a storeroom, and axes and swords and the occasional shield — its surface left blank so it could be painted with a customer's coat-of-arms — covered most of the walls.

"What can I do for ya?" a rough but undeniably female voice asked.

Kevin jumped. He could have sworn the room was empty except for Lydia and himself.

"Down here, boy."

He looked. The look became a stare.

A woman she most certainly was, but one who barely came to his waist —and who was definitely not of human-kind. Buxom and brawny, she was almost as wide around as she was tall, but Kevin suspected that little of that roundness was fat. Her flat, high-cheekboned face was no longer young, and gray streaked the red braids coiled in an intricate knot on her head, but she looked about as fragile as a boulder.

"I'm Grakka, owner of this place." The woman stopped with an amused snort. "What's the matter, boy? Never seen a dwarf before?"

"I . . . uh . . . no. I mean, yes. I mean, one of your race stopped in Bracklin once, my — my village. But he was a *he*! And all the songs say — "

"That dwarves only come in one kind: male?" She gave a sharp bark of a laugh. "Where'd ya think we came from? Jumped up outa rocks all full-grown? Bah, humans! Ya come to gawk, boy, or to buy?"

"To buy," Lydia said. "The kid needs a new weapon."

Kevin shook the fragments of the broken sword out of the scabbard. "Can you fix this?"

"What d'ya take me for, a miracle-worker?" Grakka lifted the broken blade to the light, squinting along its length. "Piece a' junk."

"A count gave it to me!"

"Then his armorer's been cheating him." She pulled aside the curtain, yelling into the back of the store, "Elli! Yo, *Elli*! Wake up, girl, we got customers! Get me the rack of one-handers — Yeah, that's the one."

A slightly smaller figure staggered out with an armload of swords, which she dropped on the counter with a clatter. Kevin stared all over again, but this time in appreciation.

Elli was almost certainly Grakka's daughter, but even though the bardling couldn't deny she was almost as squat and powerfully built as her mother, she was still as pretty in her own nonhuman way as any girl in Bracklin. Her eyes were big and blue, sparkling with mischief as she looked at him, her nose was pertly upturned, and her long yellow braids curved smoothly down her simple blue tunic and skirt and the curves of her buxom young body in a way that made Kevin swallow hard.

He froze in panic as she swayed that curvy body to his side.

"I'm Elli. But you already know that. What's *your* name?"

"I — I — I'm . . . uh . . . Kevin."

"Uh-Kevin?" she teased.

"N-no. Just Kevin."

"That's a nice name." She fixed her big blue eyes on his face. "Do you think my name is nice, too?"

"I — "

"Elli!" her mother snapped. "Stop bothering the boy. You, boy, come here."

Elli flounced away, pouting deliciously. Sheepishly, Kevin went up to the counter. "Here," Grakka said shortly. "Try this."

Kevin looked at the sword in dismay. "It's so . . . "

"Plain?" Grakka finished. "Pretty never won battles. Go ahead. Try it out."

Kevin took a few practice swings, then tried an

experimental pass or two. He straightened, smiling. "I like it. It feels . . . right."

"Good. Because from what your warrior buddy here tells me, there's no time to design a sword specially for you." She gave him a speculative glance. "Too bad. It's always a challenge to make a sword that'll be useful for a reasonable while for you younglings who are still changing build almost every day." Grakka shrugged. "Ah well, some other time. That'll be five gold crowns."

"Five . . . "

"Go wait outside," Lydia murmured to him. "I'll take care of this."

Kevin knew that an adventurer as professional as Lydia would know how to bargain much better than someone from a small town. But that didn't stop him from feeling a surge of annoyance at being sent away like a little boy.

"Hi, Kevin," a voice purred.

"Uh, hi, Elli."

She smiled up at him as brightly as a sunny day. "I have to spend all my time in this dull old place. I never get to go anywhere. But an adventurer like you must have seen all *sorts* of wonderful things."

Westerin *dull*?

"I, uh . . . " Kevin wasn't about to confess the truth about Bracklin and his drab life to this lovely creature. "Sure. Why don't we sit down " — he patted a bench along the wall — " and I'll tell you all about them."

Maybe this wasn't going to be such a painful wait after all. Kevin began weaving a tale of Bardic wonder about his adventures in Count Volmar's castle and on the road to Westerin. As Elli stared at him adoringly, he turned the skirmish with the bandits into epic adventure, spinning it out until he and his party had overcome a whole army of outlaws.

"Why, that's *wonderful*!" Elli breathed, edging closer to him.

She was, he discovered, wearing some sort of sweet, flowery perfume, a heady scent. Warily, he let his hand slide towards her, and felt a shock race through him when her own small hand, rough with work but delicate all the same, closed about his fingers. Breathless, the bardling sat frozen, not daring to move, wondering what would happen if he tried to put an arm around her. About him the bustle of Westerin seemed as distant and remote as a dream.

Kevin nearly yelped when Lydia tapped him on the shoulder. "Wake up, lover boy. Here's your sword."

Blushing, Kevin released Elli's hand and scrambled to his feet.

"You owe Grakka two gold crowns, four silver," Lydia continued blandly. "And you, Erli — "

"That's Elli!" the dwarf girl said indignantly.

"Whatever. Your mother's calling you. Here's the money we owe her. Now, scoot!"

Elli scuttled into the shop. But she paused just long enough in the doorway to blow Kevin a kiss.

Lydia chuckled. "Pretty, isn't she? Can't be a day over fifty."

"Fifty!"

"Young for a dwarf. Momma Grakka has to be pushing a hundred, if not more. Yup, little Elli's got to be fifty, all right, just about the dwarven age of puberty. Hot for marriage, too, or . . . ah . . . whatever. Grakka has her hands full!"

She glanced at Kevin, who was still staring towards the weapons shop, and chuckled anew. "Forget it, kid. These human-Other romances never work out. Besides, in a few more years, sweet little Elli is gonna be all grown up and look just like her tough old momma."

Oh. Well. The bardling sighed, disillusioned.

"Come on, Kevin. The elves must be bored out of their minds. And who knows what mischief Tich'ki's working!"

* * *

What Tich'ki had been doing was trying to teach the two elves how to play cards. She had already, it turned out, won one night's free lodging for their horses from the stablekeep.

"Never even noticed the cards were marked, eh?" Lydia murmured wryly. "And don't give me that 'innocent little me' look, either, my dear. I know you far too well! Let's get out of here before we wind up in prison."

If anything, the crowds seemed to have gotten worse as the day progressed. Kevin, one hand on his new sword, the other on his purse, struggled his way along, beginning to long for the nice, peaceful, open countryside.

All at once, a particularly rough body barrelled into him.

"Hey!" the bardling yelled. "Why don't you watch where —"

A second man hurtled into him, nearly sending the bardling sprawling. For one horrifying moment he was sure he was going to go down, and be trampled by the heedless crowd, but then Naitachal's hand closed about his arm, pulling him back to his feet. The Dark Elf gestured the whole party into an alcove where they could be out of the stream of traffic.

"Are you all right?"

"Yes, I — " Kevin broke off abruptly. Something didn't feel quite right . . . "Wait a minute." Oh no, oh no, this couldn't be! The bardling searched himself frantically, then cried in panic, "It's gone! The purse Count Volmar gave me is gone!"

Chapter X

"Oh hell," Lydia muttered. "I *knew* this was going to happen."

"That man — " Kevin gasped out, "the one who jostled me — he must have stolen my money! We have to — "

"Have to what? Do you see him anywhere?"

"No, but the guard — "

"Did you see his face? No? Can you tell them anything about what he looks like?"

"No . . . "

Lydia let out her breath in a gusty sigh. "Give it up, boy. The money's gone."

"But . . . " Kevin struggled to keep his voice from shaking from sheer panic.

All about him, the city continued its busy life, not caring whether he lived or died, and he had nothing left but the few small coins in his own purse. They weren't enough to let him survive, let alone bribe anyone. He'd failed the count. Worse, he'd failed Charina!

Hopelessly the bardling asked, "What are we going to do . . . ?"

"Well, we can't do anything without money, that's for sure," Lydia said brusquely.

"Then it's foolish to remain here." Eliathanis pulled his cloak about himself, adjusting his hood with fastidious care. "I *said* we should never have come to Westerin."

"But — "

"We've wasted enough time. I am going to do what I should have done from the start, and explore on my own."

"No!" Kevin cried. "You can't abandon — " But the White Elf had already vanished into the crowds. " — the team," the bardling finished helplessly. "Naitachal! You can't leave, too!"

"No?" The Dark Elf's eyes glinted from beneath his hood, cool and unreadable as blue ice. "There is more to be learned here if I'm not burdened with . . . anyone else."

"But — wait — " Kevin whirled to Lydia. "I suppose you're going to go off on your own, too!"

"Hell, no. I don't abandon the helpless, remember?" All at once she grinned. "Hey, cheer up, kid. It's not so bad."

"Not so bad! We don't have any money!"

"I've been stuck penniless in cities before, some of them a lot nastier to strangers than this one, and I've always managed to land on my feet. Let me think a minute . . . Ha, yes. Tich'ki, what do you think of this?"

She murmured in the fairy's ear. Tich'ki laughed and yanked a lock of the woman's hair. "Ah yes, of course!"

"All right, then. Come on, Kevin."

"Where are we going?"

She didn't answer. Kevin, struggling to keep up with the woman, who was knifing her way skillfully through the crowd, hardly noticed the buzz of fairy wings in his ear. But he *did* notice tough little fingers snatching the pouch holding his last few coins.

"Hey! Tich'ki, give that back!"

The fairy ignored him, dropping the pouch into Lydia's hands. Kevin hurried after her.

"Lydia! Come back here! Where are you going? What are you — Lydia!"

He stopped, staring up at the building blocking his

path. Where in the world . . . ? A temple? Oh yes, such an overblown stone and plaster monstrosity couldn't be anything but a temple! Kevin glanced briefly up at the busy, brightly painted facade. Over the door was an ornately carved and gilded relief of a very smug group of merchants kneeling in prayer. Praying to whom? In this city, the bardling thought drily, it could only be the Great God Money!

Ach, no, that wasn't nice. Besides, the last thing he could afford right now was getting Heavenly Powers angry at him!

Tich'ki didn't have any such qualms. She vanished into the temple with such an evil titter that Kevin stared after her, particularly when Lydia chuckled and followed.

Oh Powers, they're going to rob the temple, I know it. How can I possibly stop them before —

But Lydia strode boldly down the length of the vast inner chamber without pause, her boot heels clicking on the smooth stone floor. Ignoring the busy religious murals on walls and columns (at least Kevin assumed they were religious murals), ignoring the few worshippers and the gaudy gilded shrine (the bardling still couldn't figure out to whom the temple was sacred), she pulled aside a curtain shrouding the far wall, revealing a tiny door. The woman rapped on it three times, then two, then three again, and Kevin cried in sudden comprehension:

"You've been here before!"

Lydia grinned. "The boy's a genius! How do you think I found the livery stable and Grakka's shop so easily?"

"Oh." Feeling exceedingly stupid, the bardling muttered, "Of course."

The door swung open soundlessly. "Come on, kid," Lydia said. "Churches are always where the money is. Let's go."

Kevin warily followed her down a short flight of stairs. He paused halfway down, glancing about.

The room at the bottom of the steps was small and windowless, but elegant enough, with walls and tables of sleekly polished wood. It was full of people sitting at or standing around those tables, some of them so richly — or gaudily — clad the bardling's eyebrows rose in surprise. The only sounds were the faint rustle of cards, the clink of coins, and an occasional sigh or smothered oath.

"This is a gambling house!" Kevin exclaimed, feeling a wicked little thrill of excitement run through him. They hardly had this sort of thing back in Bracklin! "Lydia, what do you think you're doing?"

"Earning us some funds."

"B-but those are the only coins we've got left! If you lose them . . ."

Lydia shrugged. "Whatever the Fates decree." As a man threw down his hand and stalked off in disgust, the woman flopped down onto the vacant chair. "What's the game?"

No one even glanced up. "Five-card Tarot," someone muttered. "Pentacles wild."

"Fine." To Kevin's horror, she dumped all his coins out on the table in front of her. "I'm in."

The bardling had no idea what the rules of Five-card Tarot might be. He'd never even *heard* of the game before! Chewing anxiously on his lower lip, he watched as Lydia thoughtfully kept or discarded the brightly colored cards, or glanced every now and then at her equally pensive fellow players: three middle-aged human men and an elven half-blood of indeterminate age and gender. With each round, the bardling saw with a shudder, more and more of his precious coins were added to the pot.

"I'm out," one of the humans muttered suddenly, throwing down his cards and leaving.

The others never even noticed. After another hand:

"Me, too," said the half-elf with a shrug, vanishing into the crowd.

Lydia and the two remaining men never flickered an eyelash. One of the men, Kevin noted, was a bushy-bearded fellow in somber red robes, while the other was a thin, clean-shaven man, smooth of skin and dressed in an elegant tunic of blue velvet, but they were alike in their impassive concentration. The game went on, cards being selected, discarded. The pile of coins in the center of the table grew ever larger.

If she loses now, the bardling thought with a shudder, *we'll have nothing left!*

But without warning, Lydia threw down her hand with a cry of triumph.

"There! Beat *that!*"

Kevin saw that the cards she'd been holding were the King, Queen, Knight and Page of Swords, and the Five of Wands. It was obviously a good hand, because Bushy Beard and Smooth Skin threw down their cards in disgust. Smiling sweetly, Lydia raked in the pot.

"Come on!" Kevin whispered. "We've got our money back. Let's get out of here!"

"Are you joking?" she whispered back. "That's not enough to bribe anyone! Besides, I've just begun."

"What do you mean? Lydia, if you lose — "

"I'm not going to lose. All right, gentlemen," the woman added in a bright voice. "Shall we try one more time?"

Bushy Beard and Smooth Skin grumbled. But to Kevin's horror, they agreed. This time, as the winner of the last round, Lydia was the dealer, sending the cards flashing out in neat, colorful piles to the other players. "Same stakes?"

"Same stakes," they muttered, almost as one.

She's going to lose. I know she's going to lose. We won't have a coin left and — Oh, I knew it!

Bushy Beard impassively raked in his winnings.

"Lydia!" Kevin whispered frantically. "That's enough! Let's get out of here while we still have something left!"

"Hush. One more round, gentlemen?"

Smooth Skin nodded. Bushy Beard, fingering his winnings, was slower to agree.

"All right," he muttered at last.

Lydia smiled. "But we've been playing a kid's game so far. How about some real risks, eh? Major Arcana and double stakes, this time? And winner takes all?"

Both men hesitated this time. Then Bushy Beard shrugged. "Why not?"

"What about you, my friend?" Lydia crooned.

Smooth Skin sighed. "All right. But just this one hand. I have . . . other engagements."

"We'll try not to keep you too long," Lydia said drily.

Fuming and terrified, Kevin watched Bushy Beard shuffle the entire deck this time, Major and Minor Arcana together, and deal out the bright-hued cards. Fists clenched, he watched Lydia thoughtfully pick up then discard card after card, her face a studious blank.

"Raise," she said after a while, pushing a few coins towards the center of the table.

"Raise," echoed Smooth Skin, doing the same.

Bushy Beard hesitated a long time, but at last added his share of coins.

The game went on. And on. Each time it was Lydia's turn, she studied her cards for a time, then called out: "Raise."

That's the last of our winnings! Kevin realized. *If she loses this hand, we'll be beggared!*

It was Smooth Skin who hesitated this time, hand toying with the coins in front of him. "Raise," he said at last.

Bushy Beard swore under his breath. "Too rich for me," he muttered, throwing down his cards and stalking away.

Lydia smiled. "Show 'em," she said.

Smooth Skin showed his teeth in a sharp grin. "Beat this."

He held The Emperor, The Empress, The Fool, The Knight of Swords and The Five of Wands.

"Interesting." Lydia's voice was grim.

She's lost, I know she's lost. We're *lost.*

But then the woman's gloomy face broke into a grin. "What a shame you didn't have another Major Arcana card! Beat *this!*"

Her hand held The Magician, The Hanged Man, The Sun, The Tower, and The Lovers.

All Major Arcana cards. Does that mean . . . ?

It did. With a snarl, Smooth Skin got to his feet and stormed off, leaving Lydia to rake in the entire pot.

"Now can we please get out of here?" Kevin asked, sure Smooth Skin was going to return with thugs.

"Hey, kid, I know when to quit!" Lydia paused just long enough to make the bardling's heart race, then grinned. "And now, my friend, is definitely the time!"

Only when they were outside and halfway down the block did it occur to Kevin that he hadn't seen Tich'ki since they'd entered the temple. As though just thinking of her was enough to conjure her up, the fairy suddenly appeared at his side, wings fluttering, grinning her feral grin and waving a colorful piece of parchment.

"Wait a minute," Kevin said. "That's a tarot card!"

"Two points to the clever lad with the lute!"

"But — Let me see that!" The bardling snatched the card from Tich'ki's hand before she could dart away. "This is one of the cards from the deck Lydia was using! It's The High Priestess, one of the Major Ar — Ha! No *wonder* that man couldn't get all the Major Arcana cards! Lydia, you were *cheating*!"

"Shh! You want the guards after us?"

"But — but — you were! You and Tich'ki were in it together, weren't you? What did you do, Tich'ki? Use fairy magic so no one would notice you? That's it, isn't it? You looked at the other players' hands and slipped Lydia the right cards — You were both cheating!"

Lydia stopped. Placing her hands firmly on the bardling's shoulders, she told him, "My naive young friend, what did you think the others were doing? Hell, boy, we were *all* cheating, I realized that from the first hand! I just cheated better, that's all." Grinning, she released him. "You know who those two men were? The fellow with the beard — well, I don't remember his name; it's been a while. But he is a very successful gem merchant. The other one, the beardless guy, hasn't changed much at all. His name is Selden, and he sits on the city council. Neither one of them are going to miss what we took from them!"

"You stole from a city official!"

"He's not going to let anyone know he was — let's see, how does the formal term go? — participating in an illicit gambling operation! Come on, Kevin: smile! We've got our funding back, and more. Now let's go bribe ourselves somebody useful."

But just then an angry voice shouted, "There she is! That's the woman who robbed me! Guards, after her!"

"Oh, right," Kevin said sarcastically. "He's not going to let anyone know."

And then he and Lydia were running for their lives.

Chapter XI

As the guards charged, Tich'ki leaped straight up into the air, wings a blur. "See you later!"

She darted off at top speed as Kevin and Lydia raced through the crowded streets of Westerin, weaving in and out of knots of people, the guards' heavy footsteps pounding behind them. The air rang with cries of "Thieves! Stop them!" But no one even tried to block their path.

Of course not! Kevin realized. *Nobody wants to risk getting involved!*

"This way!" Lydia gasped, pointing to a narrow alley.

But Kevin stumbled to a stop, staring. In *there*? The place stank! It was filthy with piles of garbage and who knew what else. Worse, it also looked like a dead end!

He almost hesitated too long. "Got him!" a guard yelled. A rough hand grabbed at the bardling's arm, nearly pulling the lute from his back. Kevin kicked out savagely and heard a grunt of pain. The guard lost his hold, and the bardling dove into the alley.

Wonderful. Now I've assaulted a city guard. Just wonderful.

Trying not to breathe too deeply, he raced after Lydia, struggling to keep his footing on the slippery, muddy earth, telling himself the puddles he couldn't help splashing through were water, only water.

None of it seemed to bother the guards. They came pounding after him, swearing, armor and weapons clashing as they ran.

"Kevin!" Lydia whispered, snatching at him.

Where did she think she was going? That didn't even

qualify as an alley! It was only a — a crevice, a space where the backs of two buildings didn't quite meet.

"Come *on,* Kevin!"

Well, if she could fit . . .

The bardling hurried in after her, trying not to let his lute bang against a wall. How weird! None of the houses in this area seemed to meet exactly, and as a result there was a whole little maze of not-quite alleys back here. He hoped the woman knew where she was going, because if she didn't, they were going to wind up good and lost—

Lydia stopped so suddenly Kevin nearly crashed into her. She held up a hand, listening. "Damn!"

"They're still after us."

"Right. They don't usually follow anyone in here. Must be an election year." The woman shrugged. "We'll have to try something else."

She started off again. Kevin, who had just barely caught his breath, groaned and followed. They suddenly came out into a wider way, the back alley of a street of shops. The bardling noticed the rickety piles of storage crates and barrels and thought in sudden inspiration, *What if . . . ?*

"Lydia, wait!"

He pointed. She stared, then grinned in comprehension. "You're catching on fast, kid!"

As the guards charged out into the alley, they yelled to see their prey standing as if winded, leaning helplessly against a wall. "There they are! Take them!"

But the boy kicked at a crate and the woman at a barrel, and a whole avalanche of crates and barrels came thundering down, nearly burying the guards and totally blocking the alley.

"That does it!" Lydia crowed. "Let's get out of here before they can dig themselves out."

The small, open square might have been grand at one time, but Westerin had grown out and away from it long years back. Now it was a shabby little place, cobblestones cracked and broken where they hadn't been stolen outright. In the center of the square stood a fountain so chipped and worn Kevin guessed water hadn't flowed in it since Westerin had been founded.

Its rim made a fine place for two fugitives to sit and catch their breath. "No sign of the guards," Lydia said after a time. "Guess they finally lost us."

"What do you suppose happened to Tich'ki?"

Lydia shrugged. "She can take care of herself. No one's going to find a fairy who doesn't want to be found!" She glanced at Kevin. "That idea with the barrels was pretty clever. How'd you think of it?"

"I didn't," the bardling confessed. "I remembered it from an adventure ballad."

"Ha! Looks like music's good for something more than just pretty notes!"

Oh no, he wasn't going to fall into her trap. Biting back his indignant reply, Kevin asked instead, "Where are we, Lydia?"

The woman glanced about. "Pretty much where we want to be. In the . . . shall we say . . . less elegant section of town. The section that every city has, where the guards don't go too often and never alone, and where no one asks too many questions." At his raised eyebrow, the woman added jauntily, "Just trying to talk like a proper Bard!"

I will not *let her bait me!* "In other words, we're in the slums."

"Exactly. Just the spot for a few carefully placed bribes."

"*Here?*"

"Of course here. You don't find the weasels and rats we need in palaces!"

"What's to keep those rats from calling the guards?"

Lydia laughed. "The kind of folks we're going to meet are hardly going to be on the best of terms with guards. They're not going to call 'em down on us."

"Sure. Just like that city official wouldn't."

"Huh! This adventure's turning you too cynical, kid! Come on, let's go rat-hunting."

The first tavern was small and crowded, and stank of stale beer and staler humanity. But at least, Kevin thought warily, the men inside looked reasonably normal: sweaty, thick-set laborers and dock workers who'd stopped in for a quick drink.

Lydia shook her head in disapproval. "This won't do. Too honest. Come on."

The second tavern hid in the basement of a half-collapsed tenement. It was so dark in there that for one nervous moment Kevin, poised on the top of a short, rickety stairway, couldn't see anything at all. As his eyes adjusted to the gloom, he swallowed drily. This cluster of men and . . . not-quite humans lurking down there in the shadows couldn't have had anything honest to them at all.

"Better," muttered Lydia, her busy eyes checking out the clientel and scouting out possible escape routes at the same time. "Stay here."

She moved easily through the crowd, stopping a moment here to ask a question or two, slapping away a roving hand there, never losing her smile or her patience.

After what seemed an eternity to the bardling, Lydia returned to Kevin's side. "Three invitations to . . . ah . . . bed, two to sit and party a while, one to buy you — " she grinned at his outrage — " but no useful information. Besides," the woman added teasingly, "the price for you wasn't nearly high enough!"

She scurried out before he could find an answer.

The third tavern was almost as murky. The furnishings consisted only of a few splintery tables and chairs, and the thin layer of sawdust covering the floor was sticky with what Kevin prayed was only beer. The customers were an ugly lot, quite literally, hunched over their drinks like so many bitter predators, making the crowd in the last place look almost wholesome.

Not a one of them showed the slightest interest in kidnappers or a missing noblewoman. But before Lydia and Kevin could leave, a hulk of a man, big and ugly enough to be almost all ogre — lurched to his feet and staggered towards Lydia.

"H'llo, b'oot'ful. Come 'n have uh drink."

"Some other time, handsome."

"I said, have uh drink!"

"And I said, some other time."

As she turned to leave, the man caught her arm in a meaty hand. "You ain't goin' nowhere, b'oot'ful."

Lydia sighed. "They never learn," she murmured.

Before the bardling could even start to move, the woman whirled on her captor, knee shooting up with devastating force and deadly accuracy. As the man doubled over in speechless agony, Lydia pulled free and smiled sweetly at Kevin, fluttering her eyelashes at him.

"Shall we leave?" she asked.

The bardling glanced warily around the room. No one seemed to have noticed what had just happened. Even so, he had to fight the urge to back out of there, hand on sword hilt. Once they were safely outside on the street, Kevin exploded:

"What in the name of all the Powers did you think you were doing?"

"Avoiding an unwanted drink."

"But — but he might have been armed! He might have killed you!"

"And the roof might have caved in on us all. It didn't. He didn't. Kevin, credit me with enough wit to know when someone's carrying weapons. Or is sober enough to be dangerous. The poor idiot had it coming to him, and I just hope his less-than-friends back there don't slit his throat while he's helpless."

"But — you — "

"Look, kid, this sort of thing happens all the time

when you happen to be both a warrior *and* a woman."

"Well, maybe it wouldn't happen so often if you just didn't dress so—so—"

"So *what*, Kevin?"

He shook his head, miserably embarrassed, wishing he'd kept his mouth shut. "You know."

"Ah, our little bardling is a prude!"

"I am not! But you—"

"Go around asking for it? Is that what you're trying to say? Listen to me, and listen well: I am a woman in a man's world. I'm not complaining; that's just the way things are. And as a woman, sure, I could wear a nice, proper gown that restricted every step I took, the sort of thing a lady wears—and get killed the first time I needed to move quickly. I could wear full armor, too, always assuming I could afford the expensive stuff—but I spend a lot of my life on board ships. People who wear full armor on ships tend to have really short lives if they fall overboard!"

"I . . . uh . . . never thought of that. . . ."

"I realize that!" All at once, Lydia grinned. "Besides, when I *do* have trouble, the fools are generally so busy looking at my . . . ah . . . endowments that they never see my knee or fist coming. So now, enough lecturing. We still have some rat-hunting to do!"

She strode boldly away. Kevin gulped and followed, deciding that Lydia wasn't as dumb as she looked. She might be rough in manners and language—but she certainly wasn't dumb at all.

Kevin sank wearily to a bench, hardly caring that the cheaply made thing creaked alarmingly and threatened to collapse. How many taverns had it been now? Ten? Fifty? A hundred? By this point he'd seen so many roughnecks, so many weird, ugly humans and Others, so much emptiness or depravity in so many eyes, that he didn't think anything could shock him any more. If Death Itself came up to this table, the bardling mused listlessly, he'd probably just tell It to go have a nice day somewhere else.

Lydia, who in the course of their hunt had dealt with a half-dozen would-be suitors, showed not the slightest sign of weariness.

Well, sure. She's probably used to tavern-hopping. This is probably tame to her!

He looked down in dismay at the warm, watery beer in the flagon before him. At least he wasn't expected to finish the stuff. How anyone could actually want to —

"Hey, kid, look who I've found."

Lydia was returning, pulling someone with her. Kevin stared. An Arachnia! But clearly one that had fallen on hard times. Where D'Krikas had been an elegant figure, spotlessly clean, dark chitin shining with health, this being was downright shoddy, its compound eyes lacking any trace of animation, its tall body folded into a weary stoop that left it no taller than the woman. The gray cloak that seemed to be an Arachnia trademark was worn and ragged, so filthy it looked as though it had never been washed, and the being's chitin was so dull and scaly Kevin wondered if it was possible for an Arachnia to have the mange.

Lydia didn't seem to care. Slapping the Arachnia on its back, making the thin being stagger, she said heartily, "This is . . . what did you say your name was, pal?"

"D'Riksin," the being murmured.

"D'Riksin," Lydia echoed. "Sit you down here, D'Riksin, my friend, and have a drink with us."

She pushed. The Arachnia sat with a thump, as though already too far gone to resist. Kevin glanced sharply at the woman, wondering what was going on, but she was busy flagging down a barmaid. "A bottle of Mereot for my friends and me."

Mereot turned out to be a dark red wine, so sweet that Kevin nearly gagged on his first sip. He noticed that Lydia wasn't drinking much of her flagon, either. But D'Riksin guzzled down the sweet stuff with undisguised delight.

"Good," the being murmured.

"Have another, pal, on Kevin here."

D'Riksin clicked its beak in what was presumably an Arachniad smile. "Thank you, friend." It swilled down the second flagon almost as quickly as it had the first and clicked its beak with more abandon. "Good stuff. Good friends. Not like some others."

"Someone betrayed you, huh?" Lydia leaned forward, elbows on the table, resting her head on her fists. "That's tough."

"Betrayed me," the being echoed.

"Why don't you tell us all about it, pal?" Lydia's voice oozed concern. "Troubles are a lot lighter to bear when they're shared."

The Arachnia helped itself to more Mereot. "It's the king's fault," D'Riksin whined. "All his fault."

"How so?"

"Shouldn'ta supported him. Big mistake. No one'll hire me, 'cause they know I backed King Amber."

Huh? That doesn't make sense! They won't hire a supporter of the king? But Westerin is a crown city! There can't be that *many foes of King Amber here!*

Lydia didn't seem to be bothered by the weird logic, or lack of logic. "I know how it is," she purred. "Can't trust anybody, can you? Here, pal, have some more Mereot."

"Don' min' if I do." D'Riksin chittered an Arachnia giggle. "Show 'em. Show 'em all. Know something they don't know, any of them, none of the fine humans."

"Sure you do."

The Arachnia straightened slightly. "I *do*!" it insisted. "Know all about the girl."

Kevin tensed. "What girl?"

"Hee hee! *The* girl! The one who was swiped, 'course, the daughter of that fool of a count."

"Charina!"

D'Riksin tried to shrug, hampered by the lack of true shoulders. "Eck, whatever. Know who took her?" It paused, staring at them with the idiot slyness of the truly drunk. "It was Princess Carlotta, that's who!"

"That's impossible!" Kevin snapped. "Carlotta's been dead for over thirty years."

"No, no, no, no! That's what she *wants* everyone ta think! Dead, dead, dead . . . whee! Sorceresses don't die, not so easy, not she!" D'Riksin took another long swig of Mereot, then leaned forward as much as stiff chitin would allow, whispering confidentially, "It was rebels took the girl, rebels led by Princess Carlotta."

"But why?

The Arachnia chittered to itself, then tried to pour itself another drink. Nothing happened. It upended the bottle, looking blearily inside. "Empty," it said sadly. "No more Mereot for poor D'Rikish — D'Rishkin — D'*Riksin.*"

But Lydia had already ordered a new bottle. "Here, pal. Drink up. Tell us why Princess Carlotta stole the girl."

D'Riksin chittered and drank. "Wheeee!" it laughed. "She wants to use the girl against King Amber!"

"That's ridiculous!" Kevin said. "Charina may be Count Volmar's niece, but she's not all *that* important."

The Arachnia blinked and leaned forward again, studying the bardling closely. Kevin stared back, trying not to flinch at this close-up view of the being's compound eyes. "You're the one was copyin' the manshu — manshi — the book."

"How would you know — Ow!"

Lydia had kicked him under the table. She glared at the bardling, warning him to keep quiet. D'Riksin continued, heedless, "Wanna know a secret? Bet you don' know the stuff you were copyin' had a spell hid in it." The being nodded, pleased with itself. "Yup, did!"

It fell silent, staring moodily into its flagon. Lydia asked, very gently, "What kind of a spell, pal?"

"A *hidden* spell!"

"Well, yes," she said with more patience than Kevin would ever have believed, "we gathered that. What *kind* of a hidden spell?"

"Don' think I should tell ya."

"Maybe you don't know. Maybe you're making this all up." Lydia folded her arms in pretend indignation. "A fine thing when you can't even trust a drinking buddy to tell the truth."

"I *am* tellin' the truth," D'Riksin whined. "Not sure, y'unnerstand. But rumor is, it's a spell to keep Princess Carlotta from changin' shape. 'Cause if she did, if the spell works, she'd be stuck in her true self forever 'n' ever."

"Her . . . true self," Kevin said warily.

"Sure! Din'cha know? She's not human, not altogether. Naw, she's more fairy 'n' anythin' else. And she'd be stuck as a fairy!" The Arachnia chittered in laughter. "No way a fairy can sit the throne. Not legal! Gotta be a human."

"You sure about that spell?" Lydia asked.

"Eck, who knows? Thing's never been tried, never been tested. Might work. Might blow up in the user's face!"

The Arachnia swayed in its seat. "I was there," it said confidentally. "I was in the guard, you know, guard of Count Volmar's daddy. Yup, his daddy, that's who it was, Count Dalant. I saw the elves give the book to him, to ole Count Dalant. Told him to keep it safe. Guess they figured if Princess Carlotta went lookin' for the thing, she'd think the elves had it."

"But why leave it with the count's father?" Kevin asked.

D'Riksin started to pour itself another flagon full, then stopped, blinking thoughtfully. "I 'member they said something 'bout it bein' too dangerous to leave with anyone who could act'ly *use* the thing. Yeah. Just in case Princess Carlotta did think to look there. Yeah, s'right. It's keyed so only two folks can see it. One of 'em a Bard. Ardan, Aydan, somethin' like that."

The bardling tensed, heart racing. "Aidan?"

"Yeah! That's it! It'll only appear to him, or to his suchsec — shuchessor — successor!" the Arachnia finished triumphantly. "Wheeeee!" it added in glee, and fell flat across the table.

"So much for that," Lydia muttered. She glanced up. "Uh, Kevin, I think we'd better get out of here."

"Yes, but —"

"*Now,* Kevin."

Startled at the urgency in her voice, the bardling looked up. "Oh."

Six ugly . . . things were peering through the gloomy tavern, looking for something.

Things, Kevin decided, was definitely the word. None of the six was truly human, or a member of any other recognizable race, except for their leader, who was the most depraved-looking elf the bardling could ever have imagined. Pasty-skinned and gaunt, the man's fair White Elf hair hung lankly to his shoulders, and his green White Elf eyes were flat and cold and empty. Kevin wondered what depravities could have so corrupted a creature of Light, and shuddered.

"Guess not everyone liked the idea of D'Riksin talking to us," Lydia murmured.

"You don't know they're looking for us," Kevin whispered back.

Just then, the empty-eyed elf pointed their way and yelled something at the others. All six started stalking forward, radiating menace, sending customers scrambling out of their way.

"Hell I don't," Lydia said drily.

Chapter XII

"All right," Lydia said under her breath. "I've been in tighter fixes than this. Gotten out of them, too. Follow my lead, Kevin. Ready? Here we go!"

She stood up, grabbed a customer at random, and flattened him with one mighty punch. The man staggered back into another table, which collapsed, spilling their drinks all over the men who'd been sitting there.

"Hey, watch it, you stupid *Ertich*!"

"*Ertich*, is it?" growled an ogre at the next table. "*I'm* an *Ertich*, you idiot humans!"

He dove into the humans, swinging wildly, sending men and chairs flying. For one shocked moment, Kevin froze. Then he realized exactly what Lydia was doing and grabbed another man, about to imitate her.

No, no, I nearly wrecked my hand the last time I tried to punch someone! Can't risk that again!

What to do? The bardling snatched up a half-empty flagon instead, and whapped the man soundly over the head. Mereot splashed all over a heavy-set, scaly whatever-it-was at the next table. The creature sprang up with a furious hiss, only to collide with one of the men from the first table, who was blindly throwing punches right and left. The creature flattened him, and went looking for other prey. Those customers who hadn't already taken cover found themselves caught in the middle of an ever-growing melee — and joined in with savage glee. The empty-eyed elf and his men swore helplessly as the brawl engulfed them in a whirlwind of fists and bottles.

Lydia, standing safely out of the way, gave a sharp laugh. "Nothing like a good old-fashioned tavern brawl for a diversion! Come on, Kevin, let's get out of here."

She slipped out through the tiny kitchen, Kevin close behind her, struggling past harried servants who were heading out into the brawl armed with clubs and broom handles.

Hey, where had Lydia gone?

"Out here!" the woman called, and the bardling scrambled out the narrow window after her. "Now you know why I'm always scouting for ways out of places! Come on, let's put some distance between ourselves and those guys."

More running, Kevin thought wearily.

They made it all the way back to the shabby square. The bardling sank gladly to the lip of the dry fountain, panting, the lute an awkward weight on his back. He shifted it around in front of him, leaning on it. "Think we're safe?"

Lydia straightened, listening to nothing but silence. She shrugged. "For the moment. By the time old Empty Eyes fights his way out of that tavern, our trail's going to be cold."

We hope. "Now what do we do?"

"Look for the others, I guess, and — "

"*There* you are!" a shrill voice snapped.

Kevin glanced up to see the fairy fluttering fiercely overhead. "Hello, Tich'ki!"

"Never mind 'hello, Tich'ki!' I've been flying all over the city. Where the *hell* were you two?"

"Hunting rats." Lydia grinned. "Learned a lot from them, too."

The fairy landed lightly beside her. "And nearly got bit by them, I see. Oh yes, I heard all the fuss. What's the matter, the guards weren't good enough for you? Robbing a councilman wasn't exciting enough?"

"Ah, you're a fine one to scold! It wasn't me who set that inn on fire back in Elegian — "

"An accident. I never knew the spell would backfire like that."

" — or dropped the chamber pot on the mayor's head in Smithian."

The fairy grinned. "Nearly tore a wing lifting the thing. Worth it, though."

"Besides," Lydia added, "you know I didn't rob Selden. Not exactly. Look, Tich'ki, you were there! It was a game of cards, that's all. He wasn't any more honest than me."

"Tell that to the guards." The fairy glanced sharply from one human to the other. "You reek of excitement. Haven't just been eluding guards, have you?"

"Uh, no," Lydia admitted. "We seem to have gotten somebody's gang after us, too."

"Huh. And you tell *me* to keep out of trouble? Tell me, just how do you plan to get out of Westerin?"

Lydia shrugged. "We'll think of something."

"We can't leave without the rest of our party," Kevin cut in.

"Sure, but they could be anywhere."

"They're both still in the city." Tich'ki restlessly folded and refolded her wings. "Wouldn't have left without their horses. And those horses are still here. I checked."

Kevin straightened, hands tightening on the lute case. "Tich'ki, you're friends with Naitachal."

"Well . . . "

"All right, all right, maybe you're not friends. But at least you two must have something in common. I saw you doing those card tricks together."

"What's this?" Lydia asked, eyebrow raised.

Tich'ki's dusky skin flushed. "He asked me. What was I supposed to do? Tell him he wasn't bright enough to learn?"

"Teaching him tricks, eh?"

"Card tricks!"

"Of course."

"It's true!"

"And was that all you were doing, hmm?"

"Lydia, that's ridiculous! Look at the size of me! He's more than twice my height!"

"Why, Tich'ki! Aren't your people wonderful shape-changers? I should think you could be any size you want to be."

Kevin stared from Lydia to Tich'ki. "I don't understand you two! We've got all sorts of people out to get us. How can you possibly waste time in —in banter?"

They both looked at him in surprise. Lydia shook her head. "Would anything be changed if we acted like scared little kids?"

"No, but — "

"Morale, Kevin, got to keep up morale. Just as," she added slyly, "Tich'ki was keeping Naitachal's morale up."

Cornered, the fairy took to the air. Still blushing, she yelled down,

"You *know* I don't date outside my species!"

"Since when are elves and fairies separate — "

"All right! All right! I'll go look for him. You stay here."

As the fairy darted up and away, Lydia murmured a bemused, "Card tricks?"

"That's all it was, really," Kevin said.

"Oh, I figured that. But how often do I get a chance to rib a fairy?" All at once she frowned. "Eh, I know I said something about keeping up morale, but this hardly seems the time for a song! Why are you taking out your lute?"

"I'm going to try something." Kevin paused, one hand caressing the polished wood. "I only hope it works."

"What are you talking about?"

"There's a song that's supposed to draw someone you know to you. I'm going to try it on Eliathanis."

"You don't exactly know him."

"Well, no. But he's an elf after all. Even if I can't manage the whole force of Bardic Magic, he should have enough innate magic to sense *something*."

"Always assuming he wants to listen."

"If the song works properly, he . . . uh . . . won't have a choice."

Lydia raised an eyebrow. "Only hope you don't call up Empty Eye from the gang as well. He's an elf, too. More or less," she added in distaste.

"Oh. Well." Kevin hadn't thought of that. "It . . . should work only on Eliathanis." *I hope.*

Bending over the lute, the bardling tuned it carefully, then took a deep breath and began his song, trying to picture the White Elf and only the White Elf, hearing the coaxing strains soar out and out. . . .

The bardling came back to himself with a start, startled to realize he didn't know how much time had passed. It must have been quite a while, because his fingers were weary and his throat was dry. "What — Naitachal!"

The Dark Elf bowed wryly. "Surprised to see me? Returning was the only way I could get that fairy to stop pestering me!"

"Huh!" Tich'ki said indignantly. "You were the one who kept asking me questions!"

"And you were the one who wouldn't answer any of them." Naitachal grinned. "I confess: Tich'ki kept after me till she'd roused my curiosity."

"I'm sure," Lydia murmured.

Kevin nearly choked. But then the urge to laugh faded as he realized: "I guess my song didn't work."

"Oh, it did!" an angry voice snapped, and the bardling shot to his feet. "It did, indeed!"

"Eliathanis!"

"You just would *not* stop pulling at my mind! I was in the middle of learning some important information, and you — "

"What's this?" Tich'ki wondered, fluttering around the White Elf. "You're such a fair-haired fellow. What are *red* hairs doing on your shoulder?"

"Never mind that!" Eliathanis hastily brushed them from him.

"Mmm, and what's this?" She sniffed audibly. "You taken to wearing perfume, elf?"

"No!" His fair skin reddened. "It — I — "

"Oh, you were learning something, all right!" the fairy taunted. "And I'm sure it was pretty important, too! Maybe nothing to do with the stolen girl, but — "

"I was talking to a troop of dancing girls," the White Elf said with immense dignity. Struggling to ignore Lydia's delighted whoop, he continued, "They travel all over the country. I thought they might know Charina's whereabouts."

"And they really *hated* talking to such a pretty fellow," Tich'ki teased, then darted sideways in the air as Eliathanis, his face a fiery red by now, took a swipe at her. "You never *will* catch me like that, elf!" she mocked.

"Can't you be serious for even a moment?"

"Now, now, Eliathanis." Naitachal's voice was studiously serious, but his eyes glinted under the black hood. "Seems to me you're hardly the one to accuse anyone else of frivolity. Tsk, should have known there was something warmer than ice under that grim facade!"

"Don't you dare criticize me, necromancer!"

"Oh for Powers' sakes!" Lydia cried. "You two aren't going to start that again, are you?"

"What do you expect of elves?" Tich'ki laughed. "They're almost as bad as humans!"

"Hey, whose side are you on, fairy!"

"My own, of course!"

Eliathanis frowned at Lydia. "Woman, I don't need to be defended from the likes of her!"

This is getting out of hand, Kevin knew. *If we don't work everything out now, we're going to wind up in prison. Or dead.*

Kevin licked his dry lips, thinking feverishly. Maybe he hadn't acted like a leader up to now. Maybe that was because he had been trying too hard to imitate the leaders in the heroic songs, those miracles of bravery who were gifted with unfailing charisma. Well, that was nonsense! The boy who had left Bracklin might never have accepted it, but he was no longer so naive. Such marvelous, infallible heroes like that could never have existed — but those like Master Aidan most certainly did. Master Aidan and those other good, sensible, down-to-earth people who'd saved King Amber. People who tried to understand those they were supposed to lead, who brought them together and got them to concentrate only on their goal!

"All right," Kevin began.

Nobody noticed.

"I said, *all right*!"

As the others turned to him, he added sternly, "Aren't you ashamed of yourselves? Did you really mean to rob Count Volmar?"

Ha, that made them start. "What do you mean?" Eliathanis asked coldly. "I am not a thief."

"No? You certainly aren't earning your keep! You were hired to rescue the Lady Charina — *not* to fight with each other! But bickering seems to be all you can do!"

"Now, Kevin," Lydia began, "that's hardly fair — "

"Let me finish!" He glared at them all. "You, Eliathanis and you, Naitachal: I know there are long hatreds between White and Dark Elves. I know those hatreds go back for generations. I don't expect either one of you to settle such ancient grudges overnight. I don't even ask you to try! But I don't think elves of either race had anything to do with the kidnapping — and if you really mean to show your peoples' innocence the way you boasted, you had better stop fighting and show some of that famous elvish self-control! Or is that just a myth to make humans respect you?"

"It's not," Naitachal said shortly. "And you do have a point, bardling."

Tich'ki snickered. "Such a daring boy — "

"And *you*!" Kevin's finger stabbed at her with such fervor that she flinched. "You've done nothing so far but snipe at everyone else. I don't care about your background, I don't care what unhappiness you're trying to hide — "

"I'm not!" she protested.

" — but I'm beginning to wonder if you're in the pay of the enemy!"

The fairy froze in mid-air. "I most certainly am not!"

"Then stop acting like it!"

Lydia cleared her throat. "Don't you think that's going a bit far, kid?"

Kevin whirled to her. "And as for you, Lydia: look, I know I'm young, I know that compared to you I'm as ignorant of the world as they come. But one thing I am not is an idiot!"

"Oh, I never said — "

"But you think it. And as long as you go on thinking it, you're not letting me do my job."

"Which is?"

"The same as all of us: freeing Charina!"

They were getting restless. These weren't naughty children, after all. If he didn't change his tone, Kevin realized, he was going to lose them.

"Listen to me." The bardling pitched his voice as smoothly as ever he'd been taught. "Lydia and I learned something truly alarming, something that makes all our quarrelling the petty thing it is. Carlotta is alive."

"The sorceress?" Eliathanis exclaimed. "But that's impossible! Everyone knows she died years ago!"

"So we were led to think. Carlotta, I repeat, is very much alive. And you and I know there is nothing she would like better than to discredit King Amber's reign." Kevin took a deep breath, stalling, trying to figure out what he was going to say next. "Look you, we all know there's always been an undercurrent of uneasiness, of mistrust, between the different races in the realm. That's not so surprising. It may not be logical, but elf or human, we fear the unknown. And if that unknown takes the form of someone with a different shade of skin " — he glanced at Naitachal — " or a different way of life — " this time his glance took in Lydia " — well, it's all too easy to let fear turn to hate."

"True enough," muttered the Dark Elf, and Eliathanis nodded.

"But for thirty years," the bardling continued, "those different races have managed to live in peace. And why is that? Because King Amber has been such a just, impartial ruler."

This time it was Lydia who nodded.

"Well, Carlotta doesn't like that!" Kevin said. "The more popular a ruler her brother becomes, the more difficult it's going to be for her to replace him. She tried to kill him once before. We all know that. We also know how she failed. But Carlotta has had thirty years to think things over. I guess she's decided to be more devious."

The bardling paused to catch his breath, glancing at the others. They were watching him quite seriously; even Tich'ki showed no sign of her usual mockery.

"Carlotta has to know exactly how things stand between the races," Kevin continued. "What better way for her to destroy King Amber's reign than to use a kidnapping to stir up all that latent hatred? Once the land is torn by strife, what better way for her to seize control?"

"Could be," Tich'ki muttered.

"Not 'could be,' " Kevin corrected. "Will be, if we don't do something to stop her."

"Why us?" Lydia asked.

Why, indeed? He couldn't blame the woman — who, after all was a mercenary, not a subject of the king — for asking. But before Kevin could find a good argument, Naitachal said thoughtfully, "I believe I can guess why Carlotta would choose Count Volmar's niece to kidnap. His father was a true diplomat."

"He was," Eliathanis agreed. "Someone who tried his best to reconcile grievances among the races."

"But Count Volmar," the Dark Elf continued, "is . . . shall we say, a bit less friendly towards both our races."

The White Elf nodded wryly.

"That's just it!" Kevin exclaimed. "Carlotta knows about him, she must! That's why she kidnapped Charina, and that's why she made it look as if elves were to blame. Ha, yes, and she probably plans to plant hints in the count's ear — you know, that his handpicked team isn't having any success because the elves in the party are deliberately hindering the hunt, because they don't really *want* to find Charina!"

"Yes," Lydia agreed. "But you're still not giving me a good reason to risk my neck. These aren't my people or my land, after all."

"No," Kevin admitted. "But if Carlotta wins here, do you think she's really going to stop with one realm? She's a sorceress, Lydia, who can muster the forces of Darkness to her side."

"But why *us*, Kevin? How can we possibly make a difference?"

"Ah. Well. Because of the manuscript." *I'm sorry,*

Master Aidan, but I don't dare keep it a secret any longer. Hastily, Kevin told the others the reason he'd come to Count Volmar's castle — and what he'd learned about that manuscript.

"You mean Carlotta is part *fairy*?" Tich'ki yelped. "Her mother mated with a *human*?"

"So it seems."

"B-but that's disgusting!"

"Thank you." Lydia gave the fairy a sarcastic bow. "Kevin, go on. Tell us more about this manuscript."

"My Master must have realized Carlotta had returned."

"Then why didn't he go straight to the king?"

"He didn't dare!" Thinking it out as he spoke, Kevin added, "Not while Carlotta had her full powers, anyhow. No, that would be putting King Amber in direct danger. So he sent me after the spell."

"You being expendable, eh?" Naitachal asked.

"Uh, well, I wouldn't put it quite that way, but the king's life *is* more important."

"Of course," Eliathanis agreed, a little more emphatically than Kevin would have liked. "Kevin, what do you want us to do?"

What — Hey, they're listening to me! They really are! I've won!

Sure, but what was he going to do about it? "I think we're going to have to return to Count Volmar's castle," the bardling said slowly. "We have to retrieve that manuscript. If Carlotta's people really do have Charina, they might be willing to trade her for it."

"What! No!" the White Elf cried. "That's insane!"

"I'm not going to give them the *real* manuscript! No, no, I'll work up a forgery."

"They'll surely know the difference," Naitachal argued.

"They won't. You see, I had already started copying the manuscript before Charina was kidnapped. I'll put a few pages of the real copy in with the fake, and only

Carlotta will be able to tell the difference. But by the time she learns the truth, Charina will be free! Yes, and while we're in the castle, we can tell Count Volmar what we've learned. Who knows? It just might force him to rethink how he feels about elves!"

"Sooner force a stone to walk," the Dark Elf murmured. "But it's worth the attempt."

"I agree," Eliathanis said.

Lydia shrugged. "Me, too. Hey, Tich'ki, you in?"

The fairy shrugged. "Why not? Now all we have to do is get out of the city. Easy. There's only one gang out to get us, and guards watching for us at every gate." She grinned sharply. "If we can escape all that, why, anything else will be a laugh!"

"Ha," Lydia said dourly.

INTERLUDE THE THIRD

Count Volmar sat brooding before the fireplace in his solar, chin resting on fisted hand.

How could things have gone so wrong so quickly? As soon as that stupid bardling, that Kevin, was safely gone from the castle, the count had ordered the library emptied down to the bare stone walls, under the guise of giving the place a good cleaning. He had personally examined every volume, no matter how useless or bizarre the contents. By now the newly cleaned books gleamed in the newly cleaned library. But Volmar was willing to swear on every sacred relic that not one of the whole lot was the missing manuscript.

Nobody took it. It didn't walk out of there by itself. There is no place in that library for the thing to be hiding. Then where is it?

Not that it mattered. None of his plans mattered, not now, not when Carlotta was—

"You idiot! You utter idiot!"

Count Volmar leaped back from his chair with a startled yell, flattening himself against a wall, staring in horror at this sudden apparition. "In — in the Seven Holy Names," he began, tracing holy signs in the air with a hand that shook, "I bid you begone — "

"Oh, stop that! I'm not a ghost! You can't exorcise me!"

"Carlotta . . . ? Are you . . . real?"

"Of course I'm real!" The sorceress threw herself down in a chair in a swirl of green silk, flaming red hair crackling in a cloud about her. "What nonsense are you spouting now?"

"I th-thought you were dead." Volmar took a deep, steadying breath. "Carlotta, I really did think you were dead." Returning to his chair, he sat, a little more abruptly than he'd intended. "When your horse returned without you, when the court sages all swore something terrible had happened, something sorcerous — "

"Bah."

"Well, what did you *expect* me to think? You're a sorceress, dammit! Anything powerful enough to overcome *you* wasn't going to be content at stopping at a mere kidnapping. I was sure you'd been killed by a demon!" Struggling for control, the count continued, "If you had only deigned to share your plans with me — "

"You never would have been able to play your role so convincingly." Carlotta's eyes glinted with scorn. "The boy never would have believed you. This way there was genuine terror in your voice when you told him of poor little Charina's disappearance."

"But you were gone so long!"

"Poor frightened little boy!"

"Carlotta — "

"I didn't have time to hold your hand! Do you imagine it was easy to leave a false track halfway to Westerin?"

"Uh, no, I would think not."

"Ha! You *don't* think, there's the truth of it!" Carlotta sprang to her feet, green gown rippling about her as she paced. "How could you be so hopelessly, totally *stupid*?"

Volmar nearly choked himself in the battle to keep from shouting back at her. "What do you mean?" he managed.

"How could you choose that Arachnia!"

What Arachnia? Surely the woman couldn't be referring to his seneschal. "D'Riksin?" the count asked warily.

Carlotta waved an impatient hand. "Whatever it calls itself. The Arachnia in Westerin!"

"Ah. Yes." Coldness settled in Volmar's stomach. Choosing his words very carefully, he began, "Granted, D'Riksin isn't always the most reliable of my agents, but—"

"Reliable! D'Riksin is a drunken *sot*!"

"Well, yes, the creature does drink too much. It's a shame that alcohol affects the Arachniad system as it does our own. But D'Riksin has never failed me before. Besides, it was already in place in Westerin, it had its orders, and —"

"And it ignored them completely! Yes, yes," Carlotta added impatiently, "I was watching the whole thing with my magic. That stupid drunken insect was *supposed* to lead the boy and his party away from this castle, not towards it! And it was *not* supposed to tell them anything about the manuscript!"

Volmar stared in disbelief. Was that a glint of uneasiness he saw in Carlotta's eyes? Or could it possibly even be . . . fear? Just what strange magic *was* in that manuscript? Frustrating, to have to rely only on one little scrying crystal! Oh yes, the count knew it was as potent an artifact as someone with no innate magical ability could use, but it was still such a maddeningly inferior thing! He'd only been able to guess at what D'Riksin had been babbling. Something about a spell . . . a fairy . . .

A fairy?

The count stiffened in sudden comprehension. Struggling to keep the shock from his face, he thought, *Of course!* No wonder Carlotta had been in hiding for so many years! Once she had recovered her strength after the failed attempt on Amber's life, she would have sensed the existence of the magical manuscript. Ha, how that must have alarmed her! Volmar supposed Carlotta had been struggling to control the thing from afar, terrified that if she came too close she would spark the magic into life and end everything for her.

And then nasty old Master Aidan decided to up the stakes, as the gamblers say, and send for the manuscript. That forced you out of hiding, Carlotta, didn't it?

Imagine that. All these years he had been wondering at Carlotta's uncanny, precocious gift for sorcery when the answer had been so very obvious! Her mysterious, unknown mother hadn't been human at all!

Volmar only barely stifled a triumphant laugh. If news ever got out that the high and mighty princess-sorceress wasn't truly human, that she was half fairy. . . . The law stated quite firmly that no one of fairy blood could ever wear the crown. If she were unmasked, it would turn a sure thing into a very dicey proposition.

Well now, isn't that interesting? I'll keep your little secret, Carlotta. After all, if you fail, I fail, too.

But once she gained the throne, once he sat beside her, why then some changes would be made. They would, indeed!

Carlotta was still pacing so restlessly Volmar ached to order her to stand still. "You still haven't found the manuscript," she said without warning, and he started. "Don't look so surprised, man. I was watching you, too."

All at once the sorceress did stop, staring into the flames, eyes fierce with impatience. "It has to be somewhere in the library, of course it does, even if we can't see it. There are such things as Spells of Hiding, after all. But what can be enchanted can be disenchanted. With time. And without interference. Such as that fool of a bardling will provide! Damn him! We must keep him away from the castle!"

"But he's stuck in Westerin," Volmar soothed. "My hirelings are hunting for him."

"Ha! That gang of failures! If they're anything like your Arachnia, they probably can't find their own feet!"

"There's no way the boy can get out of that city," the count said flatly. "If my men don't catch him, he'll wind up in prison or —"

"I don't believe that for a moment! So far the boy's

had uncanny luck, and there's no reason for things to be different now."

"Can't you . . . ah . . . remove him — "

"Kill him, you mean? From this far away?" Carlotta gave a fierce little laugh. "I'm not a goddess, man! No mortal can throw a death-spell that far! Besides," she added thoughtfully, "I'm not sure I want him dead . . . not quite yet . . . not till I have time to lay a proper trap for him. One to catch both the boy and the manuscript. . . . Yes!"

She whirled to stare at the count, eyes wide and radiant with a cold, alien light. "You may watch this, Volmar. But do not move from that spot. Do not utter one word. On your life, do not seek to interfere."

Interfere with sorcery? Did she think him insane? "Of course not," the count said fervently.

What it was Carlotta murmured, Volmar had no idea. He wasn't even sure of the language. But each precisely uttered syllable seemed to ring in his ears long after it was spoken, seemed to prickle along his arms and ache in his bones till he longed to turn and run. But that, Volmar knew, would be the end of him, so he stood and watched and endured. And just barely kept from crying out his shock when the firelight all at once went hard and slick as ice. Or a mirror.

A mirror, indeed, though what it reflected . . . Not daring to move from where he stood, Volmar peered over Carlotta's shoulder to see a the figure of a man suddenly come into sharp focus, seen as clearly as though through an open window.

Now, who . . . ?

No youngster, this. He was a fully human man — or at least appeared to be — somewhere in late middle age, his thick-set, powerful form half-hidden by the folds of a black cloak. Its hood nearly hid the severe, harshly planed face and its graying beard. The stranger's eyes were gray, too, blazing out from the hood's shadow with sorcerous force. But an ageless weariness was there as well. As though, Volmar thought uneasily, their owner had tried and been bored by every depravity known to humanity.

Whoever, whatever he was, the man plainly knew Carlotta. No warmth lightened the terrible eyes, but he dipped his head, almost reluctantly, in reverence.

"Princess." The words were faint but clear. "What would you?"

"You have not forgotten, have you, Alatan? You have not forgotten your debt to me?"

The gray eyes flickered angrily. "No. I have not. The fools would have burned me as a sorcerer had you not intervened. Name what you would of me, Princess Carlotta. It shall be done."

"It shall, indeed," the sorceress purred. "Listen, then." She slipped back into the alien language with which she'd created the flame-mirror. The language of sorcery, Volmar thought, and wished with all his heart he was somewhere else.

But he didn't dare be squeamish. Not if he meant to sit beside Carlotta on the throne.

As the sorceress continued to give her orders to the reluctantly obedient Alatan, Count Volmar forced himself to stand proudly as any king.

But once Carlotta had banished the mirror-spell, and the flames were nothing more than flames, he let himself sag.

"Who is this Alatan?" he dared ask.

"An ally, willy-nilly."

"He said you saved him from burning as a sorcerer." Volmar said it doubtfully; charity hardly seemed part of Carlotta's character. "Someone falsely accused him, I take it?"

Carlotta's smile was deceptively sweet. "Oh no. Alatan *is* a sorcerer, indeed. A most powerful, most unpleasant one. Poor Kevin!" she added. "I find I almost . . . pity him!"

Chapter XIII

Kevin sighed. He and the rest of his group had been trying for what seemed like an age to find a gate out of Westerin: a gate that wasn't watched over either by the gang or the guards. So far they hadn't succeeded. After all this hunting, his feet hurt, his lute seemed to have picked up extra weight, his stomach was clamoring for food — and now the night was coming on.

"I think all we can do," he said wearily as they regrouped in the small, ruined square, "is find a place to spend the night and try to see if we can't figure out a way to get out of here in the morning."

"Good idea." Lydia grinned ruefully. "I can go all day on sea or land, but these cobblestones are cursed hard on the feet!"

"It is going to look rather suspicious if we all march into an inn together," Naitachal pointed out. "We're not exactly an ordinary mix of people."

"That's no problem to me." Tich'ki laughed, fluttering her wings. "All I need is a window, and I'm in!"

"The same is true of Naitachal and me," Eliathanis added. "We are elves, not clumsy humans."

"I'll remind you of that the next time you trip over something," Lydia muttered.

"I never — "

The bardling held up a warning hand. "First we find an inn. *Then* we quarrel!"

That got grudging chuckles from everyone.

Well, what do you know? the pleased Kevin told himself. *Maybe I* am *starting to get the knack of being a leader!*

But before he could congratulate himself too much, a shout from the far side of the square made them all start and whirl.

Oh no, not now.

"Well, well," murmured Lydia. "Look who found us. It's the Gang of Things."

"Ugly, aren't they?" Tich'ki mocked. "Bet they make even uglier corpses."

Kevin couldn't be so casual about it. Somewhere along the way, Empty Eyes had picked up a few more supporters. "There are ten of them," he pointed out to Lydia and Tich'ki, "and only five of us."

"They are also," the warrior woman reminded Kevin, "nicely within bowshot." She nocked arrow to bow in one swift, fluid movement. "Come on," Lydia taunted the enemy. "Come and die."

"You have only the one bow, woman," Empty Eyes purred. "And I have some tricks of my own."

Faster than a striking snake, he thrust out his hand, shouting out a savage Word of Power. Lydia cried out in shock as her bowstring snapped in two.

"That's better," Empty Eyes said. "Take them!"

Kevin had barely enough time to whip out his sword before the gang was upon them. *They've got swords!* a startled part of his mind noted. *What's a street gang doing with something as expensive as swords?*

They had to be in someone's pay. Selden? No, he had the guards at his beck and call. Then who . . . ?

No time to worry about it. Ten against five was terrible odds, no matter what Lydia and Tich'ki thought.

Naitachal had summoned up his sorcerous black blade again — but Empty Eyes only laughed, moving to counter its attack with a dead gray blade of his own. Naitachal's eyes widened in surprise and the other elf laughed anew.

"That's right, Dark Elf. Some of us have played with sorcery, too."

Kevin lost the rest of that conversation as a sinuous being that seemed some unholy cross of man and snake lunged at him, sword in scaly hand. The bardling parried, two-handed, just in time, the shock of impact shivering all the way up to his shoulders. He staggered back, closely followed by his foe, who moved every bit as fluidly and unpredictably as a serpent.

I don't know what style of fencing he's using! I — I've never seen it before and I don't know how —

Kevin's frantic thought ended in a gasp as he came up hard against the rim of the fountain. The being grinned at him, a flash of alarmingly sharp fangs, and lunged yet again. Trapped, Kevin did the only thing he could, and leaped up onto the rim, slashing down at the being, who was cutting savagely at his legs. Suddenly inspired, Kevin sprang aside and down, into the wide basin of the fountain, just as the being lunged. The creature's blade clanged harshly against stone, and Kevin, remembering the bandit back in the rocky gorge, hastily brought his foot down on the flat of the blade as hard as he could.

There was a gratifying *snap*. The being hissed — his tongue narrow and forked as that of a snake — and hurled the broken sword at Kevin's head. The bardling ducked, tripped over rubble in the basin, and went flat, narrowly missing cracking his skull against stone. Before he could catch his breath, the being came hurling down at him. The bardling grabbed a sinuous wrist, slippery with scales, and kicked upward. The being went flying over Kevin's head, landing with a crash on the cobblestones. The bardling scrambled out of the fountain, thinking in delighted wonder, *Hey, that really does work!*

He wound up just behind the grim Naitachal and Empty Eyes, even as the Dark Elf countered a vicious cut at his head. As sorcerous black and gray blades clashed together, fountains of blood red sparks flew up, casting an eerie, fiery glow over the square.

"Sorcerous games," Naitachal panted. "Some of us haven't let those games destroy our souls."

"Souls?" Empty Eyes taunted. "What are human things like souls for such as we?"

"You are not like me, you pathetic thing! You, who've forgotten your own kind!"

"No more than you, Dark Elf!" Empty Eyes retorted, and lunged.

Once more, fiery sparks lit up the square. Kevin glanced up at the surrounding houses. Didn't anyone hear or see what was going on? Didn't anyone care?

Someone did. From one side came the sound of running footsteps and the clashing of mail.

"Oh hell," Lydia said. "Just what we needed: the guards. Come on, guys, no time for heroics now. Let's get out of here!"

The gang, equally illegal, thought the same thing, scattering in all directions. Empty Eyes, panting, paused long enough to hurl his gray sword at Naitachal, but the Dark Elf struck it cleanly with his black blade. Both sorcerous things blazed up in a blinding surge of bloody light and were gone. *Oh, blast,* Kevin thought, *why was I looking that way just then?*

Vision dazzled, afterimages dancing before his eyes, Kevin staggered away as best he could, stumbling over the broken cobblestones. He gasped when someone grabbed his arm and tried to strike out, but a familiar voice said:

"It's me. Lydia. It's all right, kid, I had my head turned away. I can still see where I'm going."

Unfortunately, so could the guards. And a whole troop of them was flooding into the square, weapons drawn, far too many to fight.

"Damn," Lydia muttered. "Selden really is out for blood. No worse damage to a politician than injured pride." She looked over the grim, well-armed troop and sighed. "I hate to simply surrender, particularly since Selden isn't going to make things comfortable for us, but . . . "

"Then don't," Tich'ki snapped.

Hovering in mid-air, wings a blur, she stared at the guards, shouting out twisting, intricate, commanding Words in the fairy tongue, her eyes blazing green fire.

And to Kevin's amazement, the guards stopped in their tracks, blinking in confusion.

"Where'd they go . . . ?"

"Coulda sworn they were here a minute ago . . . "

"Who . . . ? Who are we looking for . . . ?"

"Don't know . . . can't remember . . . Hey, come on, guys! Day's not getting any younger, and we have a city to cover!"

With that, the guards turned and marched away.

"I don't believe it," the bardling gasped. "Tich'ki, what did you — Tich'ki!"

She came tumbling down into his arms, panting. For a moment Kevin gingerly held her small body, astonished at how light she was, even for her small size. *Of course she's light!* he realized. *Tich'ki's a winged creature; she has to be lightweight if she's going to get off the ground. Probably has hollow bones, like a bird or* —

A sudden sharp stab in his arm made Kevin gasp and drop her. The fairy, who'd pinched him with her hard little fingers, fluttered away, grinning in mischief even though her eyes were weary. "Whoo-oo! That, I don't mind telling you, was hard work."

"What was that?" Lydia asked. "That 'influence-their-minds' spell of yours?"

Tich'ki nodded. "You know it. And you know the thing works."

"Sure. If you can get enough force into it."

For once, Tich'ki didn't argue. "Right. It's not the sort of thing I want to do too often." But then her sharp grin returned. "It's *so* much easier lifting purses!"

"I'm sure that's true," Eliathanis cut in coolly. "But

rather than discuss thieving triumphs, don't you think we had best find shelter before one or another of our enemies returns?"

"Excellent idea," Lydia said with a wry little bow. "I need to repair my bowstring anyhow, curse that filthy excuse for an elf."

Eliathanis stiffened indignantly, plainly torn between the evidence of his own eyes and his refusal to accept that one of his people could sink so low. "Have you any idea where we should be heading?"

"Yup." Lydia pointed. "North, guys. The inn's called the Flying Swan. You'll know it by the sign. Innkeeper doesn't ask awkward questions of his guests and keeps the beds vermin-free."

"What more could we possibly want?" Naitachal asked wryly.

Lydia shrugged. "Kevin and I will register as . . ." She glanced the bardling's way, mischief in her eyes. "As friends. *Good* friends. *Very* good friends. Right, my lover boy?" She grinned as he reddened, and took his arm. "See you later, everyone!"

Ah well, the bardling told himself resolutely. *Let her have her fun. Not much you can do to stop her, anyhow.*

Lydia's teasing aside, it would be wonderful to be in a nice clean room again, with a nice hot meal and maybe even — oh miracle of miracles — a soft bed!

Chapter XIV

A half-turn of the hourglass later, Kevin wasn't feeling quite so smug. Lydia, the bardling's cloak draped not quite concealingly about herself and her scanty garb, was clinging to his arm, giggling all too convincingly as he signed the register and tried to act as though "Estban Eltar" checked into inns with attractive older women all the time.

He was still blushing even after they had settled into their room — particularly when he saw that the furnishings consisted mostly of one large bed.

"You could hardly have asked for two beds, sweetie," Lydia cooed. "Not and keep up this cuddly-wuddly pretense." To his utter mortification, she snuggled up against him, fluttering her eyelashes elaborately, and pinched his cheek. "Cute li'l' lover boy!"

"Stop that!"

"My, my, you *do* blush prettily!

"Aw, don't — "

A sharp rap on the closed shutters of the single window interrupted him. With a silent sigh of relief, Kevin unlatched the shutters and let in the rest of their party. Lydia might be a warrior, but she was far too attractive for his nerves!

"And you complain about clumsy humans, do you?" Naitachal was murmuring to Eliathanis as they climbed into the room.

The White Elf glared. "How was I to know the drainpipe wasn't secure?"

"You did make a most convincing spider, clinging to the wall with every digit."

"You *could* have helped me!"

"What, and spoil your acrobatic demonstration?" As Naitachal removed and neatly shook out the folds of his black cloak, he gave Kevin a secret but undeniable wink. "A pretty thing it was, too."

Eliathanis straightened. "I don't think — "

"A pity."

"Uh, fellows?" the bardling cut in. "I know you're enjoying this bickering, but can we please leave it for some other time? We've had a rather busy day, agreed?"

"Oh, agreed." Naitachal raised an eyebrow. "I think we'd best keep watch tonight. If Eliathanis and I could climb up here, so could someone else."

"Empty Eyes?" Kevin asked. "Ah, I mean, that elf, the leader of the gang." The bardling paused. "Whatever he is."

"Empty Eyes," Naitachal echoed darkly. "Well put, Kevin. Empty, he most surely is. I don't know what his problems might be, what he's doing here, why he's an exile from his clan — Oh, don't give me that haughty stare, White Elf, you know I'm right about that. And frankly, I don't care about those problems. I *felt* Death hovering over him. Between drugs and alcohol and botched attempts at sorcery, he hasn't much longer to live."

"Botched!"

The Dark Elf shrugged. "You've seen my conjured blade. His should have been just as impressive. But it was as dull and nearly dead as the fading life force within him." Naitachal shrugged. "Enough about him."

"I'd just like to know who hired him," Kevin cut in.

Eliathanis glanced at the bardling in respect. "The swords those thugs were carrying bothered you, too? Swords are expensive things; most brigands just can't afford them, or the time needed to learn how to use them."

"Great," Lydia muttered. "Just what we need: another enemy. The sooner we get out of here, the better we're going to sleep."

"Exactly. And," Kevin added sternly, "that's why we can't waste any more time. We have to start working on exactly how we're going to manage to escape."

"Bossy human," Tich'ki teased, but for once there wasn't much sting in her voice. "Ai-yi, I'm getting pretty tired of Westerin myself," she confessed. "Too many touchy guards for my taste. Let's see, now . . . I can *not* control every blasted guard that's going to be watching the city gates. Anyone else here able to work invisibility spells?"

Silence.

"I guess not," the fairy said with a sigh.

"What about illusions, though?" Lydia asked. "What if we cast some really terrifying illusion, something that would scare the guards away from one of the gates — "

"By 'we' you mean me, I take it?" Naitachal said drily. He shook his head. "Oh, I probably could work up something to frighten a human mind, even if illusion-casting is a bit outside the scope of my . . . art. But these are trained warriors, not children. Some of them might run, yes — but the rest would almost certainly attack. I don't care to test my body against their spears."

"We need something more tangible than illusion," Kevin mused. "Shape-shifting . . . except only one of us can shape-shift." He glanced at the Dark Elf. "What about disguising us by magic?"

Naitachal held up a helpless hand. "Now that really *is* out of the scope of my sorcery. Anyone else?"

"Hey, don't look at me!" Tich'ki said. "I can't change anyone but myself."

"I have no such talent," Eliathanis admitted.

"Well, *I* certainly don't!" Lydia added. "Besides, I've heard those spells are just as easy to break as illusions. The last thing we'd want is to suddenly change back right in the middle of the guards. And you know, Fate being the fickle lady she is, that's just what would happen! No, we need some more mundane disguises. Something that doesn't depend on magic . . . Naw, any ordinary disguises would be too easy to penetrate."

"Would they?" Kevin wondered. "Go on, Lydia. What *about* physical disguises?"

She gave him a doubtful glance, but continued, "Well, let's see . . . By now both the gang and the guards know they're looking for three men and a woman: two humans and two elves, one Dark, one White. Don't have to worry about disguising Tich'ki."

The fairy stretched her wings. "Right. I can always shrink and hide in your hair, the way we did when we were getting out of Smithian."

"But it's hard to hide elves. . . . "

"Not too easy to disguise such a . . . charmingly endowed woman, either," Naitachal added gallantly.

Lydia raised a brow. "Flattery from a Dark Elf?"

His smile was wry. "It does happen."

"Yes, yes, I know you're full of surprises," Kevin interrupted. "But can we please get back to the subject?"

"Jealous?" Tich'ki prodded.

"No! I just don't want to spend the rest of my life in a Westerin prison. Or a Westerin graveyard, either!"

"Right." Lydia returned to her musing. "All right. We agree that it's hard to disguise elves."

Naitachal held up a hand. "To disguise *male* elves . . . " he corrected slowly. "Particularly serious, combative types." He turned to look at Eliathanis, who narrowed his eyes.

"I don't think I like what you're thinking."

Naitachal shrugged. "You're the one who was . . . interrogating the dancing girls. I'm sure they'd be happy to help their dear elfy-welfy."

"They didn't call me that! And I can't — I won't . . . "

The Dark Elf smiled alarmingly. "You can. You will.

They did. Listen to me, my friends. I think we're about to find a way out of Westerin!"

Kevin squirmed uncomfortably in the saddle of the riding mule, trying to get the yards and yards of gauzy, gaudy skirts to spread out properly, grimly trying to ignore the pretty chiming of little silver bells every time he moved.

"Don't squirm, dear," Lydia cooed. "It tears threads."

Kevin glared at her. The warrior was a sugar-sweet confection, her tanned face softened with powder and paint, her lithe, muscular form disguised by a frilly bodice and layer after layer of gauzy skirts in a dozen shades of pink. A silky cloak of dusty rose shot through with gold threads was thrown over the whole thing, her black curls — and Tich'ki — hidden under its cowl. *Yes, but at least she's a* woman! *I feel like an idiot.*

What made it worse was that he knew he looked rather alarmingly like a girl in all this frippery: a slightly scrawny one, perhaps, a bit too athletic even for a dancer, but a girl nevertheless. The bardling rubbed a reflexive hand over his chin, not sure whether to be discouraged or glad right now that at almost sixteen he still didn't need to shave very often. Smooth cheeks would help the illusion.

If only the illusion wasn't *quite* so good!

Eliathanis, riding beside Naitachal, was plainly feeling the same way, sitting his mule in silent misery. Kevin bit back a laugh. What a pretty girl the White Elf made!

Both elves were, of course, slim and beardless as all their kind, and despite Eliathanis' martial calling, their long, silky hair and elegant, fine-boned faces made it quite easy for them to pass as women. Naitachal's dark skin had been lightened to a more nondescript tan with judicious use of powder, making him look more like a half-elven hybrid than a perilous Dark Elf.

Unlike the unhappy Eliathanis, he seemed to be having a wonderful time.

After all, Kevin mused, *how often does a necromancer get a chance to act* silly*?*

It had been Eliathanis' dancing girls, of course, who had lent them all this gear, with the understanding that it would be left for the dancers to gather up again outside the walls. The dancers, the bardling decided, were definitely getting the better of the deal, winding up with what was left of Lydia's not quite honestly gained coins as well as getting their gear back.

Well, actually, it was Councilman Selden who was paying for the whole thing. In a manner of speaking, anyhow.

Kevin tensed suddenly. There to one side stood Empty Eyes, the elven leader of the street gang.

"Gently," Naitachal murmured. "You're a harmless dancing girl, that's all you are." The Dark Elf straightened slightly, startled, then chuckled. "Well now, what do you know?" he continued softly. "Our disguises really *do* work! Did you feel that slight tingling just now?"

"Yes."

"That dissipated shame of an elf tried casting a Dispel Magic spell on us!"

Naitachal leaned sideways in the saddle to give Empty Eyes a flirtatious wink and a blown kiss. Kevin exploded into laughter, just in time managing to turn it into girlish titterings.

"L-look at his face! He — he — he doesn't know what hit him!"

Naitachal swept back his silky hair with a toss of his head. "Too skinny for my taste!" he declared in a light tenor so unlike his usual baritone that Kevin burst into laughter all over again.

Eliathanis shot the Dark Elf a dour glance. "Stop that! Show some — some self-control!"

Naitachal grinned. "Loosen up, dear! You look ravishing."

"Leave me alone, will you? Or are you really enjoying this?"

The Dark Elf's grin widened. "Of course I am! Come now, cousin-elf, where's the harm in it? It's rather fun to play pretend!"

Eliathanis only growled. Kevin wiped his eyes, trying not to smear his makeup, hearing Tich'ki, there in Lydia's hair, tittering so hard she was having trouble catching her breath.

"Straighten up, dears," Lydia cooed. "Here are the guards. Look pretty, now!"

Kevin tensed all over again, seeing the men's grim-faced competence, the weapons never far from their hands, hearing the guards muttering something about "Selden" and "Those thieves aren't going to get past us." Sure, their disguise had been good enough to fool Empty Eyes, who had probably been drunk or half-drugged anyhow. But these were sharp-eyed professionals. Could it possibly fool them as well?

Apparently it could. "Look at the girl in pink," one said, nudging another. "Bet *she'd* warm a cold night!"

"Warm it, hell, she'd set it on fire!"

"The one next to her's not bad, either." Mortified, Kevin realized they were discussing him now.

"Awfully stringy," someone muttered.

"But there's something to be said for those acrobatic types!" The guard who'd first spoken leered up at the bardling. "Come on, sweetie, give us a kiss for the road."

Feeling like a prize idiot, Kevin managed to work his lips into what he hoped was a flirtatious smile. To his horror, the guard reached up, trying to pull his head down. Before the bardling could panic, Naitachal leaned down to whisper conspiratorially:

"You don't want to kiss *her*."

"Oh, I don't, do I?"

"*Heavens,* no! The last man she kissed got so hot and worked up he followed her for *days*. We finally had to throw him in a lake to cool him off. You would *not* have believed the *steam*!"

All the guards laughed. "Bet *you* could raise some steam," one of them shouted.

"Oh, darling, you wouldn't *believe* what I can do!" Naitachal gave them all a dazzling smile. "My, my, *my*, what *handsome* fellows you all are! What a *shame* we have to leave just now." The very essence of a delighted dancing girl, the Dark Elf laughed and simpered and blew kisses at them all. Only Kevin caught the faint hint of contempt flickering in the kohl-rimmed blue eyes. "Now, we really *must* say good-bye," Naitachal said, pretending to pout. "We have *such* a long way to go!"

"Stay here, then!"

"Oh, darlings, I'd *adore* that. But . . . " He waved a helpless hand. "What *would* the troop do without me? They would be simply *lost*, the poor dears. Ta-ta, darlings!"

Fun was fun, but once they were safely out of sight of the city walls, the party was of one mind, searching until they'd found a small pool screened by a grove of trees. Kevin practically threw himself from his mule and gladly stripped off his girlish finery, scrubbing and scrubbing till he'd washed every last trace of paint and powder from his face.

"Ugh. Can't see how women can stand wearing all that stuff."

"Frankly, neither can I!" Lydia straightened, shaking out her damp black hair and tousling the curls dry with her hands. "I mean, I like looking nice as much as any other woman." She winked at Kevin. "You should see me when I dress up pretty! But all that stuff I was wearing just now made me feel like I was carrying a prison around with me!"

In the middle of strapping on her sword, she paused, looking out over the lake, eyebrows raised. "My, isn't *that* a pleasant sight!"

Naitachal, some distance away, had stripped to the waist to wash off the last of the disguising powder. His body was inhumanly slim and graceful but undeniably male, smooth muscles rippling and dark skin gleaming with every move. Realizing the others were watching him, he disappeared into the bushes, emerging shrouded once more in his black cloak. And now every trace of frivolity was gone.

It's almost as though he was drunk before, and now he's sober again, Kevin thought.

Maybe that wasn't so bizarre an idea. After all, for a Dark Elf, a necromancer used to a grim world of sorcery and death, being suddenly thrown into the middle of so much vibrant, busy life really must have been intoxicating!

As the bardling retrieved his lute from the pile of dancing girls' gear, he heard Naitachal mutter:

"Powers, I'm glad that's over."

"I thought you were enjoying yourself." Eliathanis' voice was cool with disapproval.

Naitachal glanced sharply at the White Elf. "Up to a point. One moment more, though, and I think I would have thrown up."

"From fright?" Kevin asked in disbelief.

"Hardly!" The Dark Elf gave him a fierce little grin. "From a surfeit of sugar!"

Chapter XV

As the party rode up the gentle slope from the river plain in which Westerin lay, Kevin suddenly reined in his mule. "Lydia, if we have to retrace all our steps back to Count Volmar's castle, we're going to waste too much time."

"Agreed. Besides, I don't want to risk going through that gorge again, either; one ambush is more than enough, thank you." The woman hesitated, chewing thoughtfully on her lip. "I do know a much shorter route. The only thing is . . . well . . . let's put it this way: anybody have any objections about riding through a battlefield?"

"A *what*?"

"An ancient one. I'm not even sure what the whole thing was all about, it happened so long ago. Shouldn't be anything left to bother us." She shot an uneasy glance at the Dark Elf. "Unless, of course, someone tries to disturb things."

Naitachal's eyes glinted coldly. "I am not in the habit of rousing that which should not be roused. Lead on."

Kevin struggled against the urge to keep looking over his shoulder. This was ridiculous! An easy ride, a nice, bright, sunny day, a smooth, grassy meadow stretching out before him without any obstructions at all and a splendid array of mountains in the distance—there was not the slightest thing to fear.

Then why oh why was his mind insisting on sending these constant thrills of nervousness through him?

"Naitachal," the bardling asked uneasily. "Is this . . . was this . . ."

"The battlefield?" The Dark Elf's voice sounded strained and distant. "Yes . . . you would sense that, too, wouldn't you, Bard-to-be that you are? So many lives lost, human and Other . . . I can feel their auras even now, calling to me. . . ."

"Well, don't answer them!" Lydia snapped, and Naitachal blinked like someone suddenly shaken from a dream.

"No," he said, and then more confidently, "no!"

But as they rode on across the meadow, the others could see shudders racking his slender frame. The Dark Elf was plainly fighting some terrible inner battle of his own, struggling against all the long, cruel years of childhood conditioning screaming at him, *You are a creature of the Darkness! Leave the light behind you!*

Unexpectedly, Eliathanis brought his mule alongside. "Take my hand," he said softly.

"What—"

"Take it. Hold fast. Yes, like that. Think of sunlight, Naitachal. Think of life and joy. They are the only realities here."

Kevin saw the White Elf wince with the force of Naitachal's desperate grasp. But Eliathanis refused to let go, as though willing peace into the Dark Elf through that link.

And little by little the tension left Naitachal's body. He shuddered one last time, then released the White Elf's hand, looking at Eliathanis in confusion.

"Thank you," the Dark Elf said after a moment. "I hardly expected you to wish to help me, but—thank you."

"Ah. Well." Eliathanis flushed, embarrassed by his own kindness. "I . . . didn't want you rousing anything undead against us."

"I wouldn't willingly." Then Naitachal added, very softly, "But it was a near thing."

* * *

Alatan, sorcerer, necromancer, paced impatiently back and forth on the ramparts of his small, square keep, glancing now and then out over the smooth, treeless expanse of meadow without really seeing it. He was alone up there, the only living being in all the keep, alone save for a few silent, soulless aides.

"Damn her!" he hissed.

And damn *him* for a fool for ever letting himself be forced to be responsible to her! So much time had passed without a word from her. He'd almost let himself believe the rumors that the sorceress was dead, or so far from here that she'd forgotten all about him and the debt he owed her: the debt of his life.

Oh no. She hadn't forgotten. All at once there had come that summons, and with it the infuriating knowledge that he still wasn't free, any more than he'd been free so many years ago . . . when the peasants had caught him weak from the aftereffects of a failed spell, had caught him and condemned him to death by fire. . . .

The sorcerer stopped short, black cloak swirling about him. Unbidden, his mind conjured up the hardwood stake as clearly as though it were with him now instead of far in the past, the stake and the chains pressing him cruelly back against it, his hands bound so he couldn't gesture, his mouth sealed with a wooden gag so he couldn't call out the slightest spell, and the flames crackling at the wood beneath him, the heat already starting to eat at his feet, his legs . . .

Alatan spat out a savage curse, forcing his mind back to the present. It was *done,* he was *safe,* and he should have banished such ridiculous memories long ago!

The sorcerer resumed his angry pacing. What nonsense this was! He had seen and done and summoned horrors enough during his career, horrors that would have sent any other man screaming — aye, and he'd seen many of those horrors do him homage, too. He would not act like some raw boy haunted by his own mind!

Ah, no. Fear wasn't the problem. What truly rankled, what stayed in his mind after all this time was having to admit that for all his Power, he hadn't been able to do a thing to save himself. Oh no, if Carlotta hadn't chanced to see what was happening, those stupid, fearful peasants would have won and he would be ashes in the wind, spirit lost in the Outer Dark. If she hadn't seen, and thought, and realized what a fine tool was about to be lost—

"Damn her," Alatan repeated aloud, but by now most of the anger was gone from his voice. A tool he was, and a tool he would remain till the debt of his life was repaid. No successful sorcerer survived by denying What Must Be. And he dare not fail.

Grimly resigned, Alatan went down from the ramparts to his private chambers, to a dark room crowded with sorcerous implements. A few careful Words of Power sparked a silver-rimmed scrying mirror into life.

Alatan focused his will, bringing into sharp focus an image of the boy, the bardling, and those with whom he rode. A woman . . . a warrior by the lithe look of her . . . and quite human. He smiled coldly. No threat there. The others . . . The sorcerer's mouth tightened. A White Elf, that one, but again, a warrior, not a mage. And again, no threat to him. But that other figure, draped all in black . . . Alatan frowned and leaned forward, staring. Whoever, whatever was shrouded under that cloak knew at least enough to block anything more than this casual scan.

You may yet be trouble, my mysterious friend.

And then again, there might not be any trouble at all. For look at the direction in which they rode! Tensing in sudden predatory delight, hardly believing his good fortune, the sorcerer urged them, *Further, ride just a little further. . . .*

With a sharp *crack!* the mirror shattered. Alatan sprang back in shock, dodging shards of glass. No doubt about it: that black-clad figure was another sorcerer! No, no, more than that: the stranger could only be a necromancer. No one else could have forced his spell back on itself so powerfully.

Alatan's laugh was sharp as the glass. So, now! It had been long and long till he'd found an enemy worthy of combat! Burning with eagerness, the sorcerer sprang to his feet, calling for his undead servants, and hurried down to the meadow below, to the field of battle-once-was and battle-yet-to-be.

Naitachal straightened as sharply in the saddle as though he'd been slapped. Eyes blazing with sudden sorcerous force, he gestured imperiously, shouting out savage, alien Words that tore at Kevin's ears and sent the mules shying wildly.

"Naitachal!" Lydia yelped, struggling to keep her seat. "What the *hell* do you think you're doing?"

Reining in his own panicky, curvetting mule, the Dark Elf said shortly, "Someone was spying on us. Through sorcery. I turned his spell back upon him."

Eliathanis tensed. "Then it wasn't my imagination just now. I really *did* sense . . . something." His hand tightened on the hilt of his sword. "Do you know who the sorcerer is, or where?"

"Who, no. Where: nearby. But I've shattered his scrying tool."

"That's not going to be the end of it."

"I doubt it." Naitachal glanced sharply about, a predator hunting elusive prey. "The sooner we are clear of this battlefield-that-was, the better."

And then the earth shook. Kevin's mule screamed in terror, rearing up so violently the bardling went flying. He twisted frantically in mid-air, landing with a jolt on his feet, lute smacking him in the side, noting out of the corner of his eye that only Naitachal had managed to keep his seat and staring as the meadow writhed, tearing itself apart. Out of the shattered earth rose:

No. That's not possible, his mind insisted, over and over.

Climbing up into the land of the living were the long-dead, the skeletons of humans and Others, the fallen victims of that now-forgotten battle returned, fleshless skulls grinning, fleshless hands gripping swords and axes. Sightless sockets stared blankly at the horrified living.

Behind them, wrapped in a cloak as black as that worn by Naitachal stood a figure who could only be the necromancer who'd dragged them forth. All Kevin could see of the face under the dark hood were a gray beard — proof the man at least was human — and fierce, pitiless gray eyes: sorcerous eyes. In the man's hand a wooden staff topped with a serpentine carving crackled with blue-white force.

To his right, the bardling heard Naitachal let out his breath in a long hiss. "So . . . " the Dark Elf said softly. "I thought as much."

He flung himself from his frantic mule, slapping it out of the way of his magic. "Get out of here, all of you."

Eliathanis' sword glinted in his hand. "Are you mad? We can't leave you here alone!"

"You can't fight what isn't alive! *Get out of here!*"

But it was already too late. The other sorcerer thrust out his staff, and the undead army charged.

"You shall *not*!" With that, Naitachal shouted out fierce, ugly, commanding Words in the harsh language of sorcery, hurling his arms up in denial. The skeletal enemy stumbled back from the force of his will — but behind them, the human necromancer cast up his own arms, staff raised, shouting out his own dark spell. Kevin, near-Bard that he was, saw the psychic flames of sorcery that blazed out from both foes, crashing together in a shower of blinding, blue-white sparks. He heard Naitachal gasp at the impact, but the Dark Elf's will held firm.

So, unfortunately, did that of the human foe.

But as the sorcerers stood locked in their savage, silent battle, both lost their hold on the skeletal warriors. They, empty things that they were, followed the only command they had received, and resumed their interrupted charge.

"Look out!" Lydia cried. "Here they come!"

Kevin gripped his sword as tightly as he could, trying not to let it shake in his hand. *Powers, Powers, how do you hurt a skeleton?*

All at once, the arch of sorcery vanished with a roar of whirling air. Naitachal shouted out new Words of command, the sound alien, hating, the essence of Dark Elf necromancy. The Words enfolding the undead bending them to his will. For a moment the deadly things hesitated, caught, quivering with the strain.

Then, slowly, they turned to threaten the human necromancer instead. His eyes widened in shock, and for a moment Kevin thought the man was going to break from sheer surprise. But after that startled moment, the gray eyes blazed up in renewed fury. The necromancer thrust out his staff with such force the undead reeled and fell back — only to be caught anew in the net of Naitachal's Power.

"Th-they're fighting each other!" the bardling gasped. "They're fighting their own battle all over again!"

Well and good, but not all the skeletal army had found foes. Some of them came spilling up towards the living. Lydia loosed an arrow — but it passed harmlessly through a fleshless rib cage.

"Damn!"

"Try for their joints," Eliathanis said grimly. "Cut those apart, and the creatures cannot move."

Kevin didn't have time to worry about it. He just barely had a chance to put his lute aside before a skeleton headed right towards him, axe raised. The bardling could have sworn that fleshless grin had sentient malice behind it.

Can't parry an axe with a sword. But an axeman can't be as quick as a swordsman; once he's swung, it has to take him a moment to recover, and — Now!

As the axe came whistling down, Kevin threw himself to one side, slashing out sideways with his sword. He missed the knee joint, the blade clanging harmlessly off bone. But at least the impact staggered the skeleton slightly; it might be an undead thing, but it was still subject to the force of gravity! Kevin swung again, hoping to knock it over completely, but to his horror, a skeletal hand shot out and closed on the blade.

Of course, of course, he — it — doesn't have any fingers to get cut!

The thing was far, far stronger than anything mortal. Kevin struggled helplessly with it, clutching the sword hilt with both hands — only to have the skeleton, still grinning its inane grin, begin reeling him in, bony hand over hand up the blade. If he kept holding onto the hilt, Kevin realized, he was going to be dragged into the skeleton's reach.

So he suddenly let go. To his relief, the skeleton, which had been braced against his weight, went right over backwards. Kevin kicked it as hard as he could, and heard ribs crack, but the thing was already climbing back to its feet, apparently unhurt.

And it's still got my sword and *its axe!*

Now, what?

The bardling backed away, looking about for a branch, a rock, anything he could use as a weapon. He found a rock, all right: he stepped on it, and the treacherous thing turned under his foot, sending him sprawling.

As the skeleton lunged down at him, Kevin did the

only thing he could think of: he caught the bony arms, and kicked his legs up with all his force, just as he had with the swordsman back in Westerin. To his amazed wonder, he sent the skeleton sailing neatly over his head, to land with a satisfying crash. It lost his sword in the fall, and the bardling snatched up the weapon, hacking and hacking at the undead thing before it could rise till he'd cut right through its skeletal neck. The skeleton collapsed in a bony heap.

I — I did it! I won!

Fierce with triumph, the bardling looked about to see how everyone else was faring. Lydia and Eliathanis were surrounded, fighting back to back, skeletal hands snatching at them from all sides, while Tich'ki, swearing savagely, tried in vain to ward off the undead with her spear.

I've got to help them before —

A bony hand closed with painful force about his ankle. Headless or not, the skeleton was still very much animated.

"No! Curse you, no! No!" Nearly sobbing with panicky strain, Kevin hacked and hacked and hacked at the hand till it shattered, releasing him. But the headless horror was getting to its feet once more.

This is impossible! The thing is never going to give up!

No, it wouldn't, the bardling realized. None of the undead would. Not while the human necromancer's spell bound them.

Panting, Kevin glanced to where the Dark Elf stood. Naitachal was still battling his foe as fiercely as ever, eyes blazing with will. But to the bardling's alarm, signs of strain showed all too clearly on the elegant face. Of course! Determined though he was, strong magician though he was, the Dark Elf had no sorcerous staff to feed him extra Power, nothing but the strength within his own slim body.

He c-can't hold out much longer, Kevin realized, *not without help! But I don't know any spell-songs to help him!*

Wait a minute . . . Maybe he didn't know any useful Bardic Magic — but maybe he wouldn't need it! Didn't all the old ballads claim when magic failed, plain common sense would save the day? There was one very practical thing he could do.

Before the headless monstrosity could grab him again, Kevin snatched up the rock that had tripped him, hefting its weight experimentally in his hand as he ran, racing past the battle of undead against undead till nothing stood between him and the enemy sorcerer.

If he sees me now, I'm dead.

But the necromancer, absorbed in his magical trance, showed not the slightest sign he knew the bardling was there.

Please, oh please, let this work. . . .

Kevin threw the rock with all his strength. Ha, yes! It hit the necromancer smartly on the side of the head! The man staggered helplessly back, trance shattered, and from the other side of the field, Naitachal gave a hoarse cry of triumph as his magic blazed free. A blue-white bolt of magic slashed through the air, engulfing his human foe in flame. Frozen with shock, Kevin heard the necromancer give one wild scream of pain and terror. Then that sorcerous flame flared up so fiercely the bardling flung his arms protectively up over his eyes.

It took no more than a few heartbeats' time. The fire vanished as swiftly as it had begun. Kevin warily lowered his arms, fearful of what he might see. But there was nothing, not man, not cloak, not staff, nothing but a small swirling of ash.

The necromancer's death shattered the binding spell. As simply as puppets with cut strings, the undead fell where they'd stood, the jumble of their bones melting quietly back into the earth. In only a few moments, the meadow had returned to grassy serenity, and nothing at all remained of the horror that had just been.

I don't believe . . . I couldn't have seen . . .

Kevin hurried back to Eliathanis, Lydia, and Tich'ki, suddenly wanting nothing so much as to be near other warm, living, mortal beings. Ah, he was glad to clasp their hands, glad to let Lydia hug him and to hug her back, glad even to feel Tich'ki tousle his hair with rough affection. All three started at the same time:

"Are you hurt? I'm — "

"I'm not, not — "

" — really. Just bruised and — "

" — tired and — "

They broke off at the same time, too, then burst into laughter.

"Hey, Naitachal!" Lydia called. "Don't you — Naitachal?"

A rigid figure swarthed in his somber cloak, the Dark Elf never moved from where he stood.

"Naitachal?" Eliathanis echoed hesitantly. "Are you . . . ?"

Without a sound, the Dark Elf crumpled to the ground and lay still.

INTERLUDE THE FOURTH

"My lord. My Lord Count."

Volmar, hurrying down the corridors of his castle, grit his teeth, trying to ignore that dry, precise voice, but it continued relentlessly:

"Count Volmar. Please stop for a moment."

The count sighed silently. When D'Krikas got an idea in its insectoid head, nothing would do but to hear the Arachnia out. Reluctantly, he turned to ask, "Yes. What is it?"

"You told me yesterday that you would read and sign these scrolls today."

Curse it! An Arachnia never forgot *anything*!

I don't have time for this nonsense now!

Carlotta was hidden in the count's solar, studying her scrying mirror, and if he wasn't there when she learned whatever she learned — He didn't dare let the sorceress gain any advantages over him.

"These are nothing," Volmar said, glancing at the scrolls. "Small matters. Sign them yourself."

D'Krikas' silence held a world of disapproval.

"All right, all right!" The count held up a helpless hand. "I'll sign them later. I don't have time now."

"No. I can see that."

Something in the dry voice made Volmar stare up at the Arachnia. And all at once, the count felt the smallest prickle of unease run through him. Usually he managed to ignore the fact that his seneschal wasn't human; D'Krikas kept pretty much to itself, after all, so quietly efficient Volmar could almost forget the being was there. Efficient, yes, meticulously so. The castle was never going to be short so much as a single copper coin or a loaf of bread as long as the Arachnia was in charge.

But in this narrow, close corridor, D'Krikas seemed to loom over him. Volmar had never stopped to realize just how tall an adult Arachnia grew, how tall and thin and alien, so alien . . . The great, compound eyes studied him without blinking, the shiny chitin, half hidden by the being's cloak, gave off a faint, spicy scent that was never a human scent, and Volmar, all at once overwhelmed, forced out a brash:

"You don't like me, do you?"

D'Krikas drew back slightly in surprise. "What has 'like' or 'dislike' to do with matters? When my home hive grew overcrowded, I left to ease the burden of feeding all. I swore the proper oath to your father. You know that. I keep my oaths. You know that, too. I served your father the count and I serve you, as I will continue to serve the master of this castle, whomever that may be. As long as honor is not compromised."

Was there a hint of warning in the precise voice? Volmar fought down a shudder. He had once seen D'Krikas save a servant's child from a rabid dog by calmly tearing the beast in two with those segmented, fragile-seeming arms, neatly and effortlessly as a man would tear a piece of parchment. And that precise Arachnia beak could sever bone. Everyone knew the one thing no Arachnia could endure was a loss of honor. If D'Krikas somehow suspected — No, no, that was ridiculous! No Arachnia wielded magic, and without magic, even clever D'Krikas would never be able to learn how his master was aiding the crown's worse foe.

"Your honor will not be compromised," Volmar said shortly.

He sent a page for pen and ink and signed the scrolls one after another, hardly bothering to read them, and hurried off, D'Krikas' speculative gaze hot on his back.

Carlotta never looked up from her scrying mirror as he entered, but Volmar knew she could tell perfectly well by her arcane senses who he was.

"I don't believe it." The sorceress straightened in her chair, voice sharp with disbelief. "I simply don't believe it."

"Don't believe *what*?" Volmar craned his neck, trying his best to see past the woman to the mirror. But to his frustration, what he could see of the images looked, to his non-sorcerous sight, like nothing more than blurs of color swirling on the smooth surface. "What's happening? What's wrong?"

"That ridiculous nuisance of a boy just killed Alatan!"

"The sorcerer?" Volmar gasped. "But that's impossible! The boy is just a bardling, a nothing! Come now, Carlotta, from what I've seen of him, he couldn't have managed enough Bardic Magic, or any other kind of magic strong enough to — "

"He threw a rock." Each word was savagely bitten off. "It was the Dark Elf who did the rest. Ahh, *damn* him, damn them both!" She glanced sharply up at Volmar. "You *would* include a Dark Elf in the party!"

"Hey now, don't blame me!" the count exclaimed. "It wasn't my idea. Not mine alone, anyhow. We both agreed having one of that cursed breed in the group would help discredit the unholy elven lot."

"Unholy, is it?" Carlotta purred, her eyes narrowing to green slits. "In all the years I've known you, Volmar, you've never yet been able to shed this obsessive hatred of the elf-kind. It is beginning to grow quite . . . wearisome."

Oh Powers. He'd forgotten all about her being half of fairy blood. Horrified, Volmar remembered the woman's quick temper, and realized he might just have doomed himself.

"I d-don't," he stammered, struggling to find the words to soothe her, "I didn't — I — I mean . . ."

Ignoring his helpless attempts at placation, she returned to studying her mirror.

"Poor Alatan," Carlotta murmured after a moment, without a hint of softness in her voice. "Poor fool. For all your Power, you never could control the weaknesses within your own mind. You let yourself be haunted all these many years by the memory of flame. And now the fire has snared you after all." Her chuckle was soft and chillingly cold. "What a pity."

She was silent for a moment longer, staring into the mirror. Volmar stood frozen, hardly daring to breathe, wondering what other bad news the woman was going to announce.

He jumped when Carlotta straightened with a sharp little cry. "So-o! Is *that* the way of it?" She glanced quickly up at the count again, one eyebrow raised in surprise. "It appears that at least the late Alatan managed to take the Dark Elf with him."

"Did he, now?" Volmar breathed an inner sigh of relief. "One less would-be hero to concern us."

With a wave of her hand and a commanding Word, Carlotta banished the images, and got restlessly to her feet. "Yes, one dead elf, but the others remain. And with that cursed hunter, that warrior-woman, to guide them, such a small party is going to be able to elude almost anything."

Well now, wasn't *this* interesting! For once the mighty Carlotta seemed to actually be at a loss! Her pet necromancer's death must have shaken her more than she'd admitted.

Volmar straightened in dour delight. Good. Let her know for a change what it felt like to be uneasy and unsure. And in the meantime, let him at last take charge of the situation!

"Never mind," the count said, his voice gentle with false concern. "Let them come."

She glared at him. "Have you gone mad?"

"Please. Hear me out. Don't hinder them, I say." Volmar smiled at her, enjoying her confusion. "Who knows? While the boy is here, perhaps he'll find that elusive manuscript for us."

"Yes, but — "

"Carlotta, my dear princess, you worry too much."

"Don't patronize me." It was all the more alarming for having been quietly said.

"I didn't mean — "

"Ah, but you did."

He could have sworn she hadn't done anything more than raise a hand. But suddenly Volmar was . . . nowhere, floating helplessly in empty grayness with no sense of *up*, no *down*, no light or dark or life . . . Choking, the count fought in vain to breathe, but oh gods, there was no air here, either. His lungs were aching, his heart was pounding painfully, he was dying. . . .

Carlotta, no! Please, no!

All at once there was a real world about him once more. All at once he was fallen to hands and knees on a hard stone floor, able to think of nothing but drawing air into his lungs.

After a time, Volmar realized he was back in his castle, with Carlotta standing over him, face impassive. "Never underestimate me, either," she murmured.

The count dragged himself to his feet, collapsing into a chair, bathed in cold perspiration. "Never," he echoed weakly.

Illusion. It had to have been illusion. He couldn't have actually left this realm. He couldn't really have just been trapped in — in that deadly emptiness.

Volmar took a deep breath. "You misunderstand me." He forced a ghost of sincerity into his voice. "I never meant to belittle you. Nor," the count added honestly, "to deny your powers."

She raised a skeptical eyebrow, then smiled sweetly.

"No. You wouldn't dare, would you? All right. Continue."

"This is my castle, these are my people. What, did you think I'd been idle all this while?" Little by little, Volmar felt self-confidence stealing back into him. Of course it had been illusion. "Once the boy and his misguided comrades are actually here, I have a few surprises of my own to spring on them. And I don't believe," the count added with dark humor, "that they will enjoy them."

Chapter XVI

"Naitachal!"

Eliathanis raced to the fallen elf's side, closely followed by the others. Kevin got there an instant before Lydia and the fluttering Tich'ki, dropping to his knees beside Naitachal's still form. The White Elf glanced across at the bardling, green eyes wide. "I d-don't think he's breathing."

"Oh no, that can't be right, he has to be!"

Kevin hastily snatched up a dark wrist. For a panic-stricken, seemingly endless while, he couldn't find any pulse at all.

Come on, come on, you can't be dead, not now.

All at once the bardling felt . . . yes. Kevin released Naitachal's wrist with a sigh of relief. "He's alive. I . . . think he's just asleep. *Deeply* asleep. That sorcerous duel must really have worn him out."

Eliathanis shuddered faintly. "Yes." He straightened slowly, fussing with the set of his now sadly tattered cloak, plainly struggling to regain his composure. "Of course it did. I should have realized that."

Well, what do you know? Kevin stared at the White Elf in surprise. *You really were worried about him!*

Not that such revelations mattered right now. Kevin glanced doubtfully down at Naitachal. Sleeping like this on bare ground couldn't be doing the Dark Elf any good. Particularly not on *this* ground. Everybody else seemed to be too battle-dazed to suggest anything, so the bardling said as firmly as he could:

"Eliathanis, why don't you see if you can coax our mules back here?"

"Ah. Yes."

"And, Lydia, can you help me lift Naitachal? The sooner we get him — and us — away from here, the better."

"Right."

For all his worry and ever-growing weariness, the bardling couldn't help but feel a little thrill of wonder at the way they were obeying him without question.

Maybe I am *a leader after all. Sort of, anyway*, he added wryly. *For now, anyhow.*

Naitachal slept without stirring all during Eliathanis' finally successful efforts to persuade the snorting, still-trembling mules to return. He slept during that entire day's ride through field and forest, alternately supported in the saddle by Kevin, Lydia and Eliathanis. He continued to sleep while they set up camp for the night, lost in so deep and still a slumber that Kevin began to worry.

He'll wake up soon enough. Of course he will.

But Naitachal continued to sleep. And at last Kevin's worry grew to the point where the bardling couldn't stand it any longer. Glancing uneasily at the others, he burst out with the question he suspected they were all thinking:

"What are we going to do if Naitachal doesn't wake up?"

"He'll wake." Eliathanis, tending the campfire, didn't sound quite sure about that.

"But what if he doesn't?"

"He will," Tich'ki said firmly. "Look, I'm the only other one of us who has any real magic, and believe me, this isn't the first time I've seen a magician overtax himself to the point of collapse. There's only so much strength in a body, you know."

"Yes, but — "

"Very true."

It was little more than a whisper, so unexpected a sound that they all started.

"Naitachal!"

"So I am."

The Dark Elf sat up, very slowly and carefully, as though he wasn't quite sure his body would obey him. Lydia made an abortive little move towards him, then stopped with a cautious, "How do you feel?"

"Like something dragged up by one of my own spells," Naitachal admitted wryly.

"But you'll be all right?" Eliathanis' eyes were oddly wary.

"Indeed."

This is ridiculous! This is Naitachal, the comrade who's been riding with us all along. He hasn't turned into a monster.

But even as he thought that, Kevin knew they were all a little leery of Naitachal now, this Dark Elf who had suddenly revealed himself as a fearful necromancer who could destroy a foe with one blast of sorcerous flame.

I will not *be afraid of him!*

After all, how could he forget how the Dark Elf had comforted him after he'd killed that bandit? Whatever else Naitachal might be, that hadn't been the act of a cruel being, or an evil one.

The bardling deliberately moved to the Dark Elf's side, and received a faint smile in return.

"That was a marvelously clever thing you did, Kevin, hurling the rock at the sorcerer to break his concentration."

"Oh, well. It was the only thing I could think to do." The bardling couldn't stop himself from adding in a rush, "Even if I didn't expect what was going to happen after that."

"Don't shed any tears for him." Naitachal's voice was suddenly cold. "I touched his mind during our battle, and it was . . . foul. The man had deliberately killed all goodness within himself, all hope of joy, deliberately turned himself into a being almost as empty as those poor dead ones he conjured. So it can be," he added, almost reluctantly, "with many necromancers."

"Not with you! Anyone who could enjoy being silly with those guards the way you did hasn't given up on life!"

That earned him a chuckle. "No. I haven't. Nor will I, Powers willing." The Dark Elf paused, eyes glinting. "He was strong, though, that stupid, evil man. So strong, with nothing but hatred left within him to drive him, with that hellish staff of his to aid him. Without your help, Kevin, I . . . don't think I would have survived."

He glanced at the bardling. "But the memory of that fire is still shocking you, isn't it? Ha, yes, you others, it shocks you all."

"Well, hell, yes!" Lydia exclaimed after a moment. "I never thought you could — "

"I didn't. Not deliberately."

"What do you mean? I saw what I saw!"

"You don't understand." Naitachal hesitated, then sighed. "I don't know if I can put this so easily into human terms. Look you, our Power was trapped, his and mine, stalemated, each against each. What happens when a dam breaks?"

Lydia shrugged. "The water bursts free and — Oh."

"Exactly. When his sorcery all at once gave way, mine — yes — burst free. Even I didn't expect it to explode *quite* so fiercely, though. A pity it did," Naitachal added grimly. "I meant only to stun the man."

"In the name of all the Powers, *why*?"

The Dark Elf's eyes glinted in the gloom. "Why do you think?"

Kevin straightened. "You don't believe he was working on his own, do you?"

"Hardly. Even a necromancer such as that isn't chaotic enough to attack at random."

"Then . . . do you think he was in Carlotta's pay?"

"Something like that." The Dark Elf stretched wearily. "But we seem to have drawn the lady's fangs."

At least for now, Kevin thought, and fought down a shudder. "I bet you're hungry."

A hint of returning humor danced in the Dark Elf's eyes. "Ravenous. As, I would think, we all are. It's been a . . . shall we say . . . rather strenuous day."

"It has indeed." Eliathanis was rummaging in their packs, coming up with a fair amount of smoked meat and some rather squashed bread. He looked ruefully at his catch. "It's not going to be an elegant meal."

Lydia rubbed sore muscles in her arms. "I've had worse. Worse days, too. Though I have to admit, I can't remember when. Most of the guys I've fought," she added with a wry grin, "had more flesh to 'em!"

They rode all the next day, still sore and weary from the battle, nerves tight. But what they rode into was nothing more alarming than a mild, sweet spring day. The land sloped gently up and up towards the mountains, so gradually that the mules climbed it without complaint. A gentle breeze played with hair and clothes, birds darted cheerfully all about them, and there was not the slightest sign of trouble anywhere.

It was so very uneventful a day that by nightfall Kevin was amazed to find himself almost disappointed.

What's the matter with you, you idiot? Do you want *to be attacked?*

No, of course he didn't. What he was feeling, Kevin knew, wasn't anything so foolish. After all they had gone through so far, this sudden peacefulness simply seemed too . . . anticlimactic to be believable.

Now that *was* silly. Maybe it was true, maybe Carlotta's fangs had been drawn. Maybe she couldn't attack them herself for some arcane reason. Maybe she'd had nothing to do with the attack at all!

Ah well, Kevin told himself, he would try to enjoy anticlimax.

Or an almost anticlimax. The only thing that was jarringly wrong in all this quiet was the way Lydia, Eliathanis and even Tich'ki still radiated uneasiness every time they glanced Naitachal's way.

I can't let that go on. If Carlotta does attack us again, we had better be able to present a united front, or she's going to destroy us!

But Kevin admitted reluctantly that he just didn't know what to do about it.

Sitting by the campfire that night, the bardling sighed, overwhelmed by a surge of guilt that had nothing to do with their quest: what with all the excitement of the past few days, he had pretty much forgotten about his music. Now, imagining Master Aidan's reproachful stare for his neglect, Kevin took out his lute and tuned it, gently since it hadn't been played for a while, then tried a few practice scales.

Ugh. His fingers were *stiff*. But as he kept after them, they finally limbered up and remembered what they were supposed to be doing. Kevin ran through his scales, from the simplest to the most complex and back again several times, till he heard Lydia give a not so subtle yawn. With a grin, the bardling switched over instead to a cheerful little springtime song common to almost all the human lands, "The Maiden's Garland."

As he played, Kevin felt eyes on him. He glanced up and caught Naitachal in the act of staring at the lute. The slanted blue eyes were, for the moment, unguarded, so full of yearning that a pang of pity shot through the bardling. He remembered Naitachal admitting that the Dark Elves had no music of their own.

What a horrible thing! What a horrible, lonely thing!

Naitachal suddenly realized Kevin had noticed him, and turned sharply away, pretending to be fixing some bit of his gear.

"Oh no, you don't," the bardling murmured, and scrambled over to sit beside the Dark Elf. Moved by an impulse he didn't quite understand, Kevin held out the lute. "Here. Take it."

"I — I can't. I mean, I wouldn't know how . . ."

"I'll show you. Take it."

Naitachal took the lute as gingerly as though it was a baby. Kevin sighed.

"Not like that. It's not that fragile, honest. You hold it like this, here, and here. Right! Now, give it back to me for a minute and I'll show you something. This is how you get single notes." He strummed a single string, running his finger up from fret to fret. "See? The pitch gets lower the further my finger gets from the body of the lute. You try it."

Warily, Naitachal touched a string. When it twanged, he almost dropped the lute in shock, then gave a rueful grin at his own reaction. But then, to Kevin's surprise, the Dark Elf ran up and down through the notes without missing a one.

"You have a good ear! Now, shall we try a chord or two?"

Naitachal shrugged uneasily. "Whatever you say."

Showing the Dark Elf the proper fingering, Kevin strummed the basic chords, then handed the lute back. Naitachal stumbled over the strings the first time, then echoed Kevin flawlessly.

"Hey, terrific!" the bardling said.

The Dark Elf grinned, this time in self-conscious delight. And to the bardling's amazement, Naitachal began to pick out, very slowly and carefully, the melody to "The Maiden's Garland."

"That — that's wonderful! And you only heard me play it once!" Kevin fought down the faint, irrational little touch of jealousy that didn't like anyone else being able to play *his* lute, and added honestly, "Do you know how long it took me to figure out what you're doing in one tiny lesson — " The bardling stopped, mind racing.

"Naitachal, listen to me, you can't stop here." The words came tumbling out of Kevin in his eagerness. "I mean it, when this is all over you've *got* to get musical training, you must! No, no, don't shake your head at me. Music would be such a wonderful comfort for you — and you've got talent, true musical talent!"

"That's the most ridiculous thing I've ever heard."

But for all his protest, Naitachal didn't surrender the lute. As though driven by some inner demon, he bent over it once more, playing "The Maiden's Garland" again and yet again, gradually bringing it up to proper speed.

Suddenly the Dark Elf stopped. With an embarrassed, delighted little laugh, he tried to give the lute back to Kevin. But Kevin was aware of how the others were staring at them in sheer confusion. The terrible necromancer wasn't supposed to be acting like this!

Oh yes, this was too good a chance to waste! The bardling waved Naitachal on. The Dark Elf frowned, but obligingly played "The Maiden's Garland" yet again. And this time Kevin sang the light, silly, happy words along with the music:

"As I was walking one spring day,
I saw a maiden fair,
Come gathering the fragrant may,
The lilac and the roses-o,
The daisies and the violets-o,
To make a pretty posy-o,
To wear upon her hair."

At first Naitachal stumbled, distracted by trying to listen to what Kevin was singing. But all at once he caught the performer's knack of hearing but not really listening to the words, and played on, smiling faintly.

As the bardling had hoped, the bouncy, cheerful melody and lyrics quickly reached out to snare the others. First Lydia, hardly aware of what she was doing, started tapping her foot in time to the music. Then Tich'ki began humming along, fairy voice high and sweet as birdsong. Eliathanis fought it for a time, but at last gave up, murmuring the words in his clear, elven tenor.

"Oh, come on!" Kevin teased. "You all can do better than that!"

They could. They did. Pushed on by the bardling's taunts, they laughed and set the echoes ringing with their singing. And Kevin, leading them on, grinned as he sang, watching the walls of suspicion come crumbling down, dissolved by the sheer joy that was music.

At last, breathless, they had to stop. Eliathanis coughed nervously, made a few abortive movements, then got to his feet and moved to the Dark Elf's side.

"I seem to be forever begging your pardon," he told Naitachal, "but . . . I must do it yet again." The White Elf shook his head. "I'm a warrior, not a magician, but that's no real excuse. Even so, I should have recognized *liathania safainias* when I saw it."

Naitachal glanced at the bewildered Kevin. "That doesn't translate very well into your human tongue. It means . . . mmm . . . 'explosion of pent-up Power' is as close as I can get, with the implication that the explosion wasn't the magician's fault."

"Exactly!" Eliathanis cut in. "Naitachal, we've fought enough foes together — and each other as well — for me to know something of who and what you are."

"A Dark Elf," Naitachal said drily. "A necromancer."

"Bah, forget that!" The White Elf waved a dismissive hand. "You had no choice in either." He paused, and Kevin could see his fair skin reddening even in the dim light. "Prejudice isn't a logical thing," Eliathanis began anew, "but it's damnably difficult to forget. As I've been proving so far."

"We are as we are."

"Don't mock me. This is difficult enough to say as it is. Naitachal, I . . . well . . . look you, I admit I've had things fairly easy all my life. I was raised with love and Light. I never had a moment's doubt about who I was or about the career I chose. But you — I can only guess at the struggle you had to be *you,* to be your own free soul."

"What are you trying to say?"

"Ah . . . I don't know. Maybe that the *you* you're creating is a being of whom you should be proud. Maybe that no matter what my people think of yours, or yours of mine, I know you, Naitachal, are not, you cannot be, my enemy. Agreed?"

The Dark Elf's teeth flashed in a sudden smile. "Agreed."

"Great," came Lydia's wry voice from the darkness. "Now can we all kiss and make up, and get some sleep?"

That created such a silly picture in Kevin's mind that he started to chuckle. The bardling was still chuckling as he settled down for the night, but mixed in with the humor was sheer relief.

Peace at last, he thought, and added a silent *Thank you* to whatever Spirit of Music might be listening.

Chapter XVII

By the second day of peaceful riding through peaceful fields and forest, climbing ever higher into the mountains, with nothing to be seen but countryside, Kevin felt his tight nerves beginning to unwind. He started to relax in the saddle, enjoying the quiet beauty of the scene around him, almost daring to hope:

Maybe Carlotta really hadn't had anything to do with the necromancer's attack. Maybe she wasn't after them after all.

The rest of the party were obviously feeling just as relaxed as he. Naitachal and Tich'ki were busily murmuring together as they rode; from what scraps the bardling could make out, they were trying to figure out a way to combine fairy magic with the Dark Elf's own to trace the missing Charina and enjoying the challenge. Lydia and Eliathanis were trading war stories, arguing good-naturedly over the comparative merits of sword and bow. Kevin smiled, and let his mind wander over various bits of music, puzzling out how he would transcribe this piece for lute or add counterpoint to that piece. It would be nice to show off some new musical skills once they were back in the castle.

All at once the inanity of his thoughts hit him like a blow. Kevin sat bolt upright. What in the name of all the Powers did everyone think they were doing?

"This is ridiculous!"

"Kevin?"

"Look at us! We're all acting as though we'd been out

for a — a pleasant little ride in the country, without a care in the world!"

"Well, yes," Lydia admitted. "But — "

"But we *know* Carlotta is alive. We *know* she had something to do with Charina's disappearance. What do you think we're going to find when we get back to Count Volmar, eh? Look you, all of you, we're talking about a sorceress who thought nothing of trying to murder her own brother! She's not going to stick at getting rid of nothings like us!"

"Nothings!" Tich'ki said indignantly.

Kevin ignored her, glaring at the others. "Think about it. For all we know, Carlotta's already figured out where we're going. Ha, for all we know, she already has agents in place in the castle!"

"Oh, you're not saying the count's in her employ!" Lydia protested. "He *paid* us to go on our hunt, for Powers' sake!"

"I'm not saying anything. Except that we don't know what we're going to be facing. So let's not be so — so — "

"So fat and lazy," Lydia drawled. She straightened in the saddle, adjusting the angle of her quiver. "You have a point, kid. Much as I hate to admit it, you do have a point."

Tich'ki came fluttering down to land, panting, on Lydia's saddle. "All right, I scouted ahead as best I could."

"And . . . ?"

She shrugged. "And all I could see was a perfectly normal castle full of perfectly ordinary humans. From what I could overhear, no one seemed to be talking about anything interesting."

"But you can't be sure," Kevin prodded.

"No, I can't be sure!" Tich'ki snapped. "I'm a fairy, not one of your heavy, earthbound breed! I don't know how you think!"

Kevin sighed. "Never mind. Just sit and get your strength back." He looked at the others. "I guess all we can do is go on."

They rode up the steep road to the castle in renewed tension, all of them wondering just how accurate Tich'ki's report might be. Could a fairy's judgment be trusted? Was this to be a refuge — or a trap?

"You're on your own," Tich'ki told them. "Once in that castle was enough. I'm not going to risk being trampled underfoot by some hulking human. See you later!"

She took wing, darting off without another word.

"Eh well, here we are," Lydia said, staring up at the watchtowers guarding the main gates.

Here they were, indeed. Kevin licked suddenly dry lips and called out their names to the tower guards. There was a brief pause, during which he had far too much time to wonder if they'd have time to get away if someone threw spears down at them. Or boiling oil. The gates creaked open. . . .

And a storm of shouting castle folk came rushing out to meet them. For one panicky moment, the bardling fumbled for his sword, sure he and his party were under attack. But before he could do anything to defend himself, Kevin made out some individual shouts amid the sea of noise:

"They're here!"

"They made it!"

"Oh, you brave, brave heroes!"

Kevin glanced at the rest of his party, seeing on their faces the same shocked disbelief he felt. "Uh, yes," the bardling began warily. "We're here, all right. But why are you — "

The rest of his question was drowned out in a storm of cheers. Eager hands reached out to grab his mule's bridle and lead it through the entryway into the crowded outer bailey.

"If it will please you to dismount, my lords, lady?"

No, it doesn't please me, Kevin thought. *This is all just too weird.*

But he couldn't think of any convincing argument that would let him turn around and ride out of here. Exchanging uneasy looks with the rest of the party, he dismounted and followed their guides.

They were led into the shadowy depths of the count's Great Hall, the sound of their footsteps muffled by the carpeting rushes. The vast, torchlit room was fairly stuffed with courtiers and servants alike. At the sight of Kevin and the others, they all burst into a frenzy of murmuring.

At the far end of the Hall sat Count Volmar himself, splendid in robes of somber blue, there on his red-canopied chair of state on its dais. And beside him was:

"Charina!" the bardling gasped.

"Kevin!" She came scurrying down the steps to Kevin's side in a wild swirling of blue velvet and long golden hair, and caught the startled bardling in a passionate hug. "Oh, you brave, brave hero! You saved me!"

"Ch-Charina," Kevin stammered, too shocked and embarrassed for anything else, overwhelmed by the soft sweetness of her. At last he managed to disengage himself, gasping out, "I'm delighted to see you're free, and I — I wish I — we — could take credit for it, but we didn't — "

"Don't be so modest, young man." Count Volmar stepped down from his chair to shake Kevin's hand. "The elven traitors who'd captured my niece released her as soon as they learned just who I had sent out to track them down." The count smiled heartily. "If it hadn't been for your reputation, all of you, and the diligent search I know you undertook, my poor dear Charina would still be a captive."

If it hadn't been for their reputation? *What*

reputation? Unless Lydia and the elves had been holding out on him . . . ?

But they looked every bit as baffled as he.

Before any of them could say or do anything, though, the count's servants swarmed down on the party.

"Hey, wait!" Kevin cried.

The last thing he wanted was to be separated from the others. But he didn't have much of a choice. Still trying to protest, Kevin was almost dragged away by the flock of eager servitors.

Chapter XVIII

To Kevin's momentary surprise, the servants deposited him not back in the chilly, barren squires' hall, but in a luxurious suite of rooms whose expensive tile floors and tapestry-hung walls marked them as the count's prized guest quarters.

"But I don't — I'm not — You can't — Hey! Isn't anybody *listening* to me?"

The servants, who were busy dragging out a hip bath and hanging the room round with heavy linen draperies "so the hero will not be bothered by drafts," stopped to stare at him.

"My lord?" one asked, glancing at Kevin's well-worn clothing and mule-scented self. "Do you not *wish* to bathe before meeting with Count Volmar again?"

"Uh, yes, of course I do! But — "

Too late. They were already off in a new flurry of excitement. Almost before Kevin could catch his breath, he was bathed and hustled into the most elegant silken hose and velvet tunic he could ever have imagined, a rich sky blue trimmed with gold thread. Somewhat to the overwhelmed bardling's relief, the whole thing was ever so slightly too big for him, especially in the shoulders: at least something wasn't totally bizarre — at least the clothing hadn't been conjured up specifically for him! A gold chain was draped about his neck, an ornamental dagger was fastened at his side, and Kevin was hurried back down to the Great Hall.

The rest of his party was already down there, arrayed in similar splendor. Lydia was truly beautiful in an amber-dark gown (Kevin could imagine what she'd had to say about having her legs hindered by skirts), her curly dark hair caught up in a net of gold thread, while the two elves looked inhumanly elegant, like some princely brothers, light and dark, out of the dawn of magic. Eliathanis' pale coloring was exquisitely set off by the softest of blue silk robes, while Naitachal's dark complexion was made yet more exotic by the deep red of his velvet robes.

Not one of the party looked any more comfortable in all that borrowed finery than Kevin felt.

"Ah, here you are!" Count Volmar cried heartily.

He, too, was more richly dressed than before, a rich blue robe trimmed with costly ermine about his shoulders, the gold chains of his office glinting across his shoulders, a jewel-encrusted velvet cap glittering on his head. At his side, in a chair only slightly lower than the count's own, sat Charina, her eyes modestly downcast, her hair caught back by a crystal circlet, and an elegantly outfitted semicircle of the count's warriors stood behind the dais.

"Now," the count announced, "we may begin the ceremony!"

"Ceremony . . . ?"

"You don't mind swearing fealty to me, my boy, do you? Just a formality, of course, but appearances must be kept up."

"Uh, yes, I mean no, I mean — "

"Good! I'm glad that's settled. Now, come along. We must do this thing properly!"

"*What* thing? What are you — "

"No, no, questions later! Now, if you " — Volmar's sweep of arm included Lydia and the elves — " will go back to the head of the Hall and reenter at the trumpeters' signal . . . "

Kevin glanced at the others in confusion. Lydia shrugged.

"Why not? The sooner we get this over with, whatever 'this' is, the sooner we can ask questions."

"Exactly," Naitachal agreed. "Come, my friends."

The trumpets blared. The blasts of sound certainly did fill the Hall, Kevin acknowledged, even if, he noted painfully, the instruments were all ever so slightly off-key. Feeling like an idiot, the bardling marched solemnly back towards Count Volmar, stopping at the foot of the dais, uneasily eyeing that semicircle of men-at-arms. One of them, he noticed, held a small, gilded lance, a ceremonial thing topped by a glittering pennon of cloth-of-gold.

Now, what?

Count Volmar stood. "Don't look so worried, lad," he murmured. "Just follow my lead. Come up here and kneel."

Sure he was going to do something stupid, like tumble over backwards down the steps, Kevin climbed the steps and carefully went down on one knee. The count extended both hands.

"Go on, lad, take them."

The bardling obeyed, feeling Volmar's palms as soft as those of any pampered nobleman but so cold he had to wonder if the count was really as at ease as he looked. Following Volmar's prompting, wondering if he was getting himself into some binding oath he might regret later, Kevin parroted:

"My Lord Count, I herein enter into your homage, and become your man by mouth and hands. I swear to keep faith and loyalty to you, saving only the just rights of His Majesty King Amber. And I swear to guard your rights with all my strength."

There. That didn't sound so bad. Nothing in there to compromise his honor or his loyalty to King Amber.

Count Volmar was returning his own part of the vow. "We do promise to you, our friend and vassal, Kevin, that we and our heirs will guarantee to you with all our power, all the rights due to you. Let there be peace between us."

"Let there be peace," Kevin echoed, then tried not to start in surprise as Volmar kissed him on the cheeks.

"Get up," the count whispered. "Take the lance."

Kevin obeyed, and everyone cheered.

"There, now!" Volmar exclaimed. "That's finished! Sorry I can't cede you any lands, my boy, but that, unfortunately, is the way of things. But from here on in, you may sign yourself as a court-baron!"

"I, uh, thank you," Kevin said helplessly. "Now, can we — "

"Now, my boy," the count cut in, slapping him so heartily on the shoulder the bardling staggered, "we celebrate!"

And celebrate they did, even if Kevin and his party still had no clear idea what they were celebrating. So quickly it seemed positively magical, the Great Hall was filled with long trestle tables spread with fine white linen and covered with elegant gold ewers, drinking cups and plates.

Plates, too! Kevin was used to the far more common thick bread trenchers. Count Volmar really was trying to impress them!

As guests of honor — for whatever reason, the bardling thought — Kevin and his party were seated at the High Table with Count Volmar. To the bardling's embarrassment, he found himself seated beside Charina, so close to her that he could smell the faint, flowery scent she wore (costly stuff, imported from the lands far to the east) and feel the warmth of her. Whenever she reached for food or drink, somehow their hands always managed to brush. Each contact seemed to burn through Kevin like flame, pleasant flame that sent heat surging through his whole body. He knew the count, sitting on Charina's other side, was asking him questions, he knew he must be answering, but Kevin, dazed by Charina's presence, was hardly aware of what he was saying, any more than he was aware of what, out of the interminable courses of fish and meat and poultry, he was eating.

The air in the Great Hall rapidly grew heavy with the varied smells of food, torch smoke and too many people crowded into one place (Kevin was vaguely aware of Eliathanis' fastidious distaste), and for all Charina's allure, the bardling found himself struggling not to yawn.

Ah, at last! Here came the subtleties, the spun sugar confections — at this dinner, a castle upon a marzipan hall and a swan swimming through a marzipan sea — that marked the end of a feast. Soon, Kevin thought with longing, he would be able to escape and get some rest.

No, he wouldn't. Dinner was followed by a seemingly endless procession of jugglers, acrobats, dancers, and an illusionist mediocre enough to make Naitachal snort in contempt. Charina oohed and ahhed over each performer, applauding vigorously, jarring Kevin awake every time he started to drift off. Powers, if this interminable celebration didn't end pretty soon, he was going to end up snoring away with his head in the crumbs.

At last, though, the ordeal did come to an end. The last of the performers bowed his way out of the Hall, and Count Volmar got to his feet, looking as crisp as ever.

"The hour is late. And so, my friends. I bid you good night." Beaming, he held up both arms in benediction. "I declare a week of celebration!"

As all the courtiers cheered, Kevin bit back a groan.

I don't know if I can survive a week of this!

Struggling not to stagger, the bardling followed a bevy of obsequious servants back to the guest quarters, blinking wearily as they fussed over him and removed his borrowed finery. As they finally left him alone,

Kevin yawned mightily, sure he was going to fall asleep the moment he fell into bed.

But of course as soon as he was settled comfortably in the big, canopied bed, his mind and body, perversely, woke up. After a time of restlessly tossing about, Kevin gave up trying to sleep altogether. Pulling back the canopies so he could get some fresh air, the bardling sat alone in the dark, puzzling over the weird events of the day.

Charina free? Himself a hero?

But I haven't done *anything!*

Nothing made sense. Oh sure, there had been the fight with the bandits and that necromancer. But everything else about their quest had been so — so easy, so ridiculously, frustratingly *easy* that —

Kevin froze, listening to the sudden faint creak of wood. That was the door! Someone was sneaking into his room.

The bardling shot off the bed, groping blindly for a weapon. His hand closed about a heavy candlestick, and he hefted it experimentally, heart pounding, trying to figure out exactly where the intruder might —

"Kid? Hey, kid?"

Lydia!

"Come on, Kevin," added a high, shrill voice. "We know you're in there!"

Wings buzzed in the darkness. Now that *had* to be Tich'ki!

Kevin put the candlestick back on the bedside table from which he'd snatched it and fumbled with flint and steel till he'd gotten the thick, expensive, beeswax candle burning. By its flickering light, he saw Lydia grin and Tich'ki come to a graceful landing on the bed. Two more figures moved silently out of the shadows: Eliathanis and Naitachal, the latter nearly invisible, shrouded once more in his cloak of necromantic black.

"We must talk," the Dark Elf said softly.

"We certainly must!" Kevin agreed. "I don't know about you, but I feel like all this glittery splendor is going to explode in my face."

Eliathanis grimaced. "Oh, indeed. The whole affair stinks, as you humans would say, like old boots."

Kevin nodded eagerly. "What it is, is that they're all trying their best to dazzle us."

"But just who are 'they'?" the White Elf wondered. "And why are 'they' doing this?"

"Why, indeed?" Naitachal mused. "I wonder . . . could someone have deceived Count Volmar? Perhaps told him of heroics we simply didn't do?"

"Why would anyone bother?" Lydia asked. "That doesn't make sense."

Tich'ki shrugged. "A weird sort of human joke?"

Kevin shook his head. "Not with Charina here. Her disappearance was hardly a joke!"

"The only other possibility," Naitachal said slowly, "is that the count himself is involved."

Lydia stirred impatiently. "Involved in *what*? All we know is, he hired us to find his niece. We returned to find said niece already free. Everyone thinks we're heroes. Yeah, it's a weird situation, but where's the crime in it?"

"Oh, Powers . . ."

"Kevin? What is it?"

He stared at them all. "I just had a horrible thought. Remember what the Arachnia back in Westerin told us? About Carlotta? Well, what if . . . what if that isn't Charina after all. I know she's no illusion, I sat next to her at dinner and all, but . . . " He shook his head in misery.

"You mean," the Dark Elf murmured, "that she might be no one else but Carlotta in disguise?"

"I d-don't want to believe it, but what if that's the truth? Then this whole thing, all this ridiculous, empty celebrating, starts making sense. It could all be part of her plot."

Naitachal swore under his breath. "Could be, no. It *is*! And here I thought I sensed something odd about that girl, a hint of sorcery hovering about her. But I told myself no, that couldn't be, I had to be mistaken. I let myself get just as bedazzled as the rest of you."

The Dark Elf straightened resolutely. "What happened, happened. If that really is Carlotta, the count is almost certainly under her sway."

"And that means they're both probably waiting for me to find the manuscript again," Kevin added. "After all, I'm still supposed to be copying it so I can bring the spell back to Master Aidan."

"Well, you can forget about all that!" Lydia exclaimed. "The last thing we want to do is play into Carlotta's hands. We've got to get out of here before it's too late. Yes, and warn King Amber, too!"

"No, wait." Eliathanis' voice was thoughtful. "If this really is Carlotta, we can't risk her finding the manuscript. That means we can't just go running off like so many frightened children."

"She probably wouldn't let us go anywhere anyhow," Kevin added, "particularly not in the direction of her brother." He hesitated, biting his lip nervously. "I — I think we have to go along with the deception, let Charina — or whoever she really is — get close to me again. And then . . . well . . . I guess then we'll see what happens."

For all his brave words, the bardling was half hoping someone would talk him out of it. But to his dismay, the White Elf only nodded. "That seems like the best idea. But since you're going to be playing the bait in what could be a most complicated trap, someone had best armor you against the weapons you're likely to encounter."

" 'Someone,' " Naitachal muttered. "That 'someone,' of course, is going to be me. Unless one of you has miraculously gained some useful protection spells? No? I didn't think so."

Tich'ki grinned, unabashed. "Now why would a fairy deign to *protect* someone?"

"Why, indeed?" The Dark Elf's voice dripped sarcasm. "Let the weak get what they deserve, eh?"

"Ha!" the fairy exploded. "Never knew your folks to be concerned with protecting anyone, either!"

"Point taken."

"Tich'ki," Lydia cut in, "couldn't you use fairy magic, though, against Carlotta?"

"How? By influencing her mind, the way I did to those guards?" Tich'ki shivered, wrapping her wings about her. "Not a chance. Look you, I know my limitations. If that really is Carlotta, she'd shrivel me like a moth in a flame."

"Never mind." Naitachal glanced at Kevin. "I'm sure you realize that when our White Elf friend mentioned armor, he didn't mean armor against anything as simple as swords."

"Uh . . . no."

"I admit I'm not the most experienced of magicians when it comes to protective spells, as our dear Tich'ki so kindly reminded me."

She tittered.

"But I shall do my best," the Dark Elf continued. "And," he added wryly, "I promise not to damage you in the process." Naitachal paused, then gave a heartfelt sigh. "It's not going to be an easy thing; if I make the spells too obvious, Charina/Carlotta will be sure to sense them. Hey-ho, who needs sleep?" He glanced at the others. "But those spells are for defensive purposes. Now let's plan what we're going to do about fighting back."

"Kevin shouldn't be left alone for a moment," Eliathanis suggested.

"That's easy to say," Lydia retorted. "I have a feeling that if Charina or Carlotta or whatever she wants to call herself really is worried about that manuscript, she's going to concentrate all her attention on Kevin."

"All we can do is our best," the White Elf said simply, and Tich'ki snickered.

"Might have known you'd say something all fine and noble and useless. Never mind the pretty words, elf! We've got some concrete plans to make: what we're going to do if the . . . ah . . . witch tries to isolate our boy here; what we're going to do if she asks him about the manuscript or makes him go get it — that sort of thing. All the nice, practical details."

Kevin nodded in fervent approval. "By all means, let's be practical!"

He and the others sat and plotted for some time. At last, satisfied with the results, Naitachal straightened in his chair.

"All right, enough of this. We all know our roles. Now, I have work to do. Lydia, Eliathanis, Tich'ki, if you can't help me cast spells, you can at least raid the kitchen and castle gardens and get me the components I'll need."

The Dark Elf rattled off a list of ingredients. Some of them, like rosemary, Kevin recognized; it was a common element of the protective amulets people wore back in Bracklin. Other items bewildered him totally.

"Naitachal? I didn't know *khafe* had any magical properties."

Naitachal's smile was wry. "That's for me, boy, not for you. This is going to be one long night's work, and I don't want to risk falling asleep in the middle of it. Oh, and by the way," he added sharply, catching the others in a warning stare, "once I begin that work, I do *not* wish to be interrupted. Understood?"

"Totally." Lydia grinned. "After all, *some* of us have to look pretty in the morning!"

She dodged as Naitachal threw a pillow at her, and scurried out of the room, her laughter trailing behind her.

INTERLUDE THE FIFTH

The night was late, at the very witching hour, and very dark, moonless and still, without the faintest breath of wind. Not a sound was to be heard without Count Volmar's castle save for the faint footsteps and chinking of mail of the guards wearily trudging back and forth up on the ramparts. Their torches were small, flickering things barely cutting through the vast mass of darkness.

Within the castle, silence reigned as well. All slept—

Or almost all. Cloistered in Count Volmar's solar, two people sat in secret conference, sharing a midnight flagon of mulled wine.

Hands cupped about his warm goblet, Volmar chuckled suddenly. "Now you have to admit," he said, glancing over at Carlotta, "that things are going nicely. Very nicely, indeed."

The sorceress, in her rightful form once more, red hair pouring over her shoulders and green gown like a stream of flame, stared broodingly down into her own goblet. "So far."

"Oh my dear princess, don't be so wary! Kevin may bear the seeds of Bardic Magic as you say, but he is still only a boy. So far it's been ridiculously easy for me to quite overwhelm him with riches and the trappings of power, you must admit."

Carlotta glanced up at that, her smile wry. "Granted. Between the two of us, he hasn't even had a chance to think."

"Exactly. And I intend to go right on overwhelming him."

The sorceress stretched wearily, graceful as a predator. "Ay me, and I will endure being simpering little Charina a bit longer, and continue casting my beguilements and love-spells on the boy."

Volmar pursed his lips thoughtfully. "Now that's something I don't understand. Carlotta, you know there's such a thing as too much caution. Why don't you just enthrall the boy in one quick burst of sorcery and be done with it?"

Her eyes flashed in sudden angry warning. "Don't be ridiculous. The only spells I dare use are subtle ones."

"But why? Surely you can — "

"Surely I can tell you not to meddle! Have you forgotten about that Dark Elf?"

The one you thought dead? Volmar thought but didn't dare say aloud. "No, of course not. But — "

Carlotta's hands tightened about her goblet. "Magic leaves a distinctive *feel,* if one has sufficient training to identify it. One magician can almost always recognize another in action, no matter which sorcerous disciplines are involved, no matter how many cloaking spells are used. I had a nervous enough moment when that elf first saw me; I swear he nearly sensed who and what I am on the spot. I only just managed to project enough girlish innocence to distract him."

The sorceress paused, staring at Volmar. "I don't have to remind you that I don't want my true identity discovered yet, not by anyone. The elf is a skillful necromancer, no doubt about it. And that makes him Talented enough to detect the working of any strong magics by anyone. And so I must limit myself to subtle spells."

"I see."

"Oh, don't misjudge me!" Carlotta smiled without humor. "The spells may be subtle, but that doesn't mean they aren't powerful. And their effect, I might add, is nicely accumulative."

"Ah, clever. Between the two of us, we should have

the boy beautifully cooperative before the week is out."

The woman's smile thinned ever so slightly. "I should think so. Assuming, of course, that you don't make some mistake."

"I won't," Volmar said as casually as he could. "And once he's under our control, of course he'll go fetch us his manuscript."

"Ah, yes. That's going to be the true test of his enthrallment. Rather than doing the copying himself, the boy must be persuaded to surrender the manuscript to one of your scribes, then let our messenger carry that copy off to his cursed Master."

The count frowned. "That's not going to be easy. He's such a disgustingly honorable boy." He raised a hopeful brow. "That isn't something that's going to change once he's enthralled, is it?"

"No. Such spells delude and lull the will, but they can't change a person's inner self." Carlotta paused. "But the boy is, as you say, still very young. If we're careful, we should be able to so beguile him that he forgets duty. Then he'll be quite willing to let the messenger have the copy of the manuscript—so that he, himself, can continue enjoying this so very flattering noble hospitality."

Volmar sat bolt upright. "Ha, I have it! If he seems reluctant, all we need to do is propose that he marry Charina."

"He *what*?"

Volmar laughed. "The poor fool is too unworldly to realize I'd never let my ward marry a mere nothing. He'll take the whole thing quite seriously. And then, of course, there will be no way he can take the copy of the manuscript back to his Master; he'll be too busy with wedding preparations even to consider doing the copy himself!"

Carlotta raised her goblet in a wry toast. "I like it. A maximum of result from a minimum of effort. Oh yes, I like it. Ah, poor Kevin," she crooned, "poor little bardling. You don't stand a chance!"

Chapter XVIX

Something that sounded like a giant mosquito was droning away in his ears. Kevin came awake with a start, ready to swat whatever. But then he sank back in his chair, realizing it was just the residue of yet another spell.

The bardling rubbed a tired hand over his face. Naitachal had been right: it *was* turning into a long, weary night's work, even if it was the Dark Elf who had to do most of that work.

Whatever it is that he's doing.

There had been a confusing barrage of spells so far, some of them briefly entangling Kevin in a whispery net of sound, some of them blanketing him in comforting warmth, some of them — the bardling shook his head. He couldn't even interpret how some of them had felt.

"Naitachal?"

"Stay still." The Dark Elf's voice was thick with fatigue. "Only a few more to go."

"Can't you stop and rest? I mean, I know I've been asleep half the time, but you haven't had a chance to so much as close your eyes."

Naitachal smiled wryly. "Thank you for your concern, but the sooner I finish the lot, the happier I'll feel."

He began murmuring incomprehensible spell-words once more, and Kevin sighed, feeling a new tingling travelling all through him, a soothing sort of sensation, odd, but not at all alarming . . . not at all . . .

As the bardling relaxed, his eyes slid closed once more. . . .

This time it was the total absence of strange sensations that woke him. Kevin straightened in his chair, blinking in confusion at the faint gray light of not-quite morning.

Morning! Powers, had the Dark Elf been working through the whole night without a pause? He glanced towards where Naitachal was slumped in his own chair, eyes shut.

Wish I could just let him sleep; he's certainly earned it!

But they'd both agreed it wasn't such a good idea for anyone to think they'd been conspiring together.

"Naitachal?" Kevin whispered, then repeated, a little more forcefully: "Naitachal!"

The Dark Elf opened his eyes with a groan. "Yes. I'm awake." He staggered up from the chair, straightening carefully, adding with wry humor, "So weary I could sleep on my feet like a horse, but awake."

"You look terrible. I wish you didn't have to wear yourself out like this."

"Ae-ye, no one ever said magic was easy. At least this way the sorceress isn't going to be able to turn you into her love slave."

Kevin assumed that was meant to be a joke.

Naitachal stretched every muscle, plainly trying to force some energy back into himself, then ran his fingers through his pale, tangled mane. "Remember, though, that these are only faint copies of true protective spells I've cast over you. Don't expect too much of them. I don't dare put too blatantly powerful magics upon you. Carlotta would be sure to sense them. But what may be lacking in force, I'm making up in volume." The weary blue eyes suddenly darkened with worry. "I hope."

"I can do it," the bardling assured him, trying to sound more certain than he felt.

"Again, I hope." Naitachal bit back a third yawn. "Ay

me, I'd best get back to my own room before I fall over. Or before the servants start wondering what's going on. Till later, Kevin."

"Till later," the bardling echoed uneasily.

"What's wrong with Naitachal?" Lydia, who'd shed her finery for more comfortable tunic and breeches, whispered that to Kevin as they stood on a wide castle balcony pretending to be engrossed in an archery contest taking place in the courtyard below.

Kevin stole a wary glance back to where the Dark Elf sat in as much concealing shadow as he could find up here on this sunny morning. Naitachal's black cloak was wrapped tightly about his slender form, the hood pulled forward to hide his face, making him look like a truly sinister figure, a sliver of Darkness amid the Light — but Kevin suspected the Dark Elf was actually just asleep with his eyes open.

"What do you think?" the bardling retorted softly. He applauded politely as one of the archers down in the courtyard below scored a near bull's-eye. "He was up all night casting spells on me."

"Ah. Right. Of course. Feel any different?"

"No, but — "

"Oh, nice shot!" the woman called out. She added so softly only Kevin could hear, "Not a decent archer in the lot. Huh, and look at the way Charina's eying you from the doorway, like a cat watching a tasty little fish."

This fish has some surprises in store, Kevin thought, *or at least I hope I do.*

The idea that the pretty young woman approaching him might really be a murderous sorceress seemed impossible on such a bright, sunny day. And yet . . . A sudden nervous prickle racing up his spine, Kevin got courteously to his feet to bow to Charina. Or whoever she really was.

"My lady."

"My! So formal!" Charina's glance at Lydia was ever so subtly edged with contempt as she took in the woman's warrior garb. "What's this? I should think you would be down there, too, Lady Lydia. Are you not an archer?"

To Kevin's ears, she made that occupation sound as unsuitable for a lady as pig-farming. Lydia couldn't have missed the snub, but she only laughed. "Oh, I hardly thought it fair to compete. I mean, I'm not one of the count's people."

"But surely you would like a chance to demonstrate your skills." It was a very thinly veiled command.

Lydia only shrugged. "Nope! Much nicer just to sit and watch. Besides, at such a short distance how could I miss? Right, Kevin?"

Thank you, Lydia! he thought gratefully. The last thing he wanted was to be left alone with Charina. "Uh, right."

"Ah, but I think you really should go down there," a suave voice purred. Kevin saw Lydia tense as Count Volmar stepped forward to take her arm. "My dear young lady, you would hardly wish to deprive us of the pleasure of watching a true professional at work, now, would you?"

She shrugged free of the count's grip. "I'll say the same thing I told the Lady Charina: it doesn't seem fair. I mean, how is it going to look if a mere mercenary like myself beats your guys?"

"That hardly seems likely," the count muttered, miffed. "My archers are not exactly children. But please," he added, urbane smile returning, "do give us a chance to judge your skill for ourselves."

It wasn't a request. With a sigh and a glance at Kevin, Lydia shouldered her bow and went down to join the other archers. Charina moved closer to the bardling with a pleased little coo. But before she could take his arm, a cheerful voice called out:

"How goes it, my lords, my lady?"

"Eliathanis!" Kevin cried in relief.

The White Elf swept down into a bow far more graceful than any human could have managed. Slanted eyes glinting with wry amusement, he said, "What a fine day for an archery contest! Ah, I see our own Lydia is among the contestants."

"You would have a better view of them down there," Charina suggested, but Eliathanis only smiled.

"Why, no, lady, if you will forgive me for correcting you. I have a much better view from up here. A better view of . . . everything." Fair face impassive, the elf crossed his arms with the air of someone who has no intention of moving or being moved.

That's all well and good, Kevin thought uneasily, seeing the anger flickering in Charina's eyes. Apparently she and the count thought more forceful measures would be out of character just now. *But you and Lydia and Naitachal can't keep watching over me forever.*

Sooner or later, danger or no, the bardling knew he was going to have to face the sorceress all by himself.

It was sooner. That night Kevin found a guard at his door "to protect him from unwelcome disturbances."

In the days that passed, the bardling caught no more than distant glimpses of his friends. But, he tried to convince himself, there was something comforting in knowing that they were taking turns watching over him, even from afar.

Not that mere watching was going to do any good if the sorceress decided to attack.

Ah, yes, but Charina wasn't showing any more interest in the bardling than a properly brought-up young lady might show in a young man she fancied. In fact, if it hadn't been for the undercurrent of uneasiness running through his mind, Kevin knew he probably would have enjoyed her attention. Or even, amazing thought, to have become a little surfeited by it. Somehow Charina was managing to almost always be at his side, the very image of a slightly spoiled but charming niece to a count, cooing and fluttering until the bardling found himself wondering just why he'd been foolish enough to be attracted to her in the first place.

But then, I didn't really have a choice about it. It wasn't really Charina I was attracted to after all. Or at least I don't think *it was.*

Or—

Ach, he didn't know *what* to think any more! Kevin wandered blindly through the castle gardens, for the moment blessedly alone, the gravel path crunching under his shoes, sweet, spicy herbal scents filling his nose, and puzzled over the fact that the girl or woman or whatever she was hadn't tried anything blatantly sorcerous on him.

Or had she? Now that he thought about it, Kevin could have sworn that from time to time during the week he'd felt the eeriest tingling, as though Naitachal's protective armor of spells was being tested again and again. So far that armor had held up.

Oh, nonsense! The whole thing was probably the product of his own overwrought imagination. How could Charina be anyone but Charina?

She couldn't.

But then again, maybe . . .

Kevin shook his head impatiently. Enough wavering! Whatever was happening or not happening, he didn't dare let his guard down. The week of celebration was over today, and if Charina really was Carlotta, this would be her last chance to try ensnaring him. And if she couldn't get the manuscript from him, then she would surely try to—

The bardling nearly jumped straight into the air when a soft hand brushed his arm. "Kevin?" Charina's sweet voice asked. "Is anything wrong?"

"Uh, n-no, no, of course not." Trying to get his

heartbeat back to normal, Kevin reminded himself that if this was truly Carlotta, she would expect him to be totally under her sway by now. He mustn't show the slightest sign of rebellion.

The bardling licked suddenly dry lips and forced himself to continue with feigned regret, "Charina, the week's nearly over. I, uh, will have to be leaving pretty soon."

"No! You can't!"

"Charina — "

"It's that musty old manuscript, isn't it? That manuscript with its dull old spells — and your dull old Master, too!"

"He's not — "

"He's dull, I say, dull, dull, dull! He's forgotten everything about what it's like being young and free and — and happy. You *can't* leave me, Kevin, you just *can't*!"

"I'm sorry," Kevin said warily, testing, pretending regret for all he was worth, "but I don't see what else I can do."

Charina's angry eyes widened in sudden delight. "I have it! I don't know why I didn't think of this before, but all you have to do is find the stupid manuscript and turn it over to one of my uncle's scribes to copy. Then one of my uncle's messengers will take it straight to your Master!" She clapped her hands. "Don't you see? After that, there won't be any need for you to go back at all!"

Kevin hardly heard her. What she'd said a moment ago was just now registering. Oh gods, she'd said that the manuscript held "dull old spells." Yet all he'd ever told Charina about the thing was that it was called *The Study of Ancient Song*. Hardly a sorcerous title.

Then how could she know it held any spells? How — unless she really is *Carlotta!*

"Kevin? What do you think?"

I think I want to run for my life. "Uh . . . I don't know . . ." He hedged desperately.

"You can trust my uncle's men, really you can. Your Master will get the manuscript, and you can stay here with me!"

Sure. As your mind-blasted slave, his mind gibbered. *Or as a corpse.*

How could she keep playing her part so well? If he opened his mouth right now, he was going to say something perilously stupid, but Kevin couldn't think of a single thing else to do except look wildly about and —

Ah, thank you, Powers! Across the garden stood a tall, slender figure: Eliathanis, wrapped in a pale blue cloak and looking, to Kevin's eyes, like a sign from the heavens themselves. Frantically the bardling tried to remember the signals they'd agreed upon earlier in the week . . . Ah, yes!

As slanted elven eyes watched him levelly, Kevin scratched his head as casually as possible, then rubbed his nose, the sign Carlotta/Charina had asked him to get the manuscript. The White Elf watched him a moment longer, face inhumanly composed, as though being sure of what he'd seen, then turned to casually study the sky.

I hope you know what you're doing, Kevin told him silently.

"I had to think it over a moment," he said to Carlotta, and forced a grin on his reluctant lips. "You know something? That's a wonderful idea! Ah, but the day's far too beautiful to spend cooped up in a library."

She looked at him strangely. "No, it's not. Kevin, it's going to rain!"

"Not for a few hours anyhow. Why don't we go riding or something and look for the manuscript tomorrow?"

"No, no, let's get it over with now!"

Carlotta seized his hand and started pulling him off towards the library. Kevin knew he could have broken her grip easily enough. But if he resisted, it was going to shout to her that he wasn't under her power as she believed. Thank the Powers that Naitachal's anti-beguilement spells had worked — and that they'd been too subtle for Carlotta to detect. Thank the Powers as well that Carlotta too had been constrained to subtlety; otherwise even his feigned cooperation would have been transparently false.

I only hope Eliathanis can let the others know I might be in trouble. The bardling glanced at Carlotta and caught, just for an instant, a suspicious glint of hardness in those lovely blue eyes, a hardness all out of place for one of her supposed youth and innocence. A hardness that smacked of sorcery.

Really big trouble, Kevin amended unhappily.

Chapter XX

"Come *on*, Kevin!"

Carlotta batted her eyelashes at him in a way the bardling might have found adorable — if it wasn't such an incongruous gesture on the part of a sorceress who'd kill him if he made one wrong move.

"Why, if I didn't know better," she chirped, "I'd think you were trying to *avoid* being alone with me." Carlotta giggled girlishly. "That's not true, now, is it?"

"Uh . . . no. Of course not." *Yes, dear Powers, yes! How am I going to get out of this alive?*

Not by letting Carlotta think there was something wrong with her beguilement spells, that was sure! But what else could he do? There wasn't much time to waste, yet his thoughts seemed to be racing around and around his mind like so many terrified wild things. The only thing Kevin could decide to do was play the befuddled bumpkin. Ha, that shouldn't be so difficult! Right now it was going to be far easier to fake stupidity and bedazzlement than to say or do anything clever!

Aren't there any servants around? Anyone who might suggest that the niece of a count shouldn't be alone with a young man?

No, of course not. That would be far too simple. The castle corridors were as empty as though there wasn't anyone else alive in the whole place. Besides, Kevin thought wearily, all the servants were probably under Carlotta's control, anyhow.

All too soon, they reached the library.

Kevin tried the handle. "The door seems to be locked," he said, stalling desperately for time.

"No, it's not. It's never locked. Here, let me see."

Carlotta tried the handle, which turned with treacherous ease. She glanced sharply at Kevin, and the bardling gave her a weak smile.

"Must have been stuck."

"Well, it isn't stuck now. Come on."

But Kevin stopped short in the doorway, hunting frantically for some other excuse.

"Ca-Charina." Gods, he'd almost called her by her real name! "Charina, I . . . uh . . . I think I'm getting a headache. Maybe tomorrow really would be a better time to — "

"Don't be *silly*! The sooner we take care of the manuscript — Oh, don't look at me with such horror, Kevin! I meant to a scribe!" She smiled teasingly. "What did you think I meant?"

"I . . . uh . . . "

"Anyhow, the sooner we get rid of the manuscript, the sooner we can do what we want. Whatever we want. Like this."

Without warning, Carlotta threw her arms around his neck, her lips all at once temptingly close to his.

Temptingly? the bardling thought in panic. Her body pressed against his, the sweet scent of her perfume filled his nose. At any other time he would have done almost anything to be embraced like this by a lovely young woman, but now — *Powers, I'd be safer kissing a spider! But if I* don't *kiss her, she'll* know *something's wrong. . . .*

Just before he forced himself to choose the lesser peril, Charina pushed him away, giggling. "You haven't got a headache. Or if you do, it will go away now that we're out of the garden. It's just the result of breathing in the smells of all those herbs." Her smile was a marvel of fake innocence. "Some of them make me sneeze every time I go near them! If the cook didn't need them for his recipes . . . Never mind. Let's find that silly old manuscript and get out of here."

Oh please, Kevin told the manuscript, *hide from me the way you did before!*

He couldn't pretend not to search, not with Carlotta watching his every move. Oh no, even though Kevin realized she didn't really know what the manuscript looked like, she certainly could tell what it *didn't* look like; he couldn't try to fool her with the wrong title. And so the bardling did the only thing he could, and examined each and every item in the library as slowly and carefully as possible.

Delaying like this was a dangerous game. Kevin was all too well aware that Carlotta's sweet expression hid barely restrained impatience. If he pushed her too far . . .

An age passed, or so it seemed, while he searched the library, then a second age, this one surely long enough to wear away rock. But at last, to Kevin's despair, he realized he had gone through every manuscript in the library save one.

As though his hand had a life all its own, the bardling watched with fascinated horror as it pulled the manuscript from the shelf, feeling the strange, magical tingling that told him what he held even before he read the title:

The Study of Ancient Magic.

Of course. You pick a wonderful time to come out of hiding, he told the manuscript with bitter sarcasm.

"Kevin!" Carlotta snapped. "What do you think you're doing? Why are you staring like that at an empty shelf?"

"But it's not— "

"Oh, stop clowning!" There was very little of the innocent young girl in that sharp command. "I don't want to spend all day here. Get on with your search!"

Bewildered, Kevin turned to face her, the manuscript in his hands.

Carlotta's eyes widened in shock. "You—you *do*

have it!" she gasped. In the next moment, the sorceress had herself back under control. "Here, let me have it."

She hadn't been able to see the manuscript until he took it off the shelf! Stunned by this new bit of magic, the bardling couldn't find a thing to say except an awkward, "Uh . . . sorry, Charina."

"Kevin? I'm not in the mood for games. Give it to me."

"I . . . uh . . . can't."

"Kevin! Give it to me!"

The bardling backed away towards the door, stammering the first words that came into his head. "I — I have to keep it, to — to — to take it to my room and — "

"I don't think so." Suspicion flickered in her eyes. "You've figured out the truth, little boy, haven't you?"

"I d-don't — "

"Oh, but you do. A pity."

There wasn't the slightest trace of youth or innocence in her voice now. As Kevin watched in fascinated terror, he saw Charina's form grow and alter in a swift, dizzying blur of shape and color. The woman who stood before him now looked nothing like the girl she'd been a few moments before: she was tall and coldly exquisite of face and form, her long hair flaming red, her green eyes hard and chill and —

Of course she doesn't look anything like Charina, his mind gibbered, *Charina was Carlotta all along!*

What had Naitachal said? Aiee, yes: if she changed to her right shape it was probably the prelude to her casting some major spell, because powerful spell-casting shattered illusions —

No time to think. But in that last midnight session, the bardling and the others had worked out every detail of what they were going to do. And oh, he was glad of that preparation now! If he stood staring at her like a fear-paralyzed fool, she'd strike him down. If he tried to run with the manuscript, like the naive boy who'd first left Bracklin, she'd strike him down.

Instead, Kevin simply tossed the manuscript out the library's open window, praying Tich'ki had had time to get into place.

That was obviously the last thing Carlotta had expected. She let out a shriek of disbelieving rage, her sorcerous concentration broken by shock.

Now's my chance!

Kevin broke into a run, praying he could get away before she regained control and blasted him. Behind him, the bardling heard her scream again, this time in sheer frustration, and felt his skin prickle as she gathered Power to her. Before she could blast him, Kevin darted out the door, slamming it behind him, knowing that wasn't going to stop her for more than a moment. He wasn't a fighter, he wasn't a magician — Powers, Powers, the others had better be ready to help out!

They were. As Carlotta tore the door open, Eliathanis appeared, seemingly from nowhere. Moving with inhuman speed, he pounced, pinning Carlotta in his arms, muffling her attempts to scream with a hand. But of course he couldn't hope to hold her for long.

"Get out of here, Kevin!" the White Elf shouted.

Then he gasped in pain as the sorceress bit him. Kevin glanced back over his shoulder and saw with a chill of horror that now her mouth was free for spell-casting. A shouted Word sent Eliathanis flying. The bardling stumbled to an anguished stop, sure he was about to see Carlotta slay the White Elf. She spat out a short, twisting sentence — and a bolt of dark fire flashed from her hand.

But before it could strike the fallen elf, Naitachal sprang forward out of the shadows, cloak swirling dramatically behind him, arms raised in denial. The sorcerous fire recoiled from a sudden, unseen wall of force, smashing instead into a wall with a roar like thunder, sending broken stone crashing down in a wild cloud of dust that forced Carlotta back into the shelter of the library. Before she could recover, Eliathanis had scrambled to his feet. The two elves slapped palms in a quick moment of triumph, then took to their heels, catching up with Kevin.

"That noise is going to rouse the whole castle!" Naitachal cried. "Hurry to the gates! Lydia should have fast horses ready."

"She'd better," Eliathanis added. "If we don't get away now —"

Too late. Carlotta had left her refuge — but she'd left it as Charina, dusty and dishevelled, pathetically calling for help.

"She — she's saying we assaulted her!" Kevin gasped. "And used sorcery to boot!"

"Wonderful," Naitachal muttered. "Just what we need."

As they came out into a courtyard, beneath a dramatically overcast sky, Eliathanis stopped short. "Here come the guards. No one's going to believe us against poor, sweet little Charina. We've got to split up." He gave Kevin a shove. "Up that stairway, hurry! Naitachal, you go that way, I'll go this. See you outside!"

We hope. Kevin scrambled up the steep stone stairway, a stone wall on his left, open space on the right, hearing a troop of guards clattering up behind him, and wound up on a narrow rampart between two towers. *Which way, which way . . . ?*

He turned left at random, and dove through the narrow door into the tower, staggering to a walk, half blinded by the sudden darkness. His foot found the lip of a narrow staircase spiralling down.

But then Kevin stopped so sharply he nearly went tumbling down the stairs. Guards were climbing up this way, too! The bardling raced back out across the rampart, blinking frantically in the sudden return to daylight — and nearly ran into the arms of the guards who'd followed him up the first stairway. He kicked and squirmed and twisted, wriggling his way through so swiftly none of them had a chance to grab him, and dove into the second tower.

Oh damn, oh damn, they're coming up this stairway, too!

He wasn't going to surrender. He didn't dare, not with Carlotta awaiting him! So Kevin took the only option open and raced up the spiralling stairway, stumbling on the narrow steps, banging knees and elbows, struggling up and up till at last, gasping, he burst out into the open on the tower's flat top.

Powers, now what do I do?

The bardling glanced wildly this way and that, a surge of vertigo overwhelming him as he realized just how high up he was. The tower top suddenly felt impossibly narrow and insecure, while the castle was spread out in a dizzying panorama far below him, swarming with frenetic life.

Kevin tensed as he recognized two people out of that swarm: Naitachal and Eliathanis, two doll-size figures from up here, looked like they were having a wonderful time. They moved with elven speed and grace, almost like a matched pair of dancers, one dark, one fair, far swifter than the merely human guards trying to catch them. The bardling could have sworn he saw Eliathanis grin, heard Naitachal's laugh come trailing thinly up to him. The elves took a moment to slap palms yet again, then scurried off in opposite directions. Kevin didn't have a moment's doubt that they were going to escape, and enjoy doing it.

Sure, great, now they can admit they're friends. I'm glad they're having fun — but meanwhile I'm trapped up here!

Here came the guards. Kevin turned to face them, back against the low balustrade, bracing himself, sick at heart, knowing that throwing himself to his death would be a kinder fate than letting himself fall into Carlotta's hands.

"Jump!"

Wonderful. Now he was hearing voices.

"Kevin! Jump!"

Strong little fingers pinched his arm so hard he yelped. "Tich'ki!"

"Come on, you idiot bardling, trust me! *Jump!*"

Powers, what if this was some truly sadistic form of a fairy joke — see the trusting human go *splat!* But the bardling knew he had to trust her. What other choice was there?

All at once dreadfully calm, Kevin climbed up onto the tower's narrow balustrade, the world a dizzy blur around him. As the guards cried out in sudden shock, the bardling jumped blindly into space.

Chapter XXI

Kevin jumped as far out and away from the castle as he could. For one wild, terrifying, thrilling moment, he was falling free, the earth surging up to meet him, and was sure he was dead.

Then Tich'ki was beside him, shape-changed to human size, catching him in her arms, her wings backwatering frantically. Those wings didn't have the strength to actually carry her weight and his together, but slowly, painfully slowly, the fairy began to check his fall. But it wasn't going to work, Kevin thought in panic, they were running out of time and space!

Tich'ki cried, "Go limp! It's not going to be a soft landing!"

Kevin hit, not as hard as he had feared, and started helplessly rolling down the steep hill from the castle, sky and ground whirling in a dizzy circle. The bardling frantically snatched at grass and rock, trying to slow his fall, only to end up with a jolt against a tough little patch of bushes.

Aching, trying to remember how to breathe, deeply afraid of what he would find when he tried to move, Kevin rolled over onto his back, eyes shut, wanting nothing but to be left alone to die. But strong hands were about his shoulders, forcing him to his feet. He opened his eyes to find himself supported by Eliathanis and clutching the manuscript that had somehow wound up in his hands again during his fall.

"Are you all right?" the White Elf asked worriedly, then added, without waiting for his reply: "Come on,

Lydia has our horses, down there where the hill levels out. We've got to get away before the guards have a chance to mount and come after us!"

"Before *Carlotta* comes after us," Naitachal corrected wryly. "As good a team as we make, cousin-elf— " he flashed a quick grin at Eliathanis, who grinned back "— I'd just as soon not tackle her again."

Kevin let all that pass without really listening to it. At least, he realized, trying to muster his stunned thoughts, he'd landed on grass, not rock. And nothing seemed to be broken after all. Tucking the hard weight of the manuscript securely inside his tunic, the bardling struggled down the hill to where Lydia waited and pulled himself into a saddle, wincing as strained muscles complained. "Tich'ki . . . "

"Here." Shrunken back to her normal size, she was draped wearily in front of Lydia. "We're all here."

"I've got your lute," the warrior woman added. As the bardling quickly slung it over his back, Lydia added sharply, "Now, let's ride!"

They went down the rest of that steep hill at breakneck speed, Kevin praying none of the horses slipped or caught a hoof. Behind him, he could hear alarm gongs starting to tear the air apart.

But we've got a good head start, we should make it into the forest's shelter before—

A brilliant flash of light made him start so violently he almost lost his seat, thinking, *Sorcery!* But when the flash was followed by a vicious clap of thunder, he realized the threatening storm was upon them. A wild, wet gust of wind slammed into the horses, making them stagger.

"We're saved!" Lydia shouted gleefully.

"No," Eliathanis cried, his eyes all at once wide and unseeing, "there is no safety. Except in the grave."

"Don't say that!" Naitachal snapped. "I've seen quite enough of graves, thank you!"

Eliathanis seemed to come back to himself with a rush. "I fear you may see yet another, my friend."

"What *are* you saying?" Naitachal laughed. "I've never yet seen a White Elf who was worth a copper coin at prophesy!"

But to Kevin's surprise, he thought he caught a trace of fear behind the mockery. And the very real hint of otherworldly sorrow lingering in Eliathanis' eyes sent a chill through the bardling and made him add in a panicky rush, "It's all right, really, you'll see. We'll be able to hide out from anyone, even an army, in the forest."

"Will you?" The sudden sharp voice made the horses shy, whinnying in fright. "Or will you die?"

With beautifully dramatic timing, a second bolt of lightning split the sky. Deafened by the following crack of thunder, Kevin stared at this sudden apparition in stunned disbelief. There was no doubt at all who it was: her elegant face was set in its cold, sorcerous lines. Her green gown whipped about her in the ever-rising storm wind that made the locks of her long hair writhe like flame.

"Carlotta! B-but how — "

"She *is* a sorceress," Naitachal reminded the bardling drily. The Dark Elf's blue eyes were flickering with their own sorcerous red embers. "I *thought* we were escaping just a bit too easily."

"Listen to me," Lydia murmured. "When I give the signal, kick your horses into a gallop."

"Don't be silly," Naitachal began, but Lydia was already shouting:

"And . . . *now!*"

The startled horses shot forward as one. But before they could reach Carlotta, she shouted out savage Words of Power — and a huge wall of flame roared up. The horses screamed in terror, shying wildly, fighting their riders. Kevin lost a stirrup, nearly smashed his nose against his animal's neck, hanging on for all he was worth.

"Told you." Naitachal's words were chopped off as his horse reared, making him look like a dark legend against the dark sky, his cloak billowing out like bat wings.

"Where's Carlotta?" Lydia shouted, clinging to her plunging horse like a burr.

"Who knows?" Tich'ki, wings beating frenetically, couldn't quite climb high enough to see over the magical flame, thermals from the suddenly heated air pushing her away every time she tried. "Somewhere behind all that."

"Illusion!" the bardling yelled, even though he could feel the fire's heat and smell its smoke. Struggling with his hysterical horse, "It's got to be illusion!"

"No illusion." The Dark Elf finally managed to bring his mount back to all four feet. "She doesn't care if she burns down the whole forest, as long as she stops us long enough for — Yes, curse her, here they come."

A new bolt of lightning blazed out over what looked like every one of the count's men-at-arms, knights and common guards alike. The wall of flame didn't seem to be giving them pause; not having seen it created, they probably just thought it lightning-strike.

"We can't fight all of them," Lydia cried over the crash of thunder. "Naitachal, how far does this fire extend?"

The Dark Elf shrugged angrily. "I don't know the spell Carlotta used. It could extend for leagues."

"Then we'll ride for leagues, dammit!"

The woman kicked her horse into a run, riding parallel to the fire, and the others followed. But a new wall of flame roared up before them, cutting off their escape. Kevin's horse screamed in panic, and the bardling nearly lost his seat all over again. Struggling to stay in the saddle, he shot an anxious glance up at the cloud-heavy sky.

The rain, curse it, where's the rain? It would put out this fire and give us a fighting chance to get out of this trap before —

"Hey, no!"

His horse had suddenly decided it had quite enough of flames. The animal whirled before Kevin could stop it, and bolted blindly back towards the castle — and the waiting enemy. The bardling frantically sawed at the reins. Wait, wait, he'd heard somewhere that if a horse ran away with you, you were supposed to pull it around in one big circle.

Oh, sure, easily said! But the animal had the bit in its teeth and a neck like iron, and in another moment horse and rider were going to be within bowshot. He was already close enough to see the flat madness in the soldiers' eyes, to wonder with a quick thrill of horror how Carlotta had managed to subvert a whole castle. Sorcery? Something as simple as drugs in the communal water supply? Oh, Powers, it didn't matter now, because this idiot of a horse was going to get him killed!

Kevin was all set to jump from the animal's back and hope he didn't break his neck when the drumming of hoofs sounded behind him and a second horse came rushing up beside his. The bardling caught a quick glimpse of an elegant profile, silky golden hair: Eliathanis!

But then the bardling got a better look at the White Elf's face, and nearly gasped. Eliathanis' eyes were blank green flame and his teeth were bared in a fierce, inhuman grin.

He's gone fey, just like a hero in an old ballad, he's gone death-mad fey and doesn't care what happens to him. . . .

No, no, that was ridiculous, because being fey meant being doomed, and surely Eliathanis wasn't — none of them were —

The White Elf flattened himself along his horse's neck, hand snaking out to catch Kevin's mount by the bridle. Eliathanis sat back in the saddle, forcing both animals out of their frantic run, turning them in a half circle back towards the fire.

He never had this strength before, never!

And the ill-omened word "fey" returned to the bardling's mind. No! He would not accept that!

Still grinning that strange, fierce, alien grin, Eliathanis released Kevin's mount with a slap on the side of its neck. Both horses raced as one as the enemy gave chase, and ahead of them, Kevin saw Naitachal's lips move in what was surely the beginning of a spell. They were almost out of range of the archers, almost—

Without warning, lightning flashed and thunder rumbled, directly overhead. As Kevin and Eliathanis rejoined the others, the skies at last opened. A heavy curtain of rain plunged down, and the walls of fire hissed under the impact, sending up vast clouds of steam.

"But there's still too much flame!" Lydia cried. "Naitachal, can't you do something?"

The sharpness of her voice made the Dark Elf start. "I was doing something," he said, biting off each word. "Till you broke my concentration." Naitachal glanced back at the dying flames, forward at the charging enemy, and swore in his native tongue. "We need more time — but they're not going to give us any!" Suddenly his dark, sorcerous sword was in his hand. "Terrible odds, my friends, but they're not going to get any better, so . . ."

"Aren't they?"

"What — Eliathanis, no!" Kevin gasped. "Oh no, don't, you can't!"

With a wild shout in the elven tongue, Eliathanis charged the foe. His hair flamed out behind him, blazing gold against the darkness, his mail and outthrust sword and the hide of his rain-slick horse were molten silver.

And time seemed to stop. There was nothing living

save for that one shining rider on a shining horse. So stunned was the enemy that they made no effective move to defend themselves. Eliathanis' sword was a brand, sweeping through their ranks, and wherever it struck, a soldier fell.

"The fire's low enough to cross," Naitachal muttered, hands clenched on the hilt of his sword. "Come back, you idiot. You've bought us enough time. Come back before they realize you're only flesh-and-blood."

As if he'd heard, Eliathanis turned and forced his horse back into a gallop. But the horse was weary from fright and effort. It stumbled on the slick grass, caught itself, stumbled again.

"He's still within bowshot." Naitachal's voice was tight with alarm. "He's not going to make it."

"Yes, he is!" Kevin heard his own voice come out high and shrill, like the voice of a child begging for a happy ending.

"No," the Dark Elf murmured, and then, in wild anguish, "Eliathanis, *no*!"

Even as Naitachal forced his horse forward, Kevin saw an arrow flash, saw Eliathanis fall. Heartsick, he watched the Dark Elf lean low over his horse's neck, urging the animal to greater speed. Naitachal dropped the knotted reins on the horse's neck, then bent out and down, catching the fallen elf and pulling him up across his saddle bow. As Kevin watched, breath caught in his throat, the Dark Elf came thundering back in a storm of arrows. To the bardling's horror, he saw Naitachal suddenly seem to falter in the saddle.

He's been hit, too! Dear Powers —

Almost directly before them, the Dark Elf's horse went down. Naitachal fell free, Eliathanis in his arms.

Lydia was first to reach their side, kneeling in the mud, staring at the White Elf. Kevin heard her sharp inhalation and saw her face pale beneath its tan. "Naitachal, come on. We've got to get out of here."

The Dark Elf glared up at her. "We can't leave Eliathanis!"

"We must."

"No!"

"Naitachal, look at him." Her voice quivered with pity. "Look. More than one arrow caught him. He's dead, Naitachal. Eliathanis is dead. He must have died almost instantly."

The Dark Elf was too well acquainted with death to deny its presence now. "Damn them." It was so low a growl Kevin almost didn't hear it. "Ahh, damn them!"

Very carefully, Naitachal let Eliathanis' body sag to the ground, then looked up. And for once his eyes were the terrible, cruel, empty eyes of a true Dark Elf. "If they want death," he murmured, "then death they shall have."

"Oh, don't!" the bardling cried in sudden panic, terrified that they were about to lose Naitachal forever to Darkness, terrified of what evil he might release.

But the elf was already on his feet, striding boldly forward into the open. Heedless of the arrows raining about him, he called out harsh, ugly, commanding Words, catching the storm winds, twisting them to his use, heightening them, focusing them, turning them to a savage, terrible frenzy. The attacking army was swept back by the whirlwind, horses screaming, men shouting as they were hurled off their feet. And still the wind's fury grew until—

"No! Naitachal, stop it!" Struggling beneath the weight of wind tearing at him, whipping the hair painfully into his face, dragging the very air from his lungs, Kevin fought his way to Naitachal's side. "You've got to stop this!"

The Dark Elf's eyes were blazing with sorcerous Power, totally wild, totally without mercy. He showed not the slightest sign he'd heard Kevin.

"Naitachal, listen to me!" Kevin shouted with all his might to be heard above the roar of the storm. "Those men aren't evil! They don't have any choice in what they're doing! Carlotta enslaved them!"

"They slew my friend." The Dark Elf's voice was inhumanly chill. "I shall slay them."

"And me?" Kevin grabbed Naitachal's arm, only to be flung aside as if he was weightless. Gasping, the bardling forced his way back to face the Dark Elf directly. "Are you going to kill me, too? Are you going to kill Lydia and Tich'ki? You will, if you don't stop this storm. Do you want us to die? Well? D-dammit, answer me! Do you want to kill us?"

A glimmer of life flickered in the terrible eyes. "No," Naitachal said, and all at once his voice was his own again, and infinitely weary. "No. Of course not."

As he removed his will from them, the unnaturally fierce winds faded . . . faded . . . were gone. In the sudden stillness, Naitachal staggered, and Kevin cried out:

"You're hurt!"

"Not badly. Not as badly as . . . as . . . "

"H-he can't be hurt now," Kevin said awkwardly. "But we can." He put a tentative hand on Naitachal's arm and when the Dark Elf didn't push him away, began to pull Naitachal with him. "It's going to take some time for the soldiers to regroup, but we've got to get into the forest's shelter before they do."

"Yes." The Dark Elf's voice was dull with exhaustion. But he stopped by Eliathanis' body. "We cannot leave him here."

Lydia tried to take Naitachal's free arm, only to let go when he hissed with pain. "There's no time to bury him," she said gently. "We don't have a choice."

"Naitachal, come on!" Tich'ki added. "I don't think Carlotta hung around to watch, but she could be anywhere! And her guys are going to come after us. We've got to get out of here!"

"We cannot leave him here! Not like this!"

"But what — "

"Stand back." The Dark Elf's eyes were wild with anguish. "Stand back, I say."

So fierce was that command that Lydia and Kevin hurried aside, and even Tich'ki kept still. Naitachal began his harsh spell once more, but this time the bardling could have sworn some of the Words were different.

He was right. Lightning lanced down out of the stormy sky, enfolding Eliathanis' body in blinding blue-white fire.

Naitachal gave a long, shaken sigh. "I don't know the burial customs of his clan. But surely they would find no shame in a funeral pyre of sky-born flame."

"Surely not," the bardling murmured.

This time when Kevin hesitantly pulled at his arm, the Dark Elf went willingly.

Chapter XXII

This was not, Kevin mused wearily, the type of adventure of which the Bards sang. Oh, Carlotta wasn't making any further move to stop them, at least there was that. For all the bardling knew, she had been blown aside by the whirlwind like her soldiers, or so exhausted by her magics she needed to rest. But that hardly made matters easy. They had only two horses left, tired horses, one of them burdened with both Kevin and Naitachal. And as the animals forced their way into the dense underbrush of the forest, Lydia said suddenly:

"This isn't working. We've got to let the horses go."

"No!" Kevin protested.

"Yes. They can barely keep their feet as it is. And this is pretty dense forest: a horse can't get through without leaving a trail any child could follow. Besides, we can hide better on foot."

"But Naitachal's too tired!"

"I can manage," the Dark Elf muttered, slipping off his mount.

Reluctantly, Kevin followed. Lydia slapped the horses on their rumps, and the animals trotted wearily away. Watching them go, the bardling thought with a flash of wry humor:

It's not fair! Heroes aren't supposed to scuttle through the underbrush!

Yes, and by any rights at all, Naitachal's sorceries should have torn the storm apart, too. Instead, the rain continued to pour unrelentingly down, and the stubbornly stormy sky turned the forest into a nearly night-black maze of roots and thorns, all of which seemed determined to trip up the intruders or tear their flesh.

"I'll scout ahead," Tich'ki said shortly. "I'm not night-blind like you humans."

As she flew, though, she trailed behind her a steady stream of what Kevin assumed could only be curses in her native tongue: even though the thick curtain of leaves cut off the worst of the rain, her wings were plainly still sodden enough to hamper her flying.

"Come on," she shot back. "No laggards."

"*Such* a caring, gentle friend," Lydia muttered.

She and Kevin followed after as best they could. Naitachal, dazed and exhausted, somehow managed to keep pace with them.

But if we don't find shelter soon, Kevin realized, *he's going to collapse — and us with him.*

But just when the bardling had decided they must have died and been condemned to an eternity of dark and wet and endless, thorny paths, Tich'ki came fluttering back. She landed on Lydia's shoulder, panting, wings drooping wearily. But Kevin saw her sharp little teeth flash in a grin.

"Shelter!" she crowed. "Just up ahead: a big old shell of a tree. Hurry up, you'll see."

She was right. The oak must have been truly ancient, incredibly vast in girth and all but dead. Time and age had worn a deep hollow in the base, a natural cave just big enough for two humans, one elf and a fairy to fit inside. It smelled strongly of animals and decaying wood, but it was blessedly dry and carpeted with a thick layer of crumbled leaves. Kevin, sure he was soaked to the very bone, couldn't make up his mind whether to remove his cloak and freeze or keep the soggy thing wrapped about him and stay wet. Hopefully, he thought, the combined body warmth of four living beings would warm the tree-cave soon enough.

"Naitachal—"

The Dark Elf had fallen to his knees with a faint groan. Lydia hastily dropped to his side. "All right, I know you're hurt. Let me see that arm."

"In here?" Tich'ki cut in. "Thought you humans couldn't see in the dark." She added in sudden alarm, "You're not going to try lighting a fire?"

"In a tree? D'you think I'm mad?"

"I—No. That's too easy a jest."

Kevin bit his lip nervously, just barely able to make out Naitachal's crumpled form in the darkness. "I'll try the Watchwood Melody again," he said in sudden inspiration. "You know, the light-spell. I . . . think I can get it to last longer this time."

There wasn't much room to take the lute out of its case, let alone play it, but by squirming his way back into the tree-cave, Kevin managed to hit the proper notes and chords. He began to sing, hesitantly at first, his singing voice feeling rusty from disuse, then more strongly, secure that the storm outside would drown out the sound and praying that his small magics wouldn't be noticeable to Carlotta.

And Bardic Magic stirred within him. The tree-cave began to glow with a faint, steady light, and Lydia nodded in satisfaction.

"Now," she told Naitachal, "you *will* let me see that arm."

The Dark Elf, eyes closed, made no move to stop her. Kevin winced at the sight of the long slash running halfway down Naitachal's upper arm, but Lydia didn't seem particularly worried.

"Arrow just grazed you. That arm's going to be sore for a time, but hopefully that'll be about the worst of it." She paused. "You aren't hiding any other wounds, are you?"

"No." It was a weary whisper of sound. "My cloak took most of the damage."

"Ah, so it did. Look at those holes." The woman held up a fold of black fabric and gave a soft whistle. "You were lucky, my friend."

Naitachal winced. "Another was not," he murmured faintly.

"Ah. Well. I — uh — don't think Eliathanis would begrudge us a chance to take care of the living before the — before we — "

"Before we mourn the dead. Lydia, do what you think necessary to this slash, then let me rest."

She blinked at his suddenly cold tone. "Sure." The woman hunted through the pouches hanging from her belt for a time. "Oh *damn*. My healing herbs are all back in the castle. Some oh so helpful lady's maid must have tried to 'neaten up' my stuff when I wasn't watching." Lydia paused, holding up a small flask. "I do still have this, though."

"Water?" Tich'ki piped up. "Should think you'd had enough of water by now."

"It's not water, believe me."

"Ah, the brandy! How'd the maid miss that?"

"I don't know, but it's a good thing she did. Naitachal, you want to take a good swig of this, then bite down on something. This is going to hurt like hell, but at least it should ward off wound-sickness."

Kevin winced in sympathy, nearly losing his hold on the light-spell, as she poured the brandy on the arrow-gash.

Naitachal never made a sound. Instead, endurance finally exhausted, he simply fainted.

"There, now," Lydia said after a moment. "That's bandaged as best I can manage, what with nothing really dry. You can stop singing now, Kevin."

The light was already fading, because the bardling's voice was quavering so much he could barely hold the tune. He broke off abruptly, and the tree-cave was plunged back into darkness.

"Kevin? What is it, boy? What's wrong?"

"I d-don't . . . I . . . Eliathanis . . ."

"Oh hell, kid, don't be embarrassed. Nothing wrong with grieving, be you woman or man."

But Kevin battled with himself till he'd fought back the tears. "I — I don't understand him!"

"Who? Naitachal?"

"How can he suddenly turn so . . . cold? Eliathanis was his friend! Why isn't he grieving?"

"Ach, Kevin." Lydia's voice was very gentle. "He is. That coldness was to hide his real feelings. Look you, I've seen a lot of people die. Too many," she added softly. "That's part of being a warrior. I've mourned a lot of them, too, and that's also part of being a warrior. True grief isn't something you can command. It comes out when and where it will."

All at once Lydia gave a long, tired sigh. "You know something? I enjoy travelling and all that but, times like this, I really wish I had a place to come home to."

She stopped for a thoughtful moment, then added with an embarrassed little laugh, "Like that castle we just left. If it wasn't already inhabited by that bitch-witch and her buddy, it might make a good place to settle. Despite all the hassle, the place itself had a nice *homey* feel to it. Or do you think that's too crazy?"

"Not at all." Kevin straightened, staring in her direction in the darkness. "There were times in that castle when I was really miserable; I admit it. But underneath it all, even with those two running things and those spoiled brats of squires, there really *is* something there that could make it a good place to live!"

Working by touch, he fit the lute back into its case. "Ah well. Let's not dream about catching the moon, as Master Aidan would say."

Lydia chuckled softly. "Oh, I don't know about that. Dreams aren't such a bad thing to have. And sometimes — who knows? Sometimes you *do* catch that moon." Kevin heard the dried leaves rustle as she stirred. "Come on, kid, enough talk. I have a suspicion we're going to be leading an active life in the next few days, so let's try to get some sleep while we can. If we huddle together with Naitachal, we should be warm enough. Hungry, bruised and battered," Lydia added wryly, "but warm enough."

"Kevin!"

The fierce hiss brought the bardling awake with a start. "Naitachal?" The tree-cave wasn't as totally dark as it had been, but even so, the Dark Elf's eyes still glinted with their eerie red light. "What — " Kevin sat bolt upright. "Carlotta! Has she — "

"She hasn't found us. Not yet. But I felt her sorcery brush us just now. And she has set loose her hunters."

"Not human hunters," Tich'ki added, perching beside Kevin for a moment, "not all of them. I sensed that, too."

"And I don't think we care to meet any of them," the Dark Elf added wryly, "so come! We must hurry."

At least it had stopped raining; they were given that much of a boon. But the day was a waking nightmare of being forever on the run, slipping on mud and wet leaves, struggling through underbrush so dense it seemed impassible, with hardly a chance to snatch a sip from a stream, hardly a chance to swallow a handful of berries. Lydia, experienced hunter that she was, led the way, showing them how to throw off anything that might be following by scent by crossing and recrossing streams, how to avoid leaving footprints by running along rock or fallen trees.

"Ha, why didn't I think of this before?" Tich'ki suddenly exclaimed during one of their brief pauses to rest. "I can help! I'll hide our trail altogether!"

"Not by magic," Naitachal warned sharply, gashed arm cradled against his chest. "Carlotta will surely sense the use of any spells."

"No, no, you don't understand! You know the trick I have of influencing minds? The way I did with the guards back in Westerin? Well, that's not magic, strictly speaking, not really; it's a — a skill of the mind, sort of an unmagic to make people unthink." She shook her head impatiently. "I can't put it more clearly in human terms. But I should be able to make the trackers unthink the trail — and there won't be a trace of magic for Carlotta to find!"

"Carlotta," Lydia reminded her dourly, "is part fairy. I'm not taking bets on anything she can or can't do. Go ahead, Tich'ki. Try your unthinking unmagic. The rest of us are going to keep right on watching our steps."

Tich'ki grinned and darted off.

"Eh, all right, Kevin, Naitachal," Lydia snapped, getting to her feet. "Rest time's over. We have some more hiking to do!"

By the time darkness began to fall, Kevin was only too glad to sink to the ground in the rocky little grove Lydia had found. Beside him, Naitachal sat in weary silence, shrouded in his cloak, but the woman paced restlessly about, checking the lay of the land in her usual wary fashion.

"We're not likely to find a better place." The Dark Elf's voice rose eerily out of the shadow of his hood.

"No," she agreed, hands on hips. "It's a pretty good spot for camping. Easily defended, too, what with the rocks making a natural wall on one side."

"And there is a stream nearby," Naitachal added. "Possibly with edible water plants."

Kevin hadn't thought anything could have gotten him to his feet, but the thought of something to eat made him scramble up. "I'll go."

"No, kid. You wouldn't know what's safe to eat. *I'll* go." She glanced around at the ever-darkening forest. "You think you can manage some sort of smokeless little fire, Naitachal?"

"Of course."

When Lydia returned with double armfuls of vegetation, it was to a rabbit cooking over the barely visible campfire the Dark Elf had concocted. "Where did *that* come from?" the woman asked.

"It popped its head up to look at us," Kevin said. He added modestly, "I threw a rock at it. I was lucky."

"So-o!" Lydia's teeth flashed in her indomitable grin. "Tonight, we feast!"

A whir of wings marked Tich'ki's return. "Just in time! I'm starved."

But it was a strangely somber meal. Now that he had a moment to relax even a little, Kevin found himself constantly expecting to see Eliathanis. He caught himself thinking, *We must remember to tell him about* — or *I wonder what he would think about* — and had to force himself not to keep looking over his shoulder for the White Elf.

At last, after their scanty dinner was done and the fire had been banked to coals, the bardling couldn't stand it any more. Hardly aware of the others, he took out his lute and let his fingers move across the strings. At the back of his mind Kevin was vaguely aware that he wasn't trying for Bardic Music: he wasn't even trying for any music worthy of a Bard at all. But somehow music took form beneath his fingers and *here* was Eliathanis stopping in surprise, the sun turning his hair to molten gold, and *here* was Eliathanis bending in worry over the fallen Naitachal, and *here* was Eliathanis grinning at the Dark Elf in sudden friendship . . .

And *here* was Eliathanis freely, joyously, giving his life so his friends might live.

All at once Kevin's vision was blurring and his hands were shaking so much he couldn't play any more. Face wet, he stilled the strings to silence with a palm, then took a deep, shaken breath and dried his eyes, drained and a little awed by what his mind and hands had evoked.

He glanced up, aware of the others only now, and slightly embarrassed at their regard. Lydia, too, was wiping her eyes, and even Tich'ki was sitting still, wings wrapped about her like an irridescent cape. Naitachal had his back to them all, huddled nearly double in his black cloak, so silent that the bardling wondered if he had even heard the music. But then Kevin heard the Dark Elf murmur fiercely, as though angry with himself:

"There is no time for this!"

"There never is," Lydia retorted.

The shrouded figure straightened slightly at that, and Kevin caught a flash of anguished eyes. But instead of the sharp reply the bardling was expecting, Naitachal asked simply, "Does it always hurt like this?"

"Always." Lydia paused, frowning slightly. "What, have you never lost a friend before?"

Naitachal glared. "Have you forgotten who and what I am? I have never *had* a friend before."

"You have some now," Kevin reminded him softly.

But the Dark Elf, plainly embarrassed by his own grief, pulled his hood savagely forward, hiding his face once more. "I intend to sleep," Naitachal said shortly. "I advise you to do the same."

Kevin and Lydia exchanged wry glances. The woman shrugged. "He's got a point." She hesitated for a long, awkward while, then added quietly, "Kevin, for the music and all that, I . . . Ah, hell. What I'm trying to say is, thank you."

The huddle of black cloak stirred faintly. "So am I," Naitachal admitted softly, then was silent once more.

Chapter XXIII

Night passed into day, and day into night, and the fugitives continued to flee through the forest. Tich'ki's "unmagic" did seem to be throwing off Carlotta's aim when it came to any direct sorcery, but her trackers remained grimly on the trail. Once Kevin, hiding flat in the underbrush, not even daring to breathe, caught a glimpse of them: squat, powerful, sharp-fanged beings, monstrous human-ogre hybrids that sniffed the ground like so many deadly hounds. If he fell into their ugly hands, the bardling was pretty sure he wouldn't have to worry about Carlotta any longer.

That time, the trackers missed their prey completely. But no place was safe for long. Kevin thanked the Powers for Tich'ki, who confused those trackers as best one fairy could, and for Lydia, who somehow kept moving her friends from concealment to concealment without their getting caught, skillfully doubling back and forth on their tracks like some hunted wild thing.

Which she is, Kevin thought wearily. *Which we all are. I can't remember the last time I had a good meal, or a full night's sleep. Ha, and if I don't get a bath pretty soon, those trackers are going to be able to just nose me out!*

What was truly frustrating was knowing he bore the manuscript holding the spell to destroy Carlotta—and yet not being able to do anything about it. When they came to a temporary hiding place, a crushed-down thicket that deer had used for a bed, Kevin pulled the manuscript out in desperation and showed it to Naitachal.

"What do you make of that?"

The Dark Elf had grown almost haggard during the chase, skin drawn tightly over the high cheekbones and eyes glittering eerily from under the shadow of his hood. "Let me see."

He barely moved the arm the arrow had grazed, and Kevin felt a little pang of worry shoot through him. "Naitachal . . ."

"It's nothing," the Dark Elf insisted, as he had every time one of the others had tried to examine the wound. "Give me the manuscript."

He studied it for a long, puzzled moment, then raised his head, frowning.

"I can't make anything of the text, Kevin. And I mean that quite literally. There's magic here, all right, but it's keyed strictly to you. The glyphs won't hold still long enough for me to read them. Only if you can copy the spell out for me can I hope to do something with it." The Dark Elf's eyes glittered with a sudden cold rage. "And once the spell is deciphered, I shall be the one to deliver it." His words were made all the more chilling by being delivered in a quiet, totally controlled voice. "We owe Eliathanis this much: his death shall be avenged in full upon Carlotta and the traitor count her ally."

"Uh, y-yes. It shall."

Kevin was almost positive that the weird, unexpected words in elfish had to be the components of the spell. He could copy those out, all right. But on what? And with what?

Wait . . . when I was making the copy back in the library, I tucked the parchment into my lute case for safekeeping.

Ha, yes, it was still there, in the pocket meant for music scores, and with it a small flask of ink as well. A twig should make a decent enough brush.

And so, every time Lydia deemed it safe to stop, Kevin worked feverishly to extract the spell from the manuscript, making as many copies as he could, hiding one each time the party had to move on.

The trackers can't possibly discover all our shelters. And hopefully someone will find the spell and be able to complete it if we're caught or — or killed.

But what a weird spell it seemed to be! Kevin, curious, showed Naitachal one elfish glyph, and wasn't really surprised when the Dark Elf shook his head.

"It looks something like elfish, yes, but you must have made some mistake. That odd notation just to the left of the glyph doesn't belong to any dialect of elfish I know!"

"That's just the way it's written in the manuscript!" Kevin protested. "See — Ah, never mind, I forgot I'm the only one who can see it."

Just what he needed: another worry, this one that somehow he was copying the whole thing wrong, making the spell useless! But there wasn't anything to do but continue.

And at last, at their next brief sanctuary, Kevin breathed a great sigh of relief. "It's done. I've got the whole spell copied out. Naitachal, now you can — Naitachal?"

The Dark Elf was sagging against a tree, as though all at once too weak to move. "It's nothing . . . a moment's dizziness."

"Nothing, hell!" Lydia erupted. "It's that arm of yours, isn't it?"

She made a move towards it, but Naitachal waved her away. "We don't have the time for this." He stepped away from the tree, now quite steady on his feet. "Let me see the spell." Taking the scrap of parchment from the bardling, he added, "Once I have it memorized — "

The Dark Elf stopped dead. "What in the name of all the Powers *is* this thing? This matches no spell I've ever seen! All these weird notations . . . "

Kevin straightened so suddenly he nearly rapped his head on a low branch. "Notations," he echoed. "Regular notations in front of every word . . . what if . . . ?" Suddenly wild with suspense, the bardling cried, "Let me see that again! Yes . . . yes . . . Dear Powers, *yes*! I never stopped to really think about what I was copying but: do you know what these notations are? They're *music notes*! This isn't elfish at all. No, no, it's Bardic Magic, and this spell is meant to be *sung*!"

Naitachal's eyes flashed with excitement. "Of course it is! I should have realized — But it's also untried. You realize what that means, don't you?"

"That it's dangerous . . . ?"

"Oh, indeed. You will have to get very close to Carlotta to even try it. And then, if it backlashes, as some spells do, it could kill you. If it doesn't work at all, Carlotta certainly will kill you!"

After all that had happened so far, Kevin knew he no longer thought of himself as a hero, not even as being very brave. But bravery had very little to do with this. Carlotta had killed a friend, and would surely kill many, many more people if she made her bid for power.

"I'll deliver the spell," the bardling said quietly, "no matter what it costs."

"Sure, but how?" Lydia asked. "We're stuck here in the forest, and even though we haven't seen a trace of those damned persistent trackers — "

"We've shaken them," Tich'ki interrupted.

"You think. I'm pretty sure they're still after us."

"And we cannot risk letting ourselves be captured." Naitachal's voice was all at once so thick with strain that Kevin stared at him in alarm.

"Are you — "

"Yes, yes," the Dark Elf said impatiently. "I'm fine. As fine as one can be without enough to eat or enough time to rest." Naitachal made what was obviously a mighty effort to rouse himself. "If we are taken, there is a good chance none of us will live long enough to even see Carlotta."

"True." Lydia shrugged. "What will be, as the saying goes, will be. It looks like the only thing we can do is just go on, and hope we meet up with someone along the way who can help us."

"Time for scouting duty!" Tich'ki said wryly, and darted ahead.

As Kevin and Lydia followed on foot, Lydia whispered in the bardling's ear, "I don't like the looks of Naitachal. If he isn't ill, I'll trade my sword for a loom."

"I know," Kevin murmured. "Even his eyes look funny."

"Yeah. Fever-glazed."

"Lydia! We've got to do something!"

"Got any suggestions? He denies there's anything wrong, and he won't even let me look at his arm." The woman gave a wry little shrug. "It's that damned sorcerer's pride."

And as the day progressed, it was surely only a sorcerer's will that kept Naitachal going. But all at once a fallen branch twisted under the Dark Elf's foot. As he struggled to catch his balance, his wounded arm struck against a tree trunk. With a choked cry, the Dark Elf collapsed to one knee.

"Oh hell." Lydia tore at the makeshift bandage even as Naitachal weakly tried to fend her off. "Stop fighting me! You're burning up with fever and — Oh hell," she repeated helplessly, staring.

Naitachal's dark skin hid any sign of inflammation, but the swelling around the still raw-looking gash was obvious even to the untrained Kevin.

"Wound-fever," Lydia murmured. "Why didn't you say something?"

"What could I say? What could you do?"

"I could have done *something*! I knew the brandy wasn't enough. Why didn't I — "

"No. This is not your fault, Lydia." Naitachal sighed.

"My people have somewhat more immunity to iron-wounds than do the White Elves, possibly from living as close as we do to the inner Earth Dark. But such things are still perilous to us."

"You still should have said — "

"No." Naitachal struggled to his feet. "To stop is to die, as simply as that. Come. I will keep up."

"I doubt it," Lydia muttered under her breath. "There's a limit even to a sorcerer's will."

"I will keep up," the Dark Elf repeated flatly.

Just then, Tich'ki came whirring back. "Strangers! A whole troop of people and wagons up ahead!"

"Wagons!" Lydia shook her head, puzzled. "Can't be soldiers or those cursed trackers. Tich'ki — "

"I know. Find out more about them. I'm gone."

She was back within a short time. "Forget any help from *them*. They're nothing but some travelling minstrels."

"Bah." Lydia turned away in disgust. "They're useless."

But Kevin, moved by a sudden wild hope, told Tich'ki, "Go on. What else can you tell us about them?"

The fairy shrugged in mid-air. "What can I say? They're a colorful lot, and their leader's a sharp-faced fellow with bright green eyes."

Kevin started. It couldn't be, could it . . . ? "D-did you happen to catch his name?"

"Ber-something, I think."

"Berak?"

"That's it!" The fairy stared at him. "You know him?"

"In a way." Stumbling over his words in sudden eagerness, Kevin stammered, "L-listen, everyone: Berak and his troupe is — are — friends of Master Aidan. We can hide with them for a while!"

"Look," Lydia said shortly, "we've been lied to and tricked along every step of this little adventure of ours. Do you really think we can trust them?"

"We can! I can be fooled, even you can be fooled —

but my Master's a full Bard. No one's going to fool *him.* Come on! Maybe we can actually beg a hot meal out of Berak. And he and the troupe might even have some valuable news to share!"

Lydia shrugged. "On your head be it, kid!"

For one brief, startling moment, Kevin could have sworn no time at all had passed since he'd first left Bracklin. There were the same gaudy red and blue wagons, the same cluster of brightly dressed men, women and children gathered around a communal campfire, and the bardling was overwhelmed by such a sudden surge of homesickness he nearly staggered. There was Berak, exuberant and arrogant as ever, pacing restlessly back and forth, as though he bore too much pent-up energy to be still.

He stopped short, staring at Kevin. "Ha! So *there* you are!"

"You . . . were expecting me?"

"Oh, eventually! At least I was hoping you'd show up! You've been stirring up enough excitement in recent days for a dozen bardlings." The sharp green eyes noted Naitachal — completely hidden in his by now tattered black cloak — and came to rest on Lydia. Berak swept down in a theatrical bow. "I had no idea you were travelling in the company of such a lovely lady."

"Ha," Lydia said, but to Kevin's astonishment, she reddened slightly anyhow.

"Ah, but from the looks of the lot of you," Berak continued without missing a beat, "you could use a good meal. Come, join us."

But Naitachal never moved. "Kevin," he said faintly, "Remember when I boasted I could keep up? I can't. In fact," the Dark Elf added, swaying slightly, "if I don't sit down, right now, I think I may do something foolish. Like faint."

Kevin and Lydia caught him just in time. In the next moment, they were surrounded by the minstrel troupe, helping hands reaching out. Berak wormed his way through the crowd and slipped a supporting arm around the Dark Elf.

"Back off!" he shouted to the others. "Give the man room to breathe! You and you, drag that bench over here. Someone go get Seritha. And you . . . "

Berak's voice faltered for an instant as Naitachal's hood slipped back, revealing his unmistakably Dark Elf features. But then the minstrel shrugged and shouted, "Seritha! Seritha, hurry!" He added to Naitachal, helping him to the bench, "She's our Healer. Have you up and well in no time."

To Kevin's surprise, Seritha turned out to be the plump, motherly woman he'd first seen in buttercup yellow: hardly the sort, he thought, to harbor any sort of Power. But she laid bare the arrow gash with quiet skill. And as soon as she placed her hands on the wound, Kevin saw Power well up about her, encircle her in a pale blue cloud, brightening to dazzling blue-white where her hands touched Naitachal's arm. The bardling thought he saw unhealthy flesh slough away under that touch, and felt his too-empty stomach lurch in protest. He hastily turned away, but after a time sheer curiosity made him look once more.

Seritha, looking worn but satisfied, was straightening. Naitachal, eyes wild with relief, was getting to his feet — and not a mark marred the smooth skin of his arm. At Seritha's wave, a little boy brought them flagons of something that smelled sharply herbal and was presumably strength-restoring. Both Healer and Dark Elf drank thirstily then smiled at each other. Naitachal bowed.

"I am forever in your debt, lady."

She beamed. "I'm hardly a lady. And I only did what any Healer should do." Seritha made a shooing gesture with both hands. "Off with you now. Go reassure your friends."

Naitachal grinned. "I hear and obey!"

As the Dark Elf approached, Kevin asked breathlessly, "How — how do you feel?"

"Healed. Absolutely, totally healed."

"Now that's truly amazing," Lydia said. "I never thought an ordinary human could wield that type of Power."

"No," the Dark Elf murmured thoughtfully, "neither did I." His glance locked with that of Berak. But then Naitachal shrugged. "So be it," he said, so meaningfully Kevin could have sworn he'd meant to say, I'll keep your secret.

What secret? What was going on between those two?

But then the wonderful aroma of roasting meat hit his nostrils, and Kevin forgot all about secrets for the moment.

"Don't gobble," Lydia warned him. "Your stomach's shrunk. You'll make yourself ill."

Oh, but it was a struggle not to wolf down the meat and bread and cheese, the wine and sweetmeats. At last, feeling alive again for the first time in he didn't know how many days, Kevin sat back with a contented sigh.

"My friends," he told the minstrels, "we can't possibly repay this."

They laughed. "No need! No need!"

"But," the bardling added, as casually as he could, "we . . . ah . . . separated a good many days ago."

"Separated!" someone teased. "You ran off, is what happened!"

"Uh, well, yes," Kevin admitted reluctantly, aware of Lydia's amused glance. "But now, what have you been doing since then? Have any news?"

Berak shrugged. "Old news by now. Count Volmar is going to be hosting a major fair at his castle shortly."

"And we're to perform at it," a boy piped up. "Before the count himself!"

Berak grinned. "That's right, Riki. Before the count himself." His grin faded slightly as he turned back to Kevin. "You know, there are odd rumors these days. Rumors that Count Volmar is going to make some sort of major announcement. You know anything about that?"

"N-no. Not really."

"Indeed. Well, rumor or no, the truth is that certainly every liegeman and ally the count has is streaming in for the grand event. Whatever it may be."

Kevin met Berak's inquisitive stare as innocently as he could. Forcing a grin, the bardling said, "Well, it's been a long day. If you don't mind, we'll spend the night here with your people."

Berak was plainly disappointed not to have learned any deep secrets from his guests, but he bowed from the waist. "Our camp is, of course, your camp. Make yourselves at home."

As soon as they were alone in the shelter of a wagon, Tich'ki popped out of hiding. "You *could* have slipped me more food!" she complained to Lydia.

"And have everyone wonder why I was feeding my hair?"

Naitachal ignored them. "What of Berak's news? That sounded truly ominous to me."

"Me, too," Kevin agreed. "This isn't just some little tourney the count decided to throw, not if he's calling in all his allies to hear some grand declaration."

"Exactly." The Dark Elf frowned. "It just might be that Volmar is gambling on Carlotta's behalf, staking all, as the saying goes, on one throw of the dice."

"If that's true," Lydia mused, "then losing one little bardling — sorry, Kevin — and one spell isn't going to stop them. They must have had this plan in motion for months."

"Sure," the bardling added, "and I'm one very small

fly in the ointment. One they think they can afford to remove at their leisure." He fought down the surge of indignant pride: he *was* small and insignificant — so far. "This could be just the chance we need to deliver the spell."

"If we can take these folk into our confidence," Naitachal said.

"If we dare," Lydia muttered.

"If we can," Kevin added quietly, "in good conscience expose them to our own danger."

"Ah. Well. There is that."

The bardling glanced at the others. "I think the best thing is for you to split up and go into hiding, first off."

"That's ridiculous," Lydia said. "We're not going to —"

"Please, let me finish. There's no point in you going into danger because — well, even if this spell works, even if Carlotta is disabled, Count Volmar won't be. And anyone who's with me is going to be in big trouble."

"For a change," Lydia said drily.

"You'll be in that trouble, too," Naitachal reminded the bardling. "I've already . . . lost . . . one friend. I don't want to lose another."

"I don't want to be lost, either! But . . . " Kevin shook his head. "To put it bluntly, I'm going to be worried enough as it is. I don't want to have to worry about anyone else. Particularly not those I care about. Or those who've helped us, either."

"The minstrels."

"Exactly. I'd like to travel to the castle with them; it does seem to be the obvious way back in. But I really want to keep their involvement in all this to an absolute minimum." Kevin gave a shaky sigh. "There's not enough time for anything other than what I think knights call desperation moves. There won't be any heroes coming out of this."

"Sounds like you've gained some sense at least," said a sardonic voice. "Maybe even enough to keep you from being killed."

Kevin nearly sprained his neck twisting about in shock. That voice . . . It was only Berak who stood there, and yet . . .

"Don't you think the masquerade has gone far enough?" Naitachal asked the minstrel.

Berak grinned. "You knew what I was right away, didn't you?"

The Dark Elf grinned in return. "Even as you recognized me."

Lydia looked from one to the other. "What *are* you talking about?"

"Just this." Berak murmured a quiet Word. And . . . it wasn't so much that his face and form changed as it was that a masking glamor seemed to fall away. Kevin stared. How could he ever have missed how high those cheekbones were, how sharply slanted those eyes? And that hair was surely far too silky to be human hair—

"You're an elf!" Kevin gasped in alarm. "You're all elves!"

Chapter XXIV

Berak chuckled. "We're all elves," he agreed, "all my troupe." The minstrel gestured to where they, laughing, had also shed their glamor of humanity.

Tich'ki wriggled out of hiding. "So *that's* it!" she exclaimed. "*Clever* disguises! So obvious, right under the humans' noses and not one of them ever noticed!"

Berak's eyes widened ever so slightly at the fairy's sudden appearance, but all he did was dip his head in polite acknowledgement and say smoothly, "Humans do tend to see what they expect to see."

Lydia snorted. "No wonder Seritha's Power was so much more than anything a human could master!"

"Exactly."

But Kevin was still staring. "I know you! You're the group who surrounded me in the forest that night! Yes, and scared the life out of me, too!"

"We were trying to scare the life *into* you, youngling," Berak corrected drily. "You were much too cocky then for your own survival."

"I don't understand something," Naitachal cut in. "You are very obviously White Elves, all of you, and yet you never hesitated to help an enemy."

"A Dark Elf, you mean?" Berak raised a brow. "And *are* you our enemy?"

"No, of course not. But — " Naitachal gave a small sigh of confusion. "I really don't understand. What clan are you? What clan can you possibly be that you don't share the usual prejudice against my kind?"

"No clan at all, or one of our own imagining."

"And what does that mean?"

Berak smiled. "Simply that we are the bits and tatters of many clans, the outcasts, the ones who couldn't fit in with all the staid and somber old traditions. We like to laugh, to rove, to sing and play our songs for others, elf or human, and share our joy with them. It amuses us, just as it amuses us to disguise ourselves as humans."

"My Master knew, though, didn't he?" Kevin asked. "What and who you really are, I mean."

"Of course." The green eyes narrowed slightly. "And it's past time you started thinking about that Master. We've been trying all this time to track you down!" He shook his head. "We woke, and you were gone. We reached Count Volmar's castle, and you were gone from there, too. We went back to Bracklin, only to learn you had never returned. Master Aidan has been frantic with worry. Why, he even considered going after you and the spell himself, despite his too-sudden age and ill health."

Ill health? Master Aidan? It was the first Kevin had heard of that. And yet . . . with a sudden surge of guilt he remembered all the times he'd thought the old Bard lazy or afraid, remembered how he'd seen his Master's pallor and shrugged it off as the result of too much of an indoor life. The signs of carefully concealed illness had been there all along. He'd simply failed, in his impatience and arrogance, to notice them.

Wait, now, what else had Berak said? "Too-sudden age?" the bardling asked hesitantly. "I don't—"

"Think, boy!" Berak snapped. "Aidan was a youngling when he rescued the king, not all that much older than you. Only some thirty years have passed. Even for you short-lived humans that's not such a vast span."

"But—but he's old!" Kevin insisted. "He's been old ever since I've known him!"

"Ai-yi, Kevin! Who do you think created that spell to destroy Carlotta? Bardic Magic is a Powerful, perilous thing: it created the spell, yes, but in the process Aidan was forced to tie up his age and health within the thing until he no longer had the strength to do anything about it."

"Then speaking the spell—"

"May restore him." Berak shrugged with true elven fatalism. "Or it may not. But either way, you must make his sacrifice worth it."

"I will," Kevin said softly. *And I'll make it up to you, Master Aidan.* "But there's something I must do, here and now. Take these, please." He gave Berak all but one of the remaining copies he'd made of the spell. "At least this way it won't be lost with me."

"What . . . *is* this thing?" Berak peered at the parchment. "Elfish, yet not quite elfish. . . . "

"It is, we pray, the spell that shall put an end to Carlotta," Naitachal said. "Berak, if you will permit it, we will ride with you. And together you and I and Kevin can set about deciphering the thing."

"Why?" the minstrel asked suspiciously. "Why Kevin?"

The bardling sighed. "Because the spell's Bardic Magic. But I can't read elfish. And unless you and Naitachal can tell me how to pronounce the glyphs properly, I'll never be able to sing them."

"You!" Berak glanced sharply from Kevin to Naitachal, then began speaking very rapidly in the elven tongue.

Naitachal held up a hand. "Kevin and I have gone over all the dangers. I agree, it's an incredibly risky thing for him to try. But neither you nor I are qualified to handle Bardic Magic. Kevin is."

"But he's *not* a Bard! The boy is just a bardling!"

"Still, I'm as close to a Bard as we're going to find in such a short time. And we've wasted enough of that time already. Will you help us, Berak?"

"So-o! The cub grows fangs! Yes, youngling, I will help you. And pray for you as well," he added wryly.

* * *

It wasn't an easy decipherment. As the wagons rolled and rattled their way toward Count Volmar's castle, the two elves spent much of the next day bent over the parchment, arguing "It says *leatal*" or "No, no, that has to read *sentaila*, not *sentailach*!"

When they were satisfied with each glyph, they made Kevin recite it till they were sure he had the intonation correct, then sing it to the corresponding note.

"When do I get to put the whole thing together?"

"You don't!" Naitachal said in alarm. "Do you want to trigger the spell here and now?"

"Uh . . . no. But if I can't rehearse the spell now, how am I going to know I've got it right?"

The Dark Elf grinned without humor. "Therein," he said drily, "lies the adventure."

"But I think you do have the component glyphs properly memorized," Berak added in what was presumably meant to be a comforting tone. "Naitachal, there is one unwoven thread to all this that bothers me."

"Eh?"

"You say Carlotta is disguising herself as the count's niece. Well then, what happened to the real Charina? There *was* one, after all . . . "

The Dark Elf shuddered as though a sudden cold draft had hit him. "I think I know what happened," he said at last. "I . . . just could not bear to . . . " Naitachal turned sharply away. "I was afraid to cast this spell. Afraid that I might find myself instead tempted to drag Eliathanis back from — I didn't dare, do you understand?"

"I do," Kevin murmured. "But Naitachal, what are you saying? That —that the real Charina is . . . that Carlotta . . . that Charina . . . Powers, what if her spirit's enslaved?"

"I thought of that." The Dark Elf slumped in

resignation. "So be it. I will do what I must. Berak, I will need a clear, sheltered place this evening, and as few distractions as possible."

The White Elf nodded. "You shall have that."

The night there in the forest grove was very dark, the only light coming from the single small campfire built between the vee formed by the two wagons. The troupe was hidden in those wagons, or out in the forest, but when Kevin and Lydia would have gone with them, Naitachal called out:

"Wait. You, as well, Berak. Say nothing, do nothing, only sit where you are until I signal you to leave. I will need your presences as an anchor."

An anchor to what? To life? Kevin felt a cold chill steal through him. What if Naitachal was dragged over the border into death? How could they possibly pull him back?

But the Dark Elf didn't seem particularly worried, though his face, picked out in stark relief by the dancing flames, was grim and his stance tense. Without warning, he began a chant, so softly Kevin almost couldn't hear him. Berak heard, though; the bardling could feel him shudder.

Somehow, soft though the words were, they weren't quite obeying natural law. They weren't fading. Instead, like so many layers of woven cloth, each new phrase fell atop the one before it, never fading, slowly filling up the night, slowly filling up the very air, calling, demanding, summoning . . .

And suddenly they were no longer alone in the clearing. Kevin was only dimly aware of Lydia's gasp, only dimly heard his own sharply drawn in breath. Lost in a mix of amazement and terror, he stared till his eyes ached at a pale glow all at once there above the fire, slowly condensing into the figure of a girl . . .

Charina's ghost . . .

She wasn't as extravagantly lovely as her counterfeit. Her hair was pale yellow, not spun gold, her face merely pretty rather than beautiful. And yet she was so much the more charming for not being perfect that Kevin felt his heart ache as though it would break, felt his cheeks suddenly wet with the loss of What Might Have Been.

"Who are you?" Naitachal said in the human tongue, his voice the essence of gentleness.

"I . . . was . . . I am . . . " The ghostly blue eyes widened in fright. "I don't remember . . . Why am I here? Where am I?"

"You must remember. Who are you?"

"I . . . I . . . can't . . . "

"You must. Who are you?"

"I can't!"

Kevin ached to shout out, "Leave her alone! Can't you see she really doesn't know?" But somehow he managed to keep from making a sound, and Naitachal continued relentlessly:

"Who are you?"

"Charina!" the ghost screamed all at once. "I am Charina!"

The Dark Elf's head drooped, and Kevin could hear him gasp for breath. After a moment, Naitachal continued, his voice gentle once more:

"Where are you, Charina?"

"I . . . don't know . . . It's so dark . . . dark and cold . . . so cold . . . I don't want to know!"

"Never mind," the Dark Elf crooned. "Go back. Back. See the day as it was. The day before the darkness. Do you see it?"

Her frightened face seemed to lighten. "Yes."

"Where are you, Charina?"

"The castle. My uncle's castle. I am up on the ramparts and — oh, look at the pretty thing!"

"What are you doing, Charina?"

"Leaning forward to see the — No! No! Please, don't! *No!*"

The sheer terror of that scream cut Kevin to the heart. *Oh, Naitachal,* don't! *Let her be!*

But the Dark Elf continued softly, "Who is it, Charina? What is he doing?"

"Uncle! Uncle, please! I won't tell anyone! You don't have to kill me!"

"Who killed you, Charina?"

"No, no, there's been a mistake, it's all a mistake, I'm alive and — "

"Who killed you, Charina?"

"I — My uncle killed me! He pushed me from the ramparts when none could see! He murdered me and threw my body down a refuse shaft!"

She burst into an anguished keening, rocking back and forth in mid-air. Without taking his glance from her, Naitachal fiercely waved the watchers away. They scrambled up and behind the wagons without any argument.

"Oh, that poor kid!" Lydia whispered. "She didn't even get a chance to live before that bastard —"

Berak waved her to silence. "Now comes the most difficult part." His voice was so soft it barely disturbed the air. "Now he must help her deal with her own death and at last find rest."

They waited in silence as the time crept slowly by. And at last Naitachal staggered out to meet them. He said not a word, but sank to the ground, head in hands. Berak moved to his side, murmuring in elfish, and Naitachal nodded. The White Elf nodded as well, and returned to Kevin and Lydia.

"It's done," he said softly. "That poor lost child is gone."

Naitachal continued to sit where he was, black cloak like a shroud about him, and all at once Kevin couldn't stand it. Seritha was already brewing one of her herbal teas, and the bardling took a flagon from her and hurried to the Dark Elf's side.

"Naitachal? Naitachal, it's me. Kevin."

The Dark Elf slowly raised his head, his eyes empty.

"H-here," the bardling insisted. "Drink."

For a moment he wasn't sure Naitachal was going to obey, but then a hand cold as the grave took the flagon from him. The Dark Elf held it for a moment in both hands, gratefully absorbing its heat, then drank. For a time he sat with closed eyes. Then Naitachal turned to look at Kevin again. And this time life glinted in the sorcerous eyes.

"Thank you. I was wise to name you an anchor."

"And . . . Charina is . . . "

"Gone. Though gone *where* I can't say. And no," the Dark Elf added with a hint of returning humor, "I'm not being metaphysical. She was a gentle girl, but she did, after all, come of warrior stock. I dare say we've not seen the last of her just yet."

"What . . . ? "

But more Naitachal wouldn't say.

"The best way to be invisible," Berak said with his usual dramatic flair, "is to be obvious. If we try to sneak into Count Volmar's castle like thieves with something to hide, Carlotta is sure to notice."

Naitachal nodded. "Just as she'd be sure to notice any manner of magic-working." He glanced at Kevin and Lydia. "Now, those two should make convincing enough members of your troupe."

"With a little judicious dying of hair," Seritha added, eying Lydia's curly black locks, "and some nice, minstrelly recostuming. But as for you," she added, studying Naitachal, "hmm . . . "

"I am *not*," the Dark Elf said flatly, "dressing up as a dancing girl. Once was quite enough, thank you."

Berak gave a shout of laughter. "A *what*?"

"You heard me. We made a pretty group, the lot of us, Kevin here and Lydia and Eliathanis —"

Naitachal broke off in mid-sentence, pain flashing in his eyes. Kevin winced, remembering the White Elf's embarrassment and the Dark Elf's teasing, remembering that silly, happy time that seemed so long ago.

Berak's sharp, clever gaze shot from the bardling to Naitachal. "Never mind," he said gently. "We won't need anything quite so . . . ah . . . drastic. Hey-o, everyone! Prepare to ride!"

The elven minstrel troupe paraded into Count Volmar's castle with cymbals clashing and trumpets blaring, and set up camp, along with all the other groups of minstrels, acrobats and stage-magicians, in the increasingly crowded outer bailey.

"How do you think I look?" Lydia, grinning, tossed her newly dyed, brazen hair, and Naitachal shook his head wryly.

"About as elven as Count Volmar. But definitely not like that wanton warrior woman."

"Wanton!" She tapped him with her fan. "I'll give you wanton, you stage-magician, you!"

The Dark Elf looked down at himself and laughed. "Stage-magician," he said ruefully. They had decided to play up Naitachal's dramatic coloring by dressing him in the gaudiest of red robes, a gold-threaded scarf draped theatrically about his head and face.

Kevin, who was dressed in fairly gaudy yellow and purple himself, wasn't really listening to their nervous banter. Instead, he stared thoughtfully up at the various castle towers. "There," he murmured suddenly, "beside the Great Hall."

"The chapel?" Berak asked. "What about it?"

"Not the chapel. The bell tower next to it."

"What *are* you — Ah. You're thinking of acoustics."

"Exactly." Kevin studied the tower for a long

moment. It was plain and square-sided, with no windows save for the great arches at the very top. "The bell can't be rung. I remember someone saying it had cracked and they hadn't gotten around to getting it down and recast."

"But that's still a pretty-looking sound chamber it's hanging in." Berak smiled faintly. "Quite nicely designed. Anyone standing in it who decided to start singing would be heard all over the castle."

"He would," Kevin agreed. "And if I have any say in things, he will be."

"That officious servant told me my troupe isn't to perform until some time tomorrow. And of course the site of the performance, of all the performances, is going to be in the courtyard. Coincidentally, right in front of that chapel. With its oh so pretty bell tower."

Berak and Kevin exchanged conspiratorial grins.

But even as he tried to act the role of a minstrel without a care in the world, calmly helping the others prepare for tomorrow's show, Kevin's hands shook. His heart pounded so fiercely he was sure the casually watching guards were going to hear it and drag him away for questioning. Berak had sent messengers off to King Amber and Master Aidan with word of what had happened, but the bardling knew he couldn't count on them to get here in time to do anything.

It—it's all up to us. To me.

Gods, gods, he couldn't make a move until after dark, and here it was only afternoon! How was he ever going to get through this day? And even after the night came, if it ever did, what if he couldn't get into that bell tower? What if Count Volmar had locked it, or set a guard, or—

Kevin battled with his growing panic. This was stupid. After all, the whole thing came down simply to this:

Tomorrow he, Naitachal and Lydia would be heroes—

Or they would be dead.

Chapter XXV

There was some mercy, Kevin thought: at least there was no moon this night. It wasn't difficult, thanks to Naitachal's elven night-vision, for three people to steal across the crowded courtyard to the bell tower without waking anyone — and without any merely human guard being able to spot them.

The bardling paused at the base of the bell tower to look nervously up and up its height: a starkly black mass against the star-filled sky. The tower hadn't seemed quite so tall from the outer bailey . . .

Don't be silly, he scolded himself. *You were higher than that when you were up on the castle tower.*

Sure, he answered himself. *And look how* that *turned out!*

Naitachal, who was quietly testing the tower door, drew back with a sudden hiss. "Curse the man and his suspicious mind!" It was a savage whisper. "I know bronze is expensive, but does he really think someone's going to try stealing a heavy bell?"

"Wh-what's the matter?" Kevin asked.

"He's bolted the cursed door!"

Lydia gave a frustrated sigh. "Can't you cast some sort of spell — "

"I'm a necromancer," the Dark Elf said flatly, "not a lockpick. Besides, you know any use of magic would bring Carlotta down on our heads."

"Wonderful," Lydia repeated. "Now what do we do?"

A snicker cut the sudden silence. "Helpless creatures!"

"Tich'ki! What — "

"Here, help me. This thing is cursed heavy!"

The fairy had stolen a whole coil of rope. "Tich'ki, this is great!" Lydia whispered. She craned her head back to study the tower. "Now, how are we going to get it up there?"

Tich'ki sighed in mock exasperation. "Do I have to do *everything* around here?"

She snatched up one end of the rope and started flapping her way up, struggling against its weight. Naitachal, watching closely so he wouldn't entangle her or destroy her balance, played the rope out, coil by coil.

"She's at the top," he murmured. "Ah! She has it!"

Tich'ki came spiralling down. "That's that. I've tied the thing strongly enough to hold even your weights! Now it's up to you."

Lydia's teeth flashed in the darkness. "All right, let's go! Me first, I think, then Kevin, then you, Naitachal in case the kid has trouble."

"I won't — " the bardling started, but Naitachal cut in calmly:

"Agreed."

Before Kevin could say anything more, Lydia was swarming up the rope with, he thought, disgusting ease.

"She made it," Naitachal whispered after a few moments. "Your turn, Kevin."

Just what I need: another chance to ruin my hands, this time with rope burns. Ah well, better my hands than our lives!

He took a firm grip on the rope, braced his feet against the side of the tower, and started to climb. To his relief, the rope was knotted, giving him something to grasp. But he'd never done anything like this. Powers, he hadn't even climbed trees when he was a child, not once he'd started studying music and had to be concerned about his hands! He could feel the ache in his arms and thighs already, and even the familiar weight of the lute on his back was threatening to pull him over backwards.

Come on! Don't be a baby! If Lydia can do it, so can you!

Hey, he *had* made it! Kevin scrambled up over the rim of one of the arches and stood aside so Naitachal — who also swarmed up the rope with disgusting ease — could join them.

"It's about time!" Tich'ki jibed. "Watch your footing. There's only this narrow strip of stone and the stairway down." She fluttered in mid-air. "The whole tower's hollow!"

Kevin shrugged. "Of course it is. They never expected anyone to stay here for very long. The bell would deafen anyone caught up here."

"That is, if it wasn't cracked so badly it couldn't be rung," Lydia said with a grin. "Lucky us!" She glanced around. "Naitachal, you don't need a clear view of the courtyard, do you?"

"No. I sense cast magic and shield Kevin from it wherever I stand."

"Fine. Then you take the left side, over here. I'll be on the right, where I can get a clear shot at any would-be snipers. And you, of course, Kevin, get the place of honor here in the center." She grinned. "Now all we have to do is wait."

Tich'ki tittered. "Nighty night, everybody! Try not to fall off the ledge in your sleep!"

"Thank you, Tich'ki," Naitachal muttered. "Thank you very much."

"You're welcome!" the fairy laughed, and darted away before he could hit her.

It might not have been the single most miserable time he'd spent; there certainly had been worse during their adventurings. But Kevin, blinking blearily in the chill light of early morning, not at all rested and not quite daring to stretch lest he lose his balance, decided he had to rate this cold, hard, precarious night just past right up there with the worst.

Naitachal was already on his feet, gaudy finery replaced some time in the night by his usual somber black, and Lydia, stripped down to her preferred warrior garb, bow and quiver within easy reach, was limbering up her muscles as best she could in that narrow space.

I wish we had something to eat other than a flask of water and some bread and cheese, something warm, Kevin thought wistfully. *Ha,* he added, looking gingerly down into the depths of the tower, *and I wish we had . . . ah . . . more refined sanitary facilities, too!*

Ah well, at least it *was* morning, and the sun would soon be warming things up. The morning he would win or die — No, curse it, he wasn't even going to think about that, not yet!

"Good morning," he said.

Lydia snorted. "More or less!" She leaned daringly out to study the courtyard far below. "At least we're going to get a splendid view of the whole event. That's got to be the count's chair, there on that dais, under the canopy. Now, if only Carlotta will just cooperate by showing up with him. . . ."

She did. Kevin tensed as the false Charina, pretty in blue silk, simpered out to take her place beside Count Volmar, who was clad in rich robes of dark red-violet.

That's almost royal purple! Kevin thought indignantly. *They really* are *planning to make a move towards the throne! Well, not if I have anything to say about it!*

Then he had to laugh at his own bravado.

Not if I'm allowed *to have anything to say about it*, the bardling corrected wryly.

Lydia was right. They really did have a splendid view of the whole event. And an endless event it was, too, with minstrels being replaced by acrobats being replaced by more minstrels being replaced by — Kevin fought back a yawn, astonished that he could feel bored even while he ached with tension. And had he really been cold before? Now it was hot in this tower, baking as it was directly in the sun, so hot the bardling envied Lydia her scanty garb.

Powers, would Berak's troupe never get to perform? Kevin took yet another small sip of water, trying to keep his throat moist. Were they going to be stuck up here until they starved or died of thirst? Would they never get to even try the spell that had cost them so much already and —

"There they are." Naitachal's voice was tight with tension. "Be ready, Kevin."

"I — I am."

Between the hopefully fine acoustics of this sound chamber and with —again, hopefully — his own Bardic Magic to provide the rest, there should be no way for Carlotta to escape the sound of his voice till the spell was cast.

Oh please, he prayed to all the Powers, *let it be so!*

In order to make the best use of the chamber's acoustics, Kevin realized, there was only one place he could stand: squarely in front of the bell, in plain view — and bowshot — of the crowd. If Lydia or Naitachal failed to protect him . . .

No. They'd been through so much together already; he wouldn't doubt them now.

Berak's troupe were performing with all their elven skill, "carrying the crowd," as Berak would put it, taking them through rousing heroic ballads and songs so light and humorous that waves of laughter surged to Kevin's ears.

Come on, he begged them. *You don't have to put on* quite *so good a show, do you? Or so long?*

But Berak was a true showman, after all. No matter how tense the situation, he wasn't going to leave an audience unsatisfied. By the time he finally sang the opening notes of the ballad he and Kevin had agreed upon, the ancient, tragic "Song of Ellian and Teris," that tale of doomed young love, the bardling was almost too numb from tension to recognize it.

Berak and his troupe sang with exquisite simplicity, barely ornamenting each line, tracing the words delicately with harp and flute, their every word filled with quiet grief and tenderness. And the noisy, restless crowd, bit by bit, fell still. The ballad came to its bittersweet ending. The lovers sank into each others' arms, their lives slowly, peacefully ebbing away. . . .

It was done. The stunned audience paid Berak's troupe that rarest, greatest of tributes: absolute silence.

They'll start cheering in a moment, Kevin knew. *It's got to be now!*

Oh gods, the bardling thought in a surge of panic, he wasn't ready, he couldn't remember the words, his voice wasn't going to cooperate —

But then Kevin realized he was doing it, he was singing out his spell, the sound chamber amplifying his voice so it rang out over the courtyard.

Yet even in that moment he knew, from the heart of his musician's being, that what he was doing wasn't enough. Oh, Powers, why hadn't he realized this before? The spell needed more than bare recitation to work! It needed heart, it needed belief, it needed a Power he simply didn't possess. The very *soul* of the music was missing, and without it Carlotta would still triumph —

No, ah no! All those poor people will die!

And all at once something seemed to tear loose within Kevin's heart. All at once he couldn't be afraid, not for himself. Wild with this sudden flame of hope, of pity, he sang for Eliathanis, he sang for Charina, he sang for all the good, kind, ordinary people whose lives Carlotta would destroy.

And magic, true, strong Bardic Magic fully grown at last roused within him. Feeling nothing but the fire surging through him, hearing nothing but the sound of the spell-song, Kevin was hardly aware of Carlotta's shriek of disbelieving rage or the count's shouts to his archers. A few arrows cut the air about him, but then Lydia and Naitachal were retaliating, fending off attack.

Suddenly the spell-song was done. Kevin sagged, drained and gasping for breath, only Naitachal's firm grip on his arm keeping him from falling as he stared, as they all stared. . . .

The silence that followed was the worse thing Kevin had ever heard — because nothing at all happened to Carlotta.

It failed after all. The spell failed.

All at once Kevin was too weary to care. He stood passively waiting to die, either from sorcery or the spell's own backlash. Dimly, he heard Carlotta's scornful laugh. . . .

But then that laugh went wrong, too shrill, too high in pitch! Kevin came back to himself with a jolt, shouting, "Look! Dear Powers, look!"

Despite all her frantically shrieked-out spells, Carlotta was shrinking. Within moments, though she still struggled to cling to Charina's form, she had shrunk to the size and shape of a fairy.

Stunned silence fell, through which Count Volmar's voice cut like a whip. "Guards!" Pointing up at the bell tower, he shouted, "Those foul sorcerers have attacked my niece! Stop them!"

"Have to admire his presence of mind," Naitachal muttered.

But Berak and his troupe were ready. As the guards rushed forward, the White Elves swung tent poles like quarterstaffs across unprotected shins. The first rush of men went hurtling to the ground, and the next wave fell over them.

"Come on!" Lydia yelled. "Let's get out of here while we can!"

The three of them scrambled down the rope, Kevin not even stopping to worry about his hands, and set off across the crowded courtyard at a dead run, people squealing and scrabbling away from the "foul sorcerers."

We're going to make it, we're really going to —

"Oh hell," Lydia murmured. "Well, we gave it our best."

A long line of the count's men had broken through the crowd, standing between the three and safety, eyes cold, pikes at the ready. Count Volmar strode forward, pushing his men aside, face so florid with rage a corner of Kevin's mind wondered if he meant to kill his foes himself.

Logic would have insisted there was no way out. Kevin, still caught in the power of his own music, wasn't ready to listen to logic. Instead, he did the only thing he could do:

He sang. He sang with all the force of his newly born magic of an innocent girl most foully slain, of a sweet young life that was the price of a man's ambition — of Charina murdered by her uncle, by the count himself!

The long, gleaming line of pikes swayed as the men murmured uneasily among themselves.

"Don't listen to him!" Count Volmar blustered. "He's a — a sorcerer trying to trick you!"

But then one of the guards cried out in shock, "Look! Look!"

The ghost of Charina, a pale glimmer in the daylight, was slowly forming, as if called by the song. But this time there was nothing soft or weak about the specter.

"Behold the murderer!" Her voice rang out, fierce as a hawk's cry, echoing in the suddenly still air. "Behold my uncle who slew me so he might steal a throne! My curse upon you, Uncle! I have come for you — and I shall have my revenge!"

She thrust out her hand as though casting a spear. Count Volmar gasped, clutching his chest, eyes wild with sudden agony. For one long moment he stood helplessly convulsed in pain, trying without breath to cry out for aid. But before any could move, he crumpled to the cobblestones and lay still.

"I am *avenged*!" the specter shrilled in savage joy, and vanished in a dazzling flash of light.

By the time Kevin's sight had cleared, one of the guards was kneeling by Count Volmar's side.

"He — he's dead," the man gasped. "Count Volmar is dead."

Kevin and Lydia stared at Naitachal. The Dark Elf shrugged. "Wasn't my doing. I *told* you Charina came from warrior stock!"

"Well now, would you look at this?" Lydia murmured.

The guards were all staggering back like men waking from a foul dream.

"I was right," Kevin said. "Carlotta really *did* have them all under her control. Her spell must have just about worn off." He stiffened in sudden alarm. "Yes, but where is she? If she got away — "

"Ha, don't worry about her!" Tich'ki suddenly tittered in his ear.

"But — but she escaped!"

"For what good that'll do her!"

"What — "

Tich'ki pinched his cheek. "Kevin, lad, I may not be on the best of terms with my fairy kin, but they *will* still heed my messages. I sent out a spell-call to them, to all of them. Every hill, every *dun*, every fairy cairn is closed to Carlotta. No one will shelter her, none give her aid. She is powerless, bound in fairy shape forever — and forever shall be in exile!"

"Uh, that's all well and good," one of the guards said hesitantly. "And we're not exactly sorry to see the end of Count Volmar, either, the murdering traitor. We're loyal to King Amber, we are!"

"We know that," Kevin said reassuringly.

"But . . . well . . . what do we do now? I mean, who's in charge and — " He seemed to notice Lydia's warrior garb for the first time. "Lady, you're the closest thing we've got to a commander right now. Will you accept our surrender?"

Lydia straightened, despite her gaudy, dyed hair looking every inch the military figure. "I will, indeed, and hold your trust in safety till King Amber does appoint a new overlord."

But then she whispered to Kevin, "How's that? Sound properly high and noble?"

He almost spoiled the whole thing by bursting into helpless laughter. "Oh, it — it does, indeed!"

"This is all well and good," Naitachal murmured. "But what happens now?"

"We get the crowd out of here, for one thing," Lydia said, and snapped out commands to the guards, who, only too glad to obey *someone*, began to make order.

"And someone has to take care of Count Volmar's body," Kevin added.

"That, I shall do," a precise voice said.

"D'Krikas!"

The seneschal bowed as best an Arachnia could. "I let myself refuse to see what was truly happening. I stained my own honor by sheer blindness. You have cleansed that honor, and won my gratitude."

"Uh . . . yes," Kevin said uncertainly. "But — "

A blare of trumpets cut into his words. A column of horsemen came riding into the courtyard beneath King Amber's gold and crimson banner.

"Well, what do you know?" Lydia said drily. "Looks like the cavalry has arrived."

* * *

The Great Hall was crowded with royal guards, castle folk — and of course, Berak's troupe, all wide-eyed with excitement. At the High Table, Kevin sat with the captain of the royal troop, a strong-faced, fierce-eyed man who explained:

" . . . and so, when my royal master received your message, he knew no man could reach this castle by normal means. The court wizards, working all as one, cast a spell to transport us, men and horses, here as swiftly as they could."

"They transported someone else," a familiar voice added.

Kevin sprang to his feet so suddenly his chair overturned with a crash. "Master Aidan!"

He raced to the Bard's side, then staggered to a stop, staring. This was still plainly Master Aidan — but he was now a man of middle years, his hair and beard only slightly streaked with gray. "It worked," Kevin breathed. "Casting the spell really did restore your years."

"It did."

Kevin couldn't stand on ceremony a moment longer. He caught the Bard in a fierce hug. Master Aidan chuckled. "Lad, lad, you're cracking my ribs!"

"Oh! S-sorry! But Berak told me you were ill. How do you feel?"

"Ah, Kevin." Master Aidan touched Kevin's cheek tenderly. "Amazingly well, now. When I sent you to retrieve the spell," he added with a laugh, "I never expected you to be the one to cast it! And you cast it so successfully, my young Bard."

"Wh-what did you — what — "

"I called you Bard, Kevin, and Bard you most assuredly are."

"He's more than that," the captain of the royal guards called out. "If you would, Bard Kevin?"

Bard Kevin! Struggling not to grin like an idiot,

Kevin returned to his place at the High Table. The captain continued:

"My royal master suspected that even with the spell of magical transport, we might well arrive after things were . . . ah . . . settled, one way or another. And since you have proven yourself a loyal subject of the Crown, a most brave and worthy subject from all we've been told, I have orders from the King himself, may the gods favor him."

"Want to cut through all the courtly talk?" Lydia asked. "Kevin's brave, all right, and worthy as they come. Get on with it, man!"

To Kevin's surprise, the captain grinned. "Anything to oblige a lovely lady," he said so urbanely that Lydia actually looked flustered. "Of course, Bard Kevin," the captain continued, "you'll have to go to the royal palace to get this all done properly, but King Amber, in gratitude for service rendered, hereby cedes to you the rank and all the lands and honors pertaining to the late traitor, Volmar."

Kevin stared. "Wh-what are you saying?"

"He's saying that you're a count now, kid!" Lydia told him. "Looks like this castle really *is* going to be your home."

"But what about you?"

"Oh, I guess I'll just go on travelling." But a hint of loneliness was in her voice.

"The *hell* you will!" Kevin exploded. "Look you, I'm going to need someone I can trust to oversee the castle guards. What do you say, Lydia: do you want to be my commander-in-chief?"

She broke into a slow, happy grin. "Sure, kid! *Someone's* got to keep an eye on you."

"And I, Bard Kevin," D'Krikas added, "will serve you as well." The being paused uneasily. "If you will have me."

"I can't see myself running a castle without you."

"Oh, I shall have help." Humor glinted in D'Krikas' great eyes.

"He means me!" Tich'ki piped up.

"Exactly." D'Krikas gave a short chitter, almost a chuckle. "I was fooled once by a count who feigned nobility and by you — a natural noble who feigned commonness. With this little one by my side, I shall not dare slip into complacency again."

Kevin laughed. "Agreed!"

"But what about Naitachal?" Lydia wondered.

Kevin glanced down the table to where the Dark Elf and Master Aidan were deep in discussion. The young Bard could have sworn he heard Naitachal murmur, "But I won't fetch your laundry. I'm a bit too old to be an errand boy." And surely Master Aidan was chuckling and agreeing?

"Naitachal?" Kevin called, and the Dark Elf looked up. And for the first time since the young Bard had known him, true, peaceful joy shone in his blue eyes.

"Kevin, Master Aidan and I have come to an agreement. I am going off with him to nice, tranquil Bracklin — as his apprentice. I shall take your advice, my friend, and study to become a Bard." His smile was a beautiful thing. "I've had quite enough of Death," Naitachal said. "I want to try the magic of Life for a change."

Kevin smiled in return. "And may you enjoy it, my friend."

"That's that," Tich'ki said in satisfaction. "All the loose ends are nicely tied up. All right, everyone, enough talk. We've some heavy celebrating to do!"

THE END

SNEAK PREVIEW

THE SHIP WHO SEARCHED

ANNE McCAFFREY
MERCEDES LACKEY

BAEN BOOKS

• CHAPTER ONE

The ruby light on the com unit was blinking when Hypatia Cade emerged from beneath the tutors' hood, with quadratic equations dancing before her seven-year-old eyes. Not the steady blink that meant a recorded message, nor the triple-beat that meant Mum or Dad had left her a note, but the double blink with a pause between each pair, that meant there was someone Upstairs, waiting for her to open the channel.

Someone Upstairs meant an unscheduled ship — Tia knew very well when all the scheduled visits were, they were on the family calendar and were the first things reported by the AI when they all had breakfast. That made it Important for her to answer, quickly, and not take the time to suit up and run to the dig for Mum or Dad. It must not have been an emergency, though, or the AI would have interrupted her lesson.

She rubbed her eyes to rid them of the dancing variables, and pushed her stool over to the com-console so she could reach all the touch-pads when she stood on it. She would never have been able to reach things sitting in a chair, of course. With brisk efficiency that someone three times her age might have envied, she cleared the board, warmed up the relay, and opened the line.

"Exploratory Team Cee-One-Two-One," she enunciated carefully, for the microphone was old, and often lost anything not spoken clearly. "Exploratory Team Cee-One-Two-One, receiving. Come in, please. Over."

She counted out the four-second lag to orbit and

back, nervously. *One-hypotenuse, two-hypotenuse, three-hypotenuse, four-hypotenuse.* Who could it be? They didn't get unscheduled ships very often, and it meant bad news as often as not. Planet Pirates, Plague, or Slavers. Trouble with some of the colony-planets. Or worse — artifact thieves in the area. A tiny dig like this one was all too vulnerable to a hit-and-run raid. Of course, digs on the Salomon-Kildaire Entities rarely yielded anything a collector would lust after, but would thieves know that? Tia had her orders if raiders came and she was alone — to duck into the hidden escape tunnel that would blow the dome; to run to the dark little hidey away from the dig that was the first thing Mum and Dad put in once the dome was up. . . .

"This is courier TM Three-Seventy. Tia, dearest, is that you? Don't worry, love, we have a non-urgent message run and you're on the way, so we brought you your packets early. Over." The rich, contralto voice was a bit flattened by the poor speaker, but still welcome and familiar. Tia jumped up and down a bit on her stool in excitement.

"Moira! Yes, yes, it's me! But — " she frowned a little. The last time Moira had been here, her designation had been *C*M, not TM. "Moira, what happened to Charlie?" Her seven-year-old voice took on the half-scolding tones of someone much older. "Moira, did you scare away *another* brawn? Shame on you! Remember what they told you when you kicked Ari out your airlock! Uh — over."

Four seconds; an eternity. "I didn't scare him away, darling," Moira replied, though Tia thought she sounded just a little guilty. "He decided to get married, raise a brood of his own, and settle down as a dirtsider. Don't worry, this will be the last one, I'm sure of it. Tomas and I get along famously. Over."

"That's what you said about Charlie," Tia reminded her darkly. "And about Ari, and Lilian, and Jules, and — "

She was still reciting names when Moira interrupted her. "Turn on the landing beacon, Tia, please. We can talk when I'm not burning fuel in orbital adjustments." Her voice turned a little bit sly. "Besides, I brought you a birthday present. That's why I couldn't miss stopping here. Over."

As if a birthday present was going to distract her from the litany of Moira's failed attempts to settle on a brawn!

Well — maybe just a little.

She turned on the beacon, then, feeling a little smug, activated the rest of the landing sequence, bringing up the pad lights and guidance monitors, then hooking in the AI and letting it know it needed to talk to Moira's navigational system. She hadn't known how to do all *that*, the last time Moira was here. Moira'd had to set down with no help at all.

She leaned forward for the benefit of the mike. "All clear and ready to engage landing sequence, Moira. Uh — what did you bring me? Over."

"Oh, you bright little penny!" Moira exclaimed, her voice brimming with delight. "You've got the whole system up! You *have* been learning things since I was here last! Thank you, dear — and you'll find out what I brought when I get down there. Over and out."

Oh well, she had tried. She jumped down from her stool, letting the AI that ran the house and external systems take over the job of bringing the brainship in. Or rather, giving the brainship the information she needed to bring *herself* in; Moira never handed over her helm to anyone if she had a choice in the matter. That was part of the problem she'd had with keeping brawns. She didn't trust them at the helm, and let them know that. Ari, in particular, had been less-than-amused with her attitude and had actually tried to disable her helm controls to prove *he* could pilot as well as she.

Now, the next decision; should she suit up and fetch Mum and Dad? It was no use trying to get them on the com; they probably had their suit-speakers off. Even though they weren't *supposed* to do that. And this wasn't an emergency; they would be decidedly annoyed if she buzzed them, and they found out it was just an unscheduled social call from a courier ship, even if it was Moira. They might be more than annoyed if they were in the middle of something important, like documenting a find or running an age-assay, and she joggled their elbows.

Moira didn't say it was important. She wouldn't have talked about errant brawns and birthday presents if what she carried was really, really earth-shaking.

Tia glanced at the clock; it wasn't more than a half hour until lunch-break. If there was one thing that Pota Andropolous-Cade (Doctor of Science in Bio-Forensics, Doctor of Xenology, Doctor of Archeology), and her husband Braddon Maartens-Cade (Doctor of Science in Geology, Doctor of Physics in Cosmology, Associate Degree in Archeology, and licensed Astrogator) had in common — besides daughter Hypatia and their enduring, if absent-minded love for each other — it was punctuality. At precisely oh-seven-hundred every "morning," no matter where they were, the Cades had breakfast together. At precisely twelve-hundred, they arrived at the dome for lunch together. The AI saw that Hypatia had a snack at sixteen-hundred. And at precisely nineteen-hundred, the Cades returned from the dig for dinner together.

So in thirty minutes, *precisely,* Pota and Braddon would be here. Moira couldn't possibly land in less than ten minutes. The visitor — or visitors, there was no telling if there was someone on board besides the brawn, the yet-unmet Tomas — would not have long to wait.

She trotted around the living-room of the dome; picking up her books and puzzles, straightening the pillows on the sofa, turning on lights and the holo-scape of waving blue trees by a green lagoon, on Mycon, where her parents had met. She told the kitchen to start coffee, overriding the lunch-program to instruct it to make selection V-1, a setup program Braddon had logged for her for munchies for visitors. She decided on music on her own; the *Arkenstone Suite,* a lively synthesizer piece she thought matched the holo-mural.

There wasn't much else to do; so she sat down and waited — something she had learned how to do very early in her life. She thought she did it very well, actually. There had certainly been enough of it in her life. The lot of an archeologists' child was full of waiting, usually alone, and required her to be mostly self-sufficient.

She had never had playmates, or been around very many children of her own age. Usually Mum and Dad were alone on a dig, for they specialized in Class One Evaluation sites; when they weren't, it was usually on a Class Two dig, Exploratory. Never a Class Three Excavation dig, with hundreds of people and their families. It wasn't often that the other scientists her parents' age on a Class Two dig had children younger than their teens. And even those were usually away somewhere at school.

She knew that other people thought that the Cades were eccentric for bringing their daughter with them on every dig — especially so young a child. Most parents with a remote job to do left their offspring with relatives, or sent them to boarding schools. Tia listened to the adults around her, who usually spoke as if she couldn't understand what they were talking about. She learned a great deal that way; probably more even than her Mum and Dad suspected.

One of the things she overheard — quite frequently, in fact — was that she seemed like something of an afterthought. Or perhaps an "accident" — she'd overheard that before, too.

She knew very well what was meant by the "afterthought or accident" comment. The last time someone had said *that*, she'd decided that she'd heard it often enough.

It had been at a reception, following the reading of several scientific papers. She'd marched straight up to the lady in question, and had informed her solemnly that she, Tia, had been planned very *carefully*, thank you. That Braddon and Pota had determined that their careers would be secure just about when Pota's biological clock had the last few seconds on it, and *that* was when they would have one, singular, female child. Herself. Hypatia. Planned from the beginning. From the leave-time to give birth to the way she had been brought on each assignment; from the pressure-bubble glove-box that had served as her cradle until she could crawl, to the pressure-tent that became a crib to the kind of AI that would best perform the dual functions of tutor and guardian.

The lady in question, red-faced, hadn't known what to say. Her escort had tried to laugh it away, telling her that the "child" was just parroting what she'd overheard and couldn't possibly understand any of it.

Whereupon Tia, well-versed in the ethnological habits — including courtship and mating — of four separate sapient species, including *homo sap.*, had proceeded to prove that he was wrong.

Then, while the escort was still spluttering, she had turned back to the original offender, and informed her, with earnest sincerity, that *she* had better think about having *her* children soon too, since it was obvious that *she* couldn't have much more time before menopause.

Tia had, quite literally, silenced that section of the room. When reproached later for her behavior by the host of the party, Tia had been completely unrepentant. "She was being rude and nasty," Tia had said. When the host protested that the remark hadn't been meant for her, Tia had replied, "Then she shouldn't have said it so loudly that everyone else laughed. And besides," she had continued with inexorable logic, "Being rude *about* someone is worse than being rude *to* them." Braddon, summoned to deal with his erring daughter, had shrugged casually and said only, "I warned you. And you didn't believe me."

Though exactly what it was Dad had warned Doctor Julius about, Tia never discovered.

The remarks about being "unplanned" or an "accident" stopped, at least in her presence — but people still seemed concerned that she was "too precocious," and that she had no one of her own age to socialize with.

But the fact was that Tia simply didn't care that she had no other children to play with. She had the best lessons in the known universe, via the database; she had the AI to talk to. She had plenty of things to play with and lots of freedom to do what she wanted once lessons were done. And most of all, she had Mum and Dad, who spent *hours* more with her than most people spent with their children. She knew that, because both the statistics in the books she had read on child-care and the Socrates, the AI that traveled with them everywhere, told her so. They were never boring, and they always talked to her as if she was grown up. If she didn't understand something, all she had to do was tell them and they would backtrack and explain until she did. When they weren't doing something that meant they needed all their concentration, they encouraged her to come out to the digs with them when her lessons were over. She hadn't ever heard of too many children who got to be with their parents at work.

If anything, sometimes Mum and Dad explained a little *too* much. She distinctly remembered the time that she started asking "Why?" to everything. Socrates told her that "Why?" was a stage all children went through — mostly to get attention. But Pota and Braddon had taken her literally. . . .

The AI told her not long ago that her "Why?" period might have been the shortest on record — because Mum and Dad answered every "Why?" in detail. *And* made sure she understood, so that she wouldn't ask that particular "Why?" again.

After a month, "Why?" wasn't fun anymore, and she went on to other things.

She really didn't miss other children at all. Most of the time when she'd encountered them, it had been with the wary feeling of an anthropologist approaching a new and potentially dangerous species. The feeling seemed to be mutual. And so far, other children had proven to be rather boring creatures. Their interests and their worlds were very narrow; their vocabulary a fraction of Tia's. Most of them hadn't the faintest idea of how to play chess, for instance.

Mum had a story she told at parties, about how Tia, at the age of two, had stunned an overly-effusive professorial spouse into absolute silence. There had been a chess set, a lovely antique, up on one of the tables just out of Tia's reach. She had stared longingly at it for nearly half an hour before the lady noticed what she was looking at.

Tia remembered that incident quite well, too. The lady had picked up an intricately carved knight, and waggled it at her. "See the horsie?" she had gushed. "Isn't it a pretty horsie?"

Tia's sense of fitness had been outraged — and that wasn't all. Her intelligence had been insulted, and she was *very* well aware of it.

She had stood up, very straight, and looked the lady

right in the eye. "Is *not* a horsie," she had announced, coldly and clearly. "Is a *knight.* It moves like the letter L. And Mum says it is piece most often sacri — sacer — sacra — "

Mum had come up by then, as she grew red-faced, trying to remember how to say the word she wanted. "Sacrificed?" Mum had asked, helpfully. "It means 'given up.'"

Beaming with gratitude, Tia had nodded. "Most often *given up* after the pawn." Then she glared at the lady. "Which is *not* a little man!"

The lady had retired to a corner and did not emerge while Tia and her parents were there. Although her Mum's superior had then taken down the set and challenged Tia to a game. He had won, of course, but she had at least shown she really knew how to play. He had been impressed and intrigued, and had taken her out on the porch to point out various species of birds at the feeders there.

She couldn't help but think that she affected grownups in only two ways. They were either delighted by her, or scandalized by her. Moira was among the "delighted" sort, though most of her brawns hadn't been. Charlie had, though, which was why she had thought that he just might be the one to stay with the brainship. He actually seemed to enjoy the fact that she could beat him at chess.

She sighed. Probably this new brawn would be of the other sort.

Not that it really mattered how she affected adults. She didn't see that many of them, and then it was never for very long. Though it was important to impress Mum's and Dad's superiors in a positive sense. She at least knew that much now.

"Your visitor is at the airlock," said the AI, breaking in on her thoughts. "His name is Tomas. While he is cycling, Moira would like you to have me turn on the ground-based radio link so that she can join the conversation."

"Go ahead, Socrates," she told the AI. That was the problem with AIs; if they didn't already have instructions, you had to tell them to do something before they would, where a shell-person would just do it if it made sense.

"Tomas has your birthday present," Moira said, a moment later. "I hope you like it."

"You mean, you hope I like *him,*" she replied shrewdly. "You hope I don't scare him."

"Let's say I use you as a kind of litmus test, all right?" Moira admitted. "And, darling — Charlie really *did* fall in love with a ground-pounder. Even I could see he wanted to be with her more than he wanted space." She sighed. "It was really awfully romantic; you don't see old-style love-at-first-sight anymore. Michiko is such a charming little thing — I really can't blame him. And it's partly your fault, dear. He was so taken with you that all he could talk about was how he wanted children just like you. Well, anyway, she persuaded Admin to find him a ground job, and they traded me Tomas for him, with no fine, because it wasn't my fault this time."

"It's going to take you *forever* to buy out those fines for bouncing brawns," Tia began, when the inner airlock door cycled, and a pressure-suited person came through, holding a box and his helmet.

Tia frowned at seeing the helmet; he'd taken it off in the lock, once the pressure was equalized. That wasn't a good idea, because locks had been known to blow, especially old ones like the Class One digs had. So already he was one in the minus column as far as Tia was concerned. But he had a nice face, with kind eyes, and that wasn't so bad; a round, tanned face, with curly black hair and bright brown eyes, and a wide mouth that didn't have those tense lines at the corners that

Ari'd had. So that was one in the plus column. He came out even so far.

"Hello, Tomas," she said, neutrally. "You shouldn't take your helmet off in the lock, you know — you should wait until the interior door cycles."

"She's right, Tomas," Moira piped up from the com console. "These Class One digs always get the last pick of equipment. All of it is old, and some of it isn't reliable. Door seals blow all the time."

"It blew last month, when I came in," Tia added helpfully. "It took Mum hours to install the new seal, and she's not altogether happy with it." Tomas' eyes were wide with surprise, and he was clearly taken aback. He had probably intended to ask her where her parents were. He had not expected to be greeted by a lecture on pressure-suit safety.

"Oh," was all he could say. "Ah, thank you. I will remember that in the future."

"You're welcome," she replied. "Mum and Dad are at the dig; I'm sorry they weren't here to meet you."

"I ought to make proper introductions," Moira said from the console. "Tomas, this is Hypatia Cade. Her mother is Doctor Pota Andropolous-Cade and her father is Doctor Braddon Maartens-Cade. Tia, this is Tomas Delacorte-Ibanez."

"I'm very pleased to meet you, Tomas," she replied with careful formality. "Mum and Dad will be here in — " she glanced at her wrist-chrono " — ten minutes. In the meantime, there is fresh coffee, and may I offer you anything to eat?"

Once again, he was taken aback. "Coffee, please," he replied after a moment. "If you would be so kind."

She fetched it from the kitchen; by the time she returned with the cup balanced in one hand and the refreshments in the other, he had removed his suit. She had to admit that he did look very handsome in the skin-tight ship-suit he wore beneath it. But then, all of Moira's brawns had been good-looking. That was part of the problem; she tended to pick brawns on the basis of looks first, and personality second. He accepted the coffee and food from her gravely, and a little warily; for all the world as if he had decided to treat her as some kind of new, unknown sentient. She tried not to giggle.

"That is a very unusual name that you were given," he said, after an awkward pause. "Hypatia, is it?"

"Yes," she said, "I was named for the first and only female librarian of the Great Library at Alexandria on Terra. She was also the last librarian there."

His eyes showed some recognition of the names at least. So he wasn't completely ignorant of history, the way Julio had been. "Ah. That would that have been when the Romans burned it, in the time of Cleopatra — " he began. She interrupted him with a shake of her head.

"No, the Library wasn't destroyed then, not at all, not even close. It persisted as a famous library into the day of Constantine," she continued, warming to her favorite story, reciting it exactly as Pota had told it to her, as it was written in the History data-base. "It was when Hypatia was the Librarian that a pack of unwashed Christian fanatics stormed it — led by some people who called themselves prophets and holy men — intending to burn it to the ground because it contained 'pagan books, lies, and heresies.' When Hypatia tried to stop them, she was murdered, stoned to death, then trampled."

"Oh," Tomas said weakly, the wind taken quite out of his sails. He seemed to be searching for something to say, and evidently chose the first thing that sprang to mind. "Uh — why did you call them 'unwashed Christian fanatics?'"

"Because they *were,*" she replied impatiently. "They were fanatics, and most of them were stylites and other hermits who made a point of not ever bathing because taking baths was Roman and pagan and not taking baths was Christian and mortifying the flesh." She sniffed. "I suppose it didn't matter to them that it was also giving them fleas and making them smell. I shan't even *mention* the disease!"

"I don't imagine that ever entered their minds," Tomas said carefully.

"Anyway, I think Hypatia was very brave, but she could have been a little smarter," Tia concluded. "I don't think I would have stood there to let them throw stones at me; I would have run away, or locked the door or something."

Tomas smiled unexpectedly; he had a lovely smile, very white teeth in his darkly tanned face. "Well, maybe she didn't have much choice," he said. "I expect that by the time she realized she wasn't going to be able to stop those people, it was too late to get away."

Tia nodded, slowly, considering the ancient Alexandrian garments, how cumbersome they were, and how difficult to run in. "I think you're right," she agreed. "I would hate to think that the Librarian was stupid."

He laughed at that. "You mean you'd hate to think that the great lady you were named for was stupid," he teased. "And I don't blame you. It's much nicer to be named for someone who was brave and heroic on purpose than someone people *think* was a hero just because she was too dense to get out of the way of trouble!"

Tia had to laugh at that, and right then was when she decided that she was going to like Tomas. He hadn't quite known what to make of her at first, but he'd settled down nicely and was treating her quite like an intelligent sentient now.

Evidently Moira had decided the same thing, for when she spoke, her voice sounded much less anxious. "Tomas, aren't you forgetting? You bought Tia her late birthday present."

"I certainly did forget!" he exclaimed. "I do beg your pardon, Tia!"

He handed her the box he had brought, and she controlled herself very well, taking it from him politely, and not grabbing like a little child would have. "Thank you, Moira," she said to the com console. "I don't mind that it's late — it's kind of like getting my birthday all over again this way."

"*You* are just too civilized for your own good, dear," Moira giggled. "Well, go ahead, open it!"

She did; carefully undoing the fastenings of the rather plain box, and exposing bright-colored wrapping beneath. The wrapped package within was odd-shaped, lumpy —

She couldn't stand it any longer; she tore into the present just like any other child.

"Oh!" she exclaimed when she revealed her prize, for once caught without a word, holding him up to the light. "Do you like it?" Moira asked anxiously. "I mean, I know you asked, but you grow so fast, I was afraid you'd have outgrown him by now — "

"I *love* him!" Tia exclaimed, hugging the bright blue bear suddenly, reveling in the soft fur against her cheek. "Oh Moira, I just *love* him!"

"Well, it was quite a trick to find him, let me tell you," Moira replied, her voice sounding very relieved, as Tomas grinned even wider. "You people move around so much — I had to find a teddy-bear that would take repeated Decontam procedures, one that would stand up to about anything Quarantine could hand out. And it's hard to *find* bears at all, they seem to have gone right out of style. You don't mind that he's blue?"

"I like blue," she said happily.

"And you like him fuzzy? That was Tomas' idea."

"Thank you, Tomas," she told the brawn, who beamed. "He feels *wonderful.*"

"I had a fuzzy dog when I was your age," he replied, "When Moira told me that you wanted a bear like the one she had before she went into her shell, I thought this fellow felt better than the smooth bears."

He leaned down confidentially, and for a moment Tia was afraid that he was going to be patronizing just because she'd gone so enthusiastic over the toy.

"I have to tell you the truth, Tia, I really enjoyed digging into all those toy-shops," he whispered. "A lot of that stuff is wasted on children. I found some logic puzzles you just wouldn't believe, and a set of magic tricks I couldn't resist, and I'm afraid I spent far too much money on spaceship models."

She giggled. "I won't tell if you don't," she replied, in a conspiratorial whisper.

"Pota and Braddon are in the airlock," Socrates interrupted. "Shall I order the kitchen to make lunch now?"

"So why exactly *are* you here?" Tomas asked, after all the initial topics of conversation had been exhausted, and the subject turned, inevitably, to Pota and Braddon's work. He gestured at the landscape beyond the viewport; spectacular mountains, many times taller than anything found on Terra or any other inhabited planet. This little ball of rock with a thin skin of dirt was much like the wilder parts of Mars before it had been terraformed, and had a sky so dark at midday that the sun shared the sky with the stars. "I wouldn't expect to find much of anything out there for an archeologist — it's the next thing to airless, after all. The scenery is amazing, but that's no reason to stay here — "

Braddon chuckled, the generous mouth in his lantern-jawed face widening in a smile and Tia hid a grin. Whether or not Tomas knew it, he had just triggered her Dad's lecture-mechanism. Fortunately, Braddon had a gift for lecturing. He was always a popular speaker whenever he could be tempted to go to conferences. "No one expected to find anything on planets like this one, Tomas," Braddon replied, leaning back against the supporting cushions of the sofa, and tucking his hands behind his head. "That's why the Salomon-Kildaire culture is so intriguing. James Salomon and Tory Kildaire discovered the first buildings on the fourth moon of Beta Orianis Three — and there have never been *any* verifiable artifacts uncovered in what you and I would call 'normal' conditions. Virtually every find has been on airless or near-airless bodies. Pota and I have excavated over a dozen sites, doing the Class One studies, and they're all like this one."

Tomas glanced out the viewport again. "Surely that implies that they were — "

"Space-going, yes," Pota supplied, nodding her head so that her gray-brown curls vibrated. "I don't think there's any doubt of it. Although we've never found any trace of whatever it was they used to move them from colony to colony — but that isn't the real mystery."

Braddon gestured agreement. "The real mystery is that they never seem to have set up anything *permanent*. They never seem to have spent more than a few decades in any one place. No one knows why they left, or why they came here in the first place."

Tomas laughed. "They seem to have hopped planets as often as you two," he said. "Perhaps they were simply doing what *you* are doing — excavating an earlier culture, and following *it* across the stars." Braddon exclaimed in mock-horror. "Please!" he said, "Don't even think that!"

Pota only laughed. "If they had been, we'd have

found signs of that," she told both of them, tapping Braddon's knee in playful admonition. "After all, as bleak as these places are, they preserve things wonderfully. If the S-Ks had been archeologists, we'd have found the standard tools of the trade. We break and wear out brushes and digging tools all the time, and just leave them in our discard piles. They would have done the same. No matter how you try to alter it, there are only so many ways you can make a brush or a trowel — "

"There would be bad castings," Tia piped up. "You throw out bad castings all the time, Mum; if they were archeologists, we'd find a pile of bad castings somewhere."

"Bless me, Tia's right," Braddon nodded. "There you are, Tomas; irrefutable proof."

"Good enough for me," Tomas replied, good-naturedly.

"And if that idea was true, there also ought to be signs of the earlier culture, shouldn't there?" Moira asked. "And you've never found anything mixed in with the S-K artifacts."

"Exactly so," Pota replied, and smiled. "And so, Tomas, you see how easily an archeologist's theories can be disposed of."

"Then I'm going to be thankful to be Moira's partner," Tomas said gracefully, "And leave all the theorizing to better heads than mine."

After a while, the talk turned to the doings of the Institute, and both professional and personal news of Pota and Braddon's friends and rivals. Tia glanced at the clock again; it was long time past when her parents would have gone back to the dig — they must have decided to take the rest of the day off.

But these weren't subjects that interested her, especially not when the talk went into politics, both of the Institute and the Central Worlds government. She took her bear, politely excused herself, and went back to her room.

She hadn't had a chance to really look him over, when Tomas gave him to her. The last time Moira had come to visit, she'd told Tia some stories about what going into the shellperson program had been like, for unlike most shellpersons, she hadn't been popped into her shell until she'd been nearly four. Until that time, there had been some hope that there would have been a palliative for her particular congenital condition — premature aging that had caused her body to resemble a sixty-year old woman at the age of three. But there was no cure, and at four, her family finally admitted it. Into the shell she went, and since there was *nothing* wrong with her very fine brain, she soon caught up and passed by many of her classmates that had been in their shells since birth.

But one of the toys she'd had — her very favorite, in fact — had been a stuffed teddy-bear. She'd made up adventures for Ivan the Bearable, sending him in a troika across the windswept steppes of Novi Gagarin, and she'd told Tia some of those stories. That, and the *Zen of Pooh* book Moira brought her had solidified a longing she hadn't anticipated.

For Tia had been entranced by the tales and by Pooh — and had wanted a bear like Moira's. A simple toy that did *nothing*, with no intel-chips; a toy that couldn't talk, or teach, or walk. Something that was just there to be hugged and cuddled; something to listen when she didn't want anything else to overhear. . . .

Moira had promised. Moira didn't forget.

Tia closed the door to her room, and paged the AI. "Socrates, would you open a link to Moira in here for me, please?" she asked. Moira would be perfectly capable of following the conversation in the other room, and still talk to her in here too.

"Tia, do you really like your present?" Moira asked anxiously, as soon as the link had been established.

"He's wonderful," Tia answered firmly. "I've even got a name for him. Theodore Edward Bear."

"Or Ted E. Bear for short?" Moira chuckled. "I like it. It fits him. He's such a solemn-faced little fellow. One would think he was a software executive. He looks like a bear with a great deal on his mind."

Tia studied Ted, carefully. Moira was right, he was a sober little bear; with a very studious expression, as if he was listening very hard to whatever was being said. His bright blue coloration in no way contradicted the seriousness of his face, nor did the frivolous little shirt he was wearing with the Courier Service lightning-bolt on the front. "Is there anything going on that I need to know, Moira?" she asked, giving over her careful examination of her new friend and hugging him to her chest instead.

"The results of your last batch of tests seems to have satisfied all the Psych people out there that you're a perfectly well-balanced and self-sufficient girl," Moira replied, knowing without Tia prompting her just what was on her mind. "So there's no more talk of making your parents send you to boarding school."

Tia sighed with relief; that had been a very real worry the last time Moira had been here. The ship had left with the results of a battery of tests and psych-profiles that had taken two days to complete.

"I have to tell you that I added to that," Moira said, slyly. "I told them what kind of a birthday present you had asked for from me."

"What did they say?" Tia asked, anxiously. Had they thought she was being immature — or worse yet, that it meant she harbored some kind of neurosis?

"Oh, it was funny, there were questioning me on open com, as if I was some kind of AI that wouldn't respond to anything that wasn't a direct question, so of course I could hear everything *they* said. There was silence for a moment, and then the worst of the lot finally blurted out, 'Good heavens, the child is *normal,*' as if he'd expected you to ask for a Singularity simulator or something." Moira chuckled.

"I know who it was, too," Tia said shrewdly. "It was Doctor Phelps-Pittman, wasn't it?"

"Dead on the target, wenchette," Moira replied, still chuckling. "I still don't think he's forgiven you for beating him in Battle Chess. By the way, what *is* your secret?"

"He moves the Queen too often," Tia said absently. "I think he likes to watch her hips wiggle when she walks. It's probably something Freudian."

A splutter of static was all that followed that pronouncement, as Moira lost control of the circuit briefly. "My, my," she replied, when she came back online. "You *are* a little terror. One might almost suspect you of having as much control as a shellperson!"

Tia took that in the spirit it was meant; as a compliment.

"I promise not to tell him *your* weakness," the ship continued, teasingly.

"What's that?" Tia was surprised; she hadn't known she had one.

"You hate to see the pawns sacrificed. I think you feel sorry for the little guys."

Tia digested this in silence for a moment, then nodded reluctant agreement. "I think you're right," she admitted. "It seems as if everybody can beat them up, and it doesn't seem fair."

"You don't have the problem with an ordinary holoboard game," Moira observed casually.

"That's because they're just little blobby pieces on a holoboard game," Tia explained. "In Battle Chess they're little pikemen. And they're cute." She giggled. "I really love it when Pawn takes Knight and he hits the Knight with the butt of his pike right in the — "

"And *that's* why you frighten old Phelps-Pittman,"

Moira said severely, though Tia could tell she didn't mean it. "He keeps thinking you're going to do the same to him."

"Well, I won't have to see old sour-face for another year and a half," she said comfortably. "Maybe I can figure out how to act like a *normal girl* by then."

"Maybe you can," Moira replied. "I wouldn't put even that past you. Now, how about a game of Battle Chess? Ted Bear can referee."

"Of course," she agreed. "You can use the practice. I'll even spot you a pawn."

"Oh come now! You haven't gotten *that* much better since I saw you last." At Tia's continued silence, the ship asked, tentatively, "Have you?"

Tia shrugged. "Check my record with Socrates," she suggested.

There was silence as Moira did just that. Then. "Oh, *decom* it," she said in mock-disgust. "You really *are* exasperating. I should demand that you spot me two pawns."

"Not a chance," Tia replied, ordering the AI to set up the game, with a Battle Chess field in front of her. "You're taking advantage enough of a child as it is."

"Taking advantage of a child? Ha!" Moira said ironically. "You're not a child. I'm beginning to agree with Phelps-Pittman. You're an eighty-year-old midget in a little-girl costume."

"Oh all right," Tia said, good-naturedly. "I won't give you another pawn, but I will let you have white."

"Good." Moira studied the analog of the board in her memory, as Tia studied the holoboard in front of her. "All right, unnatural child. Have at ye!"

Moira and Tomas couldn't stay long; by dinner the ship had lifted, and the pad was empty — and the Cade family was back on schedule.

Pota and Braddon spent the evening catching up

with the message-packets Moira had brought them — mostly dispatches from friends at other digs, more scholarly papers in their various fields and the latest in edicts from the Institute. Since Tia knew, thanks to Moira, that none of those edicts concerned *her,* she was free to watch one of the holos Moira had brought for her entertainment. All carefully screened by the teachers at the Institute, of course, who oversaw the education of every child who was on-site with its parents. But even the teachers didn't see anything wrong with History holos, provided they were properly educational and accurate. The fact that most of these holos had been intended for adult viewing didn't seem to bother them.

Perhaps it was just as well that the Psychs had no idea what she was watching. They would probably have gone into strong hysterics.

Moira had an uncanny ability to pick out the ones that had good scripts and actors — unlike whoever it was that picked out most of the holos for the Remote Educational Department.

This one, a four part series on Alexander the Great, looked especially good, since it covered only the early parts of his life, before he became a great leader. Tia felt a certain kinship for anyone who'd been labeled "precocious"; and although she already knew that Alexander's childhood had been far from happy, she was looking forward to viewing this.

Having Ted beside her to whisper comments to made it even more fun.

At the end of the first part, even though she was fascinated, she virtuously told Socrates to shut everything down, and went into the main room to say good-night to her Mum and Dad. The next courier wasn't due for a while, and she wanted to make her treats last as long as possible.

Both of them were so deep in their readers that she

had to shake their elbows to get them to realize she was there, but once they came out of their preoccupied daze, they gave her big hugs and kisses, with no sign of annoyance at being interrupted.

"I have a really *good* Mum and Dad," she told Ted before drifting off to sleep. "I really. really do. Not like Alexander . . ."

The next day, it was back to the usual schedule. Socrates woke her and she got herself cleaned up and dressed, leaving Ted to reside on the carefully-made bed until she returned. When she entered the main room, Pota and Braddon were already there, blinking sleepily over steaming cups of coffee.

"Hello, darling," Pota greeted her as she fetched her milk and cereal from the kitchen. "Did you enjoy Alexander?"

"We-ell, it was *interesting,*" Tia said truthfully. "And I liked the actors and the story. The costumes and the horses were really stellar! But his mother and father were kind of — odd — weren't they?"

Braddon looked up from his coffee with his curly dark hair over one brown eye, and gave his daughter a wry grin. "They were certifiable crazy-cases by our standards, pumpkin," he replied. "But after all, there wasn't anyone around to apply those standards back then."

"And no Board of Mental Health to enforce them," Pota added, her thin, delicate face creasing with a puckish smile. "Remember, oh curious little chick, they were *not* the ones that had the most influence on Alexander. That was left to his tutors and nurses. I think he succeeded in spite of his parents, personally, and not because of them."

Tia nodded sagely. "Can I come help at the dig today?" she asked eagerly. This was one of the best things about the fact that her parents had picked the S-

Ks to specialize in. With next to no atmosphere, there were no indigent life-forms to worry about. By the time Tia was five, she had pressure-suit protocol down pat, and there was no reason why she couldn't come to the digs, or even wander about within specified limits on her own. "The biggest sandbox in the universe," Braddon called it; so long as she stayed within eye- and ear-shot, neither of them minded having her about outside.

"Not today, dearest," Pota said apologetically. "We've found some glassware, and we're making holos. As soon as we're done with that, we'll make the castings, and after that you can come run errands for us." In the thin atmosphere and chill of the site, castings were tricky to make; one reason why Pota discarded so many. But no artifact could be moved without first making a good casting of it, as well as holos from all possible angles — too many times the artifacts crumbled to nothing despite the most careful handling, once they were moved.

She sighed; holos and castings meant she couldn't even come near the site, lest the vibrations she made walking interfere. "All right," she agreed. "Can I go outside though? As long as I stay close to the airlock?"

"Stay close to the lock and keep the emergency cart nearby, and I don't see any reason why you can't play outside," Pota said after a moment. Then she smiled. "And how is your dig coming?"

"You mean really, or for pretend?" she asked.

"Pretend, of course," said Braddon. "Pretend is always more fun than really. That's why *we* became archeologists in the first place — because we get to play pretend for months at a time until we have to be serious and write papers!"

He gave her a conspiratorial grin, and she giggled.

"We-ell," she said, and drew her face down into a frown *just* like Doctor Heinz Marius-Llewellyn, when he was about to put everyone to sleep. "I've found the burial-ground of a race of flint-using primitives who were used as slave labor by the S-Ks at *your* site."

"Have you!" Pota fell right in with the pretense, as Braddon nodded seriously. "Well that certainly explains why we haven't found any servos. They must have used slaves to do all their manual labor!"

"Yes. And the Flint People worshipped them as gods from the sky," Tia continued. "That was why they didn't revolt; all the slave labor was a form of worship. They'd go back to their village and then they'd try to make flint tools just like the things that the sky-gods used. They probably made pottery things too, but I haven't found anything but shards."

"Well, pottery doesn't hold up well in conditions like this," Pota agreed. "It goes brittle very quickly under the extremes of surface temperature. What have you got so far?"

"A flint disruptor-pistol, a flint wrist-com, a flint flashlight, and some more things," she said solemnly. "I haven't found any arrowheads or spear-points or things like that, but that's because there's nothing to hunt here. They were vegetarians, and they ate nothing but lichen."

Braddon made a face. "Awful. Worse than the food at the Institute Cafeteria! No wonder they didn't survive — the food probably bored them to death!"

Pota rose and gathered up their plates and cups, stowing them neatly in the dishwasher. "Well, enjoy your lessons, pumpkin. We'll see you at lunch."

She smiled, hugged them both goodbye before they suited up, then went off to the schoolroom.

That afternoon, once lessons were done, she took down her own pressure-suit from the rack beside the airlock inner door. Her suit was designed a little differently from her parents', with accordion-folds at wrists and elbow, ankles and knees, and at the waist, to allow for the growth-spurts of a child. This was a brand new suit, for she had been about to outgrow the last one just before they went out on this dig. She liked it a lot better than the old one; the manufacturer of the last one had some kind of stupid idea that a child's suit should have cavorting flowers with smiling faces all over it. She had been ashamed to have anyone but her parents *see* her in the awful thing. She thought it made her look like a little clown.

It had come second-hand from a child on a Class Three dig — like most of the things that the Cades got. Evaluation digs simply didn't have that high a priority when it came to getting anything other than the bare essentials. But Tia'd had the bright idea when her birthday came around to ask her parents' superiors at the Institute for a new pressure-suit. And when it came out that she was imitating her parents, by creating her own little dig-site, she had so tickled them that they actually sent her one. Brand new, good for three or four years at least, and the *only* difference between it and a grown-up suit was that hers had extra helmet-lights and a com that couldn't be turned off, a locator-beacon that was always on, and bright fluorescent stripes on the helmet and down the arms and legs. A small price to pay for dignity.

The flowered suit had gone back to the Institute, to be endured by some other unfortunate child.

And the price to be paid for her relative freedom to roam was waiting in the airlock. A wagon, child-sized and modified from the pull-wagon many children had as toys — but this one had powered crawler-tracks and was loaded with an auxiliary power unit and air-pack and full face-mask. If her suit failed, she had been drilled in what to do so many times she could easily have saved herself when asleep. *One,* take a deep breath and pop the helmet. *Two,* pull the mask on, making sure seals around her face were secure. *Three,* turn on the air and *Four,* plug into the APU, which would keep the suit heat up with the helmet off. Then walk — slowly, carefully, to the airlock, towing the wagon behind. There was no reason why she should suffer anything worse than a bit of frostbite.

It had never happened. That didn't mean it wouldn't. Tia had no intention of becoming a tragic tale in the newsbytes. Tragic tales were all very well in drama and history, but they were not what one wanted in real life.

So the wagon went with her, inconvenient as it was.

The filters in this suit were good ones; the last suit had always smelled a little musty, but the air in this one was fresh and clean. She trotted over the uneven surface, towing the cart behind, kicking up little puffs of dust and sand. Everything out here was very sharp-edged and clear; red and yellow desert, reddish-purple mountains, dark blue sky. The sun, Sigma Marinara, hung right above her head, so all the shadows were tiny pools of dark black at the bases of things. She hadn't been out to her "site" for several weeks, not since the last time Mum and Dad had asked her to stay away. That had been right at the beginning, when they first got here and uncovered enough to prove it was an S-K site. Since that time there had been a couple of sandstorms, and Tia was a bit apprehensive that her "dig" had gotten buried. Unlike her parents' dig, *she* did not have force-shields protecting her trench from storms.

But when she reached her site, she discovered to her amazement that *more* was uncovered than she had left. Instead of buying her dig in sand, the storm had scoured the area clean —

There were several likely-looking lumps at the farther end of the trench, all fused together into a bumpy whole. Wonderful! There would be hours of potential pretend here; freeing the lumps from the sandy matrix, cleaning them off, figuring out what the Flint People had been trying to copy . . .

She took the tools her parents had discarded out of the wagon; the broken trowel that Braddon had mended for her, the worn brushes, the blunted probes, and set to work.

Several hours later, she sat back on her heels and looked at her first find, frowning. This wasn't a lump of flint after all. In fact, it seemed to be some kind of layered substance, with the layers fused together. Odd, it looked kind of wadded up. It certainly wasn't any kind of layered rock she'd ever seen before, and it didn't match any of the rocks she'd uncovered until now.

She chewed her lower lip in thought and stared at it, letting her mind just drift, to see if it could identify what kind of rock it was. It didn't look sedimentary.

Actually, it didn't look much like a rock at all. . . .

Not like a rock. What if it isn't a rock?

She blinked, and suddenly knew what it *did* look like. Layers of thin cloth or paper, wadded up, then discarded.

Finagle! Have I—

She gently — very gently — pried another lump off the outcropping, and carefully freed it of its gritty coating. And there was *no* doubt this time that what she had was the work of intelligent hands. Under the layer of half-fused sand and flaking, powdery dust, gleamed a spot of white porcelain, with the matte edge of a break showing why it had been discarded.

Oh, decom — I found the garbage dump!

Or, at least, she had found a little trash heap. That was *probably* it; likely there was just this lump of discards and no more. But anything the S-Ks left behind was important, and it was equally important to stop digging *now,* mark the site in case another sandstorm came up and capriciously buried it as it had capriciously uncovered it, and bring some evidence to show Mum and Dad what she had found.

Except that she didn't have a holo-camera. Or anything to cast with.

Finally she gave up trying to think of what to do. There was only one thing for it. Bring her two finds inside and show them. The lump of fabric might not survive the touch of real air, but the porcelain thing surely would. Porcelain, unlike glass, was more resilient to the stresses of repeated temperature changes and was not likely to go to powder at the first touch of air.

She went back inside the dome, and rummaged around for a bit before returning with a plastic food-container for the artifacts, and a length of plastic pipe and the plastic tail from a kite-kit she'd never had a chance to use. Another well-meaning, but stupid, gift from someone Dad worked with; someone who never once thought that on a Mars-type world there weren't very many opportunities to fly kites. . . .

With the site marked as securely as she could manage, and the two artifacts sealed into the plastic tub, she returned to the dome again, waiting impatiently for her parents to get back.

She had hoped that the seal on the plastic tub would be good enough to keep the artifacts safely protected from the air of the dome. She knew as soon as the airlock pressurized, though, that her attempt to keep them safe had failed. Even before she pulled off her helmet, the external suit-mike picked up the *hiss* of air leaking into the container. And when she held the plastic tub up to the light, it was easy enough to see that one of the lumps had begun to disintegrate. She pried the lid off for a quick peek, and sneezed at the dust. The wadded lump was not going to look like much when her parents got home.

Decom it, she thought resentfully. *That's not fair!*

She put it down carefully on the counter-top; if she didn't jar it, there might still be enough left when Mum and Dad got back in that they would at least be able to tell what it *had* been.

She stripped out of her suit, and sat down to wait. She tried to read a book, but she just couldn't get interested. Mum and Dad were going to be *so* surprised — and even better, now the Psychs at the Institute would have no reason to keep her away from the Class Two sites anymore — because *this* would surely prove that she knew what to do when she accidentally found something. The numbers on the clock moved with agonizing slowness, as she waited for the moment when they would finally return.

The sky outside the viewport couldn't get much darker, but the shadows lengthened, and the light faded. Soon now, soon —

Finally she heard them in the outer lock, and her heart began to beat faster. Suddenly she was no longer so certain that she had done the right thing. What if they were angry that she dissected the first two artifacts? What if she had done the wrong thing in moving them?

The "what ifs" piled up in her head as she waited for the lock to cycle.

Finally the inner door hissed, and Braddon and Pota came through, already pulling off their helmets and continuing a high-speed conversation that must have begun back at the dig.

" — but the matrix is all wrong for it to be a food-preparation area — "

" — yes, yes," Pota replied impatiently, " — but what about the integument — "

"Mum!" Tia said, running up to them and tugging at her mother's elbow. "I've found something!"

"Hello, pumpkin, that's very nice," her mother

replied absently, hugging her, and going right on with her conversation. Her intense expression showed that she was thinking while she spoke, and her eyes never wandered from her husband's face — and as for Braddon, the rest of the world simply did not exist.

"Mum!" Tia persisted. "I've found an artifact!"

"In a moment, dear," Pota replied. "But what about—"

"MUM!" Tia shouted, disobeying *every* rule of not-interrupting-grown-ups in desperation, knowing from all the signs that she would *never* get their attention otherwise. Conversations like *this* one could go on for hours. *"I've found an artifact!"* Both her parents stopped their argument in mid-sentence, and stared at her. Silence enveloped the room; an ominous silence. Tia gulped nervously.

"Tia," Braddon finally said, disapproval creeping into his voice, "Your mother and I are in the middle of a very important conversation. This is *not* the time for pretend."

"Dad, it's *not* pretend!" she said insistently, pointing to her plastic box. "It's not! I found an artifact, and there's more — "

Pota raised an eyebrow at her husband and shrugged. Braddon picked up the box, carelessly, and Tia winced as the first lump inside visibly disintegrated more.

"I am going to respect your intelligence and integrity enough to assume that you *think* you found an artifact," Braddon replied, prying the lid from the container. "But Tia, you know better than to — "

He glanced down inside — and his eyebrows arched upward in the greatest show of surprise that Tia had ever seen him make.

"I *told* you," Tia could not resist saying, triumphantly.

" — so they took the big lights out to the trench, and the extra field-generators," she told Ted E. Bear after she'd been put to bed for the night. "They were out there for *hours*, and they let me wait up to hear what it was. And it *was*, I *did* find a garbage dump! A big one, too! Mum made a special call to the Institute, 'cause this is the first really big S-K dump anybody's ever found."

She hugged Ted closer, basking in the warmth of Pota's praise, a warmth that still lingered and made her feel happy right down to her toes. "You did everything *exactly* right with the equipment you had," Pota had told her. "I've had undergraduates that didn't do as well as you did, pumpkin! You remember what I told you, when you asked me about why I wanted to find garbage?"

"That we learn more from sentients' garbage than from anything other than their literature," she'd recited dutifully.

"Well," Pota had replied, sitting on the edge of her bed, and touching her nose with one finger, playfully. "You, my curious little chick, have just upgraded this site from a Class One to a Class Three with four hours of work! That's more than Braddon and I have *ever* done!"

"Does that mean that we'll be leaving?" she'd asked in confusion.

"Eventually," Pota told her, a certain gloating glee in her voice. "But it takes time to put together a Class Three team, and *we* happen to be right here. Your father and I will be making gigabytes of important discoveries before the team gets here to replace us. And with that much already invested — they may *not* replace us!"

Tia had shaken her head, confused.

Pota had hugged her. "What I mean, pumpkin, is that there is a *very* good chance that we'll stay on here — as the dig supervisors! An instant promotion from Class One supervisor to Class Three supervisor!

There'll be better equipment, a better dome to live in — you'll have some playmates — couriers will be by every week instead of every few months — not to mention the raises in pay and status! All the papers on this site will go out under *our* names! And all because *you* were my clever, bright, careful little girl, who knew what she saw and knew when to stop playing!"

"Mum and Dad are really, really happy," she told Ted, thinking about the glow of joy that had been on both their faces when they finished the expensive link to the nearest Institute supervisor. "I think we did a good thing. I think maybe you brought us luck, Ted." She yawned. "Except about the other kids coming. But we don't have to play with them if we don't want to, do we?"

Ted agreed silently, and she hugged him again. "I'd rather talk to you, anyway," she told him. "You never say anything dumb. Dad says that if you can't say something intelligent, you shouldn't say anything; and Mum says that people who know when to shut up are the smartest people of all, so I guess you must be pretty smart. Right?"

But she never got a chance to find out if Ted agreed with that statement, because at that point she fell right asleep.

Over the course of the next few days, it became evident that this was not just an ordinary garbage dump; this was one containing scientific or medical debris. That raised the status of the site from "important" to "priceless," and Pota and Braddon took to spending every waking moment either at the site or preserving and examining their finds, making copious notes, and any number of speculations. They hardly ever saw Tia anymore; they had changed their schedule so that they were awake long before she was, and came in long after she went to bed.

Pota apologized — via a holo that she had left to play for Tia as soon as she came in to breakfast this morning.

"Pumpkin," her image said, while Tia sipped her juice. "I hope you can understand why we're doing this. The more we find out before the team gets sent out, the more we make ourselves essential to the dig, the better our chances for that promotion." Pota's image ran a hand through her hair; to Tia's critical eyes, she looked very tired, and a bit frazzled, but fairly satisfied. "It won't be more than a few weeks, I promise. Then things will go back to normal. Better than normal. In fact, I promise that we'll have a Family Day before the team gets here, all right? So start thinking what you'd like to do."

Well, *that* would be stellar! Tia knew exactly what she wanted to do — she wanted to go out to the mountains on the big sled, and she wanted to drive it herself on the way.

"So forgive us, all right? We don't love you any less, and we think about you all the time, and we miss you like anything." Pota blew a kiss toward the camera. "I know you can take care of yourself; in fact, we're counting on that. You're making a big difference to us. I want you to know that. Love you, baby."

Tia finished her juice as the holo flickered out, and a certain temptation raised its head. This could be a really unique opportunity to play hooky, just a little bit. Mum and Dad were not going to be checking the tutor to see how her lessons were going — and the Institute Psychs wouldn't care, they thought she was too advanced for her age anyway. She could even raid the library for the holos she wasn't precisely supposed to watch. . . .

"Oh, Finagle," she said, regretfully, after a moment. It might be fun — but it would be *guilty* fun. And besides, sooner or later Mum and Dad would find out what she'd done, and *ping!* there would go the Family

Day and probably a lot of other privileges. She weighed the immediate-pleasure of being lazy and watching forbidden holos against the future-pleasure of being able to pilot the sled up the mountains, and the latter outranked the former. Piloting the sled was the closest *she* would get to piloting a ship, and she wouldn't be able to do that for years and years and years yet.

And if she fell on her nose *now,* right when Mum and Dad trusted her most — they'd probably restrict her to the dome for ever and ever.

"Not worth it," she sighed, jumping down from her stool. she frowned as she noticed that the pins-and-needles feeling in her toes still hadn't gone away. It had been there when she woke up this morning. It had been there yesterday too, and the day before, but by breakfast it had worn off. Well, it didn't bother her that much, and it wouldn't take her mind off her Latin lesson. Too bad, too.

"Boring language," she muttered, *"Ick, ack, ock!"*

Well, the sooner she got it over with, the better off she'd be, and she could go back to nice logical quadratics.

The pins-and-needles feeling hadn't worn off by afternoon, and although she felt all right, she decided that since Mum and Dad were trusting her to do everything right, she probably ought to talk to the AI about it.

"Socrates, engage Medic-Mode, please," she said, sitting down reluctantly in the tiny medic station. She *really* didn't like being in the medic-station; it smelled of disinfectant and felt like being in a too-small pressure suit. It was just about the size of a tiny lav, but something about it made it *feel* smaller. Maybe because it was dark inside. And of course, since it had been made for adults, the proportions were all wrong for her. In order to reach hand-plates she had to scoot to the edge of the seat, and in order to reach foot-plates she had to get right off the seat entirely. The screen in front of her lit up with the smiling holo of someone that was supposed to be a doctor. Privately, she doubted that the original had ever been any closer to medicine than wearing the jumpsuit. He just looked too — polished. *Too* trustworthy, *too* handsome, *too* competent. Any time there was anything official she had to interface with that seemed to scream *trust me* at her, she immediately distrusted it, and went very wary. Probably the original for this holo had been an actor. Maybe he made adults feel calm, but he made her think about the Psychs and their too-hearty greetings, their nosy questions.

"Well, Tia," said the AI's voice — changed, to that of the "doctor." "What brings you here?"

"My toes feel like they're asleep," she said dutifully. "They kind of tingle."

"Is that all?" the "doctor" asked, after a moment for the AI to access his library of symptoms. "Are they colder than normal? Put your hand on the hand-plate, and your foot on the foot-plate, Tia."

She obeyed, feeling very like a contortionist.

"Well, the circulation seems to be fine," the "doctor" said after the AI had a chance to read temperature and blood-pressure, both of which appeared in the upper right-hand corner of the screen. "Have you any other symptoms?"

"No," she replied. "Not really." The "doctor" froze for a moment, as the AI analyzed all the other readings it had taken from her during the past few days — what she'd eaten and how much, what she'd done, her sleep-patterns.

The "doctor" unfroze. "Sometimes when children start growing very fast, they get odd sensations in their bodies," the AI said. "A long time ago, those were called 'growing pains.' Now we know it's because sometimes different kinds of tissue grow at different rates. I think that's probably what your problem is, Tia, and I don't think you need to worry about it. I'll prescribe some vitamin supplements for you, and in a few days you should be just fine."

"Thank you," she said politely, and made her escape, relieved to have gotten off so lightly.

And in a few days, the pins-and-needles sensation *did* go away, and she thought no more about it. Thought no more, that is, until she went outside to her new "dig," and did something she hadn't done in a year — she fell down. Well, she didn't exactly fall; she *thought* she'd sidestepped a big rock, but she hadn't. She rammed her toes right into it, and went heavily to her knees.

The suit was intact, she discovered to her relief — and she was quite ready to get up and keep going, until she realized that her foot didn't hurt.

And it should have, if she'd rammed it against the outcropping hard enough to throw her to the ground.

So instead of going on, she went back to the dome and pealed off suit and shoe and sock — and found her foot was completely numb, but black and blue where she had slammed it into the unyielding stone.

When she prodded it experimentally, she discovered that her whole foot was numb, from the toes back to the arch. She peeled off her other shoe and sock, and found that her left foot was as numb as her right. "Decom it," she muttered. This surely meant another check-in with the medic.

Once again she climbed into the claustrophobic little closet at the back of the dome, and called up the "doctor."

"Still got pins-and-needles, Tia?" he said cheerfully, as she wriggled on the hard seat.

"No," she replied, "But I've mashed my foot something awful. It's all black and blue."

"Put it on the foot-plate, and I'll scan it," the "doctor" replied. "I promise, it won't hurt a bit."

Of course it won't, it doesn't hurt now, she thought resentfully, but did as she was told.

"Well, no bones broken, but you certainly did bruise it!" the "doctor" said after a moment. Then he added archly, "What were you doing, kicking the tutor?"

"No," she muttered. She really *hated* it when the AI program made it get patronizing. "I stubbed it on a rock, outside."

"Does it hurt?" the "doctor" continued, oblivious to her resentment.

"No," she said shortly. "It's all numb."

"Well, if it does, I've authorized your bathroom to give you some pills," the "doctor" said with cloying cheer. "Just go right ahead and take them if you need them — you know how to get them."

The screen shut down before she had a chance to say anything else. *I guess it isn't anything to worry about,* she decided. *The AI would have said something otherwise. It'll probably go away.*

But it didn't go away, although the bruises healed. Before long she had other bruises, and the numbness of her feet extended to her ankles. But she told herself that the AI had said it would go away, eventually — and anyway, this wasn't so bad, at least when she mashed herself it didn't *hurt.*

She continued to play at her own little excavation — which she had decided was a grave-site. The primitives burned their dead though, and only buried the ashes with their flint-replicas of the sky-gods' wonderful things — hoping that the dearly-departed would be reincarnated as sky gods and return in wealth and triumph. . . .

It wasn't as much fun though, without Mum and Dad to talk to; and she was getting kind of tired of the way she kept tripping and falling over the uneven ground at the new "site." She hadn't damaged her new suit yet, but there were sharp rocks that could rip holes even in the tough suit-fabric — and if her suit was torn, there would go the promised Family Day.

So, finally, she gave up on it, and spent her afternoons inside.

A few nights later, Pota peeked in her room to see if she was still awake.

"I wanted you to know we were still flesh-and-blood and not holos, pumpkin," her Mum said, sitting down on the side of her bed. "How are your excavations coming?"

Tia shook her head. "I kept tripping on things, and I didn't want to tear my suit," she explained. "I think that the Flint People must have put a curse on their grave-site. I don't think I should dig there anymore."

Pota chuckled, hugged her, and said, "That could very well be, dear. It never pays to underestimate the power of religion. When the others arrive we'll research their religion and take the curse off, all right?"

"Okay," she replied. She wondered for a moment if she should mention her feet —

But Pota kissed her and whisked out the door before she could make up her mind.

Nothing more happened for several days, and she got used to having numb feet. If she was careful to watch where she stepped, and careful never to go barefoot, there really wasn't anything to worry about. And the AI had *said* it was something that happened to other children.

Besides, now Mum and Dad were *really* finding important things. In a quick breakfast-holo, a tired but excited Braddon said that what they were uncovering now might mean a whole lot more than just a promotion. It might mean the establishment of a field-wide reputation.

Just what that meant, exactly, Tia wasn't certain — but there was no doubt that it must be important or Braddon wouldn't have been so excited about it. So she decided that whatever was wrong with her could wait. It wouldn't be long now, and once Mum and Dad weren't involved in this day-and-night frenzy of activity, she could explain everything they would see to it that the medics gave her the right shot or whatever it was that she needed.

The next morning when she woke up, her fingers were tingling.

Tia sighed, and took her place inside the medic booth. This was getting very tiresome.

The AI ran her through the standard questions, which she answered as she had before. "So now you have that same tingling in your hands as you did in your feet, is that right?" the "doctor" asked.

"That's right," she said shortly.

"The same tingling that went away?" the "doctor" persisted.

"Yes," she replied. *Should I say something about how it doesn't tingle anymore, about how now it's numb?* But the AI was continuing.

"Tia, I can't really find anything wrong with you," it said. "Your circulation is fine, you don't have a fever, your appetite and weight are fine, you're sleeping right. But you *do* seem to have gotten very accident-prone lately." The "doctor" took on a look of concern covering impatience. "Tia, I know that your parents are very busy right now, and they don't have time to talk to you or play with you. Is *that* what's really wrong? Are you angry with your parents for leaving you alone so much? Would you like to talk to a counselor?"

"No!" she snapped. The idea! The *stupid* AI actually thought she was making this up to get attention!

"Well, you simply don't have any other symptoms," the "doctor" said, not-too-gently. "This hasn't got to the point where I'd have to insist that you talk to a counselor, but really, without anything else to go on, I can't suggest anything else except that this is a phase you'll grow out of."

"This hasn't got to the point where I'd have to insist that you talk to a counselor." Those were dangerous words. The AI's "counselor" mode was only good for so much — and every single thing she said and did would be recorded the moment that she started "counseling." Then all the Psychs back at the Institute would be sent the tapes via compressed-mode databurst — and they'd be all over them, looking for something wrong with her that needed Psyching. And if they found anything, anything at all, Mum and Dad would get orders from the Board of Mental Health that they couldn't ignore, and she'd be shipped back to a school on the next courier-run.

Oh no. You don't catch me that easy.

"You're right," she said carefully. "But Mum and Dad trust me to tell you *everything* that's wrong, so I am."

"All right then." The "doctor's" face lost that stern look. "So long as you're just being conscientious. Keep taking those vitamin supplements, Tia, and everything will be fine." But everything wasn't fine. Within days, the tingling had stopped, to be replaced by numbness. Just like her feet. She began having trouble holding things, and her lessons took twice as long now, since she couldn't touch-type anymore and had to watch where her fingers went.

She completely gave up on doing anything that required a lot of manual dexterity. Instead, she watched a lot of holos, even boring ones, and played a great deal of holo-chess. She read a lot too, from the screen, so that she could give one-key page-turning commands rather than trying to turn paper-pages herself. The numbness stopped at her wrists, and for a few days she was so busy getting used to doing things without feeling her hands, that she didn't notice that the numbness in her legs had spread from her ankles to her knees. . . .

Now she was afraid to go to the AI "doctor" program, knowing that it would put her in for counseling. She tried looking things up herself in the database, but knew that she was going to have to be very sneaky to avoid triggering flags in the AI. As the numbness stopped at the knees, then began to spread up her arms, she kept telling herself that it wouldn't, couldn't be much longer now. Soon Mum and Dad would be done, and they would know she wasn't making this up to get attention. Soon she would be able to tell them herself, and they'd make the stupid medic work right. Soon.

She woke up, as usual, to hands and feet that acted like wooden blocks at the ends of her limbs. She got a shower — easy enough, since the controls were push-button, then struggled into her clothing by wriggling and using teeth and fingers that didn't really want to move. She didn't bother too much with hair and teeth, it was just too hard. Shoving her feet into slippers, since she hadn't been able to tie her shoes for the past couple of days, she stumped out into the main room of the dome —

Only to find Pota and Braddon waiting there for her, smiling over their coffee.

"Surprise!" Pota said cheerfully. "We've done just about everything we can on our own, and we zipped the findings off to the Institute last night. *Now* things can get back to normal!"

"Oh *Mum!*" She couldn't help herself, she was so overwhelmed by relief and joy that she started to run across the room to fling herself into their arms—

Started to. Halfway there, she tripped, as usual, and went flying through the air, crashing into the table and spilling the hot coffee all over her arms and legs.

They picked her up, and as she babbled apologies about her clumsiness. She didn't even notice what the coffee had done to her, didn't even think about it until her parents' expressions of horror alerted her to the fact that there were burns and blisters already rising on her lower arms.

"It doesn't hurt," she said, dazedly, without thinking, just saying the first thing that came into her mind. "It's okay, really, I've been kind of numb for a while so it doesn't hurt, honest— "

Pota and Braddon both froze. Something about their expressions startled her into silence.

"You don't feel anything?" Pota said, carefully. "No pain, nothing at all?"

She shook her head. "My hands and feet were tingling for a while and then they stopped and went numb. I thought if I just waited you could take care of it when you weren't so busy— "

They wouldn't let her say anything else. Within moments they had established through careful prodding and tests with the end of a sharp probe that the numb area now ended at mid-thigh and mid shoulder.

"How long has this been going on?" Braddon asked, while Pota flew to the AI console to call up the medical program the adults used.

"Oh, a few weeks," she said vaguely. "Socrates said it wasn't anything, that I'd grow out of it. *Then* he acted like I was making it up and I didn't want him to get the Psychs on me. So I figured I would. . . . "

Pota returned at that moment, her mouth set in a grim line. "You are going straight to bed, pumpkin," she said, with what Tia could tell was forced lightness. "Socrates thinks you have pinched nerves; possibly a spinal defect that he can't scan for. So you are going to bed, and we are calling for a courier to come get you. All right?"

Braddon and Pota exchanged one of *those* looks, the kind Tia couldn't read, and Tia's heart sank. "Okay," she sighed with resignation. "I didn't mean to be such a bother, honest, I didn't — "

Braddon scooped her up in his arms and carried her off to her room. "Don't even *think* that you're being a bother," he said fiercely. "We love you, pumpkin. And we're going to see that you get better as quickly as we can."

He tucked her into bed, with Ted beside her, and called up a holo from the almost-forbidden collection. "Here," he said, kissing her tenderly. "Your Mum is going to be in here in a minute to put something on those burns. Then we're going to spend all our time making you the most disgustingly spoiled little brat in known space! What *you* have to do is lie there and think really hard about getting better. Is it a deal?"

"Sure Dad," she replied, managing to find a grin for him somewhere. "It's a deal."

Pota only laughed. "If they had been, we'd have